STUCK

with the

SINGLE DAD

Stuck with the Single Dad
by Georgia Coffman

Editing by Amanda Cuff, Word of Advice Editing
Cover Design by Kate Farlow, Y'all. That Graphic
Paperback Formatting by Jill Sava, Love Affair with Fiction

"It's better to be under an umbrella by yourself than with a boyfriend." I peer at my three friends around the table.

They stare back at me slack-jawed. Of course, I don't expect them to agree with me on this, given how happy they each are with their respective smoking-hot piece of ass.

But I'm the odd one out.

"What the hell are you talking about?" Madi blinks her forest green eyes.

The mariachi music playing through the speakers and the smell of spicy fajitas fill my senses as I sip from my tangy margarita—tonight's mascot, so to speak.

It's margarita night with the girls, a standing appointment I'm ten times more serious about than my bi-weekly wax.

"Let me paint you a picture." I lick my tingling lips, coating my tongue with the last of the sweet drink, then scoot my chair closer to the table to ensure they can hear me over the restaurant buzz. This is important. "You're walking down the street in the city, and it starts raining, right? But you have an umbrella, so no problem there. You open it up and snuggle next to your boyfriend underneath it, but oh wait—half of you gets soaked, as does his half, because no umbrella is big enough to keep you both completely dry. Not to mention the crowd of other umbrellas you have to watch out for. And look at that—there's a line by the food truck on the corner that you have to maneuver around, but the sidewalk can only hold so many people, so you end up in the street, where an angry cabbie sideswipes you into a hospital bed." With gloating satisfaction, I fold my hands next to the glass in front of me and deliver the conclusion of my dating philosophy. "Now, I know y'all don't agree, but you can't blame me for preferring to stand under the umbrella alone."

"I don't know what I'm more stunned by—your surprisingly sound logic or your use of *y'all*." Tessa eyes me through thick-framed glasses. It's the look she dons while studying test scores at the career counseling center where we both work. Too bad her analytical prowess will only leave her with more questions than answers regarding my fucked-up psyche.

And where the hell did that *y'all* come from? I thought I'd wiped the word from my vocabulary over ten years ago— around the time I last drove a car. Those were two parts of myself I left behind the second I hopped on a bus up North and never looked back.

With a flick of my hand, I flip my hair over my shoulder

and use the fake, breezy laugh I've mastered over the years. I'm not proud of using it on my friends, but old habits die hard. "I guess Madison's Texan alter ego has rubbed off on me."

"I only go full Texan when I'm angry. Which reminds me—stop making me angry with your ridiculous calls at three in the morning because you can't stay off the internet." The fierce former Texan, turned New Yorker, turned LA beach bum waggles a slender finger in my face. "There's a time difference, *ma'am*."

I've never liked the use of "ma'am" on me. My friend is just messing around, but others use it as an insult. Which is why the barest of flinches twists my lips behind my margarita glass.

After a sip, I say, "If I see a new picture of your sexy movie star boyfriend online, I can't ignore it."

"It's true. Carter and I have been married for three months, and she still notifies me as soon as a new picture surfaces," Tessa chimes in, bringing her hot new billionaire husband into the mix.

"You're welcome," I joke.

"Back to the umbrella scenario." Erin claps. "While I agree with Tessa—you do make sense in a weird, Bree-like way— do you really want to stay under that umbrella alone forever? I mean, for as long as I've known you, you've preferred one-night stands over relationships, but I thought it was…"

"A phase?" Tessa ventures a guess.

Erin nods. "Like maybe you were hurt by someone in the past and just haven't been ready to get back out there—or talk about it."

Madi and Tessa murmur in agreement, and all eyes land on me.

My next gulp of margarita goes down a lot harder than the previous ones. These girls know me well, but my past has always been off limits. It's something that doesn't matter anymore, anyway, so why bring it up?

Besides, I like being single. It's why I continue living this way. They don't think plenty of guys have begged me to date them exclusively? They totally have, but I'm Bree fucking Finley. I enjoy a tryst here and there with eligible bachelors, and that's it.

It's fun and flirty, and there's no room for messy drama. None of it warrants the pity staring back at me from around the table, which I loathe more than being called *ma'am*.

"Ladies! Happy Thursday night. How we doing?" Harvey, our bartender and an unofficial member of our friend group, sidles up next to me.

"We're just trying to get the truth out of this one, but it's a difficult task." Tessa tsks.

"I bet she could use a shot," Madi adds, her eyes lighting up with bad ideas.

"I'll totally take a shot," I say coyly.

"Coming right up." Harvey raps his knuckles against the table, flashing us a generous glimpse of his tattooed forearms before retreating toward the bar.

I lean back in my chair, perfectly comfortable. They're not getting shit out of me, and it's not because I don't trust them. In fact, I trust these three women more than anyone else in the world, but again—old freaking habits.

My secrets have long been locked and secured inside the city limits of a small Georgia town, and that's where they're going to stay.

"Look, you're not going to find some sob story that jaded

my notions of love. I like the way I'm living, and that's all," I insist. "But if you really want to know what has my panties in a twist and my confidence shaken—"

Erin gasps, and Tessa lurches across the table to squeeze my hand.

"What?" I ask, thoroughly confused by their reactions.

"I didn't think even a bulldozer could rattle your confidence." Madi's eyes widen as she reaches for my other hand. "Are you okay?"

"Seriously, are you okay?" Erin repeats, her paling complexion one of alarm. "Because if *your* confidence is shaken, the universe is imploding, and there's no hope for any of us."

"Dramatic, much?" I roll my eyes and slip my hands free from my friends' ridiculous overreactions. "The universe is fine. No need for voodoo rituals to restore cosmic balance, Miss Hippie-Ki-Yay."

"Just wait until you need me to cleanse your aura. See if I come running." Erin holds her hands up as Harvey sets a new pitcher of lime margarita between us, plus a round of shots.

I chomp down on a salty chip, then point the remaining jagged half at her. "Good. I don't want you doing that shit to me anymore."

She smacks the back of my hand like I'm a kid in trouble and gasps again, the high-pitched outrage more appropriate for discovering a mouse in her closet. "You don't mean that."

I can't help but laugh. The woman and I are total opposites, but we work. I need a little kooky in my life—even if it comes with a Ouija Board. In turn, she loves my own particular brand of crazy.

"Focus. Can you please tell us what the hell is going on

already?" Madi urges, the red hair flowing over her shoulders as fiery as her personality.

"I'm trying to." I sigh and sit upright again. "The new guy in the office has been making eyes at me. At first, I thought he was cute in a Clark Kent kind of way, but there's something about him that gives me hives. Tessa knows."

"Dan is nice…"

"He's nice to you because you're married. To the single girls in the building, he stares far too long at our cleavage, like a teenage boy seeing a woman for the first time."

Tessa's face scrunches into discomfort. "He does go out of his way for some of the other single women, with their tea and thermostats. Then last week, I witnessed him totally ignore a pregnant woman who'd dropped her purse in the hall."

"For once, I wish I was wrong, but there's definitely something strange about him." I shudder as images of doll heads in his bedroom race through my mind. Dan seems like the type.

"You should go to HR," Madi declares.

"Dan *is* the HR rep."

The girls make displeased noises and threaten different ways to make his life miserable, but I wave them off.

"Truthfully, he should be more scared of me than the other way around," I state.

They nod in agreement, but Madi still rolls the ends of her sweater sleeves up like she's preparing for battle. Eyes narrowed, she grumbles as her elbow meets the table surface in a move I've only seen in wrestling. "Ian's stunt coach showed me a few moves like this. I could—and would—kick some ass. Just say the word."

I throw my head back and laugh as warmth soothes the knots in my stomach. I'd do the same for them. Hell, it's usually me offering the plan of attack to avenge my wronged friends.

As the oldest of the group, I've unintentionally taken on a motherly role—if that mother gives crude sex advice and looks the other way if they sneak into their rooms after curfew.

In any case, it's oddly—and comically—gratifying to have them jump to my aid this time. It comforts my cold gray heart.

"There's no need to storm the counseling center with torches and pitchforks, or professional wrestling moves. So far, I'm managing with my quick wit and excellent dodging skills," I reassure them, but some of it is for my own benefit since my situation acutely feels like the beginning of a horror movie.

But I could simply be paranoid.

Madi holds her shot up. "To this badass group of women."

We all follow suit, and after we gulp them down in sync, I feel Tessa's curious eyes on me. Their intensity sears a deep blush across my usually impenetrable walls.

I shoot her a glare. "What?"

We've known each other for a while now, ever since we started working together over three years ago, and I suspect I'm not going to love what she says next.

"Something else is bothering you."

Just as I suspected—I don't love it one bit.

My armor automatically clicks into place, masking any sign of what's tormenting me with a smirk. "The only things bothering me are my hormones. I need to get laid."

The girls' frowns crack into smiles, and I sink into my seat with ease. Self-preservation is my bitch, for sure.

"Bree Finley, ladies and gentlemen," Madi announces.

"If you're happy doing your thing your way, there's no reason anyone should stop you." Erin rubs my shoulder. "Not even us. What we said before about being open to a partner underneath your umbrella was just our way of..."

"Checking on you," Tessa effortlessly finishes.

It's how we are. We spend so much time together, we're more in tune than a brand-new grand piano.

"And to let you know if there is something you want to share—anything about your past or present—we're here for you," Tessa offers. It's kind and genuine, but I don't miss the suspicious twinkle in her eye.

"Cheers to you three babes." I hold my drink up for yet another toast.

Over the last couple of years, we've made plenty of them at this very table, and I cherish our weekly tradition like I did my security blanket as a kid.

Before Tessa introduced me to Madi and Erin, I didn't have a strong circle like this. I'd been living in the city for a few years before we met, and I'd only experienced fleeting friendships and acquaintances. I'm extroverted, so meeting new people has never been too difficult. But forming a connection that lasts beyond a few happy hours was the challenge.

I'm forever grateful that I found a family with these three. They've made me feel more at home here than I ever did in my own hometown.

"Okay!" I slam my empty glass down and wipe my chin free of the last of my margarita. "I'm going to get out of here and call the good doctor I met last month. I'm feeling *feverish*." I shimmy in my seat.

Tessa's the first to stand, slinging her mauve Prada coat over her shoulders—a fabulous garment her new husband spoiled her with during their getaway to Paris for New Year's Eve. Jet-setting off to Greece for their honeymoon last fall wasn't enough. Carter swept her off to freaking Paris only a few weeks later.

The lucky friend of mine.

But again, not even extravagant trips and gifts could convince me to march down the aisle to my death.

"You ladies heading out to beat the snowstorm?" Harvey reappears as I button my coat tight. "It's supposed to be pretty brutal out there tonight."

"Really? I hadn't heard anything like that." Madi checks her phone.

"I hadn't, either, until Micah messaged me to see if we're closing up early," Harvey says. "Judging from the radar, I don't think it's going to get too bad until later."

"Be careful," Erin says to the group as we wave goodbye to Harvey.

Outside, a thin dusting of sparkling snow settles on the sidewalk, but it's nothing to worry about. It's definitely not enough to make me rush home.

Once my friends are all tucked away into cabs, I steel myself against a gust of wind and let an available taxi roll by. They're all going to get some from their husbands and boyfriends. If I've taught them anything, they shouldn't be able to comfortably walk tomorrow.

And I shouldn't, either.

Time to call the doctor.

Dr. Lake worked his tongue better than his hands—and those skillful hands are what got him into a coveted surgical fellowship. He wore a stethoscope while he went down on me. It's especially surprising that I'd been so pleasantly rewarded for Christmas like that when I was definitely on the naughty list.

It was so epic, I never trashed the note with his number he left on my refrigerator.

I scroll through the images on my phone until I find the one I snapped of said note. The number never made it into my contacts, since it felt too intimate, but I'm glad I had the *sexth* sense to take a picture.

But the call goes to voice mail.

Shit.

Instead of trying to find another cab or walking toward the subway, I cross the street, stepping over a few puddles of melted snow. My nose quickly chills as I keep walking until I find a rustic little bar with deep red letters scrolled across the window. Inside, two long wooden tables occupy the center of the open floor plan, and a maroon wall is covered with shelves of booze along the back of the bar.

More importantly? It's warm. Over ten years of experience with these winters, and I still can't properly prepare myself for the sting of each gust, the numbness of low, frigid temperatures, and the sad song of my teeth chattering.

Sapphire Creek, Georgia, did *not* prepare me for New York City winters.

The bar is crowded when I walk in, and from my first glance, the demographic is varied. A fiftieth birthday party celebrates in one corner, the honoree's hat indicating as much, and another huddle of young guys appears to be having their first legal drinks.

This has the potential to be my new favorite spot to hunt for eligible one-night stands.

"Hey there," I practically coo to the late-twentysomething bartender.

As he sets two drinks in front of a couple next to me, he works his chiseled jaw back and forth, and it's actually pretty hot. I'm in my early thirties and don't tend to seduce down, but I could put his large, strong hands to work tonight.

Except he doesn't spare me a glance. Instead, he openly flirts with two girls on the other end of the bar. They toss their hair around like they're filming a shampoo commercial, and the bartender eats it up.

I manage to steal him for a clipped second and finally order a drink. "Thanks," I call after him with sarcasm because I just can't help myself.

The only response I get in return is a rude roll of his eyes.

It seems like just yesterday that a young guy like this snarky bartender would've checked me out with appreciation, offered some pickup line I've heard seven times over, and asked for my number.

But it's not like he's the only guy in here. There are plenty of other options.

The petty part of me even wants to pick up someone hotter just to show the douchebag that I can do better than him.

With my drink in hand, I maneuver through the crowd and slide onto an empty barstool, where I add a plate of loaded fries to my tab. It's not lost on me that I just left a perfectly good restaurant, but we mostly go there for the margaritas.

I tap my finger to the stem of my glass as the soft notes of an acoustic song float through the room.

Ten minutes later, the other bartender sets a fresh plate of fries with cheese and a sprinkling of paprika, parsley, and bacon on top in front of me. I deeply inhale, preparing to devour the fried heaven, but I don't get far.

A pair of stunning blue eyes lock on to mine.

Dark, sandy-blond hair curls over the tops of his ears.

His mysterious smirk makes me drop the fry between my fingers before it ever reaches my parted lips.

And he marches right toward me.

TWO

Bree

I shift to get comfortable, my fries on the bar cheering for me to dive in, but my stomach twists with something other than the hunger for food.

Heat and need curl in my lower belly like a tornado destroying anything in its path.

I'm wearing my lucky thong too. For all intents and purposes, this should be a magical night.

I sneak another glance over my shoulder, convinced the intriguing guy is headed straight for me. But he's stopped to chat and laugh with someone who seems to be a friend. It's not long before they're both swallowed by the charcuterie-eating group rising from the table behind me, laughing and holding on to the tail end of their conversation.

With a few fries in me to replace the disappointment of

still sitting here alone, I swing my legs to the side to retrieve my clutch, unhooking the strap from underneath the bar.

As I squirm back into position, my shoulder bumps into someone, and I drop my clutch.

I smell his cologne before I see him.

The sweet and spicy mix of ocean and hints of cinnamon sends a shiver up my spine. He smells like summer vacation and Christmas wrapped in one.

"Sorry about that." His low voice skitters across my exposed shoulder.

"It's fine. Although you better be glad that wasn't my plate of fries," I tease as he kneels to scoop up my clutch—a gentleman. That's two points for this handsome stranger.

He stands upright again and remains so close, the warmth of his body casts me in a hug. When I peek up at him, I'm captivated by the clearest blue eyes I've ever seen. They're framed by surprisingly long blond lashes too.

My greedy gaze roams over endearing freckles scattered across his cheeks, like he spends most of his time in the sun.

"Or what?" he plays along, dipping his head to speak in my ear as more people shuffle behind us. "What would you have done to get back at me?"

I tap my chin, keeping him guessing for just a second longer, then point to the phone in his grasp. "I'd snatch your phone and put the wrong passcode in too many times until it locks you out for the rest of the night."

He gives me a low whistle. "Sinister."

"I don't play around."

He throws an arm over the back of my seat and gives me one hell of a charming smirk. "How about you snatch my phone and put your number in it, instead?"

"You're going to have to work a little harder for that." I lock eyes with him as I slowly slide a fry between my lips. The second the delicious carb hits my tongue, my nostrils flare, and I suppress a groan.

This guy watches my every move like I'm the only woman in the room, and I have to admit—it does something to my chest.

Even though it's simple and quick, it gives my ego a boost, a special kind of aphrodisiac.

"I don't like your purse," he says in a hoarse voice, pointing a thick finger to my clutch.

"Excuse me?"

He nods toward it again like I don't know what purse he's talking about. Is he for real? I'm almost ready to take my earrings out and show him some damn manners.

"It's too small. Can't even fit your cell in that thing."

"It's big enough for mace, though, so I'd watch it." I purse my lips and turn back to my drink.

He might be incredibly handsome, with his deep tan and scruffy five o'clock shadow. His hair is tamped down, but the strands are wavy. It's almost like they're begging to be free of the gel or mousse trapping them in place. I'd like nothing more than to twist my fingers through his hair and tousle it up.

But I'm in no mood to entertain assholes.

Instead of walking away as I thought he would, taking whatever excitement of our brief flirtation with him, he orders a beer and pulls out the stool next to me, scraping the floor with it like a barbarian. "I don't like the way this sweater falls over your shoulder, either. It's too wild and sexy."

"And here I thought you were trying to get my number." I leave a question hanging in the air.

"Oh, I am."

"Is this what you call flirting, then? Because you might need to reassess your tactics."

"I would, but…"

The douchey bartender sets the beer in front of him, and then this baffling stranger wraps his lips around the top of the bottle to suck back a pull. When he fully faces me again, I glimpse the twinkle in his eye.

I lean in, my body acting on its own accord. His voice holds a unique tone, a mesmerizing lull in each hushed word out of his mouth. There's a subtle rasp in it, one that matches his rugged exterior, and for whatever reason, I'm drawn to it.

And him.

"But?" I press, confusingly curious.

"But you're too gorgeous, which is intimidating, so I needed to level the playing field."

I quirk a brow. "So, you're insulting me to make yourself feel better and more adequate?"

For the first time during our brief exchange, his confidence falters. The intensity in his gaze wavers as he hisses, "Shit. I'm sorry. That's not at all what I was trying to do. I just thought that would be… witty?"

"Is that a question you want me to answer?"

"Not really." He rubs his hands between his knees, clearly nervous, and the vulnerable change in his demeanor keeps my ass glued to the stool.

"I can't decide if you're sweet or not."

"Sweet. Let's go with sweet." He winks and flashes a crooked grin. It almost seems shy, like he's trying to plead his case through that smile.

And I almost give in but remain quiet, admittedly

interested in what he'll say next. I can usually predict what they'll say next. When their heady gaze will land on me. What they'll do with their hands.

It's not always the same, but there tends to be a pattern I rely on—one I can toy with.

But this guy is throwing me for a bit of a loop. Or, is my confidence shy tonight?

Only one way to find out.

He's the first to break our little staring contest. "What if you tell me what you don't like about me—will that make us even?"

"As a matter of fact…" I sit up a little straighter and slide my drink to the side, unabashedly giving him a once-over.

His black shirt clings to bulky muscles expanding his chest, and each time he takes a breath, he threatens to break through the fabric.

Dare I look down at his jeans?

Nope. I shouldn't have looked.

But I did, and he's just as muscular there. The denim outlines deliciously defined curves around his quads.

Jacked dudes have never really been my thing. The ones I've met in the past either had high voices, small dicks, or both, likely due to too many steroids and other shit I know nothing about.

Clearly, I just haven't met the right ones yet. Not like this guy. It's obvious he's earned these muscles, and my stomach rolls with excitement at the thought of appreciating them up close and in private.

"Well?" He raises a brow.

I lift my gaze up, up, up until it lands on his hair. "Your hair is too smooth. Not every strand needs to be smashed into place. Women like a little chaos." I cross my arms, playing his cheeky game without holding back.

He clutches one hand over his heart. "Ouch. Right where it hurts."

"You told me to."

"I did, but I didn't know you'd go straight for the jugular." He chuckles, and oh my God—what was that? Did my ovaries just burst?

There's yearning—actual fucking *yearning*—in my core, which grows hotter and hotter the more seconds I spend next to him, and I don't even know his name.

A few minutes ago, I was even prepared to send him to Hell.

I drop my arms to the bar and scoot closer to him, my sweater fluttering lower on my arm with the movement. "I believe I get a second shot too."

"You do." He sets his beer down and drops his focus to my lips, and they tingle like he's touching them.

Who the hell is this guy?

"Your eyes and smile. They're too telling."

"What are they telling you?"

When I exhale, it comes out as a mix of a sigh and a hum, and it definitely gets his attention—more of it, anyway. He visibly tenses, and his nostrils flare, much like I imagine my own did when I ate a fry.

I toy with the end of his sleeves, running my fingers over the threaded bracelet on his wrist. "They're telling me you're a nice guy. One who doesn't hesitate to help abandoned puppies or volunteer at food drives."

"But..." Grimacing, he searches my expression, his single word heavy, like there's something wrong with what I said.

There's not, although he is right. There is a *but* coming; it's just probably not what he's thinking.

"*But* you also know your way around a woman's body and can fuck one silly." I subtly hold my breath, my lungs squeezing with the hope that I'm right about my observation.

I hope my skills at reading men are as sharp as ever, but also, I want to reap the rewards of my comment.

Fire flashes across his eyes, and I smile when he rasps, "Not just *a* woman. The *right* woman."

"What makes her the right one?" I whisper, my throat dry.

He pulls my hand into his, and my core jolts from the contact. Then he uses the pad of his thumb to rub along the lines of my palm, sending electric currents throughout my body. "Tonight? It's you."

My heart flutters. We want the same thing. Just for a night—*bingo*. "We're in agreement, then."

"I'm Wade."

"Bree."

He licks his lips and stands, holding an outstretched arm for me to follow. I slide off the stool onto wobbly legs, anticipation flooding my lower stomach with fuzzy heat. Wade's hand is strong and inviting, and just having it on my hand rattles my core. What would it be like to have him touch the rest of my body?

Will I survive?

I've been with hot guys before. They've made my toes curl with a single look, and they've made me scream too. Dr. Lake was one of them, but suddenly, with this stranger by my side, I'm glad the hot surgeon didn't pick up tonight.

Wade doesn't feel any different from the likes of my past hookups, except… he might be.

I can't put my finger on it just yet, but there's something in the way he pauses, like he's deep in contemplation. Or like he's fighting with himself. His flirting definitely seems rusty.

My educated guess? He doesn't do this a lot. Going to bars and picking up women who only have their martinis for company might be as foreign to him as Spanish is to me.

And I like the idea that I may not be one of many for him, although that's a dangerous line to tread.

The first one-night stand I experienced, I thought the opposite. I was glad the flavor of the evening didn't ask for my name or any other personal detail. In truth, it was a relief. It made it easier for my fragile heart to sneak out before the sun rose. No connection. No feelings.

No heartbreak.

It was easy, and I needed easy back then, just like I do now.

Everyone else around me might be moving on with their own romantic commitments and happily ever afters, but this is what I live for in that department.

It feels good. This rush of excitement is addictive, and I wouldn't change a thing.

Whatever this guy is hiding—it's not going to make a difference.

THREE

Bree

The cab's windshield wipers work overtime as heavy flakes of snow cascade onto it during the ride to Wade's apartment. The drive is a blur of flurries, city lights, and labored breaths as we suppress the attraction between us until we get somewhere private.

He keeps his hand on my knee the entire drive, intermittently tightening and loosening his grip, and it prompts goose bumps up my legs and arms faster than ants rushing to their hill.

At his apartment, we explode.

The door slams closed, and in the dark, Wade's mouth lands on mine, his hands digging into my hair with urgency.

Heart pounding, I match his hurried energy, slanting my lips over his as I thrust my tongue into his eager mouth, enjoying the lingering taste of beer and an exciting night ahead.

He grows hard against my stomach, and a guttural sound escapes his lips, traveling across the roof of my mouth and reverberating throughout the rest of my body.

It lights a match, but I need the burn of a whole damn fire.

"Ow!" I wince as I stub my heel against something hard, the sting throbbing as my shoulder hits something else. Is that a box? I can't make it out in the dark, but it shifts and rattles like Christmas ornaments.

"Sorry." He steadies me in his strong hands. "I need to take those to storage, but I haven't had the chance since I moved in."

"You also haven't taken your damn shirt off."

With his jacket on the floor next to mine, I claw at his T-shirt, desperate to run my fingers over his abs. He grants my wish by ripping it over his head, and I swear I hear a tear in the seams.

Wade drags my sweater farther over my shoulder, exposing more skin until he finally yanks it over my lacy bralette.

"May I?" he asks hoarsely.

I don't know what he's asking for exactly, and I really don't care. I just need more of him—his kisses, his scorching touches, *him*.

"Touch me everywhere. Make me—"

Forget.

Make me feel less alone.

Make me feel special, if only for one night.

Gulping around the lump of consuming desire in my throat, I nod emphatically, and when his large hand cups the outside of my covered breast, my breath hitches.

When his mouth clamps over my tingling nipple, I lose my head altogether.

"Yes," I hiss, fisting the lean curve of his shoulder for support.

My legs are quickly becoming useless strings of noodles in Wade's arms.

I finally have the pleasure of running my hands through his hair like I wanted to earlier tonight, and it's as gloriously silky as I suspected. The strands slide through my fingers with ease, and it turns me on even more.

I love this ruffled look on him.

As my hand reaches the shorter strands at the back of his neck, I tighten my grip and tug until I bring his face back up to mine, where I fuse my lips to his again.

His hands tangle in my sweater bunched around my waist before he drags the thick material along my flushed skin, then jerks it over my head. As he frees me of it, my hair sweeps over my eyes, but through the curtain of loose strands and a flash of headlights through the windows, I make out the curve of his nose.

The chiseled angle of his square jaw.

The gleam in his eye—it twinkles with lust and seduction.

Then we're blanketed in darkness again.

I drown in another kiss, which was excitedly foreign at first, but I've quickly acclimated to his lips.

Stumbling toward the bed, I kick my leggings off, and he shucks his jeans too, revealing he's a briefs man.

Which delights me.

And we establish a new rhythm. It's slightly offbeat, but it's perfect for tonight.

Wade hauls me on top of him, and he digs his fingers into

my naked curves, his palms eagerly kneading and worshipping my full thighs.

"You're fucking gorgeous, Bree."

I lick my lips, lapping up his taste and loving the way my name falls from his mouth so easily and huskily.

He buries his head in my hair as he nips at my throat, and I grind my hips against his, greedy to free what feels like a huge cock—mine for the feasting for the next hour.

From the covered bulge alone, I'd bet it's enough of a feast to last me through the next few months.

"I want you," he confesses, and I kick my leg over to remove my panties.

But he doesn't do the same with the last of his clothing. Instead, he helps me slide the bra off and tosses it over his shoulder. Before I'm able to return the favor and tear his briefs away, he jerks me back into place on top of him.

Except he scoots farther down until I'm straddling his face.

"Um…" Through the thick fog of lust, a hint of panic taps at my temples.

"I want you like this," he states, and his tone is firmer than the one he used before. It leaves no room for debate or doubts.

Not that I have many.

The man's kisses are downright dizzying. He uses his mouth like a weapon, but in a tender, sexy way, and I'd love nothing more than to experience his hungry tongue between my thighs.

I'm just surprised it's what he wants to do first—and with me sitting on his face rather than him laying me down, instead.

In any case, it's not unwelcomed, that's for sure. If he wants to go down on me, I'd be insane to stop him.

The first swipe of his tongue is neither hesitant nor gentle, to my stunned pleasure.

It's all very arousing, and as he clenches his fingers around both my thighs, he thrusts his tongue deeper into my core with relentless power.

Like his sole mission on this planet is to bring me a record amount of ecstasy.

I lose myself in every teasing lick.

Suck.

Nip.

I bask in every feverish sensation, and it's not long before I'm riding his face into the blissful sunset of a titillating release.

He hums beneath me as I grip the headboard to steady myself. I unintentionally rise with each jolt of his tongue, but he just jerks me back down, burying himself between my legs. In the process, he spreads me even wider across his mouth, digging his tongue deeper inside me.

"Stay right here," he says, his command muffled from this position, but I hear him loud and clear. "Don't move until you come all over my mouth."

When I told him he seemed like the type of guy to fuck a woman silly, it was an educated—and optimistic—guess, but Wade is living up to it.

And he hasn't even whipped his dick out yet.

After I'm securely settled back into place, certain I'm suffocating him, his fingers roam over my back and skim the line between my ass cheeks, causing me to shudder.

"Oh… my… God." The pace of my thrusts against his face skid into a rocky wobble.

I'm practically drooling over the skill of his mouth and hands.

I even lick my lips to make sure it doesn't travel down my chin, but who even cares?

By the time I'm unraveled—death by orgasm at his mercy—I'm positive I have marks on my ass from where he gripped me so firmly and possessively. Imagining as much has me trembling harder, the bundle of nerves rubbing against the tip of his nose with wild abandon.

"Now that… is what I'm talking about," he mumbles, then places hot kisses along the inside of my thigh.

I angle my leg up to allow him room to shift, and when I peer into his eyes, the wicked mischief in them makes me feel even naughtier than I did when writhing against his face without apology or shame.

"We're only getting started," I say, panting.

"You read my mind." Smirking, he rids himself of the briefs.

The words "good boy" are on the tip of my tongue, which I nearly swallow when I get an unfiltered look at him. The lights from the city are the only source of illumination in here, but they're enough.

He's hard. Every plain of his torso is solid muscle. Curvy lines of ink decorate half of his upper body, and I wish the light was on so I could study the artwork in its entirety. The thought that I'll leave before I get a chance to gives me pause for only a second.

The loss isn't my focus.

With a condom covering his thick length, he hoists me back on top of him, using his sculpted muscles to toss me around with relative ease. I have to admit—it's impressive.

I sink onto him, eager to chase yet another orgasm. If it's anything like the one he gave me with his mouth, this might just be the best night of sex I've ever had.

Which is saying a lot.

His hands are back on my thighs, but he doesn't attempt to control my pace or movements. He seems to simply enjoy the view.

And it's obvious from the way he groans and licks his lips that he likes watching my tits bounce in his face.

I move my hips forward and backward, suspending us in the heat of friction it creates, and then I slide around for reverse cowgirl. I pick my pace back up, riding him like I might a bull as I hang on for dear sweet pleasure.

He pulses beneath me, his hips twitching to be involved, and I deliver my secret weapon. With knees firmly planted on either side of his powerful thighs, I move only my ass up and down, side to side, and round and round, finishing on a circular motion that's taken me a few years and several Pilates classes to perfect.

It's like my hips are unhinged, free of any restriction.

His groans are even louder than before. "Goddamn, Bree. You're… going to… kill me."

Wade shudders beneath me, and I smile in victory. He's at my mercy this time. The high from such power washes over me in blissful waves, crashing through me as my core clenches with another orgasm.

He follows suit, and I fall to the side with a contented sigh.

Holy fuck.

My head spins with dizzying ideas for a repeat, even though we just finished.

I'm not normally one to scramble for a place in line to ride the same roller coaster, so to speak, but I'd gladly accept another hit of whatever Wade just dosed me with.

FOUR

I flick on the bedside lamp, then settle into bed again. As I rest my back against the headboard, I interlock my fingers over my bare waist and cock a brow. "Well?"

"Well, what?" Bree sashays those mouthwatering hips to the edge of the bed, her sweater draped across her ample chest once again. Her bottom half remains bare while she spins in place as if to model for me. She's searching the room for something, but I can't stop staring.

She's a sight to behold.

Curvy legs and spunky energy.

Naturally—and devilishly—red lips.

The color of dark hair now tangled over one shoulder matches the deep amber of her eyes. The constant twinkle in them gives her an air of amusement. It's the first thing I noticed when our eyes locked back at the bar.

Even from across the room, it appeared she had a sinful secret, and I desperately wanted to know what it was. When I approached her and she didn't recognize me—well, that made this deal so much sweeter.

I thought I'd lost my chance entirely when I nearly blew it thanks to my terrible flirting abilities, but what can I say? I'm fucking rusty at the whole pickup scene.

I'm just glad she gave me another chance. How far can I push my luck with her tonight?

"Have I earned your number yet?" I ask coyly, proud as hell that at least my mouth and dick haven't lost their charms.

Bree bends at the waist and swipes her leggings off the floor, and try as I might, I can't help but drink in the peek of her lacy panties before she straightens back up. "I don't think you understand how one-night stands work," she says over her shoulder as she continues getting dressed.

And my heart rate kicks up a notch at the prospect of her walking out of here without so much as a backward glance.

I throw my legs over the side of the bed and move toward her. "Maybe I'm not the kind of guy who does one-night stands."

Not anymore.

In truth, I didn't go out tonight with the intention of finding someone, but Bree just… happened. I felt this urge to ensure I didn't let her slip away, and that same damning urge consumes me now.

"In fact, you're basically my first in… ages," I admit, thinking back to the Dutch model I met out West. Esmee was probably my last hookup before my life exploded.

I was an entirely different person last winter.

Bree clutches her chest, the leggings wadded in her grasp. "It's been a while since I was a guy's first."

I smirk. "As you could tell, this wasn't my very first *time*. I've had plenty of women in my bed, but not many have come for me like you did."

"Here's another friendly tip for flirting: don't talk about your past sexual experiences to the woman you just fucked, whether or not you'll see her again."

I slide my hands up and down her upper arms, taking note of her gaze sweeping over my naked chest and abs. Her perusal isn't subtle. In fact, it's appreciative and unapologetic as it lingers on the tattoos covering one pec, shoulder, and arm.

She doesn't say anything or move at all when I dip my head low to skim the tip of my nose along her temple.

"I'd like to see you again," I whisper in her tousled hair.

Her sharp inhale cuts through the intensity between us. "We can't…"

I hold my hands up and stalk toward the door to let her leave, but an annoying sting pricks my chest with defiance—the echo of her friendly little tip.

She doesn't want me telling her about the women I've been with. Why? Could she be jealous that others might've sat on my face like Bree just did?

Now that *was* a first.

No woman has ever chased her own pleasure with such need and enthusiasm, and it was the sexiest thing I've ever experienced. It's almost too bad I didn't prolong the moment.

My fingertips fall away from the door, and I abandon all thoughts of letting her walk out the door without at least getting her last name.

I obviously affect her, which works in my favor because the sexy temptress affects me too. I'll be thinking about her for a long fucking time after tonight, no matter what happens.

"You just rode my face—and my dick, for that matter—like I'm the last guy you'll ever fuck. What's so wrong with getting to know each other?"

She crosses her arms and purses her lips in a stance that sends a chill down my spine. This woman is tenacious and strong-willed, and I shouldn't push her. If I'm not careful, I'm going to end up on her blacklist.

What a tragedy that would be.

She's definitely making me work for her trust and patience, but I'm not unaccustomed to perseverance. I am—*was*, anyway—a professional soccer player, for crying out loud, and it was no small or wimpy feat to be successful in the sport.

I'm of a minuscule percentage to make it in this country. So many people in my life never thought I'd graduate from college, let alone become a professional athlete, but I did both. I secured sponsorships and even appeared in a few commercials during my short-lived career.

I'm confident I can convince this woman to give me one whole night.

"Learning more about you would lead to butterflies and… feelings." She releases an exasperated, if not disgusted, sigh.

"And what's so bad about feelings?" I ask. Although I don't disagree with her, I'm interested in her response. She's a mystery I need to solve, even though I shouldn't.

The reason isn't even entirely due to my past. It's Bree. She's intriguing and fun, and I'm thirsty for every drop of her.

There's also the fact that I've never had to work this hard to convince a woman to stay in my apartment.

The ones in my past have always recognized me as Wade Jameson, star striker for the LA Stars. They act like they won the lottery by landing in my bed, but Bree's attraction to me is genuine. She has no ulterior motives or interest in crossing off an item on her sexual bucket list.

She's real.

"Feelings are fucking stupid." Her shoulders slump. "They're the reason you get married at eighteen, then file for divorce a couple of years later when it's still not legal to drink those feelings. They nearly ruin your life."

"Is that what happened to you?"

She doesn't respond, but her silence is answer enough.

I study her under the soft glow of the lamp with a new perspective, one that doesn't show her as anything less than strong or sexy in my eyes, but one that explains more of who she is.

That's what I want—pieces of her to satisfy my curiosity.

Just for tonight.

I'm not trying to marry her, nor do I particularly want to catch feelings, either. After all, there's no room in my life for them or any kind of ongoing relationship.

"Who is this?" Bree shrieks, pointing to a picture on my dresser. In the frame is an image of Violet and me from a few days before Christmas—the first time we met.

Her toothy grin always makes me smile when I wake up in the morning, but it stings too.

"She's my daughter."

Bree's eyes bug out of her head as she paces by the frame like she's hesitant to ask me anything further.

But she definitely wants to know. She might still technically be a stranger to me, but I can read people. The question is on the tip of her tongue—it's unmistakable.

"She doesn't currently live with me, so we are alone," I venture a guess, and she nods, although she doesn't seem satisfied. Instead, she chews on the end of her fingernail like she's nervous. "I'm not married, either, if that's what you're wondering," I add.

"Stop!" She holds her hands up. "I'm not wondering anything, because I don't want to know."

"You don't want to know if I'm married?" I cock a brow, goading her. It's far too fun riling her up like this, especially since I get the impression it doesn't happen often.

She freezes as the lamp flickers, then dies completely, casting the bedroom in darkness. "Well, of course that's important information, and I definitely needed to know it. My moral and ethical standards are questionable, but I'm not a damn homewrecker."

"Good to know," I say.

"But don't go telling me what your favorite bagel is or how much you love your grandma. That's too much."

"You're making it so easy for me to tell you, though." I'm not buying even a teaspoon of the bullshit she's trying to feed me.

"You're right. Forget I said anything. I'm leaving." With that, she spins on her heel and disappears into the hall.

Flecks of snow stick to the window along one wall, and through the melted drops sliding down the glass, I notice the lights from the building next door are off too.

Strange.

I rush into the living room, where Bree snatches her purse

off the peninsula-style kitchen counter and marches toward the door. Behind me, I check the other buildings beyond the large windows in here, and most of their lights are out as well. It's hard to tell since my view is obscured by the melted snow and ice against the windows.

"Bree, wait—" I reach out to stop her as she throws the door open.

But she doesn't walk through it. Blocking her departure is my neighbor and friend, Tucker, who's haphazardly dressed in his police uniform. His shirt is open in the front, revealing a white tee underneath. We were at the bar together earlier this evening, but he didn't mention anything about working tonight.

Then again, he didn't have any alcohol, nor did he complain when I cut out of there with Bree, so it's possible he was preparing for his next shift.

What's more confusing is the flashlight illuminating his face like it's Halloween.

"Hey..." He glances between Bree and me, adjusting the collar of his shirt into place.

"I need out," she asserts and starts to shoulder past him.

Again, he stops her. "Actually, I suggest you stay here. There's a power outage."

"What?" she hisses.

"I just got a call from the station. The power's out across the city, and I would advise against going out there right now."

"Your concern is kind, but I need to get back to Brooklyn—stat."

"I'm not up to speed with the details yet, but I imagine the train lines are down right now. You won't be able to get a taxi or an Uber, either. No one is going to be driving in the pitch dark until police officers like myself can get out there to light up the roads for those already out. It's not safe, especially without… pants." He swipes a hand through his buzzed hair and kicks his gaze up to the ceiling.

Fuck. Bree's legs are still bare.

"Oh, God." She hunches over, and her shoes tumble to the floor as she attempts to cover herself.

I whip the blanket from the couch and lunge forward, meeting her halfway, where I wrap the fuzzy material around her lower half.

"Look away, asshole," I warn Tucker.

"Is it the squirrels?" Bree asks, her eyes wide and sober as we meet Tucker at the door again. "Before I moved up here, I read online that squirrels and raccoons can cause power outages because they chew on the wires."

I blink at Bree. Is that true? Blackouts weren't uncommon on the West Coast, but I always thought it was because of bad weather and fallen trees. I never considered mischievous furry animals were the culprits.

"You're not wrong." Tucker chuckles. "Like I said, I'm not sure of the details, but I'd say this has something to do with the weather. Have you looked outside?"

"We've been a little busy." She clings to the blanket around her.

"Right," he draws out and pins me with a shit-eating grin as if to say, *"Nice job, you dog."*

His radio crackles to life with names and codes I don't recognize, and I pull Bree farther inside as I thank him for stopping by with the news. "I'll see you in a couple of days for meditation."

"This isn't going to last a couple of days, is it?" Bree's jaw drops. "What the hell are we supposed to do?"

"I'm sure you'll think of something." Tucker wiggles his eyebrows like an obnoxiously horny teenager as he backs into the hall.

I roll my eyes at him, then shut the door and lock it. As I fish a lighter out of the junk drawer in the kitchen, I say, "I'm sure it'll be two hours at most. I'll text Tucker to keep us posted."

In the moonlight, Bree chews on her plump bottom lip. "How do you two know each other?"

"He's my neighbor, and his daughter is about a year older than mine. They've only met once, but they seem to get along." I smile at the thought of the two playing in the living room.

As the older one, Tucker's daughter, Ellie, took Violet by the hand and showed her new games to play, one of which was a fashion app on her iPad.

Then Violet begged me to buy her an iPad.

Her mother, Maggie, immediately shot it down, but I went and bought her one after they left. I plan on surprising her with it during our next visit.

"Tucker and I are both single dads, so it was easy to hit it off."

"Enough to make meditation dates?" she says with a teasing undertone.

"Something like that." I finish lighting a few candles, then inch toward her. "Since there's nowhere to go, I can just answer your earlier questions too. I know your curiosity is burning, and I'm not one to leave a gorgeous woman wanting—in any sense." I wink.

And she gulps—*bingo*.

"I like blueberry bagels, and I love my grandmother very

much. One of my favorite things about her is that she still sends me birthday and holiday cards. They're always filled with five dollars, but she never writes in them. According to her, she pays seven dollars a pop so that the message is already written for her. Otherwise, she'd send me construction paper with her scribbly handwriting like a kindergartener."

This earns me a laugh. Leave it to Gaga to be the one who helps me win over this stubborn woman.

"Now she's a spunky lady I could easily get along with," Bree says.

"You two would definitely hit it off. She'd call you her new best friend and forget I ever existed."

"I have that effect on people."

"What effect is that?"

"They tend to love me."

"I can see why—you're very humble," I joke.

She narrows her eyes and releases her hold on the blanket, letting it slump into a pile around her bare feet. Bree then grabs the hem of her sweater and slips it overhead, remaining in nothing but a matching set of pink lacy lingerie.

And I groan as my previously loose sweatpants tighten. I'm certain if I look down, the tent between my legs would be embarrassing.

But I can't look away from her.

"I think we should take up your friend's dirty suggestion. He seemed wise," she says, her voice suddenly breathy. It drips with seduction.

It's clear to me that she only wants to cut our conversation short by getting naked again, but when she looks at me and talks like that, I can't resist.

I'm only human.

"Don't tell him I told you, but the ass can be *very* wise, indeed." I growl as I wrap my arms around her waist and lick my way up to her jawline. Imagining the slick trail I'm leaving along the column of her throat fuels me.

Like I'm marking her.

She gasps, and as I cover her mouth with my own, I welcome the heat of her tongue on mine and the sting of her fingernails digging into my shoulders.

If I didn't know any better, she's trying really hard to leave a mark on me.

I nudge her backward toward the window and spin her around, then slide my hands down her curvy silhouette.

The darkness of the world expands in front of us, with the twinkling lights of the New York City skyline in the distance. Freezing rain taps against the cool glass, and the thought of casting a fog across it with our heat makes me painfully hard.

I sweep her hair over one shoulder, pull the strap of her bra down, and kiss her there as I rub my hard-on between her ass cheeks. Placing both hands on the window, she pushes against it and grinds into me.

With a groan, I whisper in her ear, "I want to fuck you right here."

"You filthy boy," she breathes.

"You have no idea."

"Do it." It's partly a command and partly a challenge.

I curse under my breath as I unhook her bra, and it flutters to our feet. My fingertips dance along her smooth skin until I reach her thong, which I slide to her ankles, completely exposing every last inch of her.

Hunched onto my heels, I kiss her calf, the back of her knee, her thigh.

I breathe her in as I knead her ass.

She might be the sexiest woman I've ever been with.

"Don't move," I say, then bite her just above the ass cheek.

With echoes of her gasp, I back away to retrieve a condom from my room. When I return, I freeze, basking in the sight of Bree arched against the window.

She's right where I left her, waiting for *me*.

Her fingers are splayed on the glass, which has already fogged. The profile of her breast and the hard outline of her nipple in the dark shadows of the city make my mouth water.

I'm fucking drooling for her.

By the time I'm done with her, there will be smears of her breasts against this window.

"You didn't move. Good girl," I growl into the crook of her neck as I line myself up to her entrance.

Straightening, I use my forefinger to trace the valley of her spine, and when I reach the top of her ass, I surge my hips forward, pushing inside her heat with ease.

"You're so wet for me, Bree," I bite out with satisfaction pulsing through me—and we're just getting started with this round. "So damn perfect."

Her head dips forward against the window as she rolls her ass into me, and her moan carries through several notes before it ends on a titillating whimper.

We start slow like this, our movements in sync as I massage her breasts one at a time, keeping my free hand on her upper thigh. I rock my hips in tune with hers, my dick coated in her aroused sex as I slide balls deep inside her.

The slapping of our bodies plays a languid beat as the chaos of the city outside increasingly drifts over us. The sirens of police cars travel up to our floor, the piercing sounds wild and alarming, and I quicken the pace of my thrusts.

She uses the glass window for balance, and I cover her breasts with both hands for my own anchor as I lose myself in this woman I just met.

Soon, she trembles in my hold, her breasts pressed against the glass just like I'd promised myself. As my own release slams into me, I slow my hands on her nipples and place a kiss in her hair, unable to stop myself.

This is no ordinary woman.

FIVE

Bree

"I saw through space and time," I whisper-scream into the phone and cling to the edge of the sink. "He moves better than any male stripper from Naked Heat. Seriously, the guy is crazy flexible and hotter than Hades. We fucked against the damn window, for God's sake." I lick my lips and cut off the incoherent sounds Erin makes on the other line. "I basically died, and his dick brought me back to life."

"What're you talking about?"

"My one-night stand."

"You never call to tell me about your one-night stands. Anytime I've asked in the past, you've told me to shut my beautiful face and toss out any ideas of learning the details like day-old meat."

"I said that? Doesn't sound like me…" I stifle a giggle. "I'm actually calling to let you know I'm still at his apartment, but I can't leave. There's a blackout."

"What?" Erin screeches, and it's followed by a deep, muffled voice rumbling in the background. I know that voice belongs to Oliver, the devilish Brit corrupting my once-innocent friend.

"I'm dropping you a pin so you have my exact location in case anything happens to me. Got it?"

"Who in the heck are you with?" Erin says, her shrill voice loaded with concern.

The winds howl outside the window as particles of sleet slap the glass, and I jolt against the sink, rattling the flashlight next to it.

"I'm with Wade—" I clamp my mouth shut. What the hell is his last name? "Wade," I assert.

Erin doesn't miss a beat, not that I'm surprised. "You chose tonight of all nights to go home with some *stranger*? When did you even meet him? I thought we all agreed to go home after margaritas because of the storm." She adds another syllable to the word *storm*, as if the magnitude of the current conditions outside is lost on me.

"I tried a new bar, *Mom*," I retort. "Which was packed, by the way. I figured if they weren't concerned about a little snow, I shouldn't be, either."

"I bet they're tucked safely in their own beds right about now," she mutters.

"You might not approve of my misguided plan, but that's not why I called. Can you answer my question now?"

"Fine," she draws out. "I have your location, and I'll check in every hour. Make it thirty minutes."

Once I thank her, I end the call to save the battery on my phone. Who knows how long this predicament will last.

I spin in place in the center of Wade's cramped bathroom, and my elbow taps the glass door to the stand-up shower. When I face the mirror again, I can only see the lower half of my face with the help of Wade's flashlight. With the power out, it's the best I can manage, which is more than I could say if I were alone. I think I have a flashlight at my apartment, but there's no telling where it is. I'm not the most organized person in the world—far from it.

I should really take note of Wade's superior preparedness, though. He jumped into action as soon as we finished going at it. Right before I disappeared into the bathroom, I saw him rummaging through a plastic tub of flashlights, candles, matches, canned foods, chips, dried fruits, and more. I didn't get a good look at the rest, but I wouldn't put it past him to have a freaking unicorn in there. It's the holy grail of survival kits.

I adjust the light over my head and study my mussed hair in the mirror.

My lipstick has long been wiped off, although if I'd known about the window special, I'd have put more on simply to smear it across the glass for the world to see once the lights come back on.

My mascara isn't in any better shape, but I can't bring myself to care about any of it. Erin's concern is a distant memory too. The sex with Wade has been… indescribably incredible. Thoughts of him will stay with me like a freaking tattoo.

My screen flashes with a new message, further illuminating the space.

Another message comes through in the group chat, with a screenshot of the pin I dropped for Erin, and I regret calling anyone. But someone close to me needed to know my current whereabouts. I watch enough *Law and Order: SVU* to know the smartest things to do in sticky situations.

Then again, if I were in fact smart, I would've gone straight home after margaritas. Instead, my stupid ego needed a boost like a dead battery in a car, and Wade was my power source.

And what do I get in return? I'm now stuck with my one-night stand. No quick getaway like I'm used to. No mumbling lies about how I need to get home because my roommate left the stove on and is out of town, or I need to feed my cat.

I don't have a roommate, and for the love of God, no cat has come within twenty feet of my apartment. I'm not a fan, to say the least.

I quickly type out another response to the girls.

I barely catch the last message before I click my phone off and exit the bathroom. I find Wade in the living room, tinkering with a… is that a record player? The simple turntable sits on top of a wooden stand, underneath which a line of records is nestled.

As he straightens back up, a soft, familiar tune dances in the air, the melody interrupted by static scratching the notes and the sleet hitting the windows.

"Patsy Cline?" I ask and lean my shoulder against the doorframe.

"She's my grandma's favorite," he answers as he stalks toward the peninsula counter.

"My grandma loved her too," I whisper after his shadow as he disappears into the darkness.

Once he enters the dim glow radiating from a few candles, I see the two glasses in his hands, one of which he offers to me. "I hope this is wine."

"Hope you like cabernet."

"I like alcohol, Wade. I'm pickier over cheese than I am alcohol, and I love most cheeses." Once I swallow my sip, I start to suggest we play cards or a board game while we ride out the rest of the power outage, and I have every intention of spicing up those games with some sort of stripping stipulation.

But Wade speaks up first. "Where are you from?"

I lick the oaky drops from my bottom lip and sigh. "Fine. We'll do this your way, and I'll tell you anything you want to know."

"But…" I can practically hear his cautious smile in the single word.

"You're learning," I praise and clink my glass to his. I try to, anyway, but I think I get his arm. It's hard to tell in the dark. "But… you can't ask for my number. You can't ask for my last name or address, and you certainly cannot ask to see me again. I'm not in the market for a relationship or anything similar. Think of me as the Antichrist of romance and commitment—the only Holy Trinity I'm interested in is alcohol, friends, and good times."

His gulp is barely audible over the music as he swallows. "I'm in no position to date, either, so we have a deal." We spend the next beat in silence as I sway to the music until he finally speaks up again. "Earlier, you said you moved here. Where are you originally from?"

"Sapphire Creek."

"I've never heard of it."

I laugh into my drink. Why is that so adorable? "I would've been shocked if you had heard of it. It's a very small town down South."

In the blanket of darkness, his fingers wrap around my wrist, and he leads me away until my knee hits the edge of the couch cushion. I hear shuffling and then, "Tell me about it."

I purse my lips, and it's not to keep the sip of wine inside my mouth. I'd rather describe to him the worst UTI I've ever experienced than talk about my roots.

But we made a deal, and I'm a woman of my word.

Besides, it's not even my hometown that I despise. The place itself is rather nice and inviting. It's a few of the people I left behind who don't deserve a second of my energy or any space in my brain.

I hike my leg up and tuck my foot under my other knee, settling in. We could be here for another thirty minutes or three hours. Either way, I plan on surviving it.

Hell, it might even be therapeutic to share these things with a stranger I'll never see again. In fact, I can't fully see him now, which makes it even easier to spill my guts.

"Sapphire Creek is the kind of Georgia town that's charming and whimsical to those passing through." I dip my head and feel a smile in the corners of my lips. "Downtown is adorable, with a bakery in one corner, an old abandoned but well-kept house across the street, and an antique store with unique gems. Everyone knows everyone, and it can be a good or a bad thing. Usually, it's a little of both. All in all, it was… the perfect place to call home growing up."

"Georgia, huh? You don't have an accent."

I'm full-on smiling now as I clear my throat. When I speak again, my mouth relaxes into the natural accent I've suppressed for over ten years, and I slow my words so that each one drips from my mouth like honey. "That's because I've worked long and hard to fit in here in the Big Apple. Otherwise, I would've been trapped in a box of the Southern Belle variety with no escape route."

"That's… very hot, actually. Can you talk with this accent while we bake a peach cobbler?"

I throw my head back and laugh, and suddenly, the sweet and spicy taste of my grandma's peach cobbler appears on my tongue. My taste buds run wild over the phantom food in my mouth.

But who can blame me? Once upon a time, the woman's cobbler was the best in the state. It's no surprise the dessert has such a supernatural effect on me.

What makes it more special—and heart wrenching—is remembering her baking it. She'd always get flour on both cheeks, but it wasn't by accident. She'd pat the white powder on her face before she started in order "to become one with the cobbler."

It made my younger sister and me laugh. We also played with the flour ourselves, much to my mother's dismay, since it was one of the many things we did that she didn't think was ladylike.

"My grandma won awards for her peach cobbler," I say, lost in thought.

"Can you tell me about her?"

I shift until my shoulder blades hit the back of the couch, and I drape a blanket over my lap. This time, I'm more than happy to answer his question. Although I miss my grandma like crazy, I love talking about her, and I don't do it enough. "She was the best. The kind of person who'd order a Christmas card in the size of a whole page instead of a postcard. The kind who'd stick every single card or invitation she'd receive onto the refrigerator until she couldn't open the door. She was quirky and loved with her whole heart." I squeeze my glass tightly between my two hands. "She never pressured me to be anything I'm not, and I was always so grateful for that."

"What do you mean?"

"Many people there dream of living at the end of a wholesome neighborhood with a cul-de-sac, where their kids can play together after school."

"That's a nice picture," he muses, his voice low in this late hour.

"I had the same dream when I got married, but it ended before we ever made it to the cul-de-sac."

"Is that why you moved away—because of your ex?"

I instinctively nod, even though Wade probably can't see me. "After we separated, the town started to feel too small.

Too suffocating. It seemed like every day, I'd run into him or one of the skanks he'd been texting while we were married. I just couldn't take it anymore. And leaving was actually a lot easier than I thought it would be, so I knew it was the right call."

"You're very brave, Bree." He squeezes my forearm, and my stupid heart lurches.

That can't be good.

"Not just that, though. The number of sympathy pies I received from neighbors was astronomical. If I hadn't left when I did, I would've been buried underneath them."

"What a way to go, though," he plays along.

And I nearly choke on my laughter as a ball of… something catches in my throat.

It's easy to talk with Wade like this. The back-and-forth. The flow. He and I are the equivalent of feng shui or some bullshit. Erin would know. She's into the earthy crap.

But this night will go nowhere, other than the occasional recollection in the distant future of a night well spent in a stranger's arms.

A stranger who listens like a saint but fucks like a sailor on leave.

"What about you? Where did you move here from?" I tip my glass back but find it empty. Sometime during our chat, I drained it.

"Southern California."

"And your daughter?"

"She lives here with her mom… and Roger," he bites out. With his face mostly obscured, it's much easier to rely on my hearing, and I definitely detect resentment.

I tense, debating whether I should suggest a sexy game,

after all. Clearly, this is a sore topic, and the last thing I want to do is make him uncomfortable. Wouldn't be a great way to return the light feeling he's given me.

A sigh drifts between us, and his foot nudges mine as he shifts. "I didn't know about Violet until last summer."

"But she's…" I hook my thumb over my shoulder toward the bedroom, where a picture of the two is displayed. "She looks to be about, what, five or six?"

"She'll turn seven in a couple of weeks." His laugh is sad and hoarse. "Years ago, I was celebrating my birthday at a club in Tribeca. My parents had flown a friend and me out here, and after our dinner, Slater and I popped into the first place with a bar, music, and people. It's where I met Violet's mother. Maggie and I hit it off, but I was in college on the complete opposite side of the country. She was a student at SUNY Binghamton. It could never work, so we agreed—"

"To a one-night stand," I finish. "I know this tale all too well."

"Do you know the one where she gets pregnant, doesn't have a way to contact him so he doesn't know, and she marries someone else, who now wants custody of his kid?"

My jaw drops. It takes a lot to surprise me and even more to render me speechless, but he's done both. Because no, I don't know this kind of story at all, although I do know of the custody struggles some of my clients at the career center experience. The more forthcoming ones share the sordid details, and they break my heart.

But listening to this situation from someone I've been naked with has a totally new meaning, and my stomach aches as if he punched me there.

"Fucking Roger is the only reason Maggie found and

told me. He claims he's the only father in Violet's life, and he deserves the right to be her legal guardian. I have to sign off on it, but—"

"You can't!" I blurt, my ears ringing.

His hand is gentle and warm when it lands on top of mine, and he says, "Trust me, gorgeous. I'm fighting for my daughter, and no prick from Wall Street is going to stop me."

"Good." I nod and repeat the simple word a couple more times as flashbacks of my own father's back while he walked away blink through my mind.

"I haven't really talked about this with many people, other than my parents and my grandma. Tucker and Slater too."

"You're still friends with Slater?"

This earns me a chuckle. "I am. Some days, it's hard to overlook the arrogance that plagues him like a virus, but he's also the most loyal person I've ever met. We played, um…"

"On the playground?" I guess, with a smile tugging at my lips as I imagine a young Wade and another boy shoving each other in the sandbox.

"Right. The playground," he answers stiffly. Is that really want he meant to say?

"So, this Maggie." I finally set my empty glass onto the coffee table, then lean back against the couch as another round of flashing blue and red lights interrupts the quiet ambiance. Once they fade, I open and close my mouth.

What is she like?

Are you disappointed you can't win her back?

Have you ever been in love at all?

Instead, I ask, "Is she why you don't do one-night stands?"

I hardly register what question I ask out loud, as the late hour, drinks, and mind-blowing sex hit me at once, my mind a fuzzy mess of jumbled thoughts. It's hard to believe margaritas with the girls was just a few hours ago.

So much has happened since I left them, and it's all weighing on my mind and body.

I briefly close my eyes to rest them as he says, "Sort of. After she told me about Violet and I realized how much I've missed out on by not exchanging information, I just haven't been able to appreciate a good time with a stranger. It's hard to get on a roller coaster after you just read about accidents that have occurred, right?" He lets out a nervous sound I can't decipher. It's somewhere between a hum and a sigh.

"One in fifteen-point-five million." With my eyes still closed, I rest my head on the back of the couch and snuggle deeper under the blanket. "Those are the chances of being injured on a ride-related incident."

"Do you work at an amusement park or something?"

"I just care about my friends, one of whom went to Coney Island last spring. I didn't know beforehand so I couldn't give her the facts, but thankfully, Madi and her movie star boyfriend didn't ride anything but each other."

His deep laugh jolts my eyes open, and I giggle too.

Until one very important piece of information rattles my brain awake.

"Wait…" I plant my hands on the couch cushion and hoist myself upright. "Is that why you've insisted on getting my number tonight? Because of what happened with Maggie?"

He doesn't immediately answer, and my heart plummets into my stomach.

"It is, isn't it?" I press, my voice more of a screech.

"It's not… exactly true," he stammers, and it's as convincing as the technician was when she told me my first wax wouldn't hurt so bad. Spoiler alert—it hurt like a motherfucker.

I curse under my breath and stand, but I only take a step before my knee slams into the corner of the coffee table.

Just great.

"Fuck," I hiss.

"Bree, please sit back down."

"I need to go."

"The power is still out. You can't be out there like this."

"I'll take a candle with me," I deadpan as I use my feet to feel around the floor for the rest of my clothes.

Shuffling sounds from behind me, and then the lights outside the windows from other buildings flicker to life as if to say, "Your time is up."

And it couldn't have come at a better moment. Maybe Erin is onto something about the universe's plan, after all.

With the help of the candle, I find the switch on the wall and flip the light on. "Look at that. Guess I don't need this anymore." I set the candle onto the counter and locate my leggings on the tiled floor.

As I slide them on, Wade meets me in the kitchen. "What's so wrong about me asking for your number in case we need to get back in touch?"

"Because I thought—" I swallow back the incriminating admission. It wouldn't do any good to share it with him, anyway. He wouldn't understand.

"You thought you'd sleep with me and leave. You figured it would be so simple to get off and run away, but I pushed you into more. Yes, I did it for my own selfish reasons, but you're no better than me," he declares, and he's not completely wrong.

"Good thing we agreed to a single night, then. Win-win."

I lift my shoulder in a defeated shrug. Fully dressed, I cling to my phone and clutch while he paces on the other side of the counter. As I reach for the door, I suppress my sudden instinct to glance back at him.

I'll never see Wade again, so it would suck to have the final picture of him in the light. The darkness was much better to hide what I didn't want to know.

During the trek back to my side of the state border, I chew on the tip of my thumbnail and face the facts: I wanted to get railed, and I did. I should be happy, even if it turned out he didn't want my number because he liked me.

And that's pathetic enough to admit to myself. I actually thought the guy liked me, and I enjoyed the adoration more than I have in the past. What was I thinking by letting myself get carried away? I know better. It's why I live and date the way I do.

I shouldn't be so hurt by the truth behind Wade's motives.

He only wanted to cover his bases out of some inherent duty he feels just because he failed to do right by a woman from his past. It's respectable, really, but it doesn't feel so knight-in-shining-armor-like when the lesson comes at my expense.

In any case, it's better this way. He's on his side of the river, and I'm on mine. We won't see each other again.

SIX

Wade

"Christ," I hiss under my breath.

Ignoring the looks tossed in my direction from the others on the subway, I end the call halfway through Maggie's upbeat voice mail message. The shrill of her tone grates on my nerves as I stew in my frustration.

It's the third call she hasn't answered in the last hour. Is she dodging me?

With anger boiling through me, I roughly tap at my phone screen and send her a message.

Call me.

The subway sways to a halt at my stop, and at least ten people shoulder past me before I hop off, barely missing my chance before the doors clamp shut. I race up the stairs, using the map on my phone to walk in the direction of the career center Tucker's cop friend recommended.

The one in Jersey City couldn't see me for another month, so I'm trying one in Brooklyn. To my luck, they had an opening much sooner. Saying it's a relief would be an understatement since I need a job stat. I've been living here for almost two months, and I have no prospects.

Between all the years on a pro soccer team and the sponsorships I secured, I have plenty in savings, but that money won't last forever, especially with the cost of living in this area, plus taking care of another human.

The legal fees funding my family attorney's beach house also need to come from somewhere. My accounts haven't taken such a hit since the first time I discovered Roulette. Shit got ugly pretty quickly.

Before I enter the building, I check my phone one last time, but there's no new message or call from Maggie.

Jaw clenched, I throw the door open and march upstairs with heavy steps, releasing my anger onto the building. I reach the office with the name Tessa Fields on the door. When I made the appointment, I was told she'd be the one I'm meeting with today. She was the only one available, and I hope to God she'll be my saving grace.

I raise my hand to knock, and the door swings open, revealing a woman with shoulder-length blonde hair and thick-framed eyeglasses perched on her nose. As she reaches up to tuck a strand of hair behind her ear, an obnoxiously large diamond ring on her wedding finger practically blinds me.

"Whoa—that thing should come with a warning," I joke.

She holds her hand in front of her, and the sparkles reflecting in her dopey eyes scream newlywed. "Carter toned it down with the engagement ring, but he insisted on the gaudy wedding band. Compromise has become our best friend."

"How long have you been married?"

"Only about four months, and in such a short time, I've already become an expert," she says with a hesitant laugh. It's the kind that suggests she's joking. I don't think there is such a thing as a love expert, anyway. "You're Wade Jameson, right?"

"Correct." I give her a tight-lipped smile. "Make me employable, please."

Instead of the grin she's worn since she opened the door, her lips sink into a frown. "Unfortunately, I need to run. There's an issue with a charity benefit I'm helping to organize, and I have to take care of it, as it's time-sensitive. I do have good news for you, though." She curls her finger for me to follow her down the hall to a different office. "My friend Bree had a cancelation and is able to fit you in, so we can get you started right away."

Her voice fades as she launches into some speech on the joys and pitfalls of the journey to the right career path, but all I can focus on is the name Bree.

That's what she said, right?

We stop in front of a closed door, and I freeze with memories of my night with Bree from over three weeks ago.

Her taste coated my tongue.

She moaned as she lost herself in the moment with me.

Her ass was perfect in my hands as she pressed her bare chest to the window.

But this is New York, with such a vast population. There are plenty of Brees in the area, so there's no way—

"Oh my God."

The whispered words of shock don't come from Tessa or me. Instead, the door is open, and standing behind the large desk is none other than my one-night stand.

"What the hell are you doing here?" she squeaks.

"This is Wade," Tessa says, but it comes out like more of a question as she looks between us, confusion coloring her tan features. "You said you have an opening right now, don't you?"

Bree clears her throat and tugs on the bottom of her hot pink blazer. "Of course. Yes. I did say that, and it's still true. As true as cheese is delicious."

Amusement cuts through my shock, and a laugh rolls out of me.

"Um…" Tessa steps between us, giving me her back as she asks Bree in hushed tones, "Are you okay?"

"Peachy."

"I'll leave you to it, then." Tessa pauses a beat as if she's unsure of Bree's answer, but when her phone in her hand bursts with a piercing ringtone, she waves goodbye.

Once the door clicks shut behind her, Bree and I lock eyes, standing frozen on opposite sides of the cramped office. It appears even smaller with the clutter hiding the surface of her desk, the crooked frames on the walls, and the dying plants in the corner.

In sum, this doesn't seem like the ideal place to make dreams happen.

But Bree herself is an entirely different story. Her bright blazer is the welcomed splash of color this space needs, although I'm surprised there isn't more of that flair and flash in here.

Her rosy cheeks and sparkling eyes are just as I remember.

But her hair is styled and silky, as if she just left the hair salon, much different than the tangled mess it was in when she left my apartment all those nights ago.

As Bree shuffles papers around on her desk, she asks, "So how does Violet feel about the state's proposed changes to the cafeteria meals? Lower added sugars is probably healthier, but it's very brutal. When I was in school, we had the same two options every day except for Fridays. That's when they really let loose and got crazy. I usually had the big breadsticks with the melted cheese inside. Kind of became my *thing* that people knew me for."

I furrow my brow. Is she… rambling?

I don't remember her going on like this during the few hours we spent together. That night, she seemed fairly relaxed, albeit reluctant to share anything personal until we made the pact.

That was before the perfectly good and hot evening blew up in my face, of course.

"Are you nervous?" I ask, trying my hardest to stifle the amused grin tugging at the corners of my mouth.

"Should I be? Are you here to off me or something? I already have a borderline stalker in this office—I don't need another."

"What? Is someone harassing you?" I lunge forward. "Give me a name."

"Don't do the protective bit. You're not my boyfriend. Besides, I can handle myself, and I feel the need to remind you—I have mace in my purse in case you're here to off me."

"Why the hell would you think that?" I gape, my heart still racing at the thought of some asshole in this building causing her trouble.

An asshole who isn't me, anyway.

"You tell me," she challenges. "I never gave you my last name, occupation, or any other identifying fact about myself. I did say I live in Brooklyn, but that's hardly enough information to go on. We were never supposed to see each other again. Yet, here you stand in my office. Creepy, much?"

I scratch the back of my head. "Okay, that sounds bad."

"Did your officer friend track me down?"

"Tucker? No. I promise, this is the weirdest fucking coincidence in the history of coincidences."

"You expect me to believe this *wasn't* planned?" She stares unblinkingly at me, and it's clear it's going to take a Herculean-level of convincing that I didn't stalk her, nor am I here to *off* her.

"I swear, I didn't know," I insist. "If you remember correctly, I'd made the appointment with Tessa. I had no clue you worked here, nor did I orchestrate some emergency for her to leave so I could see you, instead. That's bizarre."

"Not more bizarre than you being here right now." She paces behind the desk, chewing on her thumbnail. "I can't believe this."

"Honestly, I don't know how or why we ended up back in the same room, but I'm glad we did."

"Of course you are. Stalkers love when they *coincidentally* get their victims alone."

"You've obviously been watching too many cop shows."

She pauses her pacing and thumb chewing to nod. "I have been bingeing more *SVU* than normal, so fair enough." As I gloat in a moment of victory, she sweeps her curious gaze over me, then asks, "Why are you glad to see me?"

"I hate how we left things, and I've wanted to apologize ever since."

Something flashes across her eyes, but as soon as I notice it, it's gone. Does she believe me? Is she happy to know I've thought a lot about her in the last few weeks?

"I'm sorry for the dick move I made," I say. "I was scared of a repeat, and I wasn't thinking about how you might see it. I was only thinking of myself and how guilty I still feel over the whole situation with Maggie."

Bree waves me off. "I overreacted. It had been a long night, and I started talking crazy. Besides, I'm no saint. Like you said, I did use you for your body, and while you did worship me like I'm a fucking queen, that's all it was. I have no right to be upset with you, and you don't owe me an apology or an explanation."

It's a relief to know she doesn't still hold it against me, but that's not what hits me square in the gut. The part that sticks out the most is the way she says I worshipped her. The compliment makes my dick twitch with pride, and the urge to go up to the roof, beat on my chest, and scream in celebration is all too consuming.

"Um… so you're job hunting?" she asks on a gulp.

"Right. A job."

Not only do I need to start making a living and provide for the daughter I've known about for less than a year, but I also need a *respectable* job that will impress a judge when the time comes to go to court for joint custody. That's where things seem to be heading since I can't rely on Maggie alone.

There's a lot on the line here. I can't let myself be distracted by the beautiful woman in front of me.

I'm about to take a seat when my phone rings, and as soon as I glimpse Maggie's name flashing on the screen, blood roars in my ears. "I need to take this," I say, then flee from

Bree's office faster than I might if the building were on fire.

I hold the phone up to my ear as I jump down the stairs and fly outside for more privacy. Foregoing pleasantries, I grind out, "You haven't answered your phone all afternoon."

"I've been busy. I don't sit around waiting for a guy I barely know to call me. I don't owe you that kind of accessibility, Wade, and you should—"

"All right, all right." I blow out the frustrated breath I've been holding in since our mediation session this morning. "I didn't mean to sound like you need to be available to me at all times, but I do expect some decency when you show up to our session late and leave early. We didn't get anything accomplished."

"It was enough. It counted," she says, punctuating each syllable with annoyance.

"It might've counted for the mediator, but it damn sure wasn't enough for me. We didn't decide on a single compromise. I want to see my daughter, Maggie, without you lurking and overseeing the entire visit. You hover over my every move and everything I say to her like I'm a criminal."

"Well, you kind of are."

A pinch of pain throbs in my temple.

"Past aside, the last time you saw her, you brought an iPad."

"I asked you about that."

"Not before she saw it. You clearly know nothing about kids. The second they see something new and shiny, or anything full of sugar, you can't reason with them. You ambushed me into allowing her to have something Roger and I agreed we wouldn't give her for a couple of years."

"We already discussed this. It's why we made a deal to let

Violet keep the iPad at my place. She'll only use pre-approved games on it, but you hardly ever let her visit me. We always do it your way somewhere in public."

"Look, I don't know you, Wade. Can you blame me for being cautious when it comes to my daughter?"

"*Our* daughter. She's *both* of ours, no matter how badly you and Roger don't want it to be true," I clip as my temper rises.

"Fine," she snaps. "You're right, okay? I do wish you'd just sign the papers and let Roger legally adopt her. He's been the only father she's known, and you're taking that away from her. You're being selfish, Wade."

"You think gaslighting me is going to work?" I huff. "That's low, even for you."

"I'm Violet's mother. I'm trying to protect her."

"Finally—something we can agree on. That's all I want for her too. For her to be happy and healthy. But I can't ensure any of that if I'm outcasted at every turn. I'm not going anywhere, Maggie, and if you're not going to meet me halfway, I'll take you to court for joint custody. We'll let a judge settle this once and for all."

"Is that a threat?"

"No, it's a promise." I end the call with flashes of Violet's innocent grin running through my mind.

She's all I care about, and I'll do whatever it takes to be an important and involved part of her life. I'm definitely not going to let fucking Roger take over *my* role.

Immediately, I call my lawyer, who answers on the second ring. The woman always answers when I need her, which makes me more than happy to pay her astronomical fees.

After I recount the *non*-session with Maggie this morning,

our phone call, and my growing impatience of our standstill, I say, "I want joint custody. What do I need to do to prepare for court?"

"To be honest, you're not looking great."

"What the fuck does that mean?"

"What have I—"

"I'm sorry for the language. I know you've asked me multiple times not to curse, and I'm sorry. I'm just frustrated." I hold my hand up in surrender like she can see me.

"I understand," Cassidy says through my speaker. "And I'm sorry to be so blunt with the bad news, but there's no use in sugarcoating it. Frankly, it would be a waste of both our time. So, here are the issues—Maggie is right about some things."

Instead of cursing out loud, a string of unsavory words zip through my mind.

"You have been absent for the last seven years. Although it wasn't your fault since you didn't know about Violet, it wasn't Maggie's fault, either. Next, you've just moved to the city and have no ties to the community, family in the area, or experience with kids, the school system, and the like. These things matter to a judge. Those kinds of things solidify the fact that you're here to stay. It would be a different story if you were married and had a job or a career of some sort to show you were serious about living here permanently."

"I had a career," I growl. "One I loved very much and spent my entire life working for. I gave it up in order to be closer to Violet—to be her father."

"Which holds a lot of weight in your favor, but it won't be enough. Like I said, what is to keep you from finding out that being a father is too hard? That living so far from friends and family is too difficult? You need to show you are rooted here and won't pack up and run at the first sign of trouble, because trust me, parenting is not simple."

I pull the phone away from my ear and tap it against my chin as more frustration gnaws at me.

"Again, if you were married and even part of a local soccer league or something, it would be very helpful."

"I'm not either of those," I lament.

"No, you're a bachelor with several photos online of you taking shots with models during the off-season," she shoots back. "The more incriminating photo is the one where you're sporting a black eye and standing next to another guy whose crooked nose is bleeding and eye is swollen shut."

"Are you on my side? Because it's starting to sound like you're not," I grumble. "And for the record, the asshole didn't press charges. We settled our shit before we parted ways."

"There's a chance I'm being harsh with you, Carter, because you refuse to abide by the one thing I asked of you besides my fee—*language*."

I flinch at her use of my first name. No one's used it on me since my mother scolded me for getting sloppy drunk at my high school graduation party. If that alone wasn't bad enough, I drove our golf cart over her precious rose bushes that night.

On a sigh, Cassidy says, "I'm on your side, okay? I'm not bringing up anything a judge won't, so I'd like to prepare you. Please take what I say seriously."

Once I agree to do so, we make an appointment to strategize in person at her office, and I end the call, dangerously close to chucking my phone into oncoming traffic.

To my dismay, Cassidy makes several brutal but very real

points, and Maggie will use each one of them against me. I can't even blame her, no matter how badly I want to.

She and Roger have the upper hand. It's actually no contest.

Roger has a high-paying, stable job as a stockbroker. He doesn't have sloppy photos online, nor does he use the word *fuck* as often as I do. The guy is in his midthirties—he's a fucking grown-up.

And Maggie's right to trust him to be Violet's father instead of me, but I can't ignore that Violet is, in fact, mine.

I've loved her from the moment I found out about her.

The first time I saw her, I cried, which I haven't done since I fell off my bike as a kid and broke my collarbone.

A protective urge consumed me from the start, and I would do anything to care for her like a father does his daughter. I wouldn't be able to live with myself otherwise, and I sure as hell wouldn't be happy without her in my life.

No matter how badly I've screwed up in the past, I'm determined to do right by her now. To be the rock she can lean on in the future. I crave to be the one she runs to if she falls off her own bike like I did when I ran to my dad back then.

I can do her a lot of good, if I'm just allowed the chance.

SEVEN

After twenty minutes of his absence, I decide Wade isn't coming back. He probably faked a phone call just to get away from the awkwardness of working with me, and I don't blame him. I imagine I'd do the same if I were in his shoes.

As I start to prep for my final client of the day, Drooling Dan appears in the doorway of my office. Wade left it open, and I never closed it.

Shit.

"You are looking good enough to eat today, Breanna," he says, leaning in for reasons I can only assume are impure. He likely doesn't want anyone to hear.

Then again, he's established a reputation of the innocent guy next door. His nerdy glasses and dimpled smile were cute at first—even I admitted as much—but his lingering eyes behind those thick lenses tell a much different story.

One I'm tired of hearing at this point. For the last month, it's been one sleazy encounter after another, and it's making my day-to-day life exhausting.

I tap my chin sarcastically and toss back, "And you, *Un-*dapper Dan, seem to have a drop of drool on your lip that's been there since Christmas."

"Your sense of humor is such a delight."

"Yes—I'm truly a warm light on humanity," I deadpan.

Right when he's about to step into my office—and I'm fingering the zipper on my purse for access to my emergency mace—Wade reappears. Thank God.

I'm curious as to what took him so long, but mostly, he's the key to getting me out of this unpleasant trap that is Dan.

"Hi, sweetie." I rush around the desk. "Come in, come in."

Wade's brow furrows as he sidesteps Dan. His confusion deepens as I loop my arm through his and squeeze his bicep with exaggerated affection. I wouldn't even pet dogs this lovingly.

"Dan, have you met my boyfriend? This is Wade. He's my boyfriend," I repeat for good measure. Dan's skull is clearly thick, and I could use every ounce of help to make sure he understands I'm off-fucking-limits.

Even if it means lying to him about Wade.

"Your boyfriend—not husband?" Dan asks, eyeing Wade and the way I run my palm up and down his arm.

Do I detect hope in his tone?

"Well, I don't like to pressure him, but I *am* expecting a ring for Valentine's Day next week…" I practically purr in his ear, one hundred percent committing to the lie rolling off my tongue. It's easier than it should be. In leaning so close to Wade, I accidentally catch a whiff of his cologne, and deliciously filthy thoughts of our night together flash through my mind.

God, the way he owned and worshipped my body was unparalleled—a once-in-a-lifetime experience.

"I can't confirm or deny as much. I have been known to plan big, romantic surprises, so I'd hate to spoil any of the fun." Wade covers my hand with his large one.

Dan gives us a tight-lipped smile as he backs out of my office. "I think someone is calling my name," he claims, and it's safe to say, he got the message.

It's also safe to say Wade is a lifesaver. I would've hated to give Dan a painful facial with a swift punch to the eye just like Madi showed me.

Actually, I wouldn't have hated it at all. He would've deserved it.

I close the door and sag against it.

"I thought I *wasn't* your boyfriend." Smirking, Wade crosses both arms over his chest and sears me with his curious gaze.

"As far as Dan is concerned, you and I live together, fuck like bunnies, and are as good as betrothed." I exhale again and march straight for the hand sanitizer on the corner of my desk. I need a full shower after having the gross douchebag in here, but this is good enough for now. "Thank you for going along with that. You saved me—and him."

"I wouldn't go so far as to say ole Danny is safe." His amused expression slides away. "Is he the borderline stalker you mentioned earlier?"

I nod as I return to my side of the desk. "He's also the HR rep, so there's not much I can do but hope he finds someone on a kinky app to get his jollies off with."

For the first time since Wade shocked me with his resurrection into my life, I get a good look at him. At his broad shoulders and strong but lean build. The naturally full eyelashes framing devilish eyes. His wild hair, which is longer now than when we were stuck together all those nights ago.

In the clear light of day and without the fog of horny desperation, Wade appears younger than I originally thought. I don't detect many lines around his eyes, and the skin around his bulging muscles is too taut.

He seems… youthful.

With his faded denim jacket slung around the back of the chair, he starts to sit, but I stop him, blurting, "How old are you?"

He blinks, clearly surprised by my question. "Is this how you begin every counseling session?"

"No, but we haven't started yet."

He studies me while I hold my breath, then puts me out of my misery—almost. "I'm twenty-eight."

"Twenty-eight? You're twenty-fucking-eight?" I grip the edge of my desk for support.

"Why? How old are you?"

"I'm thirty-three." As I pace, I mutter mostly to myself, "I fucked a younger guy. Okay. This is okay. It's totally fine. Just a five-year difference, right? That's not too much."

The night I met Wade, the young, douchey bartender had thrown me off balance. I wanted to prove to myself that I still had my figure. My wit. My appeal.

Did I subconsciously do this? Did I unwittingly seek

Wade out because I assumed he was younger, on some level, and I wanted to prove I could still have fresh meat if I wanted?

"I've never been to a career counselor before. Is this common?" Wade points at me, and more sweat soaks through my shirt underneath my arms.

"This isn't funny." I place both hands on my hips. "How can you be so young? You're so… rugged. And your tongue knows… It's like you know every language, ancient and present. Like you speak the language of female pleasure better than sexual gods themselves. How is that possible?"

"Thank you." He winks, and my stomach flips.

"Now is not the time to be cute."

"How else am I supposed to respond when you give me such a *divine* compliment?"

I shoot him a warning glare as my heart thunders against my rib cage.

"Fine. We'll do this your way." He scoots the chair under my desk, seemingly deciding against sitting down, and widens his stance. "Bree, I'm a single dad. I have a daughter who's older than the years separating you and me. It's not like I'm underage. I can legally drink, rent a car, and—hold onto your panties—I have a seven-year-old kid, just in case you didn't hear me the first time. So, what's the big deal?"

I throw my hands up and nod. "You're right. I mean, it's not like I'm at the old age where I need reading glasses to see the writing on items at the grocery store. I still have eons until I reach that point."

"Sure?"

After one more spin in place behind my desk and a shake of my shoulders, I clap my hands and sit. I suck in a calming breath and muster my professional tone when I ask, "What can I do for you today? What do you need?"

"Other than a wife, apparently? I need a job." Wade lowers himself onto the seat across from me, and my eyes dart directly between his widespread legs.

Heat floods my cheeks, and suddenly, the three feet of chestnut between us isn't enough.

"Well," I start and busy myself with the keys on my computer. "I can't assist you with the wife, but I can definitely help you with the job. First, I need to gather some info on you, your background, and past work experience. Then I'll give you an aptitude and a personality test, which we'll go over together afterward, and I'll—"

"I'd rather just discuss it all with you face-to-face without tests," his low voice cuts in. "I've never been a fan of exams. I'm more of a… hands-on kind of guy."

I gulp over the suggestive tone in his words.

As I gather my ovaries into place, he freezes in much the same way I do when I accidentally bite my lip or hit my funny bone.

"Are you okay? Do you need some water?" I wait for a response, but the only thing I get is an odd change in his expression.

"Marry me," he blurts.

"Is this because of what happened with Dan earlier? Because I only needed you to pretend while he was here. It's not an open, ongoing role."

"This has nothing to do with Dan, although"—his gaze darts over my face as if he's in the middle of solving a complicated chemistry problem—"my proposal would get him off your back. He clearly has a thing for single women, not married ones. Did you see the way his eyes lit up when you said I was just your boyfriend?"

"I did. Isn't he so creepy? If I could show up with a husband, I could—oh my God, what am I saying? I can't marry you!" I screech.

"Hear me out." He holds his hands up, pleading. "I want joint custody of Violet, but her mother is fighting me on it. She dictates when and where I see her, and she hovers over me like I'm going to feed Violet crackers off the sidewalk. I want to be able to get to know her—*really* know her—without Maggie answering my questions for her. I haven't been to Coney Island in years, and I'd like to take Violet this summer. I want to take her to Central Park and eat ice cream until we feel like throwing up. I want to tuck my own daughter into bed at night."

He hits me where it hurts with his love and devotion for his daughter, and the room suddenly feels too cramped.

"Maggie has her husband Roger, who makes crazy good money. They're a real, wholesome family with a big house. Their backyard is bigger than my apartment. They have the stability I don't."

"I can find you a great job. It's what I do," I croak, as if I just woke up from a late night.

Wade's laugh is sad and completely the opposite of optimistic. "And I'd really appreciate your help with that, but according to my lawyer, it's not enough. I need to put down roots."

"Why don't I slide a ring onto my finger and pretend to be your wife, then?"

"They'll know it's fake if we don't have a paper trail. Maggie would light my ass on fire if she finds out I'm lying about anything, and she'll do her fucking homework. This needs to be legal."

What he's saying goes beyond logic, no matter how pure his intentions are. And my God, is Wade a saint of a man for wanting to be a good father to Violet. It makes him so much hotter. Younger men don't normally do it for me beyond a single night of fun. In my experience, they use too many slang words and spend far too much time on the newest social media apps. But Wade is giving me a whole new perspective.

And I'm not immune to his appeal.

But the idea of another marriage instantly makes my skin crawl.

"I can't be your wife!" I screech again and stand to pace a hole in the floor. "We slept together *one* night weeks ago."

"That's the brilliant part of this—you and I have a history."

"How can you call a wild night of drinks, sex, and a power outage a history?"

"It's a romantic story, right?" He wiggles his eyebrows.

"We were a one-night stand, Wade. No one is going to believe we're getting married."

"They will once they see you."

I'm wound up, cranky as hell from a night of horrid sleep and lunch from a new food truck, which I found a hair in. My apartment is raising the rent upon the renewal of my lease, and I haven't gotten laid since the man in front of me took my horny hoo-hoo to poundtown.

Those are the only explanations as to why my stupid heart skips because of his compliment. The bitch even tucks it away for a rainy day, when I'll inevitably need to feed it to my ego.

I steel myself and say, "Flattery got me into your bed, but it's going to take a lot more to get me down the aisle."

"What about steps?"

"What?"

"I'm proposing we go up the steps of a courthouse—no aisle. No spectacle of any kind, actually. Just us, two 'I dos,' and a witness."

"How magical," I deadpan.

He drops the comedic twinkle in his eyes as both hands fall to his sides. "Look, I know this is crazy, but I'll do anything to make sure I get joint custody of my daughter. I'll do anything to build a real relationship with her and make memories and be a family. It's why I'm in New York in the first place."

"What do you mean?"

"I retired from pro soccer a couple months ago in order to move up here. This is where Violet lives, so this is where I should be too."

"You're a professional athlete? You're telling me I fucked a young professional athlete?"

He holds his arms out and shrugs, and my jaw drops.

What is life? How did any of this happen to me?

In truth, I should be dancing in mini-celebration over bagging a young professional athlete, but instead, I'm two seconds away from vomiting.

Because the hot single dad I slept with is proposing to me.

I shake my head. This isn't just crazy; it's bananas. The kind of insanity used in movies and books, where a fancy schmancy writer controls the outcome.

This is not real life. It's too risky and complicated and, oh yeah, fucking *bananas*.

"I'm not your girl," I say with a frown as guilt settles in my chest. For reasons I can't decipher, I'm oddly disappointed to let him down, but I can't do this. Around the lump in my throat, I manage to say, "I'm never getting married again. Been there, done that, hated it, and vowed to never torture myself with such a thing ever again."

"That's the beauty of this arrangement—it wouldn't be real. We'd be married only on paper. As far as anyone else would know, you and I live together, fuck like bunnies, and are as good as betrothed."

Hearing my own words from earlier coming out of his mouth surprisingly brings a smile to my lips. We get along—that much is obvious. We have amazing chemistry, so it wouldn't be a hard sell to convince a judge that we're horrendously in love.

But what about Maggie? From the sounds of it, she's insanely controlling. She wouldn't take us at our word, no matter what official papers we have on our side. She'd pry into every detail with a fine-tooth comb and raging disbelief.

And what would we tell their daughter? Or my friends? We can't lie to the people who are closest to us, but if we tell them the truth, they'd all need to commit to the lie too.

There are too many moving parts here.

"You have not thought this through," I insist.

"I admit, this was a game-time decision, but we could work out the details together."

"Here's one pretty important detail: your daughter. I don't know anything about children. I literally know more about Robert Downey Jr.'s inspiring road to recovery and rise to fame than I do about kids."

Wade tilts his head, and instead of taking this as seriously as I thought he would, he chuckles. "You surprise me at every turn."

"How so?"

"When I first stepped in here, you were talking about changes in school cafeterias, and now you're talking about Robert Downey Jr."

"I'm a celebrity gossip junkie, but I like to stay current on the news as well. I have a lot of different clients, and it never hurts to be informed. That way, I can better serve them."

"I respect that. I also respect that you called your friends the night of the power outage. When you found out you couldn't leave my place, you let your friends know where you were in case of an emergency, which was smart."

"It was common sense. You're making it sound like I solved world hunger." I hook a thumb over my shoulder and point to the withering plants. "I can't even take care of a couple of plants. My friend Erin insisted I'd be good at it, but she was dead wrong. All I did was name them both. You want to know the truth about little Bob and Suzie? I forgot they were in here as soon as I left on the day they arrived. The only reason I'm acknowledging them now is because they're starting to smell, and I need to toss them out."

"They're just plants. No one I know is good at caring for plants, so who gives a fuck?" He stands up. "I can even help you get rid of them. In fact, I can help you with anything like this. Growing up, my parents traveled a lot, and I stayed with my grandma and grandpa. They taught me to be self-reliant, so I can fix anything from a sink to a car. I can put together furniture too. You name it."

I bite my lip like he's talking dirty to me. What he's offering is almost as good as sex, actually. Last month, when the pipe in my kitchen burst under the sink, I had to wait far too long for the landlord to patch it. It would've been nice to have an in-house handyman.

My protests against this whole thing dissolve, but I still have too many questions burning in my throat. "Your daughter should be part of this decision," I say, losing myself in memories of my teenage years. "When my mother remarried, I never got a say. She never said anything at all until she had a ring on her finger, and we were picking out flower girl dresses. I would've liked to have a choice."

He practically leaps over to where I stand, grabs both my cheeks, and leans in. For a second, I fear he's going to kiss me. I wouldn't stop him, not that his hold on me would allow me to jerk out of the way, but it wouldn't be a good idea.

We've just spent his entire appointment discussing a charade, and fake marriages don't involve kissing.

Thankfully, he only presses his lips to my cheek.

"You are a genius," he says, his gruff voice like freaking music from a record player. "See? You're better with kids than you think. And together, I think we'll make a good team."

I slide his hands away from me and step back, anxious for a little distance and clarity. "I haven't agreed to anything just yet. In truth, I think you're batshit crazy."

"Meet my daughter."

"That's not what I'm suggesting." My eyes bug out of my head, and I stand firm on the notion that he's batshit. Why the hell would I meet his kid? And how would he even introduce me—*Hey, sweetheart. Meet the lady I boinked a month ago. She's going to be your new pretend stepmom.*

"How else would she be part of the decision? She needs to meet you first, and you can make an informed decision too."

"I can't meet her. Then I definitely won't be able to say no. I can't resist big, innocent eyes. Contrary to what my brand might project, I'm not a monster."

"I just want you to see what you'd be getting yourself into. If it's still too much, then we'll forget I ever asked."

I scoff. "I won't forget. In fact, I'll be going to the courthouse for a restraining order instead of a marriage license."

"Fair enough."

He's totally serious. There is zero concern or indication of a bluff in his sober expression, and I don't know what scares me more—meeting his daughter or saying yes to his fake proposal.

I've never been around kids, and I wasn't a very good wife, according to my mother. Going down that road again is a recipe for disaster, even if it is just a pretense.

"Is it okay to undo the deal we made?" Wade asks.

"We haven't made a deal." Is he even listening to me?

"The deal we made the night we met—where I can't ask for your phone number." He winks, and it hits me.

Madame Horndog appreciates the saucy wink, but that's not what makes me freeze. What hits me is the deal in question. I agreed to answer anything about my personal life as long as he didn't ask for my info.

Oh, God. The things I divulged on what was supposed to be a single night together were too personal and intimate. This man knows crucial things about me, which was fine and relatively painless when I thought I'd never see him again, but here he is.

He's asking me to fucking marry him.

I can't believe it.

I can't believe the butterflies scrambling in my stomach, either. Why do I find his remembrance of our deal so damn charming? It shouldn't be, but the way he followed it up with a wink sent my vagina into cardiac arrest.

There's no way I can marry Wade. I'm attracted to him. We have chemistry. We've already slept together, and it was gloriously filthy.

Marrying him would be a huge mistake.

I'm so confused. My thoughts are more jumbled than the items in my pantry. I should really start listening to that organization podcast Tessa sent me, although it won't help me here.

But I know what I should do, right? Instead of doing the logical thing, though, and declining his proposal, the invitation to meet his daughter, and his request for my number, what do I do? I grab his phone and let my heart—the bitch—win.

I thought the fucker was dead, but here she is, screwing up my life yet again.

Wade promises to call me with the details, and I stop him before he walks out the door. "You said you'd help me with the plants."

"Right." He practically leaps for the sad companions I've shared this office with. His enthusiasm for such a tedious task is too high, but as he happily removes them from my office with a hard ass I could stare at all day, I think… I could get used to this.

EIGHT

It's a crazy idea to marry someone under false pretenses, but it doesn't mean it can't work, right?

As soon as I blurted out my spontaneous proposal, I wanted to take it back. To tell her I was kidding. But the more we talked about it, the more I convinced myself it was a brilliant fucking plan.

Besides, I meant what I said to Bree. Once anyone gets a look at her, they won't be surprised in the slightest why a man would jump to put a ring on her finger within a month of meeting her.

I could lie about that too and say we met long before then, but I already admitted to my lawyer and anyone I've met in the city, including Maggie, that I'm single. But what I do have working in my favor is Tucker, an upstanding police officer who was with me the night I met Bree. He can vouch for us in case our speedy nuptials are brought into question, and I don't see how they wouldn't be.

There will be time to figure out the details, but I need to convince Bree to do this first. After all, it's one thing to pretend to be in a serious relationship for her sleazy HR rep; it's another thing entirely to legally commit to marrying a guy she met once.

Bree agreed to meet Violet and me at a park near my apartment. It took a lot of begging on my part, and even more luck, to convince Maggie to simply drop Vi off without staying herself. The optimist in me would like to believe she might've even felt bad over our conversation the other day, where she basically told me how unreliable and possibly dangerous I am.

But it's wishful thinking on my part because I didn't get totally free reign with this visit. I had to promise to keep her here in a public place while Maggie and Roger drop into an adults-only party for his co-worker's promotion, but I'm okay with it. I'll take whatever time I can with my daughter.

Maggie will be back to pick her up in an hour and a half, so I have ninety minutes to convince Bree to do me the world's largest favor and legally bind herself to me.

I'm losing it, aren't I? It's the most logical explanation. I haven't told Tucker or anyone else what my plan is, because I realize deep down that it's insane, and it'll make me sound batshit crazy, just as Bree suggested.

I carefully watch my daughter play and giggle with the other kids her age. It's sunny today, with temperatures in the forties, and the few kids out all wear puffy jackets similar to Violet's. Her crocheted beanie has cat ears on the top, and I smile when it slips over her eyes each time she bounces with excitement. I smile harder when one of the taller girls helps her onto a whale tail, which disappears into the sandbox. Stretching across the backdrop beyond the field and playground is the New York City skyline, tall and intimidating.

It's a big, scary world out there, and I want to do everything possible to protect Violet from the ugly side of it. It's why I've been pacing back and forth, and why I've never removed my focus from her. I think I stepped in fucking gum simply because I'm busier watching her than where I'm walking.

But there can be many great things out in the world too. Those are the things I want to show her and guide her through. Teach her how to ride a bike without her training wheels and let her feel the freedom of being a kid with the wind ripping through her hair. Hold her hand on the first day of school this fall and drop her off with words of wisdom like my own grandpa and father both gave me.

I want the big and small moments with Vi.

Bree's voice jolts me when she says, "I'm here."

"I'm surprised you showed up." I cock a brow, and my shoulders relax. I'm relieved as hell to see her.

"To be honest, I am too." I hear her blow out a breath, and in my periphery, I glimpse her putting both hands on her hips, the long coat she dons hiding her gloriously curvy hips. "Which one is Violet?"

"The one with the cat ears." I point to the whale, where she still straddles the tail.

"Is she not cold?"

Vi's cheeks are tinted pink, and her pert nose matches their rosy color too. Her high-pitched squeals speak much louder than any concern over the chill in the air. "Nah. She's having too much fun," I say.

"I remember being her age," Bree muses. "The only way my mom and dad could keep me inside was to chain me to my bed, not that they ever did such a thing. But I just loved being outside so much, whether it was in the middle of summer or the dead of winter. Then again, winters in the South were nothing like these."

"I've never experienced winter in the Southeast. I remember playing against Atlanta Rising on their home turf, but it was usually summer or fall."

"Summers are a bitch down there."

I hear a gasp from another mom on the other side of Bree, and I stifle a laugh. The woman shoots daggers our way, but Bree doesn't flinch, not that I expect her to. She's a strong, independent woman with her own flair. Even though Bree herself doesn't believe she can do a young girl like Violet any good, I know she can.

She's the perfect role model for my daughter.

Since we don't have a ton of time, I interrupt Vi's playtime and call her over. "Meet my new friend, Bree."

Her head dips and rises as she sweeps her inquisitive gaze from Bree's feet up to her hair. Then she turns to me and says, "You don't have any friends."

Bree snickers behind her hand.

"Hey, I have Tucker. And the guys from the team, remember? Slater even sent you a teddy bear for Christmas," I point out.

"I've never met any of them, so how do I know they're real?"

"They are very real, little lady, and Tucker even has a

daughter around your age. Remember Ellie? As soon as Mommy lets you visit my place again, you can play with her."

"She's the one with the iPad!"

"That's right. She has one just like yours."

"Mommy and Daddy don't let me take it home, though. They say it'll hurt my eyes."

Next to me, Bree tenses, and my stomach churns as a chill snaps, stinging my cheeks. My little girl calls another man *Daddy*, and the painful slice of envy shoots through my chest.

This is why. *This* is why I fucking need Bree to agree. I can't stand by while another guy raises my kid like I don't exist at all.

"I don't think it would hurt me, though," Vi continues. "Ivy from school plays on hers all the time. There are fun games on it. That's all I want it for—the games."

"What kinds of games do you like?" Bree jumps in and leads her toward a bench while she rattles off the names of three games.

"One is for makeup. I like doing makeup. I don't wear it like Mommy does, but I help her with hers sometimes."

"That's very cool," Bree gushes. "I have a friend who loves doing makeup too. It's actually her job."

"Her job?" Vi's mouth falls open. "I want a makeup job when I grow up."

"I will have the perfect connection for you when the time comes."

I pace in front of them as they sit next to each other, talking like old friends. It hurts worse than the last time to hear her call Roger Daddy, and it takes longer than I expect to recover.

But as soon as I do, I approach them, and my chest stirs.

"You're very pretty." Vi giggles behind her tiny gloved hands.

"You and I will be the best of friends, babe."

"Did you just call me *babe*?" She scrunches her nose, but her giggles are even louder. "I kind of like that. It's funny."

Bree flashes her sparkling eyes my way, and we share a look. I don't know what it means, but it's a good look. One that causes the stirring in my chest to grow.

I clap. "How about I get us some hot chocolate?"

"Can we come with you?" Violet asks. "I might see a cookie I want."

"Oh, you are definitely my new best friend. I love the way you think." Bree stands and hooks her arm out for Vi to loop hers through it.

I imagine this is how Bree is with her girlfriends—close and fun. It's cute, really, to see her this way with my young daughter, especially when they start skipping.

Suddenly, I picture them playing like this at Vi's next birthday. Flashes of them trick-or-treating on Halloween and opening Christmas presents hit me out of nowhere too, and it all brings a smile to my face.

No matter how insane my proposal is, it feels right.

The three of us spend the remainder of our visit blowing on our hot chocolates more than we drink them. In between, we sample the five kinds of cookies we selected from the kind and patient food vendor, and we've just made a full lap around the playground area when my phone vibrates with a text from Maggie.

"Hey, kiddo," I interrupt their debate over which of Hannah Montana's songs is the best. "Your mom is almost here to pick you up."

"I'm going to the bathroom," Bree says, her words rushed. "Butterfly Vi, it was so nice to hang with you this afternoon."

Violet face palms. "Another nickname? What about *babe*?"

"I'll still call you that too, *babe*." Bree winks at her, but when she flicks her gaze to mine, I note panic.

If I had to guess, she doesn't want to meet Maggie.

It's overwhelming enough to meet my daughter, and I don't want to pressure her into meeting Maggie too. I don't know where we stand, either, which is why my heart is hammering so hard as I walk Violet toward the parking lot in search of her mother.

"Hey, you two," she calls out from the window of a gray minivan. "Did you have fun? Were you warm enough?"

I hoist Violet into the back seat as she fires off the names of the two girls she met on the playground and how one had a dog who pooped by the sandbox. "It was funny," she finishes as I click her seat belt into place across her tiny body.

"Bye, sweetheart." I slide her beanie up and press a kiss against her forehead, an ache gnawing at my heart when I stand back to wave them off.

Before they back out of the parking space, I barely spare Roger a glance, but I do thank Maggie for the afternoon. I follow their van with my gaze until it turns onto the street and disappears into the rows of other cars.

"She's precious," I hear from behind me.

I spin to face Bree, my tongue burning with the need to know if she's made up her mind. "Thank you," I say, instead.

"I'm sorry I bolted. When you mentioned Maggie showing up, I didn't want to make anything awkward for you and Violet, or for me really, so I thought it best to get off at the nearest exit—the classic potty escape."

I chuckle, but it gets caught in my throat. I didn't tell Maggie that Bree would be here to meet Vi. I never thought about it. Should I have? How would I have even explained who she is?

Fuck.

I just keep digging myself farther into a hole, don't I?

"I need to go," she says, rubbing her hands together. "I'm meeting some friends for margaritas—it's our weekly tradition—and I don't want to be late. It's also getting colder by the minute out here, and I'm freezing my ass off."

Her laugh is nervous as she brushes past me. I stand in place, a million thoughts racing through my mind, none of which I speak aloud as she stalks off. I should thank her for being so good with Violet. For having fun with her and humoring her Hannah Montana phase. At the very least, I should ask Bree if she needs a ride to this margarita date.

But nothing comes out of my mouth.

I don't even fucking move.

What the hell is wrong with me?

In my apartment, I kick off both shoes and shrug out of my jacket, my head a clouded mess.

I like Bree.

She's fun and fantastic with Violet. In fact, I'm thrilled over the effortless match between us three.

But I also think Bree is fucking gorgeous and bright too. Being with her is easy and comfortable, but there's also a strange connection between us—one where we're already communicating with eye contact.

And that's what scares the piss out of me.

I've just grabbed a beer from the fridge and run a hand through my hair when a knock sounds on my door. It's probably Tucker, so I yell, "It's open."

But the person on the other side of the door is not my friend. It's Bree.

"Answer one thing for me," she says, but she doesn't wait for my response before she asks, "Do you regret Maggie telling you about Violet?"

I nearly drop my beer at the unexpected question.

"I know it's an incredibly awful thing to ask or suggest, and I probably shouldn't be asking you at all. But I have to know—do you regret finding out?"

"No," I answer, and I fucking mean it. "If I did, I would've just signed the papers Maggie's been shoving down my throat for Roger to adopt Violet. My shitty agent even pushed for me to do as much and forget I had a daughter at all. But that's not how I was raised, nor could I have lived with myself if I would've walked away. Jamesons take care of family, whether they're on the other side of the world like my parents or they're down the street like my grandma and grandpa were when I was growing up. We are a family."

She chews on her bottom lip, and her eyes—are they welling with tears? "Then I'll do it. I'll marry you and do whatever I can to help."

My next breath leaves my mouth with a resounding *whoosh*.

This is why she barged in here like a woman on a mission. To know my intentions are genuine before she agrees to upend her life for me.

She's not afraid to challenge me, and God, I love that.

"I'm not doing it out of the kindness of my own heart or anything. I don't want my reputation tainted." Her watery laugh warms my heart. "Dickish Dan is a real issue at work, and my rent is going up next month. I can't afford to keep living on my own. I'm also too fucking old to find a random roommate who may kill me in my sleep."

I scratch the back of my head, feeling lighter than I have in months.

"I don't cook," she continues, her expression serious. "And it's not one of those hidden strengths I have like lifting a car off a child in their time of need. I don't magically cook the greatest meatloaf or chicken pot pie under pressure."

"What kind of pressure would you be under in that scenario exactly?"

"That we'd starve or something, unless I cooked an award-winning roast. I don't know." She pulls her coat tighter at her waist.

"No cooking, no problem. I have a drawer full of takeout menus."

"I won't pick up your dirty socks off the floor, either. I know people like my rich-as-sin best friend who married a billionaire have a housekeeper, but that's not my life, nor will I be *your* housekeeper."

"No dirty socks—should I be writing these things down?"

"It would be in your best interest," she teases, and even cracks a smile.

I spin in place as a building-sized weight lifts off my shoulders. This is the answer. This is the homerun I needed, and coincidentally, she can also help me find a job, which would solidify me as a capable father in a judge's eyes.

This woman… she's amazing. And selfless. And…

"I liked you," I blurt, and her eyes widen. "I mean, I *do* like you, but the night we met, I asked for your number because I liked you. It was also because it was the logical thing to do for someone with my… history, but it was mostly because I simply wanted to see you again."

She opens and closes her mouth, and my apartment thickens with nervous tension.

"But clearly, as you've seen, I'm not in a position to dedicate any time to a relationship. I didn't know if I could even commit to anything casual. I'm just a fucking mess."

Her gulp is audible, and it kickstarts my nerves into overdrive.

Why did I have to say anything?

"I didn't mean to—"

"Ground rules," she says. "We need rules for this fake marriage."

"Aside from the list you just gave me?" I rasp over the constriction of my throat.

"Those aren't rules. Those are merely facts about me, which you need to know."

"What do you suggest for rules, then?"

"I don't know. I've never done this before. But I think it would be smart to agree to terms and conditions for this arrangement. Something like whose apartment will we move into, mine or yours. We have to live together, right? For the sake of appearances?"

"We'll live here," I state.

"Why yours? I know my rent is increasing, but with two people, it's definitely doable."

"This place is near Violet and within her school district." I give her a tight-lipped smile in an attempt to avoid gloating, especially when she doesn't argue. "Besides, it's spacious and cozy in here, wouldn't you say?"

"It's… fine. You need more decorations."

"No more plants, though."

She rolls her eyes, then mumbles her agreement to move in here and adds, "I'll sleep on the couch or in Violet's room when she's not here."

"Absolutely not," I blurt.

"Where do you propose I sleep—in your bed?" She crosses her arms over her chest, folding the lapels of her peacoat in the process. We certainly should've gotten comfortable for this.

"Yes."

"And where will you sleep if I do that?"

"Also in my bed."

She purses her lips, clearly not amused, but I'm not joking.

"Violet needs to believe we're married. I'd tell her the truth, but even from the few times I've been with her, I know she can't keep a secret. We can't risk her telling anyone. *We* can't tell anyone. And if Violet notices us sleeping in separate rooms, she'll get suspicious."

"The same bed, then," she forces out with obvious reluctance.

"I barely snore." With a wink, I ask, "What else?"

"How long will we be married?"

"Five years."

"Three." She glares, and I concede. "And I think we should discuss what happens between us in the unfortunate event that…"

"That I'm not granted custody," I finish for her. Yesterday, the thought gave me a stomachache worse than when I was a kid and ate an entire box of Froot Loops in one sitting. Today, the idea doesn't bother me because I have a solid plan. I'm confident this will work.

"We'll get an annulment," she says.

"For someone who claims she's never done this before, you are awfully good it."

"Someone has to be the adult around here, and it might as well be your future sugar mama."

My shoulders tremble as laughter rolls through me.

"Actually," she starts, holding her finger up. "You're a professional athlete and must have money. Does that make you my sugar daddy?"

"I've always wanted to be a sugar daddy," I muse. "Thank you for making my dreams come true."

"You're not the first to say that," she jokes.

This afternoon has been a damn whirlwind, and the last few minutes have especially made me dizzy. We've covered a lot of ground, and although it doesn't appear she's going to take her coat off to stay a while, I don't want her to leave.

I like talking to her.

"I'm sure I'll think of more, but I have one last condition before I leave," she whispers. "No fucking against the window."

My throat tightens again, and I stuff my hands into the pockets of my jeans like I need to trap them. Otherwise, I might want to touch her.

But my soon-to-be wife is off-limits.

Because no matter how much I do like her, we can't become real. Not if we want this arrangement to be successful, and I really need it to be. Bringing feelings into the mix will just complicate it all.

It's like she said when we first met—feelings are stupid. They can ruin lives.

"No fucking or feelings of any kind." She levels me under her sober gaze. "We keep this marriage platonic. We will be less sexy than a freaking sewer, got it?"

"Agreed," I practically growl as resistance against the notion eats at me. She's unequivocally right, but it doesn't mean I have to like it. Which is the only explanation as to why I stop her as she tugs the door open. "No fucking anyone else, either."

"Excuse me?"

I close the distance between us, my heart thundering in my pea-sized brain as I reach around her to shut the door again. My chest brushes her shoulder, and her lavender aroma pulls me in like a gravitational force. "No fucking anyone else," I repeat hoarsely, speaking into her ear. I want her to really hear me and know I'm damn serious when I say, "I don't want you to be with anyone else."

Her eyes widen, and I lick my lips. Being this close to her and not kissing her is unfair, especially since I know just how sweet she tastes.

"For the sake of the charade," I croak. "I don't want you with anyone else... so we can keep the pretense."

"That's the only reason, right?"

I nod and lean down, torturing myself by bringing my mouth even closer to hers, but before I do anything stupid, I reach around her, grip the doorknob, and yank it open for her to walk through it. "I'll be in touch" is the last thing I say before she scurries away.

And I'm left asking myself one question.

Will I survive this?

NINE

I make it all the way to the Mexican restaurant to meet the girls without spilling the beans about my impending nuptials, which is more than I could've hoped for.

I've only ever kept my lips sealed about one secret in my life, so this is a true feat, not that the young girl sitting next to me on the subway would've cared I'm somewhat engaged. She was far more interested in fidgeting with the headphones that were larger than the size of her own head than what's going on with the crazy lady cramped beside her.

Because I must be crazy, right?

Me, the queen of one-night stands and resistor of love—I just agreed to marry someone.

I never expected to do this again, and I sure as shit didn't expect to fake marry a single dad athlete with tattoos and a sinfully skilled tongue.

Good thing we made a pact to avoid feelings and engaging in anything physical. It would muddle things too badly, and this mess is already complicated enough on its own.

As I maneuver through the Thursday night crowd, an array of vibrant colors blurs into a rainbow I've come to know so well. It's easy to spot Madison, Tessa, and Erin. They're at our usual table, with a fresh pitcher of margarita sitting in the center like they're worshipping it. It's been our ritual for three years or so, but tonight, it feels different.

I'm different.

Tessa's married, and although Madi and Erin are in serious relationships with the loves of their lives, they're not even engaged. Never in a million years would I have bet I'd be the second of us walking down the aisle.

Or the steps of a courthouse, anyway.

I haven't even completely sat my ass in my unofficial seat when I grab a margarita glass and chug, powering through the brain freeze like a fucking champ.

"That's mine," Tessa points out, but I don't stop.

My mouth is glued to the rim as the tangy lime cocktail hits my tongue. The explosion of the familiar and beloved drink, along with the comfortable, sentimental atmosphere, soothes my soul.

It feels like I'm home, which is a nice reprieve from the fact that I'll be moving out of my actual home soon. At least this place will never change.

The only thing that does ever change is Madi. Since moving to LA, she doesn't always join us, but thankfully, she's been in town for the entire last month, as she and Ian finally decided on a place. They'll be moving in this weekend, and I may need to ask her to lend me their U-Haul for my own move.

As I pour more into my glass, filling it to the brim, Madi cheers. "It's going to be one of those nights, huh?"

"You have no idea," I mumble.

"Oh, God. Did you already hear?" Tessa grumbles as she grabs an empty glass. "Who told you—was it Sandra? She can't keep a secret to save her life."

I glance at Madi and Erin before I set my eyes on Tessa, but I'm still completely clueless as to what Sandra would know that I don't. She's a gossip troll, but I'm far worse than anyone in our office. If there's gossip, I'm usually the first to know it.

"I was going to tell you in person tonight. I couldn't tell you I'm quitting over the phone or text. And I've missed you in the office all week, like we're playing hide-and-seek. You're very good, by the way."

"You're quitting?" I croak, nearly choking on my drink.

"Shit. You *didn't* know?" Tessa cringes as the other two sit back, exchanging frowns of their own.

"How the hell does Sandra know this and I don't? What the fuck, Rollins?"

"It's Fields now, but don't feel bad—I keep forgetting too." Erin smiles sweetly, but I just glare.

"I'm sorry!" Tessa throws her hands into a prayerlike gesture. "She overheard me on the phone with Carter, and I'm actually surprised she didn't spill the beans to everyone. She might've, but like I said, you've been MIA the last few days."

I drain the rest of my margarita like it's a shot and shake

my head, partially because I can't believe what I'm hearing, but also because this shit is so cold my brain feels like the inside of a freezer right now.

"Ava is opening her own wedding planning business, which is her true passion. I didn't know as much until she gave Carter her notice. In any case, I'm taking over her position as full-time event coordinator for Fields Company."

My head nods of its own accord. With all the insanity today, I'm surprised it's still attached to my neck at all. It should've exploded by now.

"I've just really loved working with Ava for the charity functions, and I'm excited to be even more involved," Tessa continues rambling, which is how I know she's truly happy about this change.

Although, I know my friend. I know how much she's enjoyed organizing the charity events on behalf of her new husband's company. She doesn't have to keep going on like this in order to convince me it's the right move, but since she's one of my best friends, I also know she feels bad. Like she's abandoning me at the career counseling center. It's true, the two of us have leaned on each other for years, but if this is what she wants…

"I'm going to fucking miss you!" The words burst out of me like a sneeze. I can't control them.

"I'm going to miss you too," Tessa whines and leans over the table for the most awkward but loving half-hug I've ever received.

"Hey! Watch the goods." Madi moves the margarita pitcher out from between us. With nothing but the table itself as a barrier, Tessa squeezes me tighter as she continues mumbling apologies.

"I'll forgive you if you promise to meet me for lunch at least once a week. I won't survive without my Tessa fix," I say.

My dramatics know zero bounds, but who can blame me? I've been having lunch with Tessa most days, and it's been a huge relief. I love my job and my clients, but the breaks with my friend are crucial. I'm only human, and I need to decompress with girl talk at our favorite café.

"Done." Tessa claps and shifts back into her seat.

"Wait—does this mean we should've ordered mango margarita? We're celebrating Tessa's new phase!" Erin's eyes bounce from each of us.

"You're right." I lick my lips and signal for Micah, Harvey's girlfriend, who now works here too. The petite blonde woman sashays over to our table, a small pencil adorably tucked behind her ear.

Once we order the new flavor—our go-to when we're celebrating—I sit back with a sigh as I absorb yet another change tossed my way. If I thought these girls were moving on before, here's just another thing to add to that list, and it won't be the last.

"To Tessa's new adventure!" Madi toasts. "We're proud of you, babe."

"Hear, hear," I add.

Tessa seemingly struggles to swallow her sip as she waves a finger at me. "Hang on. You didn't know about me quitting, so what did you come in here all irritated about?"

"I'm not irritated." I hesitate. After all, I'm not. I'm just… anxious for what my own future will look like, considering what I've just agreed to.

"What's going on? Is it Dan? I saw him coming out of

your office earlier this week…" Tessa cringes. "I was about to come save you, but Wade beat me to it."

"Wade? Who's Wade?" Madi rises in her seat, a twinkle in her eye.

"He was a one-night stand."

"You hooked up with him after he left your office?" Tessa gapes. "I mean, I can see why. He was dreamy as hell. The eyes, especially."

I swallow my generous gulp of mango margarita, welcoming the switch in flavor. I love the lime. It's classic for a reason, because we can never go wrong with it, but mango is spunky. The burst of fruity goodness offers comfort as I fight with my scratchy throat to say, "I hooked up with him almost a month ago—the one I was stuck with during the power outage."

"Jersey City guy?" Erin asks, and I confirm with a nod.

"You've been seeing him ever since then?" Madi ventures a guess, but her tone is laced with skepticism. Rightfully so, too.

Erin follows it up with an actual swoon. "And he surprised you at work—how stinking romantic."

"It was a total coincidence that he showed up," I clarify as I toe the line of facts. How do I tell them the truth?

Lying to them is definitely an option. It wouldn't even be lying if I don't mention Wade proposed; it'd just be omitting the details.

But I can't do it.

I've omitted enough about my life to them, and it's time I be a better friend and entrust them with this secret—as soon as I figure out how to fucking begin.

"Talk about fate!" Erin squeals. She has far too much

optimism for such a tiny person. Where does she keep any of her organs?

"How did you leave things? Are you going to see him again?" Tessa presses.

"I'll see him again at our wedding ceremony," I state and wait for the freak-out.

Except it doesn't come.

Instead of staring at me in disbelief like they don't recognize me—or like I've admitted something as absurd as murdering someone—they all rupture into howling laughter.

"What the fuck are you laughing about?" I scold, flinging drops of my drink across the basket of chips in front of me. No matter, I was going to eat these, anyway. With this offensively outrageous response, I don't care if they eat any at all.

"The joke you just…" Erin's smile falters. "You *are* kidding, right?"

"You have to be," Madi adds.

"Actually, I'm not."

And here's the look I was expecting from each of them. Totally blank stares are glued on me, and my skin crawls with all the questions they don't immediately ask out loud. I know them too well, though, and I can say without a doubt, they have hundreds of questions.

"Must've been *some* one-night stand," Tessa says, easing into the silence like any movement from her side of the table will spook me.

"That night didn't even mean anything." I lick my lips, and the lie tastes bitter. But it is the reality of how I *need* to feel. If I repeat it enough, maybe it'll finally sink in. "When he accidentally showed back up, he realized I could help him with a problem."

With a long exhale, I dive into the details of our arrangement, trusting these girls not to say anything to anyone. Besides, if I can't trust them of all people, who do I have?

Once I'm finished with the bullet points of the most ludicrous week I've ever experienced, I face Erin and ask, "This has to earn me a lifetime of good points with karma, right?"

Madi cuts in before Erin has a chance to answer. "Babe, it's a good and kind thing to help an elderly woman with her groceries or even go so far as to take brownies to a neighbor. Agreeing to legally share your life with someone and his kid is… is…"

"Just plain insane!" Tessa supplies. "If this is a money thing, Carter and I can totally help you. All you need to do is say the word."

"Or is this like a mafia thing?" Madi asks. "Did you get wrapped up in some kind of underground crime ring that involves selling yourself to an overlord? Because we've warned you about avoiding seedy places and shady people." She takes my hand and squeezes it. "If your life is being threatened, blink twice."

All three of them lean forward, studying my face and waiting expectantly.

I yank my hand out of Madi's grip and wave them off. "Guys! I'm fine. I'm only helping someone in need. It's much like Erin volunteering at the Boys & Girls Club, or Tessa organizing charity events. The main difference is that I'll have a place to live and help with rent. It'll also get creepy Dan off my case at work, and I don't have to low crawl down the hall just to avoid him."

Erin gasps. "Did you actually have to do that?"

"She did," Tessa confirms. "I witnessed the whole thing."

"Luckily, I was wearing loose trousers. If I'd been wearing a dress, Tessa here would've gotten an eyeful of the goods." I snort. If I embarrassed easily, that moment would've done the trick, but there's very little I blush over, especially when it's in the name of fending off peeping Toms and drooly Dans.

"What about *the* goods?" Madi grabs my hand again. "As in, other men? You're seriously going to dedicate the next three years of your life to celibacy for a guy you don't even know?"

"I have eight toys, and they do the trick far better than any man in this city. I've sampled enough of them to know that's more than just an educated guess." I jut my chin up with pride, steeling myself against my rattled nerves.

The truth is, Wade did rival my best battery-powered toy, but my soon-to-be husband is completely forbidden. The girls don't need to know as much, though. I can just hear the lectures I'd get in return, warning me against doing this if there are real feelings involved, physical or emotional.

They'd try to talk me out of it, but it's too late.

Besides, I'm a grown woman who can keep her physical needs under wraps—no fucking problem. I can handle pretending to be married to Wade. In fact, I'll probably even enjoy it since it'll make me feel less alone. These girls are moving on with their lives, and so am I.

"So, this is all super-duper real?" Erin asks, using her thumb and forefinger to angle my chin to face her. "This is not an elaborate joke to keep us on our toes? Because you do like to do that."

"For the last fucking time, I'm dead serious!" I say, and it's loud enough to turn plenty of heads. This restaurant should put up caution tape around our table to warn other patrons of how rowdy—and inappropriate—we can get.

Once the four of us get together, we cannot be held responsible for the things we say or do.

They exchange glances, and then Tessa is the one to break the silence again. "So, this is like… your bachelorette party, then?"

Madi claps, and Erin jolts out of her chair. "Oh my God, oh my God, oh my God."

"I drove here, for once, and I have a box of decorations from a recent event in my backseat." Tessa jumps into coordinator mode. It is about to be her full-time gig, after all. "Madi, there's a bakery down the street. It should still be open. Get anything that already looks like a dick, or something we can use to make one. Erin, get three rounds of shots from the bar and notify Harvey and Micah of our new goal for the night—to get hammered for this bitch's big night."

I try to talk them down from this madness, but it's no use. Madison's already flying out the door, her coat halfway hanging off her shoulders, Tessa's on her heels with a key fob held overhead like she's attempting to unlock her car from inside the building, and Erin's squeezing between the occupied barstools. Her animated hand gestures and smiles are too comical, and I laugh.

My friends are ridiculous, but that's them—three ladies with the biggest hearts. They're the kind of bunch who goes all out for a wedding, even when the marriage is fake.

Tessa returns with a box of bougie silver and navy decorations. With assistance from Harvey and Micah, we clear the table, stretch a silver table linen over it, and scatter navy confetti across the surface.

"Classy." Micah beams. "What else do we need?" she asks as she sets down the drinks, and Harvey reappears with the shots.

"Do you have a marker I can borrow?" Tessa asks as Erin rummages through the rest of the items in the box.

Once Micah returns with a black Sharpie, Tessa fishes out what seems to be a table runner, smooths it out, then writes on it.

"What are you—"

"We can't find a bride-to-be sash around here, so I'm making you one."

Erin whispers into her ear, and Tessa squeals as Madi returns with a white rectangular box in her hands. "I just need one second to work my magic," she says. "Every cake, even one in the shape of a sun, has a penis inside them."

"Happy to help. I know my way around a dick." Micah winks at Harvey as she and Madi make a mad dash toward the bar with the box.

And I sit back to enjoy the train wreck as these girls throw me an impromptu bachelorette party. People at the surrounding tables are also smiling now, clearly enjoying the show for once.

"Ta-da!" Madi returns shortly and opens the lid wider, presenting her so-called magic: a white iced cake in the shape of a penis, with haphazard frosting smudged along the outside. "And…" She slings a pink gift bag onto the chair and fishes out a red shimmery crown with red, pink, and white hearts bobbing across the top.

"What the hell is that?" I ask in horror as she nestles it in my hair.

"The bakery had some of these in stock for Valentine's

Day. It's the closest thing to a tiara I could find." Madi tosses her wavy red hair over one shoulder and curtseys.

"Good work," I deadpan, and I can't stop the smile from stretching across my face. "You three should really do a TikTok video on ways to improvise a party. I guarantee it'd go viral."

"Oh my God—we totally should. We could use one of those sounds that starts off slow and then slams the beat down." Erin nods with enthusiasm.

"Slams the beat down?" Tessa bursts into laughter.

"Why does that sound so dirty?" I muse.

"Everything sounds dirty to you," Madi says. "The other day, I was describing to you our new apartment over the phone, and you asked if I was having sex."

"No one is that excited about hardwood floors and a vaulted ceiling," I toss back, and margarita practically shoots from my nose.

This is how we spend the rest of the night—laughing, drinking, and creating memories. We've been doing each of those for years at this very table. May the memories keep on coming far into the future, because I don't know what I'd do without these girls.

No matter how many transitions we go through in life, I know in my bones that our friendship will remain this tight and safe. These girls are forever.

We're the last ones left in the restaurant, but I don't want to say goodbye. Sure, I'm only moving across the river. I'll be right back here next Thursday—another rule I need to make Wade agree to—but I'll have a different last name. We didn't nail down a specific date just yet, but I imagine he wants this done quickly.

On the curb outside next to Tessa's car, I hug them all and

give extra squeezes. "Thank you for tonight, you outrageously ridiculous bitches."

"Call us with updates. We'll come to the courthouse for the ceremony. We'll—" Tessa continues mumbling as Carter hops out of a taxi. She called him to come drive her car back to their place, and the yummy hunk has come to her rescue.

Madi cuts through our greetings with a slurry offer to do my hair and makeup.

"Seriously, we're keeping it so low-key. Don't get your panties in a twist about being there or not. It's not a big deal," I assure them. "But thank you."

"I have the perfect bouquet idea," Erin says as if she didn't hear me. Then again, she's as drunk as the other two. I'm sure an explosion next door wouldn't even penetrate the tequila fogging their senses right now.

"Good night," I insist and make my way toward the cab Carter just vacated, my head marginally spinning from my own buzz.

I clutch my purse in my lap during the drive to my apartment, wrapping my arms around it and my waist in order to preserve my body heat. The chilling temperatures are brutal tonight, and as we pull up to my building, thoughts of Wade's arms around me warm me better than any coat or scarf.

Speaking of him, as soon as I reach my place and trudge straight to my bedroom, I notice a message on my phone.

Wade: Looks like a New Jersey marriage license will take about three days. Free tomorrow during your lunch hour to do something crazy?

Smiling, I type out a response.

I'm ready when you are.

Wade: Here's a list of documents you'll need.

I click the link he sends and skim the obvious forms of identification I already suspected. My vision is blurry, but I read the damning item clearer than I would a dirty text.

As soon as "divorce decree" crosses my line of vision, I freeze.

Fuuuuuuccckkkkk.

I need one to prove my previous marriage has legally been terminated.

My phone buzzes again.

We should be all set, right?

Unfortunately, no.

I curse under my breath.

My divorce decree is in Georgia.

Shit. How do we get our hands on it? Anyone you can call?

I'll take care of it, but we will need to wait until Monday for the marriage license.

I squeeze my eyes closed and dig the heel of my palm into one as a headache threatens to keep me awake for most of the night. It's not from the alcohol or late hour, either.

It's because I know I need to call the one person I don't want to talk to.

"She dresses nice, and she's happy."

That's what Violet said about Bree when I called to ask her how she'd feel if we got married. Ever since Bree advised me to keep her in the loop, I couldn't stop thinking about it.

I would've rather done it in person, but this is time sensitive. On top of that, Maggie's being a stickler about Violet's "packed schedule," although I don't know any other seven-year-old who's that busy.

In any case, FaceTime did the trick. I just made sure we were alone while we chatted, which wasn't too difficult since Maggie and Roger had big plans to discuss their kitchen renovations.

Of course, those two things were the only responses I got

out of Vi before she moved on to chatter about the new nail polish she got, but it was enough of a blessing.

Bree does dress nice, and she is happy.

I spin in a circle and scan the crowd, looking for any sign of her when my phone buzzes against my palm.

"Hi" is all she says.

"Is everything okay?" I press my phone to my ear and jump down the steps, barely avoiding a run-in with a rather aggravated looking lawyer. I can't tell if he actually is one, but he fits the profile.

Unfortunately, I'm not so lucky in escaping his briefcase, which slams against my knee.

It's my wedding day, and I just got attacked by a briefcase. The man doesn't even pause to apologize.

Awesome.

"Bree—can you hear me?" I ask. Where is she? The only thing she texted me earlier was that she was here at the courthouse but needed to use the restroom. I haven't seen her at all, nor have I been able to introduce her to my grandma yet.

"I can. I just… is it weird that I wanted to hear your voice?" Her laugh is nervous, and it pierces my heart with warmth.

"Not at all." I gulp. "But wouldn't it be better if you were out here in front of me?"

"It's bad luck for the bride and groom to see each other beforehand."

"Seriously?" I chuckle. "How do you suppose we enter the building? We're going to have to see each other."

"In that case…" There's shuffling on her end, and the sound of wind whistles in the background. "You look mighty fine today, Mr. Jameson."

The deep drawl in her Southern accent—the same one she used on the night we met—makes me grin like a real groom on his wedding day.

When I glance up, I scan the scattered people along the sidewalk until my eyes lock on to hers.

Her makeup brings out the bright hazel flecks in her eyes. Her dark locks are curled and styled, blowing in the wind. The pink peacoat wrapped around her is elegant, and as she would say, totally on brand.

She's beautiful.

My grandma steps into my line of vision as Bree reaches us and hands her a bouquet of white roses. "Here you go, dear."

"Oh, I'm not interested, but thank you." She offers her a smile but doesn't spare another glance.

Which is when I realize she probably thinks my grandma is trying to sell her a bouquet.

"She's… It's not…" I stammer.

"I'm his grandmother, and we brought these for you." She places the bouquet in Bree's hand. "Every bride should have flowers on her wedding day."

Bree accepts with a wince, then pulls me aside and speaks under her breath. "You said we wouldn't bring anyone, especially not family."

"She's our witness. Did you have someone else in mind?"

"That guy. That woman. The shady teen in the black hoodie by the food stand." Bree uses the flowers to point all around us at the strangers.

And she's not wrong, but I'm not, either.

"I couldn't *not* tell her I'm getting married, so when I called, she packed two shirts and her hair products, then hopped on a plane. That's literally all she brought, so just a warning—we need to take her shopping."

"We?" Her brows rise into her hairline.

"Yes, we. As in, we, the happy newlywed couple. That's the deal, remember?"

She blows out a frustrated breath, and right when I believe she's ready, she tenses. "Wait. How much did you tell her about us? Does she know?"

"I know," Gaga calls out. "And I can also hear everything you're saying, honey, but don't be pissed with him. Wade's told me everything since he was just a boy. Couldn't even keep it to himself when he needed a larger size in jeans because his willy wouldn't fit."

My hands fly up to cover my face, and I groan into my palms, my suit and overcoat suddenly too hot, even though the temperature is in the thirties right now.

"Actually, I'm so glad you're here," Bree sings, amusement shining in her tone. "Tell me more about that."

"I'll tell you anything you want to know, but first, you two need to get hitched."

I slide my hands away and into my pockets, itching to get this over with. "If we don't get moving, we're going to be late for our appointment and may miss it altogether." I take the first three steps, but when I turn, the ladies aren't following me.

"By the way, I'm Gaga—as in Lady Gaga, but I had the name long before her. Just don't ask me to sing." She takes Bree's hand in both of hers and squeezes it.

"Sing away, Gaga. I'll be right next to you belting out the notes with zero shame myself, and whoever judges can eat shit."

My grandma throws her head back and laughs so hard the pristine twist of her hair pinned at the back of her head moves. It never moves. She laughs more hysterically than she did when my grandpa bought her a white gold lizard necklace because he thought they were her favorite.

What had actually happened was that he'd overheard her telling a friend that she'd like to kill the lizard terrorizing her from the back porch and wear it like a necklace, but she didn't have it in her heart to come clean to him.

As I recall this story, I'm reminded just how perfectly she and Bree suit each other.

"You have some balls, lady, and I love it." Gaga beams, still squeezing Bree's hand as we make our way up the steps.

Out of the corner of my mouth, I tell Bree, "No repeats of the marriage license incident, right?"

"Are you ever going to let it go? Because if you hold on to grudges like this, we're not going to make it through three years."

"It almost blew our cover."

She pauses at the top of the stairs. "Your first name is Carter. My friend just married billionaire Carter Fields a few months ago, and if you expected me not to say something about you two having the same name, then you don't know anything about me."

"I have a feeling I'll get to know plenty over the next three years."

"May the odds be ever in your favor," she chirps, flips a tuft of hair over her shoulder, and leaves me staring after her in awe.

In truth, her miniature freak-out over my first name earned us an incriminating stare from the clerk. Thankfully, she didn't say anything or question us at all. If I had to guess, it was because she's witnessed far more peculiar things in her line of work.

I hold the door open, and Gaga is the first to enter. As I follow Bree, I whisper, "I'm still surprised we were able to pull off the marriage license at all. How were you able to get your divorce certificate so fast?"

Her unsteady voice reaches my ears with hesitation, although it could be because of the echo in here. "I was able to get an overnighted copy. My hometown is small, but it is filled with willing and resourceful people."

It's a perfectly plausible explanation. Yet, I can't shake the feeling that she's hiding something.

The nagging voice in my head takes a back seat as we're directed toward our designated courtroom, where the ceremony begins almost immediately. There are no bells and whistles. No decorations or vibrancy of any kind.

Just a lot of browns, as I would expect in such a place, but none of it screams, "Hey, come get married here!" Which is fitting for our purposes.

To keep this running smoothly and neutrally, I don't hesitate to accept the justice of the peace's offer to perform the quick version, foregoing vows and such.

But when Bree slips her jacket off, I need a minute.

My soon-to-be wife stands in front of me in a pale lavender dress, and I imagine it's the material version of her perfume. The fabric is thick, and it clings to her natural curves like it's made for her. A string of pearls dangles around her neck like a true Southern belle, and the detail makes me smile.

Fortunately, I don't need to say anything other than the simple "I do." If I needed to form full sentences right now, I don't think I could.

Blood rushes to my ears as I'm instructed to place the wedding ring on her finger, and in turn, she slides a simple band on mine. Somehow, this feels more intimate than the sex we had a month ago.

Is that normal? Of course not. None of this is.

We zip through what sounds like a rehearsed script. He's likely relayed it all multiple times in the past. It's rather impersonal, but it makes this whole charade much easier. It reminds me this isn't real, although it's hard not to glance at my grandmother's ring on Bree's finger without my gut twisting.

Gaga insisted I give Bree the ring. Confessed she'd planned to give it to me all along for my bride someday, and that day has come, even if it's not what she'd pictured.

It's not what I pictured, either, but desperate times and all that shit.

"You may now kiss the bride."

I don't move. Instead, I simply blink at the justice of the peace, whose final line rings in my ears with alarm.

Bree and I discussed the paperwork, dates, locations, and the rest of the logistics, but we never reached the part where we'd have to kiss at the end of the ceremony. Should we just hug? Shake hands? High-five?

Christ.

A throat clears between us, and the officiant repeats, "You may now kiss the bride, Mr. Jameson."

Across from me, Bree shifts on her heels, and I feel my grandma's eyes on me. Sweat trickles down the back of my neck as the weight of the officiant's stare also settles on me.

It's just a kiss, right? We've kissed before. Hell, we've done a lot more than that. This is nothing in comparison.

But she wasn't my fake wife then.

Inhaling, I place my hands on both her shoulders and pull her toward me, crushing the bouquet of flowers between us as I place the most chaste kiss I can muster onto her lips.

As soon as they fuse to mine—the millisecond I feel the heat of her lips and the beginning of a very uncomfortable stiffy—I yank myself back.

My grandma snaps a few pictures on her chunky Nikon, the strap of which is hung around her neck like a professional. But she admitted to me that this is the second time she's ever used it. It was another gift from Grandpa after a misunderstanding, but she keeps everything he ever gave her. Now that he's gone, the memories surrounding each gift are extra special.

The justice of the peace holds out his hand for each of us to shake. "Congratulations to you both."

Outside, my grandma bounces ahead as fast as her aching hip will allow. I'm pretty sure my soul still hasn't returned to my body after the elaborate ruse we just pulled off, although to be honest, that was the easy part.

The trickier stunt will be taking Maggie and Roger to court.

I should call Cassidy with the news and organize a game plan in light of today's events. When I spoke with her over a week ago—when Bree and I had just reconnected—Cassidy didn't have much confidence in my case. I bet she changes her mind as soon as I tell her I have a wife, who is not only great with Violet, but who's also going to hook me up with a job.

We haven't visited the latter yet with the other chaos, but one thing at a time. Egyptian pyramids were built mud brick by mud brick until the impressive structures were finished; I can show patience too.

"Stop right there," Gaga calls out, lifting the camera to cover her face.

Bree hooks her arm through mine, adjusts the bouquet on her hip, and poses for my grandma like a pro. As we take a few different shots, Bree mumbles, "That was the most awkward kiss I've ever received. It beat out the one my stuffed lion gave me when I was a kid."

I hold her in my arms and peer down at her with awe for the sake of the picture. After all, if Maggie or anyone asks about our special day, we'll need visual proof beyond the boring documents legalizing our attachment.

It's all for show.

The silent reminder is why I steel myself when I say, "I didn't think it was appropriate to make out in front of my grandma. Plus, it went against our rules of being platonic."

"Such a good rule follower," she muses.

I take this opportunity to savor the feel of Bree in my arms. She even feels comfortable there, and by the end of our little photoshoot, I'm dazed and confused by this woman.

When she peers into my eyes, it doesn't feel fake. I just see my own emotions reflected back at me.

"All right." Gaga snaps her fingers. "Let's get out of here."

"What exactly does she mean by that?" Bree lifts a brow.

"She's cooking us dinner at her Airbnb, and there's no use in arguing against it." As I walk backward, I state, "She's already bought the chicken and the champagne."

ELEVEN

Bree

I stand in a stranger's home, which resembles a model home. There are no identifying features or pictures of any kind. The décor is far from unique, with simple grays and blues, along with the rare splash of yellow.

Even if they hadn't told me this is an Airbnb and not Gaga's own apartment, I would've guessed as much from the décor itself. A woman people call Gaga would have much more expressive and spirited paintings, knickknacks, and other whimsical features bringing the place to life.

"How long are you in town for?" I ask her.

"Indefinitely," she chirps. "I can't wait to meet my great-granddaughter."

"You haven't met Violet?"

"Not yet, but I have big plans to become the best grandma

on the block."

"Won't be hard," I say with a grin.

Wade and I follow her into the kitchen, where she squeals, holding up the bottle of champagne she promised us on the way over. The pop of the bottle makes me jerk, and my mouth drools for a sip. After the last week, I deserve the entire fucking bottle myself.

She hands us each a glass of bubbly. The French twist keeping her hair in place at the back of her head is neat and classy. The rings on her fingers are sparkly, and her makeup is flawless.

The woman could blend right in with the ladies of Sapphire Creek. The same ones my grandma hung out with. Gaga and my own grandmother would've been the best of friends, I have no doubt.

Leaning my hip against the refrigerator, I sip from my flute.

"We need to toast first!" Gaga holds up her fizzy drink and shoots her playfully scolding gaze my way.

I swallow half my sip, while the rest unintentionally slides back into the glass and along my chin. "Sorry," I manage, and I turn to Wade for… support? Reassurance? Who the fuck knows, but the one thing I do know—and despise—is how quiet he's been since our photoshoot on the steps of the courthouse.

He should be ecstatic, right? He should be the one waving champagne around, but he's kind of sulking. In truth, I should be the one doing so. I'm the one who called she-who-shall-not-be-named for the divorce decree, and it was as unpleasant as a chigger bite. While I expected nothing less, my heart hasn't stopped aching.

But instead of pouting, I'm celebrating.

"May your fake marriage be everything you hope it will be. To the Jamesons!" Gaga exclaims, and Wade and I share another look before we clink our glasses.

Once I finally swallow a full, refreshing sip, I say, "We haven't actually discussed the last name. Am I really supposed to legally change mine? Like, all my IDs should say Bree Jameson?"

"It does flow well," Gaga supplies with a wink.

"I don't know" is all Wade offers, seemingly distracted.

Is he still thinking about that kiss?

Because I totally am. It was awkward, for sure, but it was still hot because it came from Wade. The man can do no wrong when it comes to that kind of sensual stuff.

My lips tingle when I get close to him. The feel of him is still on them like a twenty-four-hour matte lipstick.

Gaga bounces over to the breakfast table, waving over her shoulder for me. "Come, darling. Let's have a chat."

"If it's okay, I need to make a call to my lawyer." Wade disappears into what I assume is the bedroom as I sink onto the seat next to his grandmother.

"Don't mind him. He's such an overthinker. And he's devilishly impatient, much like his father," she explains.

Curiosity trickles its way up my throat. "What are his parents like?"

"They're adventurers, always flitting off from one side of the world to the next for their film documentaries. I think they're currently in South Africa, where they're co-writing their first book." She smiles wistfully and toys with the stem of her glass. "They traveled a lot as Wade grew up, so he spent most of his time with my husband, Gilbert, and me." She smiles. "We did our best to fill the void his parents left. We waddled onto every soccer field for his games, even though parking was always a bitch, and Gilbert complained of his plantar fasciitis. We'd take Wade out for ice cream, play games, and eat home-cooked meals. Gilbert taught him how to drive, and I taught him how to live his life fearlessly."

"Sounds like you and Gilbert make a great team."

She lifts her glossy eyes, and I realize the mistake I've made before she confirms it. "Yes, we did, honey."

"I'm sorry. I didn't know…"

"How would you? You didn't even know Wade's first name, so I didn't expect you to know about Gilbert and his passing—and yes, I heard that too while you and Wade discussed the marriage license debacle."

We share a laugh. "We're not very good at being discreet, are we? Not sure how we're going to pull off this *holy union* with our big mouths."

"I have a feeling you'll be just fine. In fact, I doubt you'll have to pretend much at all."

"What do you mean?" I ask cautiously.

She sucks back a generous sip, then leans forward, the sun setting behind her and casting a yellow glow over her mischievous features. "I met Gilbert when I was seventeen. He was born into a vastly wealthy family, and he acted like it too. Real spoiled and entitled, and the inherent arrogance always grated on my nerves. It wasn't because I had the very opposite experience as a painfully poor child, either. He just got under my skin."

My heart stutters to life as she launches into a tale, captivating my attention much like my grandma used to. It's uncanny how much this woman reminds me of her, and the broken piece in my chest that never healed after she passed feels like it might be okay, after all.

"One day," she continues, "I was walking home from school in my pitifully worn shoes. I had holes in each of them after wearing them for three years. I even cut a hole in the front of each myself because they'd gotten too snug, but we couldn't afford new ones. In any case, I beat the snot out of anyone who dared tease me about them, and it was no different with Gilbert."

"He didn't!" I gasp.

"He was a couple years older and drove a sleek red convertible. He'd pulled up in it one afternoon with a girl sitting in the passenger seat. I heard her snickering over the obnoxious car's engine before I ever took notice of them, and when they didn't immediately drive off, I stopped and glared. He'd joined his little girlfriend in teasing me over my shoes, and I dropped my backpack on the burning sidewalk, ready to fling my entire body into his stupid expensive car and beat the crap out of them both."

"Oh my God." I cover my mouth, admittedly finding the scene equal parts hilarious and badass. I don't care for Gilbert's behavior, but given how long they were married, he obviously redeemed himself.

"I would've done hellish damage too, had Lottie Banks not come around the corner and pulled me back. I cursed her as the red convertible sped off, the jackass." She tsks under her breath. "I hated his guts and vowed to push that car into the lake if I ever got the chance."

"You're my most favorite person in the world." I beam. "But how the hell did that turn into a marriage of... of..."

"Almost fifty years before he passed."

"Wow," I breathe with disbelief.

"He liked my spunk," she brags, and I don't blame her. A spitfire like her deserves all the bragging rights. "About a week after that day on the sidewalk, we crossed paths again at a drive-in. He was there with the same bimbo as the last time. I worked the concession stand, and I refused to serve them, on principle." She shrugs.

"Of course."

"I was fired that night. Gilbert showed his first signs of having a good heart and actually offered to pay for my troubles. You can imagine where I told him to shove his money."

I giggle into my glass and fight the urge to throw my fist into the air in celebration on her behalf.

"God, I hated him, and Gilbert found my distaste for him charming." She dips her head, but when she raises it again, she's smiling. "After I lost my drive-in job, I started working at a diner, and he found me there. Started coming around every week, and the more I cursed him, the more intrigued he was. Then as soon as I turned eighteen, he told me the stupidest thing."

"What?"

"That he wanted to marry me."

I clutch my chest, finding this story oddly romantic—I can't help it.

"The dummy even went to my father for permission, and he couldn't have gotten rid of me fast enough. Like I was a damn cow in the field, my daddy sold me off to the rich man who would take care of not just me, but the whole family too."

"Seriously?"

"I married him for his money, but not before I made him drive his red convertible into the lake."

My low snort turns into a full-fledged fit of laughter that muffles her own.

I'm wiping tears out of my eyes, and as soon as my vision clears, I notice the sobriety in hers. "I didn't love him when we said 'I do,' but I pretended. I went through the motions of loving him and being his wife until one day… I realized I wasn't pretending anymore."

The last of my laugh is lodged in my throat as an unfamiliar weight settles onto my chest.

Her steady gaze pins me in place like she's trying to communicate something to me, and it's the closest I've ever gotten to a supernatural experience.

Shuffling breaks the trance she put me in, and I clear my throat as Wade reenters the kitchen. "What are you two gossiping about?"

"Your grandfather." Gaga finishes the last of her champagne as I compose myself.

"You better be careful around me, or I'll drive your car into a lake," I tease, giving him my best glare.

Next to me, Gaga smirks, and Wade stares at us both. "I leave you two alone for two seconds, and you're already plotting against me. Wow."

"Not our fault you hid away with your secret phone call." I shrug.

"Cassidy sends her warmest regards," he says to me, then continues toward the counter for his previously abandoned flute. "She's going to work on securing a court date. Meanwhile, we should have enough time for you to move your things into my place and for me to find a job."

"Right," I whisper, my chest still heavy.
I need to finish packing.
Move into my new fake husband's home.
And try not to live a repeat of the story I just heard.

126

TWELVE

Bree

With both hands on my head, I spin in circles, grumbling curses.

I curse the universe. My apartment. Wade.

Packing and moving is a torture not meant to be inflicted on a human being. It should be against the law altogether for a husband to ask his wife to do it, especially since said husband wouldn't be around to help from beginning to end.

He did promise to lift the heavy stuff, but it's the little things giving me a headache this evening. Wade and I have been married for a full week—the longest relationship I've had with a guy since my ex-husband.

It's been chaotic since I've had to work, and he's hunting for a job, running off to one interview after another. After a peek at his resume, which only includes soccer and a brief summer stint as a lifeguard ten years ago, it's going to be more difficult than I anticipated to find him a suitable job.

The most obvious to me would be for him to coach. There are plenty of youth soccer coach opportunities between Jersey City and New York. There's also the possibility of a high school soccer coach. Erin and Oliver work at a school, so we could hook Wade up.

No problem, right?

Except he won't agree to it. Evidently, he wants to explore a different route. While I'm not surprised that he has a minor in exercise science, I am shocked he has a degree in accounting. Sure, it's stable, and the world will always need accountants. I just never imagined the sexy former striker of the LA Stars would be so interested in a mundane career behind a desk.

But he insists he wants a steady, well-paying job. One that doesn't require him to travel or work late. It makes sense, but something's still nagging at me. It doesn't add up.

I sip from my glass and lick my lips, savoring the notes of black cherry as I take stock of the mess. I could—and should—organize, but all I want to do is finish this glass of wine while I watch TV.

Instead of doing any of that, I spend several minutes simply thinking about my new husband.

His tattoos and muscles are mouthwatering. I totally looked up pictures online once I learned of his past, and he's earned his physique, if the gym videos and sponsorship campaigns are any indications. He is walking, talking sex appeal, and honestly, he could've had his pick of a wife. There's no doubt in my mind that any woman off the street would've jumped at the chance.

The fact that he picked me shouldn't affect me as much as it does, but I'd be lying if I said it doesn't feel good.

I'm still thinking about the night Wade and I met too. We agreed to keep things strictly platonic moving forward. I even stupidly agreed not to go hunting for any side pieces.

I've taken countless lavender baths, sweat my ass off at Pilates and yoga with Erin, and subjected myself to the grime of the subway multiple times since I met him, but I can still feel the heat of Wade's touch on my skin. He nipped, sucked, and licked until he plucked orgasms out of me like he was playing slot machines, and he was on a winning streak—we both were.

He marked me with that tongue and those fingers of his. I won't even get started on the way he worked his dick. Those filthy thoughts will lead nowhere good. I especially can't make a habit of thinking about him in this light, either. If I get attached to him in any way, this whole charade will explode into all kinds of heartache.

Which I know all too well—been there, done that with Sonny.

A knock sounds at my door, and as I make my way over, I sidestep a few pairs of shoes. I'm still deciding whether or not they'll make the trek to Jersey City with me. At the door, I hesitate to open it. I haven't been home much this week, and it shows.

My apartment is a disaster with a capital *D*.

Half-packed boxes line one wall, I've emptied most of the drawers and cabinets in order to take stock of just how much stuff exists in the kitchen, and somewhere among the mess is my soul. It left my body days ago when I realized the massive undertaking this would be.

On top of that, I'm one of few people in the world who still buys magazines, and they're strewn about the living room as if this chaos was my poor attempt at building a paper fort. In truth, I was probably looking for a pair of my panties. Since the living room is where I normally fold my laundry while I watch reruns of *Friends*, those pesky little things tend to fall into the cracks of my couch.

Another knock jolts me forward.

Assuming it's the neighbor who usually needs sugar or the occasional chat over wine—I'm already way ahead of them on the latter—I throw the door open and freeze. I think the drink in my hand even freezes midslosh.

Maybe I swallow my tongue. Maybe I forget how to speak altogether.

Am I having a stroke? I'm too young!

Whatever madness has descended upon me, I can't escape the clusterfuck in front of me.

The woman has similar eyes to mine. Coincidentally, her hair is even dyed a similar shade as mine. Although her figure is much more slender than my own, and she's seven years younger than me, it's clear we're related.

My *sister*.

"What the—"

"I need to pee," she says, barging into my apartment and crashing my already chaotic life.

She doesn't ask where the bathroom is, nor does she offer any greeting. Considering we haven't seen each other in almost eight years, I don't think it's unreasonable to expect a "Hey" or "Mind if I use your restroom, *please?*"

Moments later, Harper flushes the toilet, and the hair at the back of my neck stands. What could she be doing here? We talked on the phone last week. As a last resort, I begrudgingly called her in order to overnight the divorce certificate, but that's it.

We didn't share pleasantries, nor did I even offer an explanation as to why I needed the damn piece of paper. I thought the extent of our non-reunion would've ended peacefully right then and there. I definitely didn't expect my selfish little sister to pop up on my doorstep.

I pour more wine into my glass, even though it's nowhere near empty. I simply know I'm going to need it.

When she returns, she points a manicured finger toward the living room. "Did a tornado come through here? Do y'all even have those in New York?"

I eye her over the rim as I all but hide myself in the red drink. "What are you doing here, Harper?"

"I had to congratulate my big sis in person."

"On what?"

"You got married again."

I stare blankly at her as I sip, sip, and sip some more.

"That *is* why you wanted your divorce certificate, right? What other explanation could there be?" She glides over to the couch as if this is her home too, but she's never been here before. The only reason she knows my address is because I had to give it to her in order to receive the certificate. Which I needed for my fake wedding to a single dad I fucked over a month ago on a whim.

Well, I guess he's technically no longer single, thanks to me and my big, traitorous heart.

Harper chucks her shoes off, sets aside a stack of magazines, and wiggles herself into a comfortable spot on my couch like she's going to stay awhile. "So? What's my new brother-in-law like? Tell me everything!" She grins, and I hate how genuine it appears.

It can't be, right? I don't trust it, or her.

I lick my lips and clip, "Is this some kind of joke?"

"No." She gapes and has the audacity to look offended.

"Did Mom send you? Are you checking up on me to make sure I don't blow it like the last time?" I ask sarcastically.

I might be deeply aware that I made no mistakes last time. I didn't run Sonny off, nor did I make him text pictures of his dick to other women. I worked myself to the bone to provide for us while he and "his band" gained momentum, and what thanks did I get in return? People around town snickering behind my back, while others took pity and sent me homemade pies.

My mom and sister weren't of the latter variety. They were actually pissed that I "drove him away," claiming I should've been a better wife. *Ha!* The fucking audacity of those two, and now, Harper sits in my living room with her feet propped onto my coffee table like she has any right to be here.

I'm actually insulted she asked about Wade at all, especially since she's asked nothing about me. Does she even care how I'm doing? What am I saying—of course she doesn't. She never gave a rat's ass about how I'm doing. It's why I haven't heard from her in so long.

"Mom doesn't know I'm here," she whispers.

"Then why? Why are you here?" I press.

"I know we've had our issues in the past, but you're my sister. You got remarried, and I had no idea until you needed something from me. How do you think that made me feel?" She slides her feet off the table, bringing along a few magazines that drop to the floor. "It's why I left Ruthie in charge of the nursery for a few days and flew up here. I want to make amends."

"Yeah right." My heart pinches below thick walls, which were strong before she walked through the door. Now, they're trembling.

"I hate how I acted the last time I saw you." She dips her head, fidgeting with the hem of her shirt as my stomach lurches. "Gran would've been so disappointed, and I've felt so guilty ever since."

I purse my lips.

"Mom pushed me to fight you on the house. I didn't even want it that badly, but I trusted her… until it was too late." She chews on the inside of her cheek, and tears build in her eyes, chipping away at my resolve. "I shouldn't have trusted her at all about anything."

I scoff. "You got that right."

"She wanted Gran's house for herself. It's why she manipulated me and convinced me it was just as much ours as it was yours, but when I realized she and Farley had planned on edging me out, I cut them off. What I actually did was tell them to fuck off, which is what I should've done years before that." A tear slides down her cheek, and it might as well be a knife to my chest.

As a teen, there was nothing worse than seeing my baby sister cry, and even though we're estranged in adulthood, it doesn't hurt any less. "Why didn't you tell me any of this back then?"

"I was embarrassed." She clutches her chest. "When you came home for Gran's funeral, the things I said and did to you were so fucking horrible. I let Mom control me, and it wasn't fair to you. I was just nasty as hell, and I didn't think you'd ever forgive me, no matter what I said."

"And what are you saying now?"

"I'm sorry, for starters."

"For the nasty things you said, trying to talk me out of living in Gran's house, even though she left it to me, or for running me out of town altogether?"

"I was thirteen when you and Sonny divorced," she says, clearly knowing exactly what I'm referring to. This feud between us is only partially thanks to the fight that broke out the night of Gran's funeral. It was one of the few times I'd gone home after my divorce, and it was the last. After my grandma passed, I had no reason to go back.

Sometimes, I do miss Mrs. Marilyn's stories about the pieces in her antique store, Conversation Pieces, and the lemon squares from Bready or Knot. I even miss the humid summers and excessive pollen. But none of those sentimental things from my childhood have been enough for me to step foot back into that town.

"I remember," I snap. "I also remember how you and Mom fucking terrorized me. I didn't care about Sonny's skanks laughing at me around town. They meant nothing to me. I cared that my own family didn't have my back."

"I was a child," she shoots back, and her nose reddens much like my own does when I'm frustrated. "I didn't know any better. I lived with Mom. I only understood her twisted, fucked-up version of your story. What was I supposed to do?"

"You should've believed me. I'm your sister. All I ever did was look out for you, and you stabbed me in the back the first chance you got. You kept doing it too." I drain the rest of my glass and slam it onto the counter, then pour more wine, except it's not enough to fill up my glass. Digging into a box off to the side, I retrieve a new bottle and get to work.

"I'm sorry, Bree." She frowns, and again, it appears genuine.

In truth, this woman looks a lot like me. We share the same eyes, bow-shaped lips, and hair too, although hers is shorter than mine. We grew up together. Shared a bed during the nights she felt alone or scared. Talked extensively about how much we hated Farley when Mom married him, but we'd made a pact to try to be a family again after Dad abandoned us.

We leaned on each other after Dad left a void in our house.

Once upon a time, I shared all my ups and downs with my sister. Yet, I barely know her.

It doesn't change how badly I want to believe her, though. How much I want to accept that she's truly here to make things right, for old time's sake and for our future.

"I'm really, really sorry. I shouldn't have let Mom poison me. I should've taken your side, and I regret it. I regret everything so fucking badly."

I set a fresh stemless wineglass in front of her and plop down on the love seat by the window. "You're making it too easy to want to forgive you, but I don't. Not yet."

"That's fair. I'm here to earn it. It's why I didn't apologize over the phone."

"I respect that." I purse my lips and point to the glass.

"Thanks." She picks up the metaphorical olive branch but stops with it halfway to her lips. "You have more of this, right? We're going to need a lot more if we're going to talk about everything we need to get out in the open."

She does have a point, although I'd rather just drink in silence than work through our baggage. That's *not* the night I had planned.

As I sip from my own glass, Harper speaks up again. "What are your panties doing in the couch? And don't tell me you lost them while your husband was fucking you every which way to Tuesday, because seriously, I'll want to switch places."

Instantly, as if it's from reflex alone, a giggle tickles my throat, but it doesn't reach my lips. Not when thoughts of Wade fucking me in his own apartment flash through my head—again.

I really need to stop doing that.

There will be no fucking around with my *fake* husband, but Harper doesn't need to know the truth. She hasn't earned as much, but as we get reacquainted, I must admit—I've missed my sister.

THIRTEEN

Wade

Grunting like a hungry bear, Tucker hurls a punch, but I thwart his gloved fist with my own and bounce back.

In the ring next to ours, two men do the same, except the coach and his protégé talk strategy through each swing, while Tucker and I gossip.

"You got married? *Married*? You're telling me you got married?" he says, stumbling over his words like he does his feet. Foot work has never been his strong suit, but thankfully, neither of us is going pro.

We're simply here to blow off steam.

I throw a quick combination, most of which he dodges, but I manage to land one on his side. "You can repeat it however many times you'd like. Won't make it any less true."

"A woman's pussy is never good enough to put a ring on

her finger after one night, although from what I saw, I guess I could believe it in your case. She was hot as fuck."

We've been in this boxing gym for over an hour, and seconds ago, I was ready to call it quits. Any more sparring and I'll collapse long before my interview in the morning.

But hearing my friend talk about Bree like this sends my nerves into overdrive. I launch my entire body into the next combination like this is the start of our round, and I'm not tired in the slightest. I give it my all, firing away at him until he leaps backward into a corner, his hands tossed up in what I can only assume is a white flag. His lips move as he pants, but I don't hear anything over the ringing in my ears.

I stalk toward my water, and as I sip, the noises in this place finally filter back through. "Fuck," I mutter.

"Did you hear me?"

I turn to face Tucker and use the back of my hand to wipe the stray water trickling down my chin.

"I forgot we were talking about your wife now, and not some random chick. I respect it, and her, all right? I'm sorry." He holds his hands up in surrender.

"We're good," I say, my voice hoarse as remnants of jealousy course through me, even though I don't have the right.

But as long as Bree's wearing *my* ring on her finger, I have all the fucking right.

Tucker talks over the scratchy tear of Velcro coming loose around our gloves. "We won't be single dad superheroes anymore, man."

I smirk. "And that's a bad thing?"

"It's catnip for the ladies, and two is always better than one. You're my wingman."

"Not anymore." I stuff my shit into the bag. "You could help my new lady move her stuff into my place this weekend, though."

He mutters a curse.

"I'll bring beer, and I'll even buy the UFC pay-per-view for us to watch Saturday night," I offer to sweeten the deal.

"Oh, you're so on." He whistles as sweat drips down his forehead. "I need to make my bets first."

He continues mumbling about doing his research. Apparently, he's been out of the loop on most of the fighters on the card this weekend.

With our bags slung over our shoulders, we emerge onto the sidewalk, where the midday sun is bright and further warms my already-heated cheeks.

"You're married, with prospects of a job. It's like magic, man," Tucker muses.

"No magic involved. I'm just good at making shit happen."

Tucker places a large hand on my chest and brings us to a stop. "Don't take this the wrong way, but out of curiosity, this marriage is… legal, right?"

"Would you like me to show you the documentation?" I shift, uncomfortable under his scrutiny. His gaze is too intense and unwavering. He's locked in on me like a target. The guy is going to make one hell of a detective someday, that's for sure.

"It's just hard to believe you were single a month ago, and now you have a wife."

I scratch the back of my head. "You saw her, and you said so yourself—you don't blame me."

"I believe you, Wade, but if there's anything you want to tell me about this, you can. I don't think I need to remind you how risky and sticky this could get if anything you've done isn't… kosher."

I lift a brow. "Is this Officer Marks talking, or are you my friend Tucker, who threw up in my closet on New Year's Eve?"

"Tequila shots and I really don't mix."

"It's about the only thing in the world that can penetrate your rigid exterior," I joke.

His expression sobers again.

"I know the risks, trust me." My stomach sinks. "But here's another truth. When I played soccer, we never canceled a game if the opposing team was bigger, faster, more experienced, or whatever. We rose to the challenge."

"And I've known you long enough to know you'd do anything to overcome that challenge. That's what concerns me."

"No need to be concerned. I know what I'm doing," I say, confidence coursing through me at warped speed.

I'm about to follow it up with a more solid defense to ease his worries, but we're interrupted by my phone vibrating with an incoming call. I thank Tucker for the chat and afternoon, and we split into opposite directions. He rushes off to pick up his daughter from his mom's, and coincidentally, the call is from my own family matters.

"Hey, Maggie. How—"

"You brought a random woman to the park with Violet, and I'm just now finding out about it?" she asks incredulously, her words rushed and clipped.

My gut twists. Maggie's angry. I thought we were making progress when she dropped Violet off at the park with me over a week ago, but I botched it because I didn't tell her Bree would be there. The idea never even crossed my mind beforehand, but it was harmless.

It's definitely not worth the argument I know is coming. In fact, most of the arguments Maggie and I have are blown out of proportion. It's like she's locked and loaded at all times, ready to chew my ass out for anything and everything.

Is it always going to be like this?

"This is why I can't trust you, Wade," she continues. "You should've told me you and Violet wouldn't be alone. Actually, you shouldn't have brought a random freaking woman to meet her in the first place. It's not healthy for Violet to meet your girlfriend of the day. She needs stability, which you clearly cannot provide. Your lifestyle is not appropriate for Violet, and if you think I'll be leaving her with you again anytime soon, then you have another thing coming."

"Are you finished?" I bite out, my adrenaline from the workout still pumping through my bloodstream with vigor.

"No," she hisses. "There's plenty more I'd love to explain to you about how inappropriate it is to bring random women—"

"She wasn't a random woman, Maggie. She's my wife," I growl.

"Your *what?*" she screeches, and I have to pull the phone away for fear she busted an eardrum.

"Bree is my wife, and Violet had every right to meet her. *I* had every right to introduce them. Don't forget—*I'm* Violet's father. Not Roger. And I'm going to legally remind you of that fact when I take you to court. You'll be hearing from my lawyer *very* soon."

I end the call, which in Maggie's eyes, probably falls under the claim that I'm immature, irresponsible, and selfish, but I'm fucking tired.

This time last year, I was kicking off the new season with my team, tumbling through a tunnel created by the guys lining up and joining hands, their fingertips touching in pyramid-like fashion. We'd each take turns rolling through headfirst while we all yelled "wooooo" in Rick Flair fashion.

It was our sacred tradition—one I held very fucking dear.

I wasn't aware of a daughter. I lived in a house by the beach in California, where winters were nothing like the one I've survived here. I was part of a team, and the other players were like my brothers. I was single and living like it too, without a care in the world other than making it to the playoffs.

A year ago, I wasn't watching the team in Slater's videos from my Jersey City apartment, nor was I preparing to be an accountant for a sports apparel company with headquarters in the Financial District of Manhattan.

Every bit of my life has been turned on its damn head, but I meant what I said to Bree when she asked if I regret any of this. I don't. I don't regret a single part of it, but I do miss the team. I even miss California sometimes.

This transition would be a hell of a lot easier if Maggie would stop crawling up my ass over every little thing. If she would've been the tiniest bit agreeable about things regarding Violet, I wouldn't have taken such extraordinary measures to fulfill the role as Dad.

I'm fucking exhausted over it all.

As I slide into the driver's seat of my car, my phone vibrates with a new text. If it's Maggie again, I'm going to scream.

But to my pleasant surprise, it's Bree.

Bree: Does your building allow ferrets?

If you tell me you have a pet ferret, that might be the most surprising thing about you.

I don't, but a neighbor has one for someone to adopt. I thought I might be interested. For Violet, of course. Furry creatures and I myself don't mix. Then again, I've done my fair share of good things lately. I should stop now.

I feel like you're talking about me…

Was I that obvious? ☺

I have so many questions.

I'm sure the most pressing one is about how many pairs of shoes I'm bringing over.

You read my mind.

I wouldn't be a decent wife if I wasn't good at that.

I'm not being a very decent husband, am I? I'm sorry I haven't been there more to help with the packing.

Don't sweat it. You've been busy yourself. Did Gaga find a place?

I swipe at the corners of my lips with my thumb and forefinger, the subtle taste of salt from my sweat lingering there. Once I confirm that Gaga has found a new home in Jersey City, I send Bree the link to the online listing too.

When it was time for my grandma to leave the Airbnb to head home to Florida, she was so misty-eyed, she bumped into a wall. According to her, she didn't feel right about leaving. Not when all she'd return to would be an empty house, where she'd be all alone.

My heart cracked at that.

She wanted to stay here, so I picked her up the next morning to hunt for a suitable apartment. She's down in Florida now, getting her affairs in order and preparing for the move, which means I'll be hauling boxes for the foreseeable future.

Returning my attention to Bree's texts, I tap out an offer.

> If you still need help packing, I can come by now.

> We're pretty much done, except for the essentials. My sister's actually been really great.

I furrow my brow as I type out several messages, decide against them, then finally call her.

"You have a sister?" I ask as I pull onto the road. "How did I not know this?"

"We hadn't spoken in years, but I guess Hell froze over, because here she is." A strangled snort crackles through the speaker.

"So, you're close then," I tease.

"The *closest*. We share clothes, braid each other's hair, and sing duets of Reba's biggest hits," she says with a heavy dose of sarcasm.

I let out a deep laugh as she continues. "We're actually two Southern women who prefer the petty, avoid-confrontation-at-all-costs route. It's why I gave her our grandma's house, even though she left it to me. It was my way of sticking it to my sister because she can't live there without thinking about me."

"Savage."

"What's savage is her ruining our ways and showing up here in person to work out our issues. It's a torture I've never experienced before."

"You better be glad I showed up, you bitch. Who else would've taken the precious time to toss the ugly clothes from your closet?" I hear from the background, presumably from her sister.

"You did what?" Bree barks.

"I did you a favor, so you're welcome."

"No, the favor you're going to do is to take me shopping— on Fifth. Not the cheap stores. Fifth. Avenue." There's a hint of amusement in Bree's tone, which makes me laugh again.

She might claim they're not close, but they sure sound like they are.

"You'll be happy to know that Vi loves your clothes," I cut in.

"Ha! A seven-year-old has better taste than you," Bree says.

"I'll let you two hash this out." Chuckling, I come to a stop in an open spot on the curb near my building.

"Can't wait to meet you, Wadey Baby," her sister calls out. "Tell…"

"Harper. Her stupid name is Harper."

"Tell Harper I said hi."

As I click to end the call, I shift in my seat, the sweat soaking through my T-shirt giving me chills, but that's not what stops me. It's the dopey grin on my face.

How does she do this? Bree instantly makes me feel… happy. And it's over silly things like bagels.

The way she and my grandma talked like old friends.

How easily she connected with my daughter.

If I didn't know any better, I'd say Bree has magic powers, but it's who she is. I enjoy talking to her, whether it's about jobs or random hypothetical pets. And she's moving into my place in two days, after which she'll be in my space at all times.

We're going to share a bed, for Christ's sake.

It's dangerous to feel this good about my fake wife.

FOURTEEN

"**D**o you think he likes a kink or two in bed? I feel like he does." Harper peeks around the box of pillows in her arms and licks her lips.

When the elevator door opens, we step into the hallway and cross the short few feet toward the open door of Wade's apartment.

Well, I guess it's mine too now, so *our* apartment.

"I bet he has a filthy mouth on him," I say.

"I'd die if a cop used the law to talk dirty to me."

"Officer Hot Ass at your service," I say in a low, suggestive voice, impersonating Tucker for Harper's benefit. She appreciates it, too. In fact, he can probably hear her cackling all the way downstairs.

It's move-in day, and Wade and Tucker are lifting the

heavy stuff, as promised, while Harper and I carry as little as possible. We'd contribute more if we weren't too busy laughing over old memories and new hunks in the building, including Tucker. The guy's dark eyes are downright devilish, and the man can work a pair of Levis better than the guys back home.

He's also a sweetheart, with manners for days.

"I'd let him handcuff me to the bed while I bagel blow him." Harper snorts.

"What are you two talking about?"

My spine stiffens at the sound of Wade's voice coming from his bedroom. Shit. How much did he hear?

"Nothing," I chirp, but Harper has no chill. Instead of following my lead, she answers honestly.

"Your friend Tucker. He's a looker, as the old biddies down South would say."

I roll my eyes. "You have said as much about every guy we've come into contact with," I say in an attempt to backtrack in case Wade overheard me gawking over his neighbor's ass.

Would he even care?

"This city is full of sexy men. Do you know what my options are back home? Jeremiah, the arthritic seventy-year-old owner of a car shop, and the sleazy group of middle-aged lawyers who play golf every week and talk about how rich they are."

"Sounds like you've got a winner there—the rich men would treat you *real* nice," Wade muses as he crosses the room toward the door, and Harper flips him off.

The two might've only met for the first time an hour ago, but they're more comfortable than a margarita and the lime on its rim. My sister has that way about her, and Wade possesses his own charms too, so I'm not surprised over their instant friendship.

We're all one big, happy family now.

"What about Cole Rivers?" I ask Harper, feeling oddly nostalgic as the name rolls off my tongue with such ease, even though I haven't thought about him in years. I barely even knew the guy when I lived in town. "You always had a crush on him."

"I do have a thing for bartenders, but some slut from out of town snatched him up," she laments, and I read between the lines.

The "slut" is probably an average woman who's likely super nice, but my sister hates her for snagging one of the few eligible bachelors in town.

"Oh!" Harper drops the box at her feet like it's full of bricks instead of light pillows. "Do you remember Austin Kyle?"

"Doesn't ring a bell."

"He's closer to my age, so you wouldn't have crossed paths in school. But he was snatched up by some girl from Nashville. I mean, Caroline is originally from Sapphire Creek, but she moved, which totally makes her a slut too."

"What is with these whores rolling into town and stealing your men?" I play along.

"My thoughts exactly! I should go out of town and find me a hunk." She places both hands on her hips over the plaid shirt dangling from her slim waist. Paired with black wool leggings, Doc Martens, and a bandana headband, she effortlessly makes this look work.

I, on the other hand, would look ridiculous in such an outfit, which is why I have nothing like it in my closet. Is that why she got rid of my stuff—because she thinks she dresses better?

We have a lot of work to do on our relationship, and a fashion war will throw a wrench in it. *She better watch her back...*

"Speaking of a hunk." Harper's voice trails off as Tucker enters with a load of boxes on the dolly, his red T-shirt tight around his biceps. If she's liking him in this getup, Harper would absolutely freak if she got a glimpse of him in his uniform.

And if that happens, there's no keeping her hands off him, and there's no chance I'd like to share a bedroom wall with her. I'd hate to find out for myself what she meant by "bagel blowing" earlier. If she's anything like me—and she totally is—it's something hella dirty, which would completely ruin the pleasant and cherished memories I have of the food.

Seemingly unaware of us and our conversation, Tucker backs out the way he entered, with Wade on his heels, and we're alone again, admiring their backsides.

"He's a single dad too, you know," I say absentmindedly. "Tucker—he has a daughter. I haven't met her yet, but she's around Violet's age."

"Oh my God." Harper grabs my arm like she needs me to hold her steady. "He's a girl dad?"

Suddenly, my body vibrates as she shuffles her feet in delight, her grip on my arm tightening. Her mini dancefest is cut short when the guys reappear, much to my disappointment. It's a treat when Harper stumbles over her awkward moves. The woman has zero grace or coordination, which is one of about three differences between us. I can throw down with the best of them, whether I'm at a club in Manhattan or a hoedown at the annual Peach Festival in Sapphire Creek.

"That's the last of what's on the truck," Wade announces, and as if in sync, the four of us scan the small space, cramped from the boxes labeled with garish handwriting. Harper got zealous with the Sharpie earlier.

A makeshift narrow path leads from the door to the living room, cutting off the entrances to the bathroom and the two bedrooms on either side of it.

We're all staring at the mountain of boxes in that direction when Harper says, "I need to pee."

Maybe it's the exhaustion or delirium—or both—but we break out into a chorus of laughter, especially when she tries to parkour the piles like they're part of an obstacle course.

"Shit!" she hisses as her foot crashes through the top of a box.

I check the label and tsk. "You better be glad those are just bath towels and nothing breakable."

"I'm pretty sure I saw two other boxes with towels." She shimmies her foot free, but not without the help of a gallant knight in shining *muscles*.

Tucker rushes to her side while Wade and I sidle up next to each other to witness what transpires between the pair. They make googly eyes at each other like a couple might in a cheesy romantic comedy. Once she's free of the cardboard, he holds her like she's just been saved from oncoming traffic.

Next to me, Wade snickers, and I can't help myself, either, although I do try to stifle it in the palm of my hand. It's enough to break the spell between them, though, and Harper practically jolts out of her skin, as if she forgot we were even standing here.

The pool of men in Sapphire Creek must, in fact, be slim pickings if she's losing her shit over this ridiculous, otherwise innocent, encounter. Then again, Tucker is just that hot, so who am I to judge?

Harper all but launches herself onto the other side of the wall of boxes toward the bathroom, and Tucker turns to us. "So…" He shifts back and forth on his heels. "Bree, are you excited about Jersey City? It's a little different than Brooklyn."

"Tell me about it." I snort. "What will be even more different is sharing a bed with a guy every night, let alone the entire apartment. I never saw that happening. Not in a million years did—"

I feel Wade's wide eyes on me before I see them for myself.

Clearing my throat, I wrap my hand around my new husband's arm and retrace my proverbial steps. "What I mean is, I never saw any of that happening before *this* guy." I beam up at him. "Just takes… the right one."

But I'm putting on a show for no one, because Harper returns from the bathroom, and it's clear we've lost Tucker's attention.

"We should take the truck back." Wade pats my hand before I tear it away from his impressive bicep.

"I'll grab the keys." Harper skips over a few rogue boxes with my magazines in them, which Wade insisted we keep in storage the moment he noticed. Given the limited space, I might have to agree. "Just keep them away from that one over there." She tosses the keys to Wade.

"You don't drive… big trucks?" he asks me as he cocks a brow.

I'm either super horny or pathetic—or both—but the sexy undertone of his question lights a fire between my legs.

"I drive them fine, but they just can't handle this much woman," I say with a wink.

Harper's abrupt laughter interrupts, effectively zipping my hormones up tight. "The last time Bree drove anything remotely the same size was a combine through Sonny's father's cotton field. Well"—she waves her arms, speaking through snorts—"she *tried* to drive it through the field, but she ended up crashing into his shed. Minimal damage, but old man Pemberton was pissed."

My throat constricts at the mention of Sonny. It's like she's just invited his ghost into my new home—with my new husband, however fake he might be.

That's the thing about having my sister here. She's bringing my past into my present, and I wasn't prepared for the clash of my two worlds.

I haven't been prepared for any of the memories this new arrangement with Wade has conjured. I've thought about Sonny more in the last month than I have in the last fourteen years altogether.

Unfortunately, I've also thought about my dad a lot. I vowed long ago to myself that I wouldn't give him the satisfaction of remembering his mere existence, but the last couple of weeks have made the hole he left in my life impossible to ignore.

It all makes me uneasy, to say the least.

"You were a wild child, huh?" Tucker chuckles, spreading his arms out on both sides. "Believe it or not, I got into loads of trouble as a teen myself."

"Oh, I believe it…" Harper narrows her eyes suggestively.

And I roll my own. "So, the truck?"

"Right." Tucker holds up the jingling keys and backs away toward the door.

Wade follows him out as my nosy sister pilfers through

his—*our*—kitchen. "There has to be wine around here, right? We need to celebrate!"

"I'd definitely prefer the wine over unpacking these boxes. Maybe I could leave my clothes and take the rest to storage…"

"What will you do without your hundreds of bath towels and magazines?" Her sarcasm floats all the way over to me in the living room.

Flipping her off, I sink onto the couch, my muscles aching from the treacherous physical labor I put them through this week, all in the name of domestication.

Me, fucking domesticated.

Next thing I know, I'll be printing out pictures from the wedding to put up on the walls.

Which is actually not a bad idea, for the sake of appearances. When Violet comes over, it'll be comforting for her to see them and have a sense of family, even if she doesn't yet know us very well.

"Aha!" Harper rises from behind the counter, a black glass bottle of wine in her hand.

"Thank God."

"Here you go." Harper wiggles her tiny ass onto the couch next to me as I take the swishing wineglass from her. "And cheers," she chirps, which is followed by a healthy gulp.

I'm right behind her.

This is how we spend the rest of the hour, sipping Merlot with our feet on the edge of the coffee table while we talk about Sapphire Creek. She fills me in on the Christmas parade, which is always a big hit with the community, and the big high school reunion they threw at Buchanan House last fall. The old armory usually hosts them, but they wanted to try something different. It's the first of many reunions that'll be held there, including Harper's next year.

"We'll create a new tradition, you know?" she continues. "Buchanan House is not only big enough for our class, but it's also absolutely gorgeous. The pictures we'll take on that stairwell—it'll feel like we're throwing a whole new prom."

I giggle along with her, but my chest clouds with turmoil as we continue swapping stories.

This is how it was always supposed to be with us. This is what sisters do—gab about boys, real and fake proms, and share old memories while we create new ones.

It's surreal sitting here with her like this, but I can't say I don't love it, because I totally do, even if she does remind me so much of the place I left behind.

My life has changed so much since then. Here, there are no Buchanan Houses, combines, or peaches, but the words themselves are familiar. They conjure foggy images in my mind beyond yellow cabs, skyscrapers, throngs of people, and everything else I've grown accustomed to.

The old memories are simply buried underneath piles of new ones, and I'm about to make tons more. I'm about to be a kid's stepmother, for fuck's sake.

Sure, it might be in name only, but it'll be a title I'll hold for the very first time. What the fuck do I know about being a stepmother?

For starters, I should probably stop using the word *fuck* so much.

The sun has set by the time Tucker and Wade barrel through the door, announcing in their best Bruce Buffer impressions that it's time for the fight.

"Oh, God," I mutter.

"UFC is up next, ladies!" Tucker's cheeks split into a boyish grin I've never seen on him before as he stalks toward the TV on the wall across from us.

At some point during my chat with Harper, she chucked her shoes off and made herself right at home. Wiggling her red-painted toes, she asks, "What's going on?"

"Fight Night," Wade and I answer in sync. His confused gaze snaps to mine, but I glimpse a hint of awe too.

He obviously didn't expect me to know anything about the barbaric sport.

"How cute are you two! You have like, one brain," Harper gushes.

"Shit," Tucker mumbles, spinning on his heel to face us. "Did you two want the place to yourselves tonight? We can take a raincheck on the fight…"

"Oh my God—he's totally right," Harper chimes in, but I'm pretty sure she would've agreed with the "hunk" had he suggested we get our assholes waxed.

I did it once years ago, and ten out of ten, I would *not* recommend. I keep my waxes to bikini, and that's it.

My sister hops up, her hands flailing like she just found a spider in her lap, but it's more likely that she's had too much wine. There's a chance her hormones are on fire for Tucker too, which is cutting off circulation to the calm part of her brain. "I didn't even think about this being your first night together in your home. I mean, I know you two have spent many nights together, but this is different." She waggles her eyebrows in sync to her accusatory finger, which she waves in Wade's face. "I found the rogue panties between her couch cushions."

Wade sears me with a heated stare, and my nostrils flare.

Why does he have to be so damn hot? More importantly, why do I wish those panties *were* from a night of sex with him, as Harper is suggesting?

I jump up, swipe Harper's empty glass from her hand, and stick my tongue out. "No more for you."

"Fine," she draws out with exasperation.

Tucker clears his throat, but I suspect he's hiding a laugh. "Seriously, we can go and leave you two to do… your thing."

I snort as I return from the kitchen, sans glasses. "There's no *thing* here. We're not even—"

Another glare from Wade stops me.

"I'm on my period, anyway," I blurt, and the room wears matching expressions of confusion with a touch of disgust from my overshare.

Wade might be my husband, but he does not know me like that. Tucker sure as hell doesn't.

It's not even my time of the month, so I don't know why I said it other than to justify why Wade and I are "not even" anything. Being on my period sounded like a good excuse in my head.

I really need to get a freaking grip on this arrangement before I give the lie away in court or something equally disastrous happens.

"No more wine for you, either, sis." Harper smirks, and I welcome the save.

"I promised Tucker I'd get the fight," Wade swoops in. "Plus, Ellie's with your mom, right? No kids at home for either of us, so UFC night it is. If that's okay with you, baby?"

I tuck myself into his open embrace and squeeze his side. "Of course," I nearly squeak as we step into the roles of doting newlyweds.

It's only been a few hours, and I've slipped up twice now. This is going to be harder than I thought, isn't it?

"Besides, we're also celebrating your new job," I gush, but this time, I don't need to fake it.

I'm truly excited for him, although accounting still doesn't seem to fit him in my eyes. Nonetheless, it's a well-paying job, and it's going to work wonders with a judge.

"Congratulations, man." Tucker slides onto the chaise on the other side of us.

"When do you start?" Harper takes the love seat I brought from my apartment. It's purple, which fits right in with the slim décor around here. It's the exact splash of color this place needs.

Wade gulps down a large swig of beer before answering with a short, "Monday."

As my sister pries more information out of him and what kind of job this is, Wade's cologne holds me in a trance.

His tattooed arm is warm and teasing around my shoulders, his hand dangling over my upper arm. It's relaxed and seemingly innocent, but my frustrated nipples are too aware of how close his fingertips are to them. It would be so easy and satisfying to turn right into his touch.

I try to focus on the bloody fighters on the screen, but when that doesn't work, I thwart my attention onto the upholstery of the love seat, and not because it's one of the few pieces from my former single life.

It's because the moment Wade's hand lands on my upper thigh, my breath hitches. The heat radiating from the contact travels up my body and takes residence in my core.

While Tucker holds a beer up and cheers for whomever he bet on, and Harper's too busy checking Tucker out, I attempt to shift away from Wade's touch for my own sanity. If I sit like this much longer, my resolve will snap, so I need to distance myself.

But he only grips me harder.

FIFTEEN

Wade

During the long night of fights on the TV, Bree and Harper alternated between squeezing their eyes closed and making gagging sounds of disgust over the blood shed in the ring while Tucker and I high-fived each other.

"There is nothing sexy about cauliflower ears and busted noses," Bree said, and I didn't hear Harper's response because I was too busy noticing all the sexy things about my new wife.

The fitted cotton top clinging to her perky breasts.

The teasing way she bites her bottom lip.

How both nostrils flare when her eyes meet mine.

My balls were fucking blue by the time Tucker offered to give Harper a ride to wherever she's calling home while she's in town, and now, I'm alone with Bree.

Who's in the shower.

Soapy, wet skin flashes through my mind as I imagine her scrubbing every inch of her sinful body, and I'm suddenly envious of the damn soap.

My fingers itch to busy themselves. I should reorganize the boxes or do the dishes stacked in the sink. Instead, I simply stand in the middle of the kitchen, suspended in a special kind of purgatory of my own making.

The shower squeaks to a stop, cutting off the steady flow of water, and instantly, more images of a naked Bree slam into me.

Steam rising around her bouncing breasts as she emerges from the stand-up shower.

Hands smoothing her wet hair out of her face.

Her pouty lips parted as she sucks in a breath.

Gripping the edge of the counter with both hands, I hang my head and utter a curse. I should go work on my car, shouldn't I? It's crazy late, but I should leave this apartment altogether.

Instead, I maneuver around the boxes and disappear into my bedroom, where I peel my shirt off and over my head. The cool air hits my flushed skin, and even that turns me on. Feels like my fucking tattoos come alive.

How am I supposed to make it through the entire night without touching Bree? Without wanting to feel her smooth skin against mine?

Without kissing her lips until they're swollen and marked by me?

After all, she's my wife now. She's wearing my grandmother's sacred ring. She's mine.

But she isn't, is she? Outside of the law binding us together, we're not truly a married couple.

"Fuck," I whisper as I toss my shirt into the growing pile of dirty clothes on the floor. I have a hamper. Why don't I use the damn thing?

Sighing, I decide this would be as good a time as any to do just that. I scoop the clothes into my arms and reach the hallway right as the bathroom door swings open.

Good timing, as the hamper is in the bathroom.

"Can I get—" I swallow the rest of the question as Bree shrieks.

She shuts herself into the bathroom again, leaving me stunned and frozen in front of the door with a pile of dirty boxer briefs and sweatpants in my arms.

She was naked.

Completely fucking bare.

The only thing on her was the towel holding her hair in a twisted knot on her head.

It was a quick flash, but I got an eyeful of her puckered nipples and the light trail of hair between her legs.

I've had those legs wrapped around my head before, and the urge in my dick to recreate the first night we had together wrestles with the logic in my mind.

With a quiet drop of the clothes at my feet, I drift back into my bedroom, hands covering my face as if it'll help me unsee what I just saw, because what I did just see doesn't help the tent pitching between my legs.

Why did I have to see her naked?

"Um, Wade?" she calls out meekly from the short hallway.

"I'm in the bedroom," I croak worse than a teenage boy hitting puberty. I can tell her I'm in the bedroom. It's an innocent fact. It's not like I'm in here jacking off.

But I sounded as embarrassed as if I actually did have my hand in my pants.

"I'm in the bedroom," I call out more firmly.

"I heard you." She stands in the doorway, and her smile catches me off guard.

Then again, why should I be surprised that she seems completely relaxed? She's always confident, as she should be.

Besides, she knows as well as I do that her naked body is nothing new to me. I shouldn't be so shaken up over seeing it again, but I so am, because this is in a totally different context. Our agreement insists we keep things platonic, and having her naked in front of me makes it extremely difficult to uphold the necessary boundaries.

"Sorry about my little peep show." She hooks a thumb over her shoulder in the direction of the door as if I'm not perfectly aware of what just happened and where. "I kind of forgot there's another person living with me," she admits, gripping the sides of her robe tight around her.

"You already forgot about me? Ouch." I clutch my chest in exaggeration, easing into the comfort I've come to expect with Bree.

"I've lived alone for years, so it's going to take longer than one night to get used to this, okay? Plus, the shower was so hot and relaxing, I got super dazed."

Her hips sway as she saunters to a box by the dresser, and I bite my scuffed knuckles as she bends over. I try not to stare. God, I try harder than I would to lift a fucking boulder off the ground, but I fail miserably.

I can't help but take in the sight of her bending over in search of… something. What the hell is she looking for that's taking so long?

And why is she wearing such a short, scant robe? The thin material is too revealing, and it's just cheering my dick on.

I'm close to offering her my wallet to go buy whatever she needs just to stop torturing me with the view, but fortunately, it doesn't need to come to such measures. She rises with a rather colorful cosmetics bag in her hand and a twinkle in her eye.

Pressing the bag to her chest, she sighs. "That was a close one. I thought I was going to have to tear through all the boxes tonight to find this."

"Is there gold in it?"

"Better. My face creams." With a lazy shrug, she practically dances her way back into the bathroom for another fifteen minutes.

While I just sit on the edge of my bed.

Does she take this long in the bathroom every night? Oh, fuck. How long does it take her to get ready in the mornings? There's only one bathroom, and there'll be three of us sharing it when Violet stays over.

The mornings before work will be chaos enough, but if Bree takes forever and a day in there, I'm in deep trouble.

When she emerges again, her skin is smooth and glistening, presumably from these magical face creams. She's also ditched the robe, thank fuck. Instead, she's in a loose T-shirt and gray pajama bottoms with a couple holes around the ankle—the epitome of comfort.

And I'm jealous of her peaceful state.

I open my mouth to ask about her morning routine, but something else entirely comes out. "How are you feeling?"

"I'm great after that hot shower and the mini facial I just performed."

"Performed?"

"It's a beauty ritual, which is basically a self-care production. Ergo, *performed*." Her giggle floats over to me, along with a minty scent.

"So, you're… okay? Because I can run to the store for whatever… feminine… products you might… need." I wince. I'm such a fucking guy, aren't I?

Both of her hands fly to her mouth, but the crinkles around her eyes are still visible. She's grinning. "I totally forgot what I said earlier, but it was a lie. I'm not due for my period for another week, and trust me, you'll know when it hits because the only company I'll want is that which only Netflix and Hershey's can provide."

"Netflix and chill is out, and Hershey's is in—got it." I chuckle, but it gurgles in my throat as Bree moves toward me.

When she places both hands onto my shoulders and levels me with a gracious tilt of her soft smile, I tense, clamming up worse than I did during my one and only theater role in a Christmas play as a nine-year-old.

"Thank you for asking. That's very sweet." She leans in like she's going to kiss me. She wouldn't, would she?

She licks her lips, and it drives me wild. Does she want *me* to kiss her? I fucking want to.

Before anything escalates between us, though, she pats my arms and tiptoes away, leaving a void in my personal space.

"Good night," she calls over her shoulder.

It's not until she's left the room that I register she's not crawling into my—*our*—bed.

"Where are you going?" I ask, following her into the living room, where she unfolds a fluffy purple blanket, the color of which matches the love seat. Is everything she owns purple?

I'd hate to find out the hundred bath towels she brought over are all purple.

Then again, a part of me thinks purple towels overflowing from our shared bathroom would be… charming. So very Bree.

"It's after one in the morning. I'm going to sleep." She curls underneath the blanket, her head resting on—unsurprisingly—a purple pillow.

Blinking, I stalk toward her, but before I can protest this little arrangement, she rises on her elbows and tilts her head. "I guess we should've discussed this earlier, but are you a morning person on the weekends? If so, all I ask is that you're quiet while I'm asleep out here."

"No."

"I'm not asking you to tiptoe around like a robber, but a little consideration would be appreciated, please. I'm not a light sleeper, but I can hear cabinets if you were to bang them repeatedly."

"No," I draw out slowly, internally gliding over her word choice. I cannot dwell over any kind of *banging*, or I'll lose my shit completely. "You're not sleeping out here."

"I'm not going to impose and kick you out of your own room. That would be insane."

"You're sleeping in there with me," I declare and snatch the blanket off her.

"That's even more insane!" She shoots upright and paws at the blanket, but it's no use. There's no chance she's getting this back as long as she insists on this ridiculous plan of hers.

"We agreed we'd share a bed," I remind her.

"When Violet is around—yes. But she's not here, nor

will she be until we go to court in a couple of weeks. That's multiple nights of bed-sharing, and it's unnecessary."

I clench my jaw. "We need to get used to sleeping in the same bed. I don't want to wait until the first time my daughter spends the night to find out you snore or spread yourself across most of the bed."

Bree holds up a finger. "I do *not* snore, but I do like to get comfortable. If that means I'm taking up most of the bed, so be it."

"And where am I supposed to sleep in that case?"

"You're a big boy—figure it out."

"I'd like to practice doing just that by having you sleep in bed with me."

Is she serious? I've never had to verbally spar with a woman to convince her to sleep in my bed. In my experience, women have always *wanted* to sleep in my bed. It might sound arrogant, but it's true.

"This isn't a sport you need practice to be better at!" She lunges for the blanket again, but I hold it out of her reach.

"It's a different kind of sport—the dreaming kind. It needs practice all the same." Fuck, am I grasping at straws, or what?

Bree's nothing if not persistent, a quality I might admire at any other time. Right now, though, she's being plain stubborn.

Or I am. I can't tell anymore, but I'm too far into this to back down now.

Right when I think she'll give in, she wraps her fingers around as much fuzzy fabric as she can and tugs, but I don't concede.

Which is how we end up playing tug-of-war in our living room.

"This is ridiculous," I clip.

"You're being unreasonable," she shoots through gritted teeth.

Time to end this.

Up until now, I was polite and let her think our physical strengths matched, but they do not. I yank on the blanket, overpowering her, but instead of letting go, she comes along for the ride.

And she staggers to a stop two inches from me.

Our panting breaths mingle.

Her eyes dart all over my face.

I lick my lips and conjure the incredible taste of her on my tongue.

The apartment fills with the intensity of our heat. Our chemistry is as natural as a heart beating, and mine knocks against my ribs as if to say, "You've made a horrible mistake."

My stiffening dick thinks otherwise, but that's the problem, isn't it? Because the mistake I've made is insisting Bree sleep in the same bed as me. How can I lie next to her without touching her?

"I'll sleep in the bedroom," she whispers, then jerks a finger into my chest. "But no funny business. We made a deal."

"I remember," I grumble as I follow her out of the living room.

The view of her backside is bad for the arousal partying in my pants, and I need to repeat, "No funny business."

But the extra reminder does nothing to curb my desire for this woman.

My wife.

My *fake* wife.

SIXTEEN

Bree

’m almost thirty-four years old. The last decade zipped by in a flash of margaritas, laughs, and of course, the glue that's held me together—one-night stands.

When Wade and I first entered our arrangement, I figured I'd blink and three years would fly by faster than I could say, "I'm fucking horny for a megahot former soccer player with tattoos deliciously scattered over his muscular body."

But it's only been a single night, and it has felt like an eternity. I'm fucking horny for a megahot former soccer player with tattoos.

And he's touching me, but I can't do anything about it. I shouldn't, anyway.

Next to me in a cloud of white pillows and sheets, Wade's soft breaths leave his parted lips with blissful ease, and his large hand cups my right breast like it belongs to him. Like a freaking safety blanket or something.

Every now and then, he squeezes it as if to gain comfort from it. Is he dreaming? Is he having a dirty dream?

Because the filthy things racing through my mind would make even him blush.

But I can't act on it, no matter how loud my ovaries scream at me. No matter how tingly and wet I am. We have to set the precedent, or the next three years will be a disaster.

Chances are, we wouldn't make it through the full three years at all. What would that mean for his daughter? What would it mean for me? I only have a few weeks left on the lease at my apartment in Brooklyn, and the landlord has already secured new renters for it.

If Wade and I blow up this deal we made, I'd technically be homeless.

Glancing over his shoulder toward the window, I note it's still dark. No sign of dawn or the sun at all. I refuse to become an early morning person on a Sunday simply because my fake husband cups my breast in bed.

So, for once, I do the rational thing and peel his hand off me as gently as possible to avoid disturbing his obviously deep sleep. Then I slide out of bed, tiptoe from the room like I used to when escaping strangers during my hookup era, and resume the spot on the couch. This is where I'd planned to sleep last night before Wade flashed those baby blues and convinced me sleeping in the same bed would be harmless.

Out here, it's much easier to avoid a breast cupping, or accidentally grazing my husband's hard-on.

Which I did.

Wade was hard as a rock in the middle of the night, and

the rigid tip of him poked me in the ass like a stern finger—if that finger was enormous, anyway.

With less stress over physical contact with him, it's not long before I'm fast asleep again. I only wake when the shining sun blasts its light in my face like a laser beam.

We should really get blinds for these windows. They're too large to be bare. The light is too disconcerting.

But when I blink the sleep away and force my heavy-lidded eyes open, my breath catches.

The view outside is gorgeous, with the New York City skyline standing tall in the distance. The sliver of water visible glistens under the morning sun. White wispy swirls of clouds decorate the sky, and although I'm cooped up in here, the open windows make me feel like I'm part of the world.

I decide against the blinds. I could get used to this view.

Rubbing the tips of my stiff fingers over my face and through the matted strands of my hair, I stand and stretch. It's during this moment that the smell of fresh coffee hits my nostrils, and glee floods my body. It's as natural and immediate a response as running into Bradley Cooper in the city and gushing over him.

Well, I did more than gush. I inappropriately groped his arm, complimented his singing voice from *A Star is Born*, and possibly tried to invite him out for drinks just so I could stare at him. I would've been remised if I hadn't tried.

"Wade?" I call out. I asked him to keep it down this morning, but he's too quiet. When did he even make the coffee? Did he use the bathroom at all? I would've heard a toilet flush.

But he's nowhere to be found.

Is he a jogger? As a former athlete and a guy in possession

of chiseled abs, it wouldn't surprise me to learn he's one of those people who goes out for morning runs, but he better not freaking ask me to join him.

"Wade?" I try again, but still, only silence answers.

I grab my phone and check my messages, only to find he hasn't called or texted, but the girls sent me plenty last night. I just forgot to check my phone for the first time in ages since I was actually enjoying myself with Wade, Tucker, and Harper.

There's a sentence I never thought I'd confess, even to myself.

> Tessa: How's your first night going, MRS. JAMESON?

> Erin: Are you wearing your faded old pajamas with the holes in them like I suggested? You never get sexy when wearing those.

> Madi: Who are you kidding? Bree would get just as sexy wearing a potato sack as she would a low-cut little black dress.

> Erin: I don't think you understand how hideous these pajamas are, Mads.

The next eight messages debate what each of their version of my old pajamas is, and by the time I reach the end, I'm cackling like a maniac. I barely manage to send a response.

> Actually, we fucked like bunnies. It was epic.

Bubbles pop up at the bottom of my screen, then disappear.

> KIDDING. General 'Gina did not get any action last night.
> We slept in the same bed, he grabbed my tit in his sleep, and then I moved my ass to the couch. SO HOT, right?

When the bubbles appear again, I play a game with myself

and guess who will be the first to respond. My bet is on Tessa, but I'm wrong.

> Erin: Sounds like the beginning of one of Ian's rom-coms.

> Your endless positivity is sickening, even for a Sunday.

> Tessa: You haven't had your coffee yet, have you?

I hold the steaming mug I poured while skimming their messages and snap a picture to send them, my smile forced and a bit psychotic, if I'm honest. My wide, puffy morning eyes are more suited for a serial killer's.

> I have coffee, but the General needs to storm Wade's castle.

> Tessa: Ah, the joys of sexual frustration...

> I'm so horny I'd even take just the tip at this point.

> Erin: Mold, cats, tie-dye tees, wrinkled pages of your magazines.

> What are you doing?

> Erin: Making you picture your least favorite things so you'll stop being horny for your husband.

I smirk into my coffee, but any hint of amusement disappears as I read the next message.

> Tessa: Remember what you told us—this is a platonic arrangement, and it'll only work if you keep it that way! Remember Violet. She's the priority here.

> I got this. I'm keeping my hands to myself.

> Tessa: For the children!

I shake my head and click my phone off. I wish they

weren't right. In fact, I wish I didn't want Wade at all, but I'm a mere mortal.

He just doesn't need to know how badly I want him. That, I can keep to myself and the girls, in which case this attraction won't escalate. Not to imply he would reciprocate these feelings. He's made it perfectly clear where he stands, but something—*his boner*—tells me he wouldn't be opposed to a little sexy fun.

"Enough," I mutter and shimmy in place, ridding myself of any dirty notions.

We can't. Period.

With no sign of Wade, I sync my phone to the Bluetooth speaker on his counter next to a newer picture of Violet, turn the volume down a few notches for our neighbors' benefit, and unpack a couple boxes of my clothes. I'm going to need easy access to them for work tomorrow.

Wade has cleared out space for me in his dresser and closet. I didn't even have to ask him to, and the idea that he's so thoughtful further warms the once-icy plains of my heart.

The painful sting that follows comes from knowing he'll be such a considerate husband… for someone else.

Long after I'm gone, the drawers and closet space will be filled with some other woman's clothes, but that's the deal. I was fine with it two weeks ago, and I'm perfectly happy with it now.

With my favorite outfits hung up, I bob my head to the music and shimmy out of my pajamas—my old, faded set Erin rooted for. She was right about the advantage of them. They're the equivalent of a cold bucket of water dousing a flame.

But I don't know if they could've saved me had I not moved

to the couch this morning. The boob cupping was the most action I've gotten in ages. I'm smart, but I'm not a robot.

A ding sounds from my phone with a new message, but it's not in the room. "The kitchen," I mumble as I drift toward the counter. I've just read Erin's text to stop trying to name my vagina when the front door swings open.

Wade's eyes widen as the chorus of the song bursts through the speaker with a loud "fuck" in the lyrics.

"I was just unpacking, and—" The last word rides the wave of a squeak as I realize he's not alone. "Oh my God." I fumble with the phone to turn off the inappropriate song as Maggie covers her tiny daughter's eyes and ears. Once the music cuts off, I square my shoulders. "There!" I celebrate.

Wade steps in front of Maggie and Vi, blocking their view as he clears his throat. "You, um, don't have…"

If I was horrified before for subjecting Violet to the language in the song, no matter how unintentional, I'm absolutely mortified to find I never got dressed before waltzing out here into the open.

"Shit," I hiss as my hands fly over the flimsy bra and panties barely covering Thelma, Louise, and Lady Boom Boom. "Oh! I'm sorry for that too," I offer as I walk backward, bump into a stack of boxes, then disappear into the bedroom.

I might stay in here forever. That's the only option I have, right?

Frantic, I search the drawers for anything to wear, forgetting where I just put everything since my mind is now mush. Over my shoulder, the door opens, and I jump.

Wade enters, then shuts it behind him. "Do you ever wear clothes?" he whispers. His voice is low, but it doesn't muffle the harsh emphasis in his scolding question.

"Yes," I snap with a few extra s's for good measure. "Where have you been?"

"I was downstairs… working on my car." He slides his palms down the sides of his sweatpants the same way I've witnessed clients do when they're nervous for an interview. Is Wade nervous?

Oh, God. I'm still fucking naked—that's probably why.

I turn my attention back to the drawer, grab the first shirt and pair of shorts I find, and stumble into them like I'm drunk. "You never told me we'd have visitors this morning," I chide.

"Maggie didn't tell me, either." The sharp edge of his tone simmers but takes on a sarcastic one when he says, "She just popped in to meet my new wife."

"Who was buck naked in the fucking kitchen," I whisper-scream. I've never been as embarrassed in my life as I am right now. Sure, if it was only Maggie, I could make a joke, and we'd all laugh. But Violet? She got an eyeful of a body not even grown men can handle.

"Language," he warns. "Do you need help?"

I fall onto the bed with an exasperated grunt and wrestle my shirt into place. "Got it."

"Are you going to be okay to do this?" He searches my face as I stand. "I need your A-game here."

"And A-game you will get." I plaster on a bright smile—one I hope doesn't look like the psycho Joker grin in the picture I sent to the girls earlier.

Seemingly satisfied, Wade nods and holds his hand out for me to lead the way.

Maggie stands right where we left her, clinging to Violet, who's smashed against her mother's side. The woman's lips are pursed, and her posture is more rigid than a freaking lamppost. Is she… scared of us?

Rather, is she wary of *me*?

"I told you two to make yourselves at home, but the boxes ruined it for you, huh?" Wade jokes, although it doesn't sound light and funny. Those two are definitely not laughing.

I force a laugh of my own. "Sorry. I have a ton of stuff. Still getting settled."

"It was extra fun moving it all inside, but hey, that's what husbands are for," Wade adds, and his deep voice holds more relaxation this time.

I, on the other hand, momentarily freeze when his fingertips brush the small of my back before he rests his palm there. Leaning into the gesture, I playfully place my own hand on his chest. "And sorry about before." I point to where I stood mostly naked as if we *really* need the reminder. I'm not one to beat around the bush, though, so I might as well address it head-on. Rubbing circles on his chest, I blurt, "The special newlywed bubble, where clothes are optional, am I right?"

Wade clasps his hand over mine to stop the way I'm practically groping him—another *oops* on my part. It's not my fault it's so easy to get carried away. He should try having a less muscular chest.

Fuuuuuucckkkkkk.

I'm ruining this. I'm here to make things easier on him and his daughter, which means I should be playing extra nice and clean with Maggie too, but I'm doing a piss-poor job of it.

"Wade, can I speak to you for a moment?" She steers her pointed glare to me. "In private."

"Look, Maggie, we weren't expecting you, okay?" Wade sighs. "Bree was just—"

"No, no. It's all good. Violet and I can, um, play in her new room," I suggest with a show of jazz hands. Where the hell did those come from?

Violet's mouth falls open, and a squeal pierces the tension between us.

But Maggie doesn't immediately let go.

"We'll be right in there," I reassure her and point to the door five feet away. It'll be Violet's room after the court date, provided all goes as we hope.

And it should. Wade's lawyer, Cassidy, was unusually optimistic when she learned of his new bride. Add that to the new, wholesome job Wade is starting tomorrow, and Cassidy believes we're golden.

It's why she set the court date for two weeks from now. She's confident we have nothing to worry about, or she would've pushed for a later time.

"Can I look in your closet after?" Violet asks me as we walk away from the friction crowding the kitchen. "You have really pretty clothes."

"Next time you see my sister, be sure to let her know."

"You have a sister?" She gasps. "I want a sister."

"You can have mine." I let out a snort, and it turns into a full-on burst of laughter when Vi takes me up on the playful offer.

Once I close the door behind me, she twirls in the middle of the room, gushing over the cream-colored bed frame with the seashells on the headboard. "This is exactly like the one I told Wade I wanted!"

I suppress a flinch over her use of his first name, but I

can't expect her to call him "Daddy" just yet. Neither can Wade himself, although he never talks about it.

There's no timeline for this sort of thing.

Violet doesn't know him as a person, let alone as her father, especially since she's believed Maggie's husband to be that figure for her since she was two. It'll take time, and I have no doubt Wade will get to a good and peaceful place with Violet.

It just hurts my heart for him right now.

"And this is my favorite book I told him about!" She skips to the shelves along the wall in the shape of tree branches. Painted on the wall is the tree trunk and leaves. It's like Pinterest threw up in here.

Who helped Wade do all this? Someone had to have helped, right?

The man can look as sexy as he does, be a phenomenal athlete, and know how to work on cars. He has the rare quality found in very few men of being considerate and paying attention too. But if he can decorate a little girl's room like this, then it's just unfair to the rest of the male population.

Violet bounces her miniature body onto the bed and scrambles to her feet like she's going to start jumping. That's bad, right? I should stop her.

"I don't think that's—"

The door opens behind me as Violet takes the first jump, and Maggie gasps. "What are you doing? You know better than to jump on the bed. You could hurt yourself."

As Violet's smile droops into a frown, she slides off the bed.

Anger and accusation flare in Maggie's eyes as she casts them on me. "*You* should know better. Kids can't jump on the bed like that."

"I was just about—"

"She won't let it happen again," Wade cuts in as he bends down to scoop Violet into his arms. He coos in her ear, and whatever he says unearths a hint of her previous smile.

When I watched him with his little girl in the park the first time I met her, my heart flipped over and over again like cheerleaders at a football game. It was such a special sight.

Hot too. It was definitely hot seeing a father with his daughter.

But now, instead of my heart turning into a gymnast again, fury lights my stomach on fire.

Wade could've—and should've—stuck up for me just now with Maggie, rather than implying I don't know what I'm doing. I mean, I don't, but I'm not so much of a ditz that I'd let Vi jump on the bed like it's a trampoline.

I was just about to tell her to get down, but the woman has such bad timing. I mean, what is that about? Does she lurk in the shadows until she knows she'll catch me doing something stupid and irresponsible?

Shit.

No matter what supernatural forces—or snarky baby mamas—might be against me, though, Wade should've had my back.

SEVENTEEN

Wade

"*That's the kind of stepmom you want for Violet? One who gallivants around the house naked?*"

That's what Maggie pulled me aside to talk to me about. No, she didn't just *talk* to me. Rather, she scolded me like I'm even younger than Violet. And I said nothing, even though I knew in my bones that it was all bullshit.

It's why I'm pretty sure my face turned redder than my fucking Mustang. I couldn't see it, but I could definitely feel the hot rage burning my skin.

"Did you two get married on Valentine's Day?" Violet asks as her mother practically drags her toward the door.

"No, it was not on Valentine's, sweetheart." When they stop, I kneel down to meet Violet at eye level.

"I meant, *for* Valentine's Day." She peeks over my shoulder, and I don't have to follow her gaze to know Bree's standing behind me. I can almost feel the heat of her against me.

That, and the tension.

"Is that how you celebrated?" Violet asks.

"Oh, well, we…" I trip over my words.

"It was part of it," Bree swoops in, thank fuck. "You see, on Valentine's Day, your da—"

I stiffen. At the mention of calling me her dad, I freeze on the spot with my knees aching for reprieve, but I can't move.

"Wade," she corrects. "Wade brought me a box of chocolates. No flowers, because he knows I don't like them."

"And because you can buy your own?" Vi giggles and sways like she's dancing to a song in her head.

"You've listened to the Miley Cyrus song, huh?" Bree doesn't miss a beat, and it all makes sense.

"I know all the words!"

"That makes two of us." Bree hunches down on her heels next to me. "I *can* buy my own flowers, but also, I just prefer the chocolate."

This exchange eases even Maggie's apprehension. I can't tell for certain what she's thinking, but she's still here. That tells me all I need to know.

"We had dinner at a super cute rustic Italian restaurant, which I'd hinted at weeks before," Bree continues. "The candlelight, wine, and food were all so romantic. Afterward, Wade and I ate the chocolate while we walked around the city. I'd tucked it away in my purse because I'm always prepared like that." She gives Violet a wink. "It was freezing, but the chocolate kept us nice and cozy. While we were snuggled up, he whispered in my ear that he wanted to marry me."

My gaze meets hers, and the frozen bones in my body

thaw. The story she spins makes us sound much better and far more romantic than my pathetic plea in her office to make a deal with me.

Instinctively, I place my hand over Bree's and squeeze.

"How spontaneous," Maggie mutters.

"Very." Bree's gaze doesn't waver from mine as she laughs. "But when you know, you know, right?"

"You know what?" Vi tilts her head, and the wheels turn behind those pure eyes.

Eyes that are so similar to mine it's crazy.

"I'll explain when you're older, honey." Maggie softens her tone. "Well… congratulations, you two. It was, um, nice to meet you, Bree."

"You too."

"See you both next weekend." I wave to Maggie, who spares me something between a smile and a grimace, and to Violet.

My little girl playfully wiggles her fingers in my direction as she asks her mother to stop for chocolate on the way home.

As soon as the door shuts, I whirl around to Bree with arms open. "You're brilliant! You just thought of that whole story on the spot?"

She folds her arms across her chest, her makeup-free cheeks reddening with… anger? "I did. I'm glad it was up to your standards."

"What do you mean?"

"Nothing, other than I'm super pumped I did *something* right this morning."

I furrow my brow, still stumped. Other than the crude song and wardrobe mishap, the impromptu visit went as well as I could've hoped. We certainly ended on a high note, at least, one I'm still riding, but the longer Bree looks at me like I've insulted her, the more my stomach churns.

She has the same dip in her frown as Coach did after a loss, right before he laid into us for all our mistakes to improve on.

"Violet jumping on the bed?" Bree sticks an incredulous finger in the direction of the bedroom. "She'd just hopped on there when you two walked in. I was right in the middle of asking her to sit down. I wouldn't have put her in danger, and I need you to know that."

"Of course…"

"You didn't have my back when Maggie snapped at me like I'd given your daughter a knife to play with. And besides, jumping on the bed is hardly dangerous. When I was her age, the neighborhood crew and I would tie rope to the backs of our bikes and pull each other on a skateboard down the street."

The image of a young Bree being so wild lifts the corners of my mouth like a puppet string.

"We didn't even wear helmets. I mean, we should have, but that's not the point."

"You're right." I close the distance between us so she can look me in the eye and hopefully accept my sincerity. "I'm sorry I rolled over when I should've stuck up for you to Maggie. It's just that after the naked kitchen dance, I wanted to play nice."

"And that's the other thing, come to think of it." She paces in front of me, her arms still folded tightly over her chest. "It was hella embarrassing, but I wasn't doing anything wrong. I'm allowed to walk around my own home naked. It's not like I was strolling through Times Square with my tits and ass out. I was in *my* kitchen."

I saw tits and ass, all right. The thin material of her bra and panties was basically see-through, and I got a frustratingly sexy view of her body. Which did nothing to help my sexual frustration that has my muscles in a twist.

"There was no kitchen dance, either." She narrows her eyes.

"Really? Because I saw a little twerk in your step," I tease.

"I was so not twerking!"

"You were right there doing this move." I run my hands through my hair and gyrate my hips, exaggerating the moves I glimpsed from her earlier, but I'm not sure she can tell what I'm even doing. I've never been a great dancer.

"First of all, I was not doing… whatever this is." She circles her finger over me as I stop my embarrassing attempt to recreate the sensual dance she was doing. "And second, that's not twerking. You don't even know what twerking is, do you?"

"It's the thing I just did." I shrug.

"There's no name for what you just did, but it's not twerking." She spins around, bends at the waist, and wiggles her ass in a move I've only seen on the internet, but experiencing it like this with Bree gives it a whole new meaning.

Dear God, what have I done to deserve this torture?

"*That* is twerking." She straightens and faces me again, a twinkle in her eye as she laughs.

"What an inspiring lesson," I strain.

Her own smile slides into a firm line as her chest rises and falls in a steady rhythm.

I gulp, and she follows the movement with her gaze before it settles on my lips.

Her inhale is sharp as it slices through the electric current traveling between us. Is she panting? She wasn't before this—what is it? A moment?

We can't have moments.

"Now that I know what it is, I'll warn Violet against partaking in the trend," I rasp.

Bree licks her lips. "Then she should probably stay away from Miley Cyrus, since she's the twerking mastermind."

Bree is definitely panting, and I'm dying my own sexual death over here. I'm three feet away, and it's not enough distance.

"Good to know." I inch backward. Space will do us good, and with an extra two feet between us, maybe I won't be able to smell the sweet scent of her.

It's the same damn scent that had me racing out the door this morning to distract myself by working on my car. It didn't even need anything except a little wiper fluid, but after I added it, I checked the tire pressure, antifreeze, and oil too.

I needed anything to help me escape the lavender all over my bed, which had me in a fucking chokehold.

"I am sorry I jumped to Maggie's side instead of sticking up for you," I offer as guilt furls in the pit of my stomach.

She twists her lips, shifting on her feet. "It's not about me."

"It's not?"

"I never meant to bring it up like it hurt my feelings or anything, if that's what you think." She shakes her head, and the nervous sound akin to a laugh hits my ears as if it's a cover-up. "I only said something because… well, we're playing the part of a happy newlywed couple who wants custody of a little girl, right? I want you and Maggie to know I'd be good at taking care of Violet. That I'm responsible. So, this is all really about… you. Because while this marriage might be fake, Violet is real, and I don't want my supposed recklessness to ruin anything for either of you."

I nod slowly. What she's saying makes sense, but it's not the whole truth. Something's bothering her, and my need to know is as stubborn as she is when keeping her secrets. "Did Sonny think you ruined your marriage back then?" I whisper, inching into unknown territory.

Her back pops into a rigid stance like it's glued to a wall.

Her sister mentioned his name only once last night, but it was enough for it to stick in my head. Before that, my desire to dislocate his jaw was bad enough, but putting a name to the guy who hurt Bree gives that violent desire twice as much fuel.

I didn't even mean to bring him up now, but the insight she provides has to come from somewhere, right? And since she's the only one between the two of us who's been married before, I assume her experience comes from Sonny.

After a long pause, she finally says, "Yes. He did, and my mom and Harper agreed with him."

"You know you didn't do anything wrong, right?" The urge to hold her enters my nervous system, but is that what she wants?

"I know." Her smile is weak as she adds, "But it's not as easy to truly accept it. There are still times when I wonder if I should've fought harder. Communicated better. Dolled up my hair and makeup more—I don't know."

"Bree, it's not your fault he was texting other women. That's on him. He was the one who was unfaithful. He might not have been physical with any of them, but it's cheating all the same, as far as I'm concerned."

"And I agree. Which is why I left him. But sometimes I think I could've done more to keep him from even going so far as texting them."

"What do you mean?"

She sighs. "Are we really doing this right now? Because this entire morning has been a far cry from what I had planned, which involved much more coffee and a lot less chatting about the past."

Nodding, I march toward the coffeepot, discard the used filter, and pour out the cold coffee. Then I stick a pod into the single-serve side of the machine, which gurgles to life. While it brews, the kitchen fills with the nutty aroma once again.

Quietly, I hand her the fresh mug, place my hand on the heated small of her back, and guide her toward the couch to get more comfortable. "We're doing this," I state definitively.

Thankfully, she doesn't challenge me again. Much to my delight, she blows on the coffee, occupying herself with it instead of how much she doesn't want to do this.

"He was in a band, right?" she starts. "Sonny and three of his dimwitted friends played at a local bar most Fridays during their open mic nights, and I sincerely hope that place curates who plays there now, for the sake of their business."

"So, Sonny and the dimwits were bad?"

"How do I put this?" she mumbles under her breath. "They weren't just bad. They were *so* bad that even their parents were ashamed. Their sets cleared out half the bar to the point where the bartenders and servers would complain to the owner. The band didn't even know the names of chords. They'd just play for hours until they believed something sounded good. Took them two months to put together a single song."

I furrow my brow, and as if reading my mind, she answers my unspoken question.

"If you're wondering why I put up with it, I've asked myself that very thing countless times over the years." Her sad laugh sucks the energy from the room. "I stupidly believed in the impossible. I was young and excited for adventure. I had faith in Sonny and his dreams. We were going to take on the world together."

Oh, to be young and in love. I remember my own teenage relationship. I didn't marry Eloise Farmer, but there was a time when I seriously thought we'd eventually make it down the aisle. That was before her father demanded she end things with me before we went off to different colleges, or he wouldn't cover her tuition. She took less than an hour to humor alternative solutions before she ripped my heart in two.

I don't like to place total blame on her, but that breakup had a lot to do with my loose morals in college when it came to one-night stands. But I'm reasonable enough now to acknowledge that she's not why I kept up the habit. After I was drafted, I simply enjoyed the attention that tagged along with being a professional athlete.

And I'm certainly paying for the trail of broken hearts I left in my wake as well. That's the reason I'm being tortured now, isn't it? That's why my balls are so damn blue—it has to be.

"It's not stupid to believe in something like that, especially at a young age when your whole life is in front of you," I say honestly.

Bree sips from her mug and licks her lips, leaving behind a glossy sheen. "Maybe not, but I sure felt stupid after the fact. I mean, I should've pushed him to get a real job while he worked on his music. At the very least, I should've insisted he take a few guitar lessons."

I can't help the snort bubbling free.

"Instead, I worked myself to the bone to make up the difference, while he lived his best fucking life." She fingers the letters scrolled across the side of the mug as a curtain of hair shields most of her face from my view. "The stupidest thing of all was accepting his dumb excuses for texting those girls."

"What?" I blink.

When her eyes land on mine, the shame in them guts me. "I didn't immediately leave him after I found out about the texts." She purses her lips. "He claimed it was all part of his *brand*. The rock star image was all about flirting with the fans and remaining *just* out of reach. He loved how it drove them crazy."

I cringe.

"I bought into it all because I was too afraid to blow up my marriage—and my life. I'd been with him since I was a junior in high school. He was a senior. All the girls wanted to be with him, and they were insanely jealous when he'd asked me to the senior prom. We were inseparable ever since, and I, for one, took our vows seriously."

"What changed your mind?"

"Not what, but who." This time, Bree's smile turns wistful and maybe even a little grateful. "His antics quickly escalated from cheesy, flirty texts to full-on sexts, and my grandma ultimately guided me toward the light. The saint of a woman sat me down one night, flicked me on the forehead, and asked what the hell was wrong with me."

"She did?" I ask, surprised.

"I'd just finished a back-to-back shift at a local diner, and my feet were throbbing with the force of a thousand hammers. The last thing I wanted to do was go to my grandma's, but she insisted. I actually thought something was wrong, so I rushed over, and it was the most considerate, selfless thing anyone's ever done for me. She didn't believe in divorce. She refused to support it, but she got out of her comfort zone because she wanted what was best for me. I loved her even more after the harsh but much-needed intervention. She even rubbed my feet after she said her piece and let me cry until I was ready to leave."

"Sounds like she was one hell of a woman."

"She was a lot like Gaga, actually." Bree smirks. "Those two women would've caused some trouble together, for sure."

"Christ, can you imagine? I'm sure we would've had to bail them out of jail on numerous occasions."

"Without a doubt."

I steal a glance at her as she sips her coffee, seemingly lost in nostalgia while I lose myself in her. She's the most sensational woman I've ever met.

Strong-willed and passionate.

She might insist she doesn't have anything to offer Violet as her stepmother, but she's proven over and over again that she definitely does. Moreover, I have an indisputable feeling she's going to teach me a lot more than she already has, too.

"I'm going to put a matching outfit on." Standing, she gestures toward the striped sweatshirt hanging loosely over her breasts and the black-and-white polka-dotted shorts, which look like pajamas.

A low chuckle rumbles out of me. "I didn't even notice." And it's true. To be honest, the woman can make anything look good.

"Yeah right." Bree rinses her mug in the sink, then wipes her hands on the towel hanging over the stove. The whole thing feels so natural, like we're a real couple living together.

"Very disgustingly domesticated," as Slater jabbed in his message the other day in response to the end of my bachelor status.

"It's just a good thing Harper isn't here to notice what a disastrous outfit I threw on. She'd never let me live it down."

"You said she wasn't supportive of the divorce, but now, you're both... good?" I rub my chin, unsure if I'm crossing a line with all this prying, but Bree doesn't visibly react. I wouldn't have asked at all had she not mentioned their past turmoil.

In fact, after spending a few hours with them last night, I'm surprised over their unpleasant history altogether. They seemed very close, and happy, even.

Bree lets out a contented sigh as she glances at me. "I think we will be."

"She's something else, huh?" I meet her in the kitchen as she steps around the counter.

"You have no idea."

Before I know it, I'm standing a couple inches away from her. When I dip my head, we breathe the same air.

Her lips part.

My hands tremble to cup her cheeks.

I want to kiss her so badly my mouth fucking stings.

Over her shoulder, the clock on the microwave ticks to the next minute as we stare at each other, exchanging nothing but increasingly quick puffs of air.

My arms lift of their own accord.

They wrap around her arms.

I tug her to me—and it's the most awkward hug I've ever initiated. Her arms are glued to her sides, so she can't hug me back, if she even wants to. Her chin is smashed against my right pec, digging into my chest like the heel of a foot.

And when she talks, it's muffled, but I still make out a cautious, "What are you doing?"

Jerking away, I scratch the back of my head as I struggle to suppress the growing ache between my legs. "I was just, um, giving you a hug."

"Why?"

"As a—as a thank you. For sharing. You shared, and it was hard for you, and I want you to know you can… talk to me whenever you want."

"You are surprisingly a very good listener. I brag to my friends about it all the time." She lifts a brow. "So, you and I are like… friends, huh?"

The idea of being *only* friends with her makes my already squirmy dick scream in protest. Nonetheless, I manage to croak, "Sure. Friends. There's no reason you and I shouldn't be friends."

"Agreed," she says, but there's a hint of doubt in the simple word. Maybe it's the way she slightly draws it out, or it's all in my damn head.

Racing toward the door, I mutter, "I need to work on my car."

EIGHTEEN

Bree

It's been years since I've had this thought, but I need my sister.

I wish Harper didn't have to get back to Sapphire Creek. Her job. Her own life.

While I previously would've thought ten whole days with her would be my own special torture, it was actually not enough. By the time she left, I was surprised we'd gone so long without talking before.

How did the bitch do that? She got under my skin and wormed her way back into my life—and my fucking heart. This organ has been causing me a lot of trouble lately.

The traitorous thing couldn't stop thumping in my throat during Wade's awkward hug a couple weeks ago. Before I met him, I was floating from one guy's arms to the next. I was sowing my wild oats and enjoying myself too.

The guy before Wade was a freaking doctor who dressed in a lab coat and a Santa hat like a sexy holiday snack. It was a dream to be on the naughty list with Dr. Lake. The things we did with his stethoscope were totally X-rated.

Now, the extent of my sex life is a weird hug in the kitchen of my new home with a husband who's not really in love with me. How did I get here?

"Ready for this?" Wade holds his hand out for me.

Happy newlywed couple.

That's who we need to be today of all days.

"Almost." I force a smile and hit send on my message to Harper. I won't be checking my phone for her response, but I know she's thinking about us today. That's enough to get me through this court hearing.

Before I tuck my phone away, I treat myself to another glimpse of all the kind messages from the girls too. They're all my rocks.

"Let's do this," I say and squeeze Wade's hand.

I've held it enough times over the last few weeks, all for show at Violet's piano recital. At Cassidy's office. At a cute pizza joint with Tucker and his daughter.

But holding Wade's hand now feels extra genuine, like he needs my physical support, and I cling to his hand in hopes he realizes I'm here for him—not as his fake wife, but as his friend.

That's what we've become.

I thought he was kidding when he first brought it up, but we've done a hell of a job making it a reality. We're co-existing pros. We've established a routine at home, where I limit my time in the bathroom in the mornings before work, and we commute into the city together, although he hops off the train a few stops before me.

We even binged Netflix and Hershey's together last week.

Gaga has moved into a place near our apartment. When Wade asked her if she was sure she was okay with giving up her condo in Florida to live here, in a city so different than her low-key, sleepy retirement community, she answered, "You and Violet are my family. Where else would I be?" She then smirked and said, "Besides, the old farts back in Florida only talked about their gardens and how life used to be. I was one juniper tip away from screaming, so really, you're saving me. It's far more exciting up here."

God, I love the woman.

I spot her and Tucker in the front row and wave. Before I leave Wade's side, I whisper in his ear, "We'll be right behind you. Let us know if you need anything. A water or a distraction—anything."

"Distraction?"

"Like if I need to pull the fire alarm, I'll do it," I tease, but I'm also very serious. Knowing Gaga like I do, she'd be my accomplice without hesitation too. I kiss Wade's cheek, adding, "You won't need me to, though, because we've totally got this."

I say *we* because it's him and me. We're in this together now, and that fact is equally scary and exhilarating.

Silently, Wade squeezes my hand and peers at my mouth. For half a second, the thought enters my brain that he's going to freaking kiss me in front of everyone. That I've been locking up my attraction to him while we're alone in our home, only for him to cross the line here in public.

But instead of a kiss I won't have time to savor, he wraps me in a tight embrace. It's meaningful all the same, and when he kisses my temple, I know he's nervous.

"We've got this," I repeat, then peel myself away in the direction of my seat next to Gaga.

As she clings to my hand, I peer over to the other side, where Maggie and Roger speak in hushed tones. His suit is as impeccable as his hair is smooth, and the pinch between his brow hasn't moved since we arrived. He's put together, for sure, but there's an air of coldness surrounding him too. It's likely the side effect of this stressful day, but if the other two times I've interacted with him are any indication, he's always like this.

On the contrary, Wade exudes warmth and love. He plays with Violet, and I just can't imagine Roger hanging from the monkey bars like Wade did at the park two days ago. To my surprise, Maggie's been agreeable in letting Violet come around. I suspect she's on her best behavior in an attempt to show the court she and Roger are reasonable, and they allow Wade plenty of time with his daughter.

I don't like the smell of it.

"All rise," the bailiff says with gusto. The hearty announcement pulls us all onto our feet as the judge enters.

The only experience I have in a courtroom was the day I showed up for my divorce, and the day Wade and I got hitched. Although it's not the same room as the latter, it is the same building, and this is the time to pull an Erin and believe magic exists between these walls.

One way or another, after today, Violet's world will change, and so will ours.

The proceedings begin in similar fashion as the law shows I watch, and the first thing they address is Wade's absence. Normally, a father would lose his rights after a few months without contact, but since Maggie never told Wade about their child, this is a unique circumstance.

Their backstory requires only a few minutes to share. Although the effects of their situation are long lasting, they're not discussed now. Shouldn't they be, though? I'm no expert, but it seems to me that they should spend longer than it takes to mix a margarita to talk about how confusing this all is for everyone involved.

How emotionally damaging it can be for a young girl to be separated from her father. I could speak to the latter from gut-wrenching personal experience, so it's probably best they don't linger on the topic, after all.

Roger spares us exactly half a glance during all this, but when I get a better look at Maggie, she doesn't share an ounce of rigidity as her husband. Her skirt is flowy and friendly, unlike the tight pencil skirts I imagine the women around Roger's office wearing. She's also chewing a hole through her bottom lip as the lawyers make their cases.

By the time we're thirty minutes in, sweat drools down the back of my neck like a waterfall.

They've already discussed mediation, and from the sounds of it, the judge was sympathetic toward Wade since Maggie was the one who flaked on trying to settle custody outside her courtroom.

Maggie's lawyer bounces right back with less-than-stellar facts of her own, one important piece I wasn't aware of until this moment.

"Your Honor, Mr. Jameson spent a night in prison last year for aggravated assault against a Mr. Holden. He clearly has a temper. How can we be assured he won't let it affect the well-being of my clients' daughter? His visits need to be supervised."

The judge peers over her eyeglasses at Wade, and my heart

collapses into my stomach. How did I not know about this?

"The charges were dropped," Wade says.

"And why were they dropped?" the judge inquires. It's a fair question, admittedly, but her accusatory tone still makes me wince, like I'm the one she's targeting.

I'm also curious, though. Why wouldn't Wade have told me this himself? I thought we were always honest with each other, as *friends* who live together would be.

But the charges were dropped, so that's a good thing, right? Probably a misunderstanding? In the last few weeks, I've watched plenty of soccer games. I've seen the occasional fight break out, so this thing with Wade could very well be related to the sport. An argument on the field that landed them both with a red card.

It's plausible, although it's probably just my rare optimism rearing its meager head. Logically, if the incident was during a game, would there be legal charges?

Fuuuuuuckkkkk.

"I pled my case to Mr. Holden, Your Honor. I explained that I wasn't myself and that I was deeply sorry for what happened between us. I truly regret my actions. He was honest with me too and admitted he was out of line himself. He confessed to his own wrongdoing. Even though we reached an understanding and he changed his mind about the lawsuit, I didn't sleep for months. I vowed I'd never let such a thing happen again."

"You didn't plan on it happening then, though, did you?" the judge asks. "That's the very definition of reckless, isn't it, Mr. Jameson? When a person is reckless, they do things like repeatedly punch a man in the face without thinking of the consequences."

Cassidy places a firm hand on Wade's chest to stop him from speaking up again. His lips tighten into a grim line, and he squares his shoulders like he's steeling himself for whatever punishment this woman has in store for him.

That's what's happening, right? She's about to punish him by denying him the right to be a father to his daughter.

I have to do something.

I can't just sit here while she tears into him like this.

I need to—

"We all make mistakes," I blurt, jumping up to my full height.

"Please take your seat, ma'am."

She did *not* just call me *ma'am*.

Eye twitching, I remain firmly in place as Wade eyes me questioningly. The entire room is probably staring, but he's the only one who matters. I might feel duped by his lack of sharing, but from the sounds of it, it's not as bad as the judge implies. Wade definitely doesn't deserve to lose over this.

"We all make mistakes," I repeat. "Just a few months ago, I dyed my own hair, and I didn't rinse it out like I was supposed to because I got distracted with a Buzzfeed quiz and finding out if my current career is right for me. Which is ironic since I'm a career counselor, right?"

"Listen, this is not—"

"Also ironic is that I have a perfectly capable hair stylist at the top of my call log. She's my best friend. She's Ian Brock's girlfriend too. You'll see him in *Ghost Predators* in theaters this summer. She totally did the makeup for that movie."

"If you don't sit down, I'll hold you in contempt."

Oh my God—I didn't think judges said that in real life, but she totally did. It's not just a *Law and Order: SVU* thing!

Nonetheless, this is important.

"I just need to say one more thing," I plead. "Wade is amazing, and he's so handy too. I never realized how important it is to have such a handy man around. He can fix a leaky sink without googling it or calling a guy. I always had to call a guy, but not anymore. Whether it's the sink or smoke coming out of the hood of his car, he just knows how to fix them, just like he knows how to be an incredible father. He's not just a pro at making Violet laugh or showing her how to kick a soccer ball, either. He's great at doing what's best for her, and he'd do anything for her. *Anything.*"

"That's enough, Mrs...."

"Jameson," I supply without a thought or hesitation.

"Right." The judge shoots me a forced smile and a glare. "You'll have your time to shine during the character witness portion, so please sit down now."

I don't back away from many challenges, but my luck with this judge has run out. Knowing what's best for me, I plop my ass back onto the hard bench before she makes good on her earlier threat to throw me out of here.

My heart thunders, muffling their subsequent arguments like words delivered through a storm.

Thankfully, the judge doesn't harp on Wade's past indiscretions.

Unfortunately, Maggie's lawyer is a force to be reckoned with. "Mr. Jameson himself can attest to the fact that my clients have been extremely flexible in allotting quality time for him to see his daughter. Over the last three weeks, Mr. Jameson has had eight visits, which is far more than many custody agreements I've overseen."

"Noted." The judge shifts, and the tip of a pen moves.

That's all I can tell from where I sit.

I knew Maggie was full of shit. Every time she's brought Violet over the last few weeks has been a proverbial chess move, strategically played for her own interests.

I have to bite my freaking tongue before I jump up and interrupt the hearing again. How could I not want to say something? Maggie's been nothing but controlling and judgmental ever since Wade first mentioned her. She might've been agreeable lately, but there's nothing stopping her from cutting Wade off in the future.

That's the whole point of today—to make sure she doesn't have that power.

The back-and-forth like a tennis ball lasts for another hour and a half. Wade speaks. I testify. Roger's monotonous tone echoes around the small room, and Maggie's tears come alive while she's questioned.

Through it all, more and more hope blossoms throughout my body. I'm biased toward Wade, but even without it, he's looking and sounding like grade-A father material. He has a plan with the right home, which provides a whole room for his daughter, he has a job, and he has Gaga, Tucker, and me on his side—a loving support network. His grandmother and I will help pick up Violet from school and serve as strong female role models.

That's right—*I'm* a fucking role model.

Nerves and tempers rise toward the end, and my palms clam up as the judge leans forward, her fingers interlocked in front of her.

I'm about to ask Gaga if this is it, but they continue speaking, inadvertently answering my unspoken question.

There's no warning. No big production, spotlights, or the

like. If I would've ducked out to use the restroom, I probably would've missed the whole outcome.

As the lawyers and parents stand, the judge states, "Our job here is to do what is best for the child. That's all we want, right? So, here's what we're going to do."

My heart thunders in my ears as she delivers the verdict.

NINETEEN

Wade

Muffled cries echo from the shower behind the closed bathroom door.

"Bree?" I call out from the other side, but another hiccup answers me.

I pace in front of it, my emotions conflicted. What a fucking day this has already been, and now Bree is sobbing in our bathroom. I should go in, right? She could be hurt. I wouldn't be a very good *friend* if I did nothing.

And I'm a damn good friend. No matter how badly I've wanted more from her, I've upheld our boundaries like a good little Samaritan for weeks.

But I draw the line at tears.

"I'm coming in," I announce and inch the door open. I don't hear any protests, so I step inside. "Bree?"

Steam escapes through the cracked door, clearing the

small room. Sniffs and sharp pants sound from the shower, painfully audible over the running water, and my jaw tightens.

I can't fucking take this anymore.

I open the foggy door to the shower, and my lungs cease functioning. Bree's body sags against the opposite wall from the flow of hot water. Sparse bubbles of shampoo stream down the side of her head and neck. My body trembles with the urge to comfort her and figure out what's going through her head. Why is she so distraught?

Reaching a hand inside, I cup Bree's cheek, whose tears blend with the water bursting from overhead, but it's not enough to hide her red eyes.

"I'm sorry I didn't tell you about the… incident." I grind my teeth as I search her expression for any indication that my past indiscretion is why she's upset, but all I get staring back at me are two dark amber eyes filled with anguish.

Fuck. Does any of that change her mind about me? We were getting along so damn well. In truth, we were getting along *too* well, and I didn't want to ruin it by bringing up something that might change Bree's perception of me.

In hindsight, it was extremely selfish. I knew it would come up in court, but I didn't think about how it would affect Bree. I'm an ass, aren't I?

With the weight of my shortcomings on my shoulders, I scramble for an explanation. "The guy was being a dick. He was harassing the bartender, and I was a fucked-up mess after a brutal loss—one that could've been avoided had I not gotten too greedy and kicked the ball over the goal. It was my fault, and I took it out on the pig at the bar."

Another sob breaks loose as the water cools.

I cut it off completely and plead, "If it makes you feel

better, I wasn't lying in court. The guy did drop the charges, and he even apologized to me for the whole thing. Evidently, he'd been drinking too much because his father had just died, and he felt guilty over the way he acted. I was surprised we handled it so peacefully, but I don't shoo away a good thing when it comes knocking."

"It's not… that," she manages as she hugs her waist, both naked breasts spilling between her arms. "It's about today, in general."

"But we won, Bree. We have a set custody schedule and everything. It's what we've been working for."

"I know… I'm just…" She hiccups as more tears burst free. "I'm sorry I'm crying so hard in the shower. I've never even sobbed like this at the end of *The Notebook*, and I should because Allie and Noah deserve these tears much more than—"

I blink, waiting for her to finish her sentence, but I'm left on the edge. "Is this about Sonny?" I clench my jaw. Why is she crying over the bastard? On this day, especially.

She covers her face and shakes her head.

But it's not a relief in any way. She's still crying.

"Who hurt you?" I squeeze the door until my knuckles turn white. Whose ass do I need to kick? That's what I really want to ask, but in light of my incident, it's best I steer clear from promises of violence, no matter how badly I want to punch whoever's responsible for my wife's tears.

Through a gap between her palms, she gives me a small, sad smile that breaks my fucking heart. "My father."

"You never talk about him."

"With good reason. But today just… triggered a lot of emotions. Actually, you fighting for Violet has." She wipes at her eyes. "It's true—I agreed to marry you because of the lovesick-bordering-on-stalking HR rep at work and the raised rent at my own apartment. It felt like all my friends were moving forward, and it seemed like I should too, even if it's not real. At least I'm doing something to butter up my karma. I also thought it would be a lot better to come home to a rugged former soccer player instead of an empty apartment."

"Who wouldn't want the latter?" I try to joke, but it doesn't come out as light as I hoped—I don't like where any of this is headed.

"But the biggest reason was that I wanted to give you and Violet the chance I never got with my own father." She chokes on her sobs again. "He left us when Harper was around three, and he didn't fight for us. Never came back around at all. He just disappeared from our lives when I was almost ten. Then he popped up at my high school graduation as a proud, doting father."

"Did he try to make amends? Apologize? Anything at all to make me not want to twist my hands around his tiny throat?"

She turns her defeated, teary eyes up at me, and it further fuels my need to strangle the embarrassment of a man between my bare hands. "My father was only there because he was dating a classmate's mother. He wasn't there to see me."

Since this piece of shit isn't here for me to punch him in her honor, all I can think to do is hold her.

Fully clothed, I step inside the shower and pull her into me. Together, wrapped in each other's arms, we sink to the floor as the bathroom fills with more of her sobs.

I don't know how long we sit here as I lose myself in the soft echoes of her pain. I can't imagine abandoning Violet like that. Sure, she has Roger, but *I'm* her fucking father. I want to be in her life as such.

What I don't want is to wake up in ten years and realize Violet and I don't even recognize each other. That's why today was so important.

As I wipe the last of Bree's tears from her flushed cheeks, she sniffles. "I'm sorry I spoiled this day. We're supposed to be celebrating, but all I'm doing is crying over my daddy issues."

"Are you kidding? You have absolutely nothing to be sorry about. I'm just sorry your dad is such a sack of shit."

Her shaky laugh bounces along the acrylic walls of the stand-up shower. She's still tucked into my side. We've been huddled into the corner for a while, and the ass of my jeans is soaked.

It doesn't matter, though, and neither does the cramp in my thigh. Being here for Bree is worth every twinge in my muscles and more.

I kiss the top of her head and whisper, "Let me grab you a towel."

Bree curses under her breath. "Oh, God. I'm totally naked again. Maybe I don't wear clothes as often as I thought."

The chuckle gets lost in my throat as she holds onto me for support while she stands. My clothed chest grazes her nipples on the way up, and my throat constricts as we stare at each other like two long-lost lovers reuniting after years apart.

"Thank you," she whispers, gripping my arm.

Reaching around, I finger a purple towel that didn't make it to storage and stop. "You were right before. He doesn't deserve your tears, nor does he deserve to know you at all. He doesn't deserve your kindness or your smiles."

This seemingly relaxes her.

"But he is missing out by not getting to know you, because you, Bree Finley, are incredible. You're loyal, generous, and hilarious. *I* don't deserve any of your kindness, and I count myself so damn lucky that it was you at the bar that night."

"It's Bree Jameson, remember?" she whispers with a warm smile. "It's on a legal transcript and everything from the hearing today."

"You are correct." I kiss the side of her face, my mouth hovering over that spot as emotions swirl in my stomach like a hurricane. "Is it weird that I fucking love the sound of that?"

She shakes her head, the wet strands soaking through my already wet shirt, and her gaze travels over me, starting with my eyes, then my cheeks and mouth.

She stares at my lips as she licks her own. The drops from her shower have long dried, but instantly, I imagine her tongue soaking them up as she swipes it along her lip.

"Thank you," I rasp, cupping her cheek. "Thank you for what you've done for me and for saying what you did in court today."

"I meant it," she states, and the simple words send a shot of adrenaline throughout my body.

"I know." My hoarse voice cracks as I add, "That's why I'm going to kiss you now."

Energy whips around us in waves, and it kicks up a notch when I back Bree up to the wall, pressing against her bare body. With zero space between us, my shirt wrinkles, especially when I lean down and tug her top lip between my lips and suck.

Her aroused gasp squeezes my dick like a hand might, and I chase the feeling.

I chase this thing between us. Whatever it is, it's real.

It's been taunting us for weeks, and kissing her now feels so fucking right.

Angling her head to the side, I cover her mouth with mine and press my tongue into hers, playing with it through languid, pleasurable strokes like I'd move my hips during sex—smoothly and full of passion.

I savor her taste, drowning in it as I slip my fingers through her wet hair and pull her closer, burying my tongue inside her mouth.

Moans from deep in her throat echo freely in a seductive song.

"I don't know why I ever thought we could just be friends," I mutter with a nip along her bottom lip. "I was kidding myself."

"So was I." Her eyelids flutter.

"There will always be *more* between us." The admission is more like a confession, one I know to be true deep in my bones.

I only step away to strip my clothes off. Bree bites her lip the entire time, and her nostrils flare. I haven't seen this look on her in too damn long, and I'm sure as hell not going to waste it.

She moves into the spot I occupied seconds ago and turns the knob with a squeak.

I practically lunge inside and cup her cheeks again, planting a firm kiss to her lips, then blurt, "I work on my car so much because it distracts me from wanting to touch you."

The water warms as it drips over my head and shoulders. I dip my hand between her legs. I almost wish the water was still off. That way, I could feel how soaked she is.

If her labored breaths are any indication, though, she's aching for me.

With the tip of my finger, I tease her slit, and her legs fall open. Bree's head lulls lazily until she rests it on my shoulder, her breath hot against my skin.

"Fuck," I hiss as I sink my finger into her. She immediately clenches around me, and I bite out another curse as memories of our one-night stand flood through me.

We're not even having sex yet, and I already know this is going to be better than anything we've done before. We know each other better.

We've been to battle together, so to speak.

We've slept in the same bed night after night without crossing the line. But Bree and I have been dancing along that tantalizing line since our eyes locked from across the room for the very first time.

Being with her now is natural, like we've been this intimate the whole time.

I add a second finger, gloriously stretching her, and when she bites my shoulder, I groan.

She mutters in my ear, but I can't make out anything coherent. As the water pours over us, steam rising up to the ceiling, I curl my fingers inside her, working my wife until she shudders against me.

"Ah!" Her head falls back against the shower wall, her lips parted and chest rising like she can't suck in air fast enough. "Oh... my... fuck..."

I skim my nose along the column of her throat, sharply inhaling as hot water pelts my back. My blood runs even hotter as it shoots straight south, turned the hell on by my woman coming so hard for me.

And Bree is *my* woman.

I repeat it in my head over and over again as she kisses me.

My hands skate over her slippery body until I reach her hips and spin her around so her breasts are pressed against the opposite wall. My fingers trace a line along her spine between the wet streams traveling down her smooth skin.

"Fuck me." Her command reaches my ears alongside dinging bells like I've won the lottery.

"I need to grab a condom," I strain. I'm surprised I even remember such a detail, important as it is. I'm surprised I remember how to form full sentences at all—I'm so damn entranced under Bree's spell.

She reaches behind her to grab my wrist, shaking her head. "I said, *fuck me*." Her eyes shine bright with resolution and reassurance. "I'm tested regularly—all negative."

"Same here," I say absentmindedly. I'm distracted by her curves until the weight of what she's saying finally sinks in. "You want me to fuck you… bare?"

Nodding, a wicked smile breaks free across her beautiful face. "You are my husband, after all."

"Damn right." A guttural sound rips from my throat as I grip her hips and thrust into her pussy, claiming it and her in the process. "Say it again," I practically bark as I grind my hips, my dick twitching with pleasure inside her.

"You're… my… husband." She slaps the wall with her palms and backs her ass into me, meeting my vigorous thrusts like none of this is enough.

I snap into a violent, caveman-like pace, driving into her as I roughly yank on her hair to angle her head toward me.

Her eyes blink through the spray of water, which slowly cools the longer we fuck in the shower, but it doesn't stop me.

Not until we both explode.

I sink lower onto my knees and drive upward, sliding deeper inside her.

The walls of her clench around me, and the sensations are too overwhelming. Too good to slow down.

The slapping of our wet bodies slows as we come in sync. She trembles against me, and my own release thrums throughout my body, which rumbles with a satisfied vengeance.

As Bree sags into my arms, I curse myself for not indulging in this sooner.

TWENTY

Wade

"A butterfly!" Violet chases an orange-and-black butterfly across the sidewalk and onto the grass. When it flies away, she only pouts for a second before saying, "I colored a butterfly purple, like Bree's favorite color. I like when she calls me Butterfly Vi."

My smile is immediate.

"She'll be excited to see the drawing," I say, and Violet scurries ahead toward an open spot on the field.

It's the first day of our custody arrangement. I left work early, which wasn't difficult since my boss cares more about his golf swing than my Friday plans, and I picked up Vi from school. Her friends *oohed* and *ahhed* over my red Mustang, and Vi actually blushed. It was so damn cute, I texted Bree as soon as I parked the car next to the field.

Violet will be staying with Bree and me for the weekend. It will be the first time she and I spend more than a couple hours together. Maggie will be nowhere in sight, and I'm in charge.

I drop the youth-sized soccer ball at my feet and tap it toward my daughter, warming her up. She had never played before she met me, and the urge to fine-tune her skills is as strong as a hunger cramp.

When I played my first high school varsity soccer game, I was nervous. My fucking toes were sweating in my cleats, and my jersey felt too tight. The captain's band around my arm was completely suffocating.

Both of my parents were there. They didn't make it to many school functions, but they rearranged their travel schedule in order to attend my very first match of the season. They knew it was important to me, and while it was thoughtful, it made me ten times more nervous too. Like I had all the more pressure on me to play well and lead the team to success, or my parents would regret interrupting work for me.

It occurred to me that if I played horribly, they wouldn't attend another game. They'd come to others before that day, but I still felt like it was all on the line.

But when the whistle blew, its echo bouncing off the surrounding trees and scaring the birds, I tuned out my concerns. Nothing mattered other than the ball at my feet and my teammates.

We won that day, and my parents told me how proud they were of me. How glad they were to be in the stands. Gaga hugged me all afternoon because she was so happy for me.

And I was relieved I hadn't let anyone down. It was comforting that they'd had a good enough time to gladly return for future games.

As I kick the ball to Violet in the park, similar apprehension crawls up my spine. I just hope I have a "fun dad" gene to keep her coming around.

Vi chases after the ball, dribbles once, and seemingly uses every ounce of strength to kick the ball into the child-sized goal Bree and I bought earlier this week. Violet throws her fists into the air and cheers.

"You're almost ready for the draft," I call out as I jog over to her.

"What's a draft?"

"One of its meanings is where you're selected to play on a pro team," I explain in the best way I can think of on the spot. Instinctively, I search the sidelines for any sign of Bree. She's supposed to meet us here, but her final appointment might've delayed her.

She'd be good at answering Vi's questions, but in her absence, I'll have to do.

"What's another meaning for it?" She sits cross-legged on the grass like she's hunkering down for a school lesson.

"Draft could be another word for pull, or it could mean the depth of water needed for a ship to float." I reach into the recesses of my mind for the latter, which was something my grandpa and Gaga taught me. They'd had a boat at one point, and Granddad would often take me out on the water with him on warm summer days. "Draft is also beer."

"Beer?"

I freeze. Should I be talking to a seven-year-old about alcohol? Probably not. "It's grown-up juice."

"Can I try some when I'm a grown-up, or would I not like it?"

I hang my head and chuckle as sweat drips down my back.

"That's very far into the future, so no need to think about it now."

"Mommy and Daddy talk about the future a lot." She picks at the grass, and my scattered nerves from before fire at warped speed again.

I lower myself onto the grass across from her and mimic her seated position. "What about the future?"

"About you, mostly. She says you're my dad too."

"How do you feel about that?" I ask with caution, adding an extra syllable to each word.

This isn't news to Violet. Her mother and I didn't immediately tell her the truth about who I am, opting instead to ease the kid into the idea. We did tell her after the new year, though, and it seems like she's still having trouble grappling with exactly what that means.

"I like having two dads." She shrugs. "Daddy wears cool suits and does puzzles with me. But you have a cool red car."

I chuckle. "What else do they talk about?"

"Bree." At the mention of her name, Violet's cheeks split into a grin. "She's funny."

"Is that what your Mommy said?"

She shakes her head. "Mommy doesn't trust the floozy."

"Is that right?" I arch a brow and make a mental note to address that little comment the next time I see Maggie. Clearly, Violet's just repeating what she heard, and it doesn't seem right to selfishly skew the young one's perception of her stepmom just because Maggie doesn't see Bree's brilliance.

I don't run around bad-mouthing Roger, even though I really, *really* want to, so fair is fair.

"Is a floozy a kind of flower?" Violet smooths her hand over the prickly tips of the blades of grass. "It sounds like a kind of flower. Maybe a red one. Bree looks pretty in red, especially when she wears lipstick. Can I wear lipstick too?"

A moving figure sways in my periphery. On the sidelines, Bree paces, holding her phone to one ear. She catches me and waves, and a warm grin teases my lips. "She *is* pretty," I mumble to Violet, my eyes glued to my incredible wife. "But no, you can't wear lipstick at your age."

"When can I?" she presses as I stand.

I hold my hand out to help her up and answer, "Around the same time you can drink your first beer."

Groaning, she rises to her feet, then dips down to pull her tall socks up to her knees.

As we resume passing the ball back and forth, my attention often wanders back to Bree. She's probably talking to one of her many friends, or Harper. I like that they've patched up their relationship. That they've become a family again.

If they can put aside their hostilities, then maybe Maggie and I can too, for Violet's sake. But we have a long way to go, that's for damn sure.

The sweat on my back and underarms grows aggressive as the hot sun beams down on us, but in a way, it's comforting for me. This is the kind of weather I'm used to. It reminds me of afternoons in LA, and when we arrived out here today, I even felt like I was home.

It feels like all is right in my world as my daughter and I play my favorite sport—something I'd dreamed of for months.

I wish I could fully enjoy it without my insecurities nagging at me, though. Hearing Violet call Roger Daddy still stings. I should be used to it by now, but I can't help the droves of envy knotting in my stomach.

Just once, I want to hear her call *me* that. I'd cut off my arm to be *Daddy* to her.

It's why I'm so fucking nervous today. I want Violet to enjoy herself while she's with us so that she'll *want* to come back of her own accord and not simply because the court requires her to.

I need to show her a good time. That we can have fun together, no matter what we're doing. It's why I suggested soccer. This is something we can have in common that she and Roger don't. The man has probably never played an outside sport. He's too sophisticated to get a speck of dirt on his T-shirt, if he even owns one. Every time I've seen him, he's worn a button-down like he's too good for plain cotton tees.

Why does that bug the shit out of me?

"Tag me in, coach," Bree calls out, her phone nowhere in sight.

"You want to play?" I smirk.

"What? You don't think I can?" She places both hands on her hips, and I temporarily lose myself in the memories of us in the shower the other day.

Us tangled in the sheets of our bed.

Filthy goodnight moans and kisses.

"I think you can do anything." I hold my hands out and kick her the ball.

Which rolls right between her legs.

Violet claps, shrieking, "Goal!"

I throw my head back and laugh with my girls.

Rolling over, I throw my hand onto Bree's side of the bed, but instead of her warm body, only icy sheets greet me. Is she already awake? Saturday and Sunday mornings are her sacred days to sleep in. The last time I suggested we wake up to run together, she tossed her phone at my head, which she narrowly missed.

She didn't even care to check if the screen had cracked, and she loves her phone more than shopping.

I yawn in the open doorway of our bedroom as crackling sounds drift from the kitchen. She hums along to the record playing, and I can't help the swelling of my chest.

Bree's hips sway as she cracks an egg. She beats the fragile thing against the countertop like it's a jar whose lid is glued shut, and she curses when the yolk splatters and drips onto the floor.

My low chuckle draws her attention.

"It's not a golf ball you need to break open," I tease as I rush toward the paper towels to help her clean up.

"I wasn't kidding or exaggerating when I said I don't cook."

"Even if I thought you were kidding, the nightly DoorDash meals would be proof enough."

"Jarvis treats us so well," she muses, referring to our delivery guy, whom she knows by name. She also knows he works for DoorDash while attending Columbia for a writing degree. He wants to be the next Stephen King and is working on a mystery thriller novel, in which a food delivery driver helps the FBI catch a serial killer.

Because she's so vehemently supportive and sweet, Bree reminds him every visit to bring her a signed copy once it's published.

While she wipes down the disaster zone one final time, I plate the bacon and toast, keeping my hands busy. All I really want to do is touch her, but we agreed it would be best not to be too gropey when Violet stays with us.

She could wake up any minute. The little girl is unnaturally quiet when she enters a room, and the thought alone of scarring her scars *me*.

"I thought I'd give eggs a shot this morning," Bree says, opening the fridge. "You know, start with the breakfast basics. But I'm worse with eggs than I am chicken pot pie."

As she steps close to me, new eggs in hand, I sweep her hair over her shoulder and lean in for a quick and innocent peck to her lips. "You just need some practice," I say, my voice low and far more seductive than I intend.

Her shaky inhale sends blood straight south like birds for the winter—an inherent response.

This woman drives me crazy, and it's a miracle I've been able to keep my hands to myself for the last eighteen hours.

I cup her cheek and slant my mouth over hers again, but this kiss lingers on longer than the previous one. "Last night was fucking torture," I grumble with a flex of my jaw.

"Did your dick miss me that much?" she whispers, teasingly running her free hand over the bulge between my legs.

I growl into the crook of her neck, losing myself in her messy hair and the way she turns me on. I shouldn't love a brief rubdown over my pants as much as I do, and I definitely shouldn't grind against her hand. It's embarrassing how enthusiastic I am over this morning handy, and I'm—

"Wade? Bree?" a tiny voice interrupts.

We snap apart, and the eggs Bree was holding hurdle to the floor in another display of shattered shells and yolks.

"Hey, sweetheart," I coo, angling my body away from her while my stiffy dies a slow and painful death.

"Are you having an egg fight?" Vi points to the mess.

"No, no. It was an accident. I'm just clumsy this morning." Bree giggles as she cuts off half a roll of paper towels.

"Eggs are *not* for throwing," I warn Vi, my lips twitching as she rubs the sleep out of her eyes. Her lids are still heavy over shiny blue eyes, and my heart swells at the sight of her here, first thing in the morning.

Relief eases the tension in my shoulders.

Until Violet's smile twists into a frown, and a sob bursts loose.

"Hey, hey." I ease into a crouched position in front of her and reach for her arm, but she snatches it away. "What's going on?"

"I want to go home," she whines.

"You are, sweetheart. This is your home, too. Two homes with two different bedrooms all to yourself. Isn't that fun?"

Violet shakes her head, furiously swiping at the tears flooding her cheeks, and the quiver in her bottom lip slices through my stomach. "I want my mommy."

"You'll see her in a couple of days. Until then, we—"

Another cry racks her tiny body.

I clear my throat and search for help from Bree, but she's rummaging in the pantry like we're not in the middle of a brutal meltdown over here.

"Sweetheart, we can go to the trampoline park today. Have a picnic in the park. Ride the ferry into the city. Whatever you fu—" I catch myself just in time. My desperate pleas almost get me in trouble with the cussing police. "We can do whatever you want today."

"Bagel bar!" Bree announces from behind me. "Who's ready?"

On the counter, she's spread out various sliced bagels, along with three cream cheeses I never noticed in our refrigerator. I didn't know we had so many bagel options, either.

Suddenly, I register the silence of the apartment. Violet has stopped crying, and she's now tiptoeing toward the carb-loaded buffet, blinking away the last of her thick tears like it's a Build-A-Bear Workshop.

"What do you think?" Bree asks with a wide grin.

"I can't see it all." Violet attempts to climb onto the barstool, but her legs are still a little too short.

As I assist her, I remain speechless. Is bread seriously all it takes to soothe Violet? It can't be this simple, right?

Bree leans onto her elbows to level Vi with her gaze. "So, here's how it works. When my grandma did this for my sister and me, she'd let us choose two favorites, and we'd smear whatever cream cheese we wanted on each half. Then we'd swap with each other just so we wouldn't choose the same one to eat every time. While we tried different flavors, my grandma would tell us five jokes of the day."

"Let's play." Violet claps.

I tear my gaze away from Bree and search my daughter's face. There's no sign of her earlier meltdown, except for a touch of red under her eyes where she fought with her tears. At this rate, I imagine she'll be as good as new by the time she hands over the bagels she chooses.

Bree uses show hands like a model on *Wheel of Fortune* when she describes every bagel. "Over here is poppyseed. This is blueberry, and that's a salt bagel. Over there, we have the everything bagel."

"Everything?" Violet repeats somewhat skeptically.

"It's got garlic, onion powder, sea salt, and"—she squints

her eyes toward the bagel in question and finishes with—"some other things too."

She clearly forgot the rest, and it's so damn adorable. The whole production is.

"Oh!" Bree tosses her hands up. "I can't believe I almost forgot we have one more." She bounces back from the pantry with the mother of all bagels, which puts the biggest smile on my daughter's face.

"Rainbow?" she squeals. "There's a rainbow bagel?"

"There sure is, and thankfully, it's not as hard to find around here as I thought." She shrugs in my direction.

"I hope you or Wade picks that one for me." Violet shoots us each a wide-eyed, hopeful look.

"Ready to play?"

Instead of answering Bree, we all three practically attack the bagels as if we're limited on time.

When one half tumbles to the floor during our dash to make a choice, Bree bursts into laughter. "It's not a race, y'all!"

"Whoa. Is the Georgia girl coming out to play this morning?" I cock a brow at her, and she laughs harder, especially when Violet chimes in with her own rendition of "y'alls," the chorus ranging in pitch from low to high.

"It's a funny word," Vi manages through her fit of giggles as she struggles to smear the strawberry cream cheese with a plastic knife. A glob twice the size of a normal amount ends up on one side of the rainbow bagel, so I lean in to help her smooth it out.

"Thanks, Daddy," Violet chirps, then resumes the game.

But I stand frozen. *Did she just…*

My gaze shoots to Bree, and she stares right back, a light sheen of joyful tears in her eyes. I clutch my chest, which swells with pride, and I kiss my daughter's head with a newfound sense that I'm right where I need to be.

Last week, I might've questioned my choices. After Slater texted and my agent left a voice mail, I might've even envisioned being on the field with the team this summer.

But right now, I have zero doubts about the course I've chosen for my life. This is where I'm meant to be—with Bree and Violet. We're simply eating bagels with cream cheese, but the magnitude of it all reaches the moon and the stars.

If I were traveling with the team, I'd miss most of these moments.

"Looks like we've all picked rainbow." There's a tremble in Bree's voice, and I'm sure if I tried to speak, I'd sound the same as her. So many emotions clog my throat.

"We all get to try it!" Violet throws her victorious fists into the air so hard she almost falls off the stool. I catch her just in time and sigh with relief.

"Careful." I set her upright again.

"I got too excited." She covers her mouth with one small hand. As she drops it, I marvel over the sparkle in her eyes. It matches the glitter on her shirt.

The sparkle even brightens as she bites into the rainbow bagel with glee.

"Who's ready for the first joke?" Bree asks. When Violet raises her hand, Bree continues. "Why do hummingbirds hum?"

Violet and I both shrug, wiping cream cheese from the corners of our mouths in sync.

"Because they don't know the words."

The sounds of our laughter carry into the rest of the jokes while we finish our bagel breakfast. The Patsy Cline record continues in the background. Vi loves watching the spinning disc, as if it's a game, and the classic country songs fill the apartment with wonder.

When Violet disappears into the bathroom, I approach Bree from behind and wrap her in my arms as she turns off the kitchen sink. "Where did all these bagels even come from?"

"I told you—I can't cook. I had to get a backup breakfast to ensure little miss thing in there had something to eat this morning."

Resting my chin on her shoulder, I beam. "You are amazing."

"Tell me something I don't know." She snorts as her damp hands cover mine beneath her breasts.

I shower her neck with open-mouthed kisses, all the way up to her ear. "Seriously, thank you for this. You have no idea…"

She turns in my arms and interlocks her fingers behind my neck.

As I kiss her lips, I drink her in, deepening it for one stolen moment.

My wife.

It's like a new, all-consuming chant that fills my life with a joy I've never known before.

"I was so focused on reaching this point—on fighting for custody of Violet—that I didn't think about what would happen once I got it," I say, my voice low. "I didn't realize I have no fucking clue how to be a father until this morning when she completely lost it."

"Good thing you don't have to do this alone. I'm here." Bree rises onto the balls of her feet and holds me in a comforting hug. There's nothing sexual or erotic about it. It's a sweet and simple gesture. Yet, it turns me on because it's so genuine.

So relieving.

So *Bree*.

How does she do this to me? The way she so easily affects me should be illegal.

The hug coupled with her words reach a part deep inside me and take up residence, where they make me fantasize about a future just like this. One where Bree, Violet, and I are a real family.

TWENTY-ONE

've never seen a grown man lose his shit, and I definitely never expected to witness brooding, grumpy Oliver Westbrook like this.

The posh British man is positively giddy.

"I can't believe I'm in the presence of Wade Jameson, the best striker in LA Stars history. Where have you been hiding him, Bree?" Erin's boyfriend asks.

With Violet on one side, I loop my arm through Wade's and sigh. "We've just been keeping him all to ourselves, I guess."

"Biggest congratulations to you on your recent wedding. I'm sorry I didn't say so before. I'm just chuffed to be here today, and my nephew will be too, once he arrives. He doesn't have any other uncles, but if he did, I'd undoubtedly be his favorite." He rubs his hands together in victory.

"I didn't realize you were so competitive," I tease.

"Mainly when it comes to soccer," Erin chimes in as a stunning woman approaches, her arm slung over a young boy's shoulders.

"Malcolm!" Oliver scoops the kid into his strong arms, and I can't help the shell-shocked state freezing me in place. I've seen more emotion from him in the last fifteen minutes than I have in the several months I've known him.

I'm not much for sports, but if nothing else, I'm glad we came back out today to kick the soccer ball around just so I could experience this colorful side of Oliver. It was Violet's idea to return to the park since she had such fun yesterday, and of course, Wade teared up a lot like he did when she called him Daddy.

It's been a big day for him, and the sun's still out.

I just wish we could celebrate with our birthday suits tonight, but having Vi with us for the next two nights means no funny business.

At least I have the glorious pleasure of watching Wade run around the field, sweat magnificently glistening on his golden skin. As he plays, he lights up in ways I've never seen. It's obvious from the glimmer in his eye how much he loves this sport, and it does something to me knowing he left it all behind in order to be as present as possible for Violet.

My own father didn't even hug me when we ran into each other at my high school graduation. All I got was a quick nod, and I'm not sure it was even meant for me. He very well could've been shooing a bug off his nose.

As Oliver continues gushing over Wade's presence today, repeatedly telling Violet how talented her father is, I nudge Erin to the side and speak through one side of my mouth.

"The sex must've been good today if he's acting this *chuffed*."

Erin lets something between a gasp and a laugh loose. "We got creative this morning and had a breakfast buffet."

"Scandalous," I deadpan. "So, you had croissants and—"

"He licked pancake syrup from my belly button." She clasps a hand over her mouth, her eyes wide like she's equally as surprised she confessed such a thing as she is that she did it in the first place.

I couldn't be prouder. This woman is my mini-me. My delight over her naughty success practically lifts me off the ground. I throw my arm over her shoulders and squeeze. "I have nothing left to teach you."

"Speaking of good sex…" She eyes Wade as he, Oliver, his sister Rebecca, and the kids run after the ball. Other families and couples litter the park with their own games, picnics, and what appear to be photo sessions.

Birds ascend from the trees, and my heart soars along with them.

For the first time in years, I feel light and hopeful.

"You and Wade still having naked sleepovers?"

"We're fucking, Erin." I roll my eyes, mumbling, "Maybe I do have a few things left to teach you."

"And?" Her clear, shiny eyes are greedy for more juicy details.

"You know when you're in an airplane, and it descends, you spend a moment where you fear you won't safely touch down?"

"I have flashes of the entire contraption bursting into flames upon contact with the ground." She shudders.

"Exactly," I agree, turning my focus back on Wade, who lifts his shirt to wipe the sweat from his brow. The action gives me a delicious peek of his abs and tattoos, which makes me bite my lip. "But when you do arrive at the gate unharmed, a strong sense of euphoria overcomes you. That feeling is what it's like being with Wade."

"Wow," she whispers. "I never thought I'd see the day…"

"Well, you're seeing it, babe. I'm finally fucking happy with a guy. I don't know how he did it. I'm even a little pissed that it was relatively easy for him to end my single streak, but I don't hate it one bit." I can't help the smile gracing my lips.

Erin squeezes my arm. "And I'm happy for you, Bree. You deserve this."

I search her eyes. The previously suggestive twinkle has been replaced with caution. "But?" I prompt.

"You know me—I'm ever the optimist, but I worry." She shrugs with a downward tilt of her mouth. "It was one thing to fake the marriage, but it's another thing to actually fall for each other. If you're both in the same place, then that's amazing. One big, happy ending for all. But if this is just a thing of convenience, then I think you should know what you're getting yourself into. You should make sure he's on the same page as you, whatever it might be."

Alarm bells blare in my head. In truth, we do sleep in the same bed, so having sex *is* convenient. But the word choice cheapens what I believe to be a meaningful connection.

And it is meaningful, right?

I fucking hate that Erin's not wrong, but when I look at Wade, I see nothing but warmth and devotion. I can even practically feel both radiating off him from several yards away. Am I insane to think this thing between us is real?

"I need a break!" Rebecca hollers to the guys and Violet, then strides over to Erin and me, fighting with the wisps of her hair as they blow in every direction.

"You're holding your own out there. Very impressive," I say.

"As a single mom of a ten-year-old boy, I've learned a lot of things I never expected, including how to keep up with him in soccer." She laughs through a rough exhale.

"I could use some lessons," I try to joke, but Erin's earlier comment sits on my chest like a boulder.

Violet races across the patch of grass we've indirectly claimed for our little game. Her arms flail as she hurries to catch up with the guys, but then she abruptly stops. "I need to potty!"

Giggling, I use this moment for a reprieve to catch my breath and compose myself as if I've been playing too. "Come on, babe. Let's go to the restroom." I wave her over.

"Thanks, babe," she tosses back with a giggle.

Next to me, Erin beams. "So stinking adorable."

I nod toward Wade to make sure he knows she's not wandering off by herself, and the grin he gives me is more than enough to melt the North Pole. Violet links her hand in mine, and my chest warms further.

She's so small and gentle. So innocent and full of joy.

Wade might not have been part of her life until last year, but I see a lot of him in her, beyond the eyes and similar dark blonde hair.

"Did I run fast?" she asks, hopping over the cracks on the sidewalk.

"You sure did, Butterfly Vi. Just like your dad."

"Really? He's *so* fast."

Once we're finished in the restroom, we start our short trek back to the group, but a familiar face stops us.

"Bree?"

"Oh my God," I whisper to myself, my heart leaping against my rib cage.

It's Dr. Lake.

He's here in the park.

I haven't seen him since last Christmas, when I was living a much different life than I am now.

It's strange seeing him in such a relaxing place, wearing a graphic T-shirt and shorts. It's almost weird that he's not here in a button-down and slacks, which he wore the night he introduced himself to me.

What a cold blast from the past.

I offer a screechy greeting and clutch Violet's hand more tightly.

"And who is this?" He stuffs his hands into his pockets and grins down at the little girl, whose ponytail is charmingly crooked thanks to her enthusiasm over soccer.

"My name's Violet," she chirps. "What's yours?"

"I'm Vince."

"That starts with V, just like mine."

The tall, rugged man chuckles. The sound is deep and endearing, which is one of the reasons I was instantly attracted to him. It held me under a tempting, sexual spell once, but now, it's more of a pleasant, friendly laugh. It's… nice.

Good sweet Lord, how things have changed.

He straightens back up and faces me. "Is she your niece?"

"No, she's my, um, stepdaughter." I lift my left hand up to swipe the hair out of my face, and I inadvertently display my ring in the process.

"You're… married?" His jaw drops, but he recovers almost instantly. "Wow. I had no idea. No wonder you haven't been answering my texts."

Next to me, little eyes snap up to mine, and I nearly choke on my own spit. "It was nice to see you again," I say, in a hurry to escape.

In my haste, I don't immediately realize I'm practically dragging Violet behind me. Her muffled pleas to slow down finally filter into my ears through the ringing in them.

"Sorry, babe." I relax my steps into a leisurely stroll.

"You're trying to be fast like me, aren't you?" she teases, and it eases the sudden tension in my shoulders as we make our way toward the others.

I can't help but look over my shoulder, a wave of varying insecurities rolling through me.

I've changed, right? I'm not the same person I was when Dr. Lake and I met, am I? I'm totally capable of being a one-dick woman.

Erin's words of caution rush back. She mentioned being on the same page, and my first concern was in regard to Wade's feelings for me, not the other way around. But I like him so much—this I know to be true.

I've also known myself to get bored, which is partly why I kept my past sexual repeats to a minimum. It's why I've kept men at a distance altogether. I won't lose interest in Wade, right? It's not possible. He's… different.

Or, do I just really want him to be?

Shit.

What am I doing? Things are great with us. I shouldn't be questioning a damn good thing when it smacks my ass and fucks me in the shower like there's no tomorrow.

Violet and I approach during what appears to be a hydration break, water bottles clutched in each of their hands. Oliver and Wade stand a few feet apart, deep in conversation.

Clearly uninterested in the topic, Malcolm leads Vi back out onto the miniature "pitch"—I'm becoming a freaking expert on soccer lingo, and I wouldn't do that for just anyone.

There. Take that, insecurities.

"I was absolutely devastated when I heard you were retiring, but I completely understand such a necessity," Oliver tells Wade. "I left my home as well when I learned I had a sister, and I've never looked back."

Rebecca's head lulls backward, like she's speaking to a higher power when she asks, "Here are two men with admirable priorities. Where can I get me one?"

"England and California, apparently." Erin points to the two. "Here in New York, though, I can tell you the spots to avoid so you don't catch the eyes of creeps like I used to."

"That's equally important." Rebecca nods.

"We have a lot in common, don't we?" Wade fist-bumps Oliver in a gesture of true camaraderie. "Now, could you be a good new *mate* and convince my agent to understand? He's become more aggressive in the last week about getting me to come back."

"He has?" I cut in. This is news to me. I've learned through him that Mick is persistent, but I thought he'd given up on his dream of Wade returning to the Stars. In fact, Wade's been referring to the guy as his *old* agent. As in, *not* his current agent.

Wade shakes his head and asserts, "He's wasting his time. That part of my life is in the past."

One glimpse of the clarity in his eyes, and I believe him. He's not going anywhere, and neither am I. I was being silly before. It's natural to doubt a good thing, but Wade and me? We're solid.

"The LA Stars' loss is our gain," Oliver muses.

"You two have struck up quite the sweet bromance this afternoon, huh?" I laugh with the girls as we all sneak glances in the kids' direction, keeping an eye on them and their safety. "It's a good thing I didn't introduce you two before. Seems like you would've left Erin and me for each other."

"I could do a lot worse in a guy," Wade plays along, then scoops me into his arms and plants a sloppy kiss onto my mouth.

Our friends erupt into a mix of cheers and mock gagging noises, and my heart fucking flutters.

We arrive at our apartment, smelling of fresh grass and steeped in joy. We embody the scent of early spring.

"I met Bree's friend today," Violet announces as we shut the door behind us. As much as she loves all the girly things, like fashion and nail polish, she's surprisingly unaffected by the dirt stains on her clothes.

"I met her friends today too." Wade chuckles and places a chaste kiss to my cheek as he moves toward the refrigerator for a few bottles of water.

"No," Vi draws out. "I'm talking about Vince. His name starts with V too."

Wade's curious gaze lands on me, and I freeze.

"We met him on the way back from the bathroom," she continues.

"Why don't you go clean up?" I scrunch my nose in exaggeration. "I can smell you from here."

"I can smell *you* from space!" she shoots back.

I clutch my chest and deeply inhale a fistful of my shirt. "I smell like roses."

"If roses were covered in poo!"

"How dare you." I jokingly gasp as she takes off toward the bathroom, trembling with her giggles.

With her out of sight and earshot, I inch toward Wade. "Listen, Vince was someone I knew before I met you and Violet."

"Was he like a…"

I blow out an unsteady breath. "In the name of honesty and transparency, he and I slept together once, but that's it. It meant nothing."

He rubs his large hands up and down my upper arms, and to my surprise, he smiles. "Bree, I know you had a life before me, and I'm aware we might run into some of the guys of your past. If we were in LA, we'd definitely run into some of the women from my own past too. There's no need to explain, but…"

"But?" I hold my breath. I don't love what he's implying with his own sexy history, but it's true. Before we met, we led different lives, and there's no changing them, not that I'd want us to.

Whatever happened back then shaped who we are now, and these versions of ourselves are in a good place. It's a hard lesson to embrace, and although I still falter, it's taken me a long time to accept it all as best I can.

Finally, Wade leans in, takes a deep whiff of my shirt, and tsks. "Vi was right. You do not smell like roses."

I playfully shove him back, and he teeters on his heels.

"You need a shower, young lady."

"I'm your sugar mama, remember?" My cheeks split into a grin.

He sways back into my space and uses the tip of his nose

to trace a teasing line up my neck and into my hair. "All I want to do is make my sugar mama come like a porn star." His dirty desire expressed with such a gravelly voice wakes my core with a violent jolt.

"And I'd do filthy things to you that porn stars have never heard of," I whisper back, an air of mystery in my own voice.

"I'd kiss your—"

"What are you whispering about?" Violet bounces back into the kitchen with more energy than I'd expect from a girl who's just spent hours running around kicking a soccer ball.

She's indestructible.

"We were considering a pizza for dinner!" I burst like I'm talking over a rowdy crowd.

"Can I talk that loud?" Vi practically screams back with glee.

Wade covers his ears in exaggeration. "Maybe we stick to our inside voices."

Two hours later, the apartment smells like the pepperoni pizza we've destroyed, and Violet has fallen asleep on the couch. Turns out, she's not indestructible after carbs and half a movie, and I'm right there with her.

While Wade tucks her into her own bed, I use the opportunity to occupy the bathroom, rushing through the motions of brushing my teeth and hair.

I never thought it'd be possible, but I've pared down my precious bedtime routine, all for Wade.

I have most certainly changed.

I've just burrowed under the covers in the bedroom when Wade enters, a sigh on his lips. "Today was…"

"Everything you hoped for?" I supply.

"And more. I don't even know how to describe it." He

wrestles a shirt over his head, covering his muscles and tattoos, much to my chagrin.

But we agreed we'd go to bed fully clothed while Violet stays with us, a conversation we had to repeat as soon as she fell asleep on the couch. We cannot be tempted to "engage in filthy acts like we're horny miscreants," as Wade said. The line was similar to one I'd expect from Oliver. Their budding new friendship has already widened Wade's vocabulary after a single day. I can't imagine how it'll further change the more they hang out. They've already made plans to get together again soon.

"I just hope she's having a good time," he says, and I detect a hint of fear in his voice.

"Of course she is," I reassure him. "She had enough fun playing soccer yesterday that she wanted to do it again today. She's having a blast."

He sits on the edge of the bed, his back muscles tense. "What about the next time she visits? Will she want to play, or will she be bored? I don't know how to keep her entertained enough to *want* to come back."

And suddenly, it all makes sense. He's worried her visits here will dull, and they'll lose the progress they made today.

I lean up to massage his shoulders, fidgeting with a few knots here and there as I gently offer, "You don't have to constantly make big gestures, Wade. You're enough for her just as you are."

The back of his head falls to my chest.

I keep working the stress free from his bulging muscles without causing too much pain. After all, I'm trying to help reduce the aches he's clinging to right now, not make them worse.

"She's young," I say. "She might not always appreciate a simple pizza-and-movie night, but when she's older, those bonding moments will be special to her. She'll look back on those times and smile because she was comfortable and safe and loved. You're creating a family, and they're not all made from filling every moment together with some over-the-top experience. You can have a balance of both the fun and relaxing stuff. As long as you're together, she'll know you love her and that it won't change. That'll keep her coming back."

He finally sags against me without the weight of this fear bogging him down as much. He kisses the palm of my hand and murmurs against it, "Thank you. You always know what to say, and I only hope I can be as wise someday."

"You're doing just fine," I reassure him and crawl back to my side of the bed.

He switches the bedside lamp off, but as soon as the room darkens, it lightens again from the same lamp. "I finally understand the bagel question." Wade slides under the covers next to me, his pajama bottoms loose over his corded muscles.

"What bagel question?"

"The first night we met, you told me not to tell you how much I love my grandmother or what my favorite bagel is."

"And you told me both the literal second I finished warning you."

"Couldn't help myself." His chuckles send vibrations through the bed.

"My grandma used to play the game to distract Harper and me from whatever fight my parents were having. If we were laughing and telling jokes, she figured we wouldn't register the yelling and name-calling." Facing him, I tuck my hand under my cheek.

I feel the distance of that time in my life. Of how many years have passed since then, but the pain of it still hovers in the recesses of my heart. Just because I've learned from my past, and it has shaped me, it doesn't mean I'm not still affected by it from time to time.

I was older than Harper, and I could make out most of our parents' arguments, especially when Grandma wasn't there to entertain us. I felt like it was up to me to step in and do that for Harper, so I'd make up songs for us to learn and sing together. I'd read to her. If there was daylight, I'd squeeze her hand and guide her into the backyard, where we could escape the hostility.

"I'm sorry you had to experience that," he whispers.

"Bagels are a good memory for me. Even though they're a little tainted with the real reason, I'll always appreciate those times with Gran. They were small, but they meant the world to me, especially now that I'm an adult. That's how I know Violet will be grateful for you no matter what." I smile into the dimly lit room.

The bed dips under the weight of him as he shifts, rustling the sheets in the process. "I don't want Violet to think Maggie and I only fight. I don't want her to remember us like that when she's older."

"I get that."

"I just wish I didn't get so damn frustrated, but I swear Maggie does it on purpose. It's like she seeks out all the ways she can push my buttons and goes all Whack-A-Mole on them."

I can't help my snort as I find his hand in the dark. Lacing my fingers through his, I offer, "I don't think she's doing it on purpose. I just feel like you're trying to find your rhythm, you know? Change is hard, especially when it's so different than what you had planned."

"Don't I fucking know it," he grumbles and slips his free arm under my neck, tucking me into his side. "But change can also be a good thing," he says in such a low whisper, I wouldn't have heard it had I not been glued to him.

"Like when we change our underwear—that's good," I joke. Wade needs a laugh, and I deliver.

"Exactly. You're always so good at reading my mind."

"Among other talents." I suppress the urge to slide my hand into his pants to prove just how skilled I truly am. Then again, I'm sure he remembers. *Wink, wink.*

Groaning, Wade shifts yet again. "We can't," he says and repeats it a few more times.

I know we can't, but it doesn't stop me from wanting him.

From wanting to experience each sensation his fingers elicit.

The way every growl leaves his parted lips like a curse and a prayer all in one.

How hard he gets in my grip.

It's all so sexy. But I should really stop picturing it, or I can't be held responsible for the dirty things I do to him.

"Good night, Bree," he says, and the warning in his tone echoes around the room until I finally give in to the dreams waiting for me.

TWENTY-TWO

Wade

I pace outside my apartment building, grinding my teeth like a blender does to ice.

The phone is hot against my ear, heat radiating from it as my agent's pleas echo through the speaker. Mick has reached an entirely new level with his tactics.

"You can't seriously tell me you're happy playing house in New York, can you?" he spits, and I'm glad this is only a voice mail. If he were on the phone himself, I would've barked my disdain for him, LA, and returning to the team with words that would make Gaga equally proud and ashamed of me.

I have half a mind to hop on a plane today and go out there to reject him in person.

"This role you're playing isn't you, Wade. And if it is, fine. I respect it." Nothing in his nasty tone suggests he's sincere, and my fury only grows wilder. "But in that case, you can easily be a father on the LA Stars, or any other team. You could have your pick. You're not the only player out there with a spouse and a kid. You could do both, and you'd be fucking happy. If you can tell me I'm wrong, I'll leave you alone."

I curse under my breath, the afternoon humidity bogging my body down.

"Stop dicking me around, and get your ass back where you fucking belong."

That's it. That's the end of the message.

Up until now, Mick has been persistent, but this voice mail is just brutal. The tone. The words.

The harsh truth.

It is true, isn't it? For over two weeks now, I've been running myself ragged trying to be everything—father, husband, and accountant. Add friend, grandson, and co-parent too.

Yesterday, I fell asleep at my desk at work, partly out of mind-numbing boredom and partly from exhaustion. I'm no stranger to hard work and exertion, especially that of the physical variety, but this new routine I've created is kicking my ass.

Fueled by anger with a lot of daylight left to fill—it's Maggie's weekend with Violet—I tap on my phone screen and place a call.

"You've reached the better half of the former single dad superheroes. What can I do for you?" Tucker's voice booms through the speaker, and I roll my eyes. The guy and his over-the-top salesman impression are both ridiculous.

"I need to meditate. You in?"

"I'm always down to kick your ass," he says. "And you're

in luck—my mom is on her way to pick up Ellie for a shopping day. The girl is growing like a weed. Nothing fits her anymore."

"That's what happens with kids, Tuck, or do you need me to draw you a flow chart of how the human body works?"

"I'll keep your smartassery in mind while I'm kicking your ass," he shoots back.

"Are you coming down, or what?" I chuckle as I move toward my car. My gym bag with the gloves and other necessities is already nestled in the back seat, and the anxious energy coursing through me is ready for a fight.

Once Tucker and I end the call, I slide into the driver's seat, huffing a rough exhale.

My head is still a little foggy from a night of beer with Oliver at his favorite British pub. He's twelve years older than me, and he can throw back beer like I've never seen. He didn't lose focus or sharp enunciation for a second.

He also never missed a beat in offering sound advice on adapting to the city and a new life. When we first met, I thought it odd that I had so much in common with him, but the rigid guy really fucking gets me, no matter how many beers he's had.

It was all very impressive, but also dangerous, because I stupidly tried to keep up. Now, I'm paying for it, but it's nothing that can't be helped by a few rounds in the ring.

While I wait for Tucker, I shoot Bree a quick text.

How's the hair appointment?

Bree: Spent most of it chatting over champagne.

What kind of salon does Madi have?

The best kind ☺

> Tell her she owes me for that dumb game of pool on her birthday. I accept all forms of payment, including a bottle of champagne.

> She says she has no recollection of pool...

I lean my head against the seat and laugh under my breath. Bree and I celebrated her friend Madison's birthday around St. Patrick's Day. We decked ourselves in green and completed a bar crawl of epic proportions. I saw a whole new side to the city, and I actually really loved it.

Most of all, I loved seeing Bree so happy and full of life. She lit up as soon as we connected with her friends, who welcomed me like I was one of them. I even have inside jokes with Tessa's husband, Carter, since we share the same first time, coincidentally.

I felt like my old self. Carefree, reckless, and flirty. I wasn't solely a father, which has been my priority since I arrived in New York. I was simply a guy out with a rowdy group of friends.

I was a horny guy too. I couldn't keep my hands off Bree, and the more I drank, the more I clung to her, not that she complained.

It was, indeed, nothing like how a wholesome father would act. I'm not even sure it's how a husband would act.

Mick's accusations slam into me again.

The guy on the bar crawl, wearing a green top hat and beer stains on his shirt—that was me. In fact, I celebrated the holiday in similar fashion last year in Southern California.

I hang my head until it hits the top of the steering wheel, cursing myself. I never assumed this transition would be easy. It's natural to have doubts, but I won't give up. I can't.

This is too important.

Bree and Violet are way too fucking important to lose my shit now. I just need a good boxing session to let out my frustrations—that's all.

I send Bree another text.

> I'm headed to meditate with Tucker. Care to join us once you're finished?

She sends several puking emojis.

> Bree: Erin's been begging me to meditate with her forever. She hasn't convinced me, and neither will you, no matter how sexy your ass is.

> This sexy ass still has your fingerprints on it from last night.

> I'll be making more tonight.

> You better.

> Have fun meditating...

> I'll send you the address in case you change your mind. It'll be worth it. You've never meditated like we do.

> What do you mean?

> You'll have to find out for yourself.

The passenger door swings open, and Tucker ducks inside.

"It's about time," I grumble, and he's barely closed the door before I race away toward my favorite place for stress relief.

"What's with you?" He shoots me a glaring side-eye.

"Nothing. I'm fine." It's not lost on me that I sound like a toddler, and immediately, I backpedal. "Okay. I'm not fine."

"I know," the dick says, gloating.

"I don't know if I'm meant to be here. Do you ever... question if being a father is right for you? I mean, I hardly have time to do the things I love for myself since I'm always thinking about Vi. Bree. My stupid job." My temples throb. "Fuck. I know how that sounds, and I don't regret anything. I'm just… lost. Do you ever feel that way?"

"All the time," he states, dropping any amusement he previously held.

His honest and vulnerable admission gives me pause. He's not going to judge me? Ridicule me for sounding selfish? Is it possible that he senses how broken up I am about this, so he doesn't want to make me feel alone?

As we pull up to the gym, all I can follow up with is "Really?"

His chuckle is light as he levels with me. "Being a parent isn't easy. In your case, you're a husband too, and I can't imagine how difficult it is to balance it all."

"Exactly, but being a parent is so overwhelming in itself."

"You want a break every now and then, but it never happens. Even if the kid doesn't live with you one hundred percent of the time, you're always a parent. You're always on the job, worrying, calculating, and thinking. Are we making the right choices for our kids? Are we balancing loving them and disciplining them when needed? I could go on."

"Please don't—it's bad enough I'm constantly asking myself these same questions. I don't need you working me into a sweat before we even go inside."

"It's a lot, man."

"I just hope I'm what's best for Violet."

Tucker grips my shoulder. "Here's what I've learned: if you're that concerned over whether you're doing it right or not, then you're doing just fine. At the end of the day, all the kids need to know is that you love them unconditionally, to infinity and beyond."

Bree gave similar advice. How did I get so lucky to have such insightful people in my life? I don't know what I'd do without my circle—my new, unique team, so to speak.

"We've been watching a lot of *Toy Story* this week," he says, cutting through my thoughts.

"Classic."

"But seriously, I know it's all new for you. You became a father overnight, and I can imagine it's been a shock."

"That's putting it lightly."

"We can't truly prepare for parenthood, anyway. It helps that I had nine months to try, though. Then again, I never expected to do any of this alone." A dark shadow crosses his features, and I know he's thinking about his late wife.

He doesn't talk about her much. During the first month we met, we had a beer, and he told me she died due to complications while giving birth to Ellie. He never married again, using all of his energy to raise his daughter.

"One day at a time, man. One day at a time, and you'll get the hang of it." Tucker offers a tight-lipped smile. "Like I said, you're doing great just by showing up."

I fist-bump him over the console. "Thanks for the talk. It's nice to know I'm not the only one fucking this up."

"I never said I'm fucking it up. I just admitted I sometimes think I am, but it's hard to ruin something when I'm so good at everything."

"Get out of the car, so I can show you just how terrible you are at one thing—boxing."

We jump out and meet in front of the door, bags slung over our shoulders. I'm about to yank the door open when he grips my shoulder, the pinch in his brow serious again. "I know you have Bree, but I want you to know you can always come to me too. Happy to help however I can."

"Thank you." I nod and blow out a relaxing breath. His offer, plus the mere mention of Bree, both put me at ease. "She has been a fucking godsend. The woman is a damn child whisperer. You should see how effortlessly she diffuses Violet's meltdowns. She could win awards."

"There's something special about a Finley girl, isn't there?" he muses as he enters, and the wistful tone in his voice reaches my ears in strong waves.

Although it seems innocent enough, a ball of jealousy lights my stomach on fire. Where the hell did that come from?

It's probably because he called Bree "hot as fuck" right after we were married. He said as much in the ring, after which I clobbered him with a rear hook, uppercut, jab combination.

Are we going to have a repeat today?

Tucker and I finally slide into the ring after another pair finishes. After thirty minutes, I haven't seen the need to pummel him for anything inappropriate. The trash talk has been minimized to include my weak upper body and his puny calves. Tucker is surprisingly insecure about his calves, although they're nothing to be embarrassed about.

We're just shooting the shit.

During a break, I check my phone and find a message from Bree saying she's on her way. It was sent a while ago, and I've just clicked off when a shadow approaches.

"What am I doing here?" Bree asks.

My wicked grin spreads slowly until my eyes crinkle in the corners. "Welcome to meditation, baby."

"I was certain this was a mistake until I saw your car

outside." She studies the rest of the gym, spinning in place. "This is what you call meditation?"

"Better than sitting still in a quiet room, huh?" If possible, my cheeky smile only grows, especially when her eyes narrow with intrigue.

"I'm in."

"Get your sexy ass up here."

She kicks her shoes off, and I hold the rope up for her to duck underneath it.

"Are you replacing me, man?" Tucker covers his chest with a large glove. "I'm hurt."

"Actually, I think I'll let her practice on you while I take a piss." I wink toward Bree. "Give him hell."

I hop down and reach my bag for an extra pair of gloves. They're a little small, which is why I don't use them, but I also can't return them at this point. They should fit Bree just fine.

"On second thought, I can't do this…" She backs away, but I jump back into the ring and stop her.

We've drawn some attention by now, but it doesn't matter. We pay to be here just like everyone else, so if I want to have my wife punch one of my friends, it's my prerogative.

"I'm too pretty to hit—I get it," Tucker brags.

"Now, I need you to take him down because his obnoxious love for himself is nauseating." I dry heave with an exaggerated gagging sound as I finish wrapping Bree's hands, then slide her gloves into place. "Gloves up."

She imitates my position, half her beautiful face obscured by the gloves. I stand in the corner as a coach might, while she practically tiptoes toward the middle of the ring like she's in ballet. I've never seen her so skittish, and it's fucking with me.

I'm close to telling her she doesn't have to do this. If she's this uncomfortable, I need to give her an out. But I think she'd love this if she gave it a chance.

Bree throws the first punch, but it doesn't land. If I had to guess, Tucker's instinct to leap out of the way kicks in, but it doesn't take much. Her strikes are limper than if she had the flu.

"Put your back into it," I call out as I walk toward the restrooms. "Hit him like you mean it."

When I return, Bree's punches don't appear to have gotten any meaner.

With a rough exhale, she drops her hands to both sides and faces me. "I think it would help if I got angry. What would make me hate him enough to punch him?"

From the opposite corner, water spills down Tucker's chin as he scoffs.

"I thought what I said earlier about how in love he is with himself would've done the trick," I joke.

"Self-love is important," Tucker calls out in defense.

"He's not wrong." Bree giggles.

"What about this—he hates *The Notebook*, and he'd rather drink poison than listen to any podcast, especially one about organizing your closet." I hit her where it hurts, bringing up a long-time and a more recent love, respectively, but it had to be done.

It works too, because the hesitant shadow in her eyes instantly transforms into vengeance. She charges after him, flicks the bottle from his hand, and yells, "You're a dead man."

She wails on him with the force—and clumsy chaos—of a dozen geese after their prey.

I'm laughing so hard, my sides ache.

Tucker manages to flee her physical tirade, but she just chases him down. "What the fuck, what the fuck, what the fuck…" he repeats as he runs in circles.

As if she's possessed with the ghosts of Noah and Allie themselves, she avenges the couple by landing an uppercut like a fucking pro. It's actually a good thing Tucker has a great chin, as boxers might say, and it hardly fazes him.

"Okay, okay!" Tucker stammers as his chest heaves. "You've convinced me—organization podcasts are the shit, and I will never disrespect them," he vows, holding his right hand up as he slows to a jog.

"That's what I thought," Bree warns.

"I didn't even know those were a thing." He huffs out a breath.

"I didn't, either, until I moved in with your friend there and needed professional-level help with combining our things into one apartment."

"This was so much better than anything I had in mind." My abs squeeze as laughter racks my body, and Tucker continues cursing.

He flings his gloves off and flashes me with two middle fingers.

"Looks like it's my turn, but I can't promise to make you hate me," I tease, but Bree's reaction isn't the lighthearted one I expect.

Her eyes are still a few shades darker than usual, and they resemble the kind of amber when she's… turned on.

Jesus—is she horny? We're not exactly in a place where I can take care of business, and I can't ignore her in this wanting state. Not when something feral blazes through my gut with the urge to tend to her every need.

"I need to go to the restroom now," she announces, and I don't miss the suggestion in her voice. *Does she…*

As I help remove her gloves, my dick twitches in my fucking gym shorts.

With both hands free, she leans in and whispers, "Meet me in the back."

Christ.

I'm about to get frisky in a public place with my fake wife.

"Shit," I hear from Tucker behind me as Bree sashays away. "I need to go. My mom needs me back at the apartment."

"Sure, sure." I wave him off, hardly registering what he's saying. He mentions something about a kite, or a cat. He could be talking about an impending apocalypse, but I would still have only one dirty thing on my mind.

"You're going to have sex with your wife in the bathroom, aren't you?"

Now that, I hear. I flash a smirk in his direction for confirmation. It's useless to deny it, anyway.

"We rode here together, man."

I retrieve the keys from my bag, toss them his way, and walk backward toward the sexy vixen waiting for me. "I'll find my way back."

In the deserted hall, I tap on the door to the restroom, my blood pumping at an ungodly speed. I barely hear the click of the lock, signaling for me to join her. I even stare at the doorknob a moment as I float outside my body.

When I finally enter, shut the door, and lock it behind me, low, heady moans reach my ears, and my jaw drops to my chest. If it could fall farther, it would.

Because Bree is naked from the waist down with her hand between her sprawled out legs. Her back slides up and down the wall as she works herself to the brink, and I'm pretty sure I'm drooling.

I'm definitely hard as a rock as I stand witness to this erotic display of sexuality.

"You started… without me," I manage, my husky voice mixing with the growing whimpers of her pleasure.

"What are you going to do about it?" As if her eyelids are far too heavy with lust, it takes a moment for her to lift her gaze to meet mine in an arousing challenge.

"I'm going to watch some more before I join the party."

She bites down on her bottom lip like she just loves the sound of that, and she works her finger inside her even faster.

My mouth fills with saliva. She's a work of art.

"I don't know why, but boxing… makes me hot." She pants, her lips parted. They beckon me to join her. "New kink unlocked."

"I'm going to bring you to the ring every day then," I promise—and I'm mostly serious. If this is the reward I receive, then I'm more than happy to keep that promise.

As she hums, a teasing smile graces her lips. "Think you can handle that?"

"Why don't I show you how perfectly I can handle that?" I cross the short distance and lock my mouth onto hers. When she tries to remove her hand from between her thighs, I shove it back down. "I didn't tell you to stop."

I swallow her moan, guide her hand along her heat, and slide my own finger inside, along with hers too. We move inside her together, our pace languid but so damn carnal. My head spins as we reach a level of intimacy we have yet to share.

Her wetness coats both our fingers, and right when I

believe she's going to burst, I clamp my hand over her mouth and plunge our connected fingers deeper inside her.

Bree's release sizzles through her, and she explodes against my body, her mouth wide open against my palm.

With no time to waste, I jerk my shorts down and yank her toward the sink. With a grip of the edge, she positions her ass out to me like a salacious offering, and I push inside her dripping heat.

I meet her gaze in the mirror as I fuck her like a wild man. I'm an animal.

This woman reaches somewhere inside me and pulls out a completely different person, one that makes me soar into space.

This is fucking paradise.

Her bottom lip pales under the firm grip of her teeth, and I smirk, feral pride coursing through me like a shot of a drug.

"Need to scream?" I groan, my own low cries on the tip of my tongue as my tightening balls slap her ass. The flesh of her cheeks is pink where I hold her, and a new wave of bliss overwhelms me.

"Yes… yes… yes." She pants through each syllable in a breathless cheer, chanting and rooting for us.

My body clenches, then falls off the edge with a reverent curse on my lips.

Her eyelids flutter, and when they finally latch on to mine in the mirror, I'm captivated.

I might have my doubts on occasion, but right now, all I can think is that this life I've created with Bree is all I need.

The woman is insatiable. She makes me want to be better. She's the reason I strive so hard to be better.

No matter what Mick or anyone else says, this is the guy

I want to be for her. This is the guy I *should* be. Someone I'm proud of, and judging from the dopey grin on my wife's face, she's happy with it too.

TWENTY-THREE

"**A**ny update from Lionel?" another accountant from our department asks, poking his head into my office. I shake my head.

And before he disappears, he offers me a disappointed frown.

I tap a pen on my desk and bite out a curse.

I'm good at a lot of things, but one quality I don't possess is patience.

How much more of this can I take?

If my boss isn't running behind on the expense reports, he's delaying his approval of vendor invoices or arriving late to our budget meetings. This morning, he's too "swamped" to discuss the quarterly taxes.

If he was truly busy, I'd be a tiny ounce's worth more

understanding, but the asshat has been in his office tweaking his short game. What makes him such an asshat is that he knows I can fucking see him through his floor-to-ceiling windows—he's putting.

He has a small green set up in his office, where he's been putting while the accounting department bites its tongue. It would be less insulting if he'd slap us right across our faces.

It's been two months of this.

I'm not one to put up with anyone's shit. When Coach yelled at me, I knew it was because he was trying to help me. The same with Mick, although he's downgraded from a motivating son of a bitch to just a son of a bitch.

They both wanted the best for me, but my current boss is essentially laughing in my fucking face.

I can't take it. My tie suddenly grows too tight, and the walls of my office feel like they're closing in on me.

I have to say something, right? Of course, I'm just a low-level accountant. Lionel is much higher on the corporate ladder. When I took this job, I unofficially agreed to stay on my own rung toward the bottom.

But it's perfectly professional to point out we're all waiting for him. I can be professional. I won't call him an asshat to his face.

Except, knowing myself, I'd take one look at his sunburned face from playing too much golf during his extended "lunch hour," and I'd tell him to fuck right off.

I *can't* say anything.

I can't risk being suspended, or worse. Getting fired is not on the horizon for me, no matter how enticing that glowing horizon might appear in my head.

With a few deep breaths, I imagine Bree and Violet—my girls always calm me down, even when they're not present. I'm doing this for them, anyway.

And it's working out great. I can't mess it up just because I'm temporarily restless.

Besides, the antsy feeling is nothing new. The nerves have been the same all month, but when I get home to Bree and Violet, nothing inside this office matters. I cling to that freeing feeling of relief and calmly walk to Lionel's office, where I knock on the door.

"Hey, boss," I say, rather proud of how even my voice remains through both words of greeting.

He taps on the pod in his ear and stands upright, his putter dangling at his side. "What's up, superstar?"

Another reason I'm so short-fused with him is because of that exact nickname. He calls me that because of my former life, which is a constant reminder of how much everything has changed and how restless I am.

I clench my teeth, nearly biting my tongue. "Any progress on the quarterly taxes? I'm about to head to lunch but wanted to check in first."

"Go on and eat. I'll have them ready for you by the time you're back." He tips an imaginary hat, but before I leave, he stops me with a wave of his hand. "Check this out," he says, getting back into a putting position over the ball with his arms bent into a diamond shape. "He shoots… and he scores. Goal!"

"Very impressive, sir," I offer with a forced smile. Good thing he's not paying attention to me, though, as he taps his ear and begins a new conversation with whoever's on the other line.

I slip away undetected and rush to lunch. As I walk along the sidewalk, basking in the fresh air, I loosen my tie, along with the top button on my shirt, and I feel better.

My bento box settles surprisingly well in my stomach, and I even have enough time for a stroll. I make it all the way to the harbor, shoulder to shoulder with a few tourists, whose cameras are held high during each step.

The Statue of Liberty appears small in the distance. Even though it's only a short boat ride away, I haven't found time to ferry over and see it up close. Has Violet? Have they been on a school field trip or something to see it?

When I first announced I'd be moving here, Slater made me a list of all the touristy places he and I never visited during our trip up here eight years ago. The Statue of Liberty was one, and I still haven't gone, although I've been living here for several months.

Then again, these last few months have felt like years with as much complicated shit as I've packed into them.

As I walk away, I draw up a mental note to sightsee in the future. To take Violet to museums and historical sites. To take Bree to romantic dinners in Manhattan like she described to Violet when we first got married.

Feeling lighter and more resolved in my life's intention, I stalk back toward the office. I'm a block away when I receive a Snapchat from Slater with an image of himself and a couple other guys from the team. They're all in jerseys, and the text over parts of their faces reads "Miss you, buddy!"

I wish a simple picture of my former life wasn't all it took to bring back my nerves.

But it sends a wave of nausea through my stomach, nonetheless, as I ride the elevator back up to my office. I shouldn't think of it as a prison, but I do since that's what it feels like today. *Most* days, in fact.

Instead of locking myself away in there, I stop by my boss's office with another knock. This time, I don't wait to be let in. "You ready for me?"

He scoffs. "What are you doing to me, Jameson? You interrupted my shot."

He's moved onto hitting his driver. The left part of his office is set up like one of the bays at a sports store where they test different clubs. A large screen of a fairway gives the impression of being outside, and set up next to it is a contraption to measure ball flight, speed, and angle.

Perfect.

"I just need to get the quarterly taxes done and was—"

"I'll have them ready for you later today."

"They need to be submitted later today. We're waiting on you before we make the necessary deposits, and the bank closes at five."

"You're really harshing my vibe over here, superstar." The grown man pouts, which takes off about fifty years of his life. He resembles a toddler.

My team is waiting on this. We've been waiting on it like this guy had no idea of the deadline, but he did. He's been reminded several times over the last two weeks.

Yet, he's in here playing golf.

So instead of marking this task off our to-do lists for the day, we're going to spend the rest of the afternoon filing for extensions, prolonging this matter when we should be doing other things. How has Lionel accomplished anything in his life with such an apathetic attitude? He exudes zero sense of urgency and motivation.

It's not the work ethic I'm accustomed to, and I don't want to become like him.

Just to piss him off, I wait until he's about to swing when I clap and announce, "I quit."

The driver, which likely cost him more than my monthly rent, flies out of his hand with a thud against the screen. "Excuse me?"

"Consider this the start of my final two weeks."

His laugh is maniacal and nothing like the carefree spirit he previously embodied, and it catches me off guard, although my resolve doesn't falter. "You can't quit," he snaps.

I scratch the side of my head with sarcasm. "That's funny because I think I just did."

We've drawn attention from the staff milling the halls, but it doesn't matter. I'm used to an audience. I'm used to thousands of rowdy fans yelling both positive and negative things at me from the stands. I don't freeze under scrutiny or criticism.

After all, this is a good thing. I'm definitely not going to freeze in fear over a good thing.

I wrap my knuckles against his door with finality and retreat. Curious stares burn holes through my back as I reach my office and get to work on the extensions.

I would leave, but I don't want to dump the workload onto the rest of the group. It's what being a team player means, whether I'm on the pitch with the guys or in a Manhattan office on the sixteenth floor.

My heart pumps with heavy, exhilarating beats, and joy washes over me like a wave from the Pacific Ocean. During the rest of the afternoon, I finish my work with fantasies of different beaches in LA. The sun setting over the water. Cyclists cruising down the boardwalk in Venice.

And I leave work with a smile on my face for the first time since I started this job.

"Work must've been memorable." Bree gives me an enthusiastic once-over.

"Hmm?" I blink.

"You're wearing the same dazed look you do after sex, especially when that sex is in the public restroom of a gym." She wiggles her eyebrows, and a twinkle sparkles in her eyes like she's peering at a diamond necklace. "When are we *meditating* again, by the way?"

I should tell her I quit my job. That's not the sort of thing I should keep a secret. It's too big to hide, and besides, we live in the same house now. This change affects us both. Or does it? We're a fake married couple, even though we're kind of a real couple. We've certainly been playing the part of one, but does she consider us real? I don't know what she thinks or wants.

Telling her about my job feels like something a real husband would do. In any case, it would be the *right* thing to do. I don't want her to find out from anyone else like she did about my past indiscretion with physical violence.

Rather than devise a speech or excuse to tell Bree what happened today during the entire commute back to Jersey City, all I did was sit back and enjoy the jostling ride, my mind in the damn clouds. It was like I was outside of my body.

How would she even respond? Would she be pissed?

If I blurt it out now, would she try to find me a different boring job? In her defense, she only did what I asked when she found me this accounting position. She suggested multiple times that I might like something in the outdoors, and she was right.

I just thought I needed to do—and *be*—someone else.

The embarrassing truth? I was trying to compete with fucking Roger.

"You name the time, and I'm always up for meditating." I wink and slide my arms around her, my nerves more skittish than a cat in the rain.

"How about a sexy shower right now?"

"I'm definitely feeling dirty." I breathe her in as I place a soft kiss on the side of her neck.

This is insane. I can't act like nothing's changed. Besides, Bree is amazing. She was crazy understanding and patient about the whole incident of my almost-felony, and she would be the same with this new piece of information.

But the former was in the past. My resignation is in the present. There's a difference.

When she rises onto the balls of her feet to kiss me, I simply cover her mouth with my own and disappear into her warmth and safety.

All thoughts of being jobless scatter, leaving nothing but desire coursing through me.

"I want to take you on a date tonight," I say in a scratchy, uneven voice. Her effect on me never ceases, and I always lose my head around her just as I lose my own voice.

Her fingers dance along the expanse of my chest as she hums, the tune reverberating between us. "What did you have in mind, Mr. Jameson?"

I tease her with the softest kiss, nuzzling my nose against hers as I say, "I'd like to keep that a surprise."

"You've convinced me," she whispers, and the sultry breath slipping between her parted lips wraps around my tongue, inviting me in.

I kiss her more fully, reveling in the special brand of salvation she offers, and I don't stop. I lead her toward the bathroom, where I turn the hot water on in the shower and strip her bare.

I escape into her heated gaze, sinful curves, and hot touches.

It's pure heaven.

And an hour later, Bree completely consumes me when she saunters into the kitchen wearing a fitted black dress that accentuates her sexy figure, a high ponytail swaying from side to side on the back of her head. The neckline dips into a *V*, teasing me with her cleavage. Also making me bite my knuckles are her fucking heels. Outside, they click along the sidewalk, each step reminding me how hard I still am for her.

"You look good enough to eat," she whispers as she slips her hand into mine.

I dip my head until my lips meet her temple. "I was just thinking the same about you."

She holds my hand the entire ride into Manhattan, where we walk side by side toward a "super cute rustic Italian restaurant," as she'd said when she'd first described it to Violet. Inside, the hostess seats us at a table next to a wooden ladder, at the top of which are organized wine bottles. They're nestled above a brick arch, and together, it all feels nostalgic somehow.

"I hope I got it right." I chuckle under my breath as I settle onto my seat across from Bree and smooth my hand over the charcoal button-up I've tucked into black slacks.

"What do you mean?" The candlelight casts a glow over her furrowed brow.

"The date you described to Violet all those weeks ago—I tried to get the restaurant right. You didn't give a name, so I got creative."

The confusion in the pinch of her thick brows smooths away as she soaks in our surroundings with visible awe.

"We're going to stop for a box of chocolates at the shop on the corner after this too, since you don't like flowers."

When she smiles, it's watery, and for a moment, I think she might cry. "This is… fucking lovely."

I grip her hand across the table next to the flitting candle and wholeheartedly live in this moment with her.

This is a time to live in the present and worry about what I've done later.

TWENTY-FOUR

Bree

It feels like I'm living in a dream.

This can't be real, right? Ever since our date a week ago, Wade's been more charming and thoughtful than ever. He's been more handsy too, much to my delight, gripping my thigh under the counter while we sip our coffees in the morning.

Showering together every day we're alone.

Kissing me extra hard each time we part ways from our commute to work. The effects of each goodbye kiss linger with me from nine to five. I don't even notice Tessa's absence since she quit anymore, although lunch still sucks without her. But not even Dan has gotten to me at all in a while.

It's been a fucking fairy tale.

When I described our date at the last margarita night, the

girls thought I was high, and truthfully, I wondered as much myself. Who even am I? I've been gushing about Wade for days, to them and anyone else who will listen.

I'd be furious with Wade for the change in me if I weren't so happy.

"How about we go to the Statue of Liberty today?" Wade asks, entering the living room, where I'm sprawled on the couch with a magazine and pen in my lap. I just finished taking a quiz while he and Violet got dressed for the day. "I've been wanting to do it ever since I got here but always have an excuse not to. Now I'm thinking, why put it off when we can do it today?"

"Sure. I thought it was going to be a lazy Sunday, but…" I close the magazine with the pen still inside and glance up at him, his bright eyes nearly blinding me. "I could do a little sightseeing."

"Me too! Daddy said we can take the boat there." Violet peeks out from behind him and scurries to sit next to me.

"Do you like boats?"

"The only one I've ever been on was my other Daddy's. He's in something called a yacht club."

"Of course he is," Wade mutters, but if Vi hears it, she doesn't seem fazed. "What do you two ladies think?" He claps with enthusiasm like he really needs to sell this.

"I'm in," Violet says without hesitation. Doesn't surprise me. She's usually up for anything, especially if it involves being outside. She's like Wade in that regard.

And ever since Wade and I got married, I've become quite the outdoorswoman myself.

Seriously, who the fuck am I?

"We're going to need sunscreen." I slide the magazine onto

the coffee table and hop up to search for the bottle of SPF 50. It's around here somewhere. It's because of all the time I've spent outside lately that I've come to realize the importance of sunscreen. As I exit the bathroom with the bottle in hand, I say, "Oh, and we should invite Gaga."

Violet pumps her little fist in the air. "The last time I saw her, she gave me ten dollars for my piggy bank."

"Ten? The most I ever got was one." Wade feigns offense.

"Sounds like I'm her favorite, then." The little girl shrugs.

"You've really changed since you turned seven and a half," he teases.

She skips to her room, tossing over her shoulder, "I need my new unicorn backpack!"

Wade sneaks a kiss to my lips while she's gone, then disappears into our bedroom. As I call Gaga, I make my way to the kitchen to clean up the rest of our bagel bar mess. The drawings of purple butterflies stuck to the fridge make me smile. Vi drew them specifically for me, and my fragile heart just about bursts every time I walk past them.

A few minutes later, Violet dances back into the kitchen with a white fuzzy bag strapped to her shoulders.

"What did you put in there?" I ask, extremely curious. I don't think I even have enough stuff to fill an entire backpack myself, and I'm the adult between the two of us. Should I have more stuff?

"My princess coloring books, crayons, headphones, and a brush. My hair always gets tangled, and Mommy says I have to keep it brushed. She says if I get too many knots, I might have to cut it short, and I do *not* want to cut it short." A hint of horror flashes across her expression, but it quickly passes. "Can we get ice cream today?" she asks.

"Of course." I lean my elbows onto the counter and meet her at eye level. "It's not a fun family day without ice cream."

Her toothy grin makes me smile even wider, especially as the joy of *family day* sinks in. That's what we are, right? No matter how this arrangement started, it's morphed into something true and beautiful.

"Until one day… I realized I wasn't pretending anymore."

That's what Gaga said about her marriage to Gilbert, the love of her life.

That's what's happening to me. I'm not simply playing the role—I *am* the wife. The stepmom. The family woman. A year ago, a day out in the sun doing something so touristy would've been a no go. It would've sounded like torture.

Today, it sounds like heaven since it's with Wade and Violet.

"Let me see how heavy this thing is." I lift up Vi's bag on her back, raising her shoulders in the process, and frown. "Are you sure you need all these things?"

"I can't leave here without them. I never know if I'm going to need to color. One time at a restaurant with pizza, my other Daddy was outside on the phone for so long, while Mommy and I waited. I didn't have anything to do, so I have to take my coloring books just in case."

I giggle. She's already learning from experience. "How about you only take one coloring book, though? That'll lighten your load quite a bit."

"Okay, but you have to help me decide." Her eyes widen like I just asked her if she'd rather give up ice cream or pizza for the rest of her life.

As we discuss the pros and cons of each—princesses vs. unicorns and other cute animals—I notice Wade leaning against the wall by the bathroom. He watches us with such obvious affection I could probably feel it from across the street.

He doesn't weigh in on the debate. Instead, he simply witnesses the scene with arms crossed and a smile tugging at his lips.

Violet and I finally settle on one, after which I convince her to leave two of the three boxes of crayons as well. *Victory.*

When we arrive at Gaga's to pick her up, she has a backpack of her own filled with snacks and a couple waters.

"I need to get me a backpack, I guess. I'm feeling totally left out," I say.

"Can we shop for one today? I want to help you pick it out." Violet holds up her tiny hands in a pleading manner. "Please, can I help you?"

"I would *love* your help, babe."

"Score! Let's go," she draws out, clearly ready to get this show on the road.

Gaga is on her heels, and before Wade and I climb into the car, he gives my ass a smack, followed by a quick squeeze. "I'm going to devour you later," he growls into my neck, and the hair back there stands with delicious anticipation.

"You're going to have to wait until tomorrow," I whisper, tilting my head toward the direction of the giggles from the back seat.

"I can be quiet if you can." He winks. "Plus, this is why there are locks on bedroom doors."

"We can't…" I narrow my eyes, but I can't deny how much I fucking want him.

I can't get enough of him, especially with this newfound energy of his. He's kicked this chemistry between us up a hundred notches.

And we were already pretty hot before.

With filthy images flashing through my mind, I walk toward the car and fan myself with my hand, a wave of heat burning through both of my cheeks.

Five hours later, thick, angry clouds roll across the sky as we enter our apartment. Vi runs straight to the windows, stretches her fingers against the glass, and watches slack-jawed as the raindrops trickle on the opposite side.

"Look at that cloud," she says, pointing in the distance. "I think I'll call it Triton, like Ariel's father. He was mean at first, but he came around. That's what the cloud is doing."

"How astute," I whisper toward Wade, who appears equally impressed by the young girl's imagination.

Our day was cut short from the unexpected weather, and although I hated the disappointment on Violet's face, it doesn't seem like it got her down for long. She's bounced into a more positive mood like her feelings are on a trampoline.

As she hums a soft tune, she's mesmerized by the streams of rain decorating the windows.

I can't help but notice how Violet finally feels comfortable with us. She seems to even look forward to returning here on our scheduled days.

Gaga has become a true grandmother to her, large birthday cards and all, although she actually writes in the little girl's. Wade felt miffed, but it was all in good fun.

She's become a grandmother to me too.

Wade seems content at home and with his new job. I had my doubts at first, convinced an office wouldn't fulfill his soul, but this week, he seems different. Happier. Less restless.

As for me, I survived an entire day of walking, getting soaked from the rain, and trying a fried pickle for the first time. Wade insisted I'm missing out on some precious gem, and I couldn't say no. After I caved, I wouldn't agree to the phenomenon he described, but the sour food was okay.

"Do you love your new backpack?" Violet spins around and beams over the new accessory she picked out for me. Unsurprisingly, it's pink with sequins. It's like something we'd find in a Disney store instead of a place on Fifth, and I proudly wore it through the city.

Slinging it off my shoulder and onto the counter, I answer with gusto, "It's perfect."

"Oh my goodness." Gaga flings a couple water droplets from her hair and trudges toward the couch. "What a day."

By the door, I hang up the two umbrellas we bought from a Walgreens we passed after the first sign of a storm. Wade and I shared one, and although it didn't keep me completely dry—a fact I tirelessly shared—I was content underneath my half because he was the one next to me.

How did he manage to completely change my perception of romance? I might even believe in happy endings, after all.

"I'm hungry. Can we have ice cream now?" Violet scurries toward me in the kitchen, seemingly unfazed by her drenched shoes. They squeak along the tile, leaving a trail of chaotic shoeprints.

"First, we need to get you changed. Then, we need actual food."

"And *then*, ice cream?" She raises her eyebrows.

"You're relentless." Behind her, Wade scoops her into his arms, his damp hair curling over his forehead. My heart sputters as he tickles Violet's sides, and her gleeful shrieks fill the apartment.

As he sets her back onto her feet, she peers up at him, curiosity pinching her brows together. "What's *relentless* mean?"

"It means you're nonstop and determined. You never give up," he explains.

"Like you?" Violet asks. "Mommy says you never give up."

Wade's smile falters a fraction, but it returns full-fledged with an air of wistfulness. "I guess I don't. Not when it comes to the people and things that matter to me."

"Hanna's relentless too." Vi bends down to retrieve a doll from her backpack. As she smooths her hand over the shiny hair, I presume this is Hanna. "She always wants to drive in her car without a roof and have lattes."

"Is that right?"

Vi nods. "Chai tea lattes are her favorite."

"Why don't you tell me more about Hanna while you change?" he smoothly offers.

Her voice wanes as they disappear into her bedroom, and I smile as I join Gaga on the couch. "I didn't know what a chai tea latte was until last year. Where does she get this stuff?"

Gaga doesn't return the playful sentiment. Instead, she turns her grave eyes on me.

"Are you okay? You can borrow some of my dry clothes and stay for dinner, if you'd like."

"I'm fine, dear." She pats my hand, but it doesn't ease my concern. "What I'd like to know is if you and Wade are okay."

A blush fills my cheeks. "We're... amazing. You were totally right when you said it would stop feeling like we're pretending."

She offers me a soft smile. I even detect a touch of nostalgia. Is she thinking about Gilbert?

"I never wanted to get married again," I continue. "But with Wade, it feels like this was always supposed to happen. You know?"

"He's hiding something," she says in a faint voice, as if she's saying it to herself.

"What do you mean?" I ask with sudden caution.

"He tells me everything, but today, when I asked how he was, he didn't answer with as much… enthusiasm as you just did. There was something off about him."

I gulp.

"I'm probably worrying for no reason. Part of my job is to worry." She pats my hand again and shakes her head. "I just thought I'd ask you as well, just in case. You both know that if you ever need anything, you can call me."

"Of course." My voice sounds far away even to my own ears.

What could any of this mean? I've been living and sleeping with Wade for weeks—could I have missed something? Sure, I've noticed a change in his mood, but it's a good one. I've been glad over the extra spark in him, but should I have been questioning it?

Wade steps out of the bedroom and clears his throat with exaggeration. "Presenting… Princess Peach!" he booms like he's an announcer at a ball game.

Violet appears in a silky pink dress that flares at the waist, and the emerald pendant around her neck glimmers like the crown on her head. It's the costume we bought right after we watched *The Super Mario Bros.*

Her smile shines as she shows off her costume, spinning slowly like a pageant contestant.

"I'm going to wear this to Halloween. I want to trick-or-treat here," Vi says.

"You got it, babe." I beam. "Are we eating dinner in the Mushroom Kingdom tonight?"

She raises her wand and uses it to tap her chin in contemplation, then nods. "I'll allow it, Mushroom Queen."

"Are you staying for dinner?" Wade asks Gaga.

With a hand on the armrest, she hoists herself up. "I should be going home. It's been a long day, and I have to put my frail old body in a warm bath."

"I'll give you a ride. And maybe some Aleve?" he thoughtfully offers.

"I have my own good stuff." She winks, and I've learned that the "good stuff" is a CBD gummy. "I don't mind taking a cab, either. Stay and have dinner in peace with your family, darling."

"How about I give you a ride home, stop by the store for noodles, and make us some spaghetti?" Wade glances at Violet and me.

"Only if you promise to also bring garlic bread," I say.

Vi shoots me an appreciative grin, and Wade bows. "As you wish, my queen."

Having a rugged man cook for me and call me queen? I can definitely get used to this, which is probably the only explanation as to why Gaga's words of worry sink to the back of my mind so easily.

TWENTY-FIVE

Wade

I mentally check off the items I need for spaghetti tonight—tomato sauce, onion, noodles, Italian seasoning, and the rest of the ingredients from the recipe I memorized at eighteen. It's easy to make and delicious, which is the best option after the full day we've had.

After the stress overwhelming me this week, a fun day with my family was exactly what I needed to lift me up. It distracted me from the fact that I still haven't told Bree I quit my job. The timing never feels right, and at this point, I figure I'll secure a new job before I come clean. In this case, I can justify my transition by explaining one led to the other.

It sounds a lot better than admitting I quit on a whim simply because my boss grated a nerve ten too many times.

It's fine. It makes sense. Bree will understand and even be happy for me.

None of this has anything to do with Mick's unanswered calls and voice mails, or Slater's pictures of the team on the bus I used to travel on alongside them.

The growing ache of the void in my gut doesn't play a part at all.

This is what I keep telling myself, anyway.

I've just added the garlic bread to my stocked cart when my phone pings with an incoming message. Thinking it's a text with a last-minute request, I smile, but it's from Violet. As I skim the short message, my good spirits quickly sink into a flustered panic. My fingers fumble to place a call, but Violet doesn't answer.

I try Bree, but she doesn't pick up, either.

I receive another message from Violet, though, saying she's at Tucker's.

What the hell is going on?

After another call to Bree goes to voice mail, I drag the full cart behind me and abandon it at the door, barely registering the cashier talking to me as I pass. I think I mutter an apology, but I can't be certain. My feet run of their own accord toward my car, and the ride to our apartment is a blur.

My heart hammers away like it's being chased as I ride up the elevator, leap into the hallway, and reach Tucker's door.

I don't pause to knock. The door is unlocked, much to my relief, and I barrel through it like a madman. But I don't know what to make of the scene in front of me.

Tucker and Bree sit side by side at the island, their knees an inch apart, and two half-empty wineglasses rest in front of them.

The smile gracing Bree's lips is genuine and—is it flirty? I blink, bringing her in and out of focus as her smile transforms into a confused frown.

"Wade?"

She sounds like she doesn't know what I'm doing here. I went to the grocery store, not to Europe, for fuck's sake. She knew I was coming right back. Yet, here she is, settled in with our neighbor.

Hot blood floods my veins, bringing me to the edge of an explosion.

Giggling erupts from the corner of the living room, where Violet and Ellie are huddled together over two iPads.

Alarm bells echo in my head. "What's going on here?" I clip, the bite in my question harsh.

"The girls are having a little impromptu playdate," Bree explains casually. It's far too damn casual. The storm brewing inside me is the exact opposite of her calm and collected state. "Since we're out of wine at our place, Tucker offered to share his, so I thought I'd hang out."

"You should've texted me to bring more. I was at the store," I state. Wasn't that an obvious thing to do? Shouldn't she have asked her *husband* for more wine before she ran to another guy like a damsel in distress?

But Bree is neither a damsel nor is she in distress, from what I can tell.

"I actually haven't seen my phone..." She half-heartedly searches the counter in front of her, but I lose my patience.

"Violet," I call out, and her smile radiates from across the room. "Why did you message me that you needed me?"

"She did?" Bree asks, sliding off the barstool. She finally displays an ounce of concern.

"Hi, Daddy!" My daughter hops onto her feet and skips over. The amount of time it takes for her to reach me probably spans across three seconds, but it feels like an eternity as I study her from head to toe for any sign of trouble.

But she looks fine. Happy, even.

"Why did you message me that you needed me right away?" I repeat, my ears ringing.

"Ellie thought it would be a fun prank. Got you!" She claps, and next to her, Ellie joins her.

But I don't share in their celebration.

"You scared the shit out of me," I bark, and the whole room freezes.

"Hey…" Bree folds her hand over my arm, and I whip it out of her grasp, anger boiling inside me and taking over.

"Let's go," I command.

"My shoes," Violet draws out as she points over my shoulder.

But my patience is on hiatus. Instead of helping her find her shoes, I scoop Violet into my arms and haul her out of here, not bothering to pause when Tucker offers apologies and promises to talk to Ellie about what happened.

"Daddy!" Violet wails.

"We'll get your shoes later," I tell her, ignoring Bree too as I stalk to my apartment. During the entire seven steps, Violet launches into a story about how a friend of Ellie's from school played this "prank" on her mom last week, and they had to try it on me.

I don't imagine the mother in question was thrilled. That is, if she's even still breathing. I almost had a heart attack myself.

We reach our own kitchen, where I set my daughter onto the counter and level her with my gaze. "Violet," I start, my breathing erratic. "I left a cart full of groceries at the store. Do you know what's going to happen to them now?"

"Another family will make spaghetti tonight. They might have a dog who eats the leftovers too," she chirps. "Do you want a dog?"

I grind my teeth.

"I think I'd name her Sparkle if you got one. And I'd give her a pink bow that matches my favorite headband. You know the one, right, Daddy?"

"*Enough*, Violet." I pound my fist onto the counter next to her and suppress the curse on my tongue.

Her eyes widen, and guilt chews on the edges of my heart.

"I'm sorry," I say, then pinch the bridge of my nose as I deeply inhale. "But I need you to understand why this so-called *prank* isn't funny and why you should never do it again to me or to Mommy." She doesn't move a muscle as I continue. "I left the cart full of food because I thought you were in danger. Now, a nice worker has to clean up the mess I left behind, and it's not fair. It's also not fair to scare Daddy like that for no reason. Do you understand?"

She nods, but she averts her gaze. If I had to guess, it's because she wants to hide the tears in her eyes, and I can't fucking stand the thought of her crying.

"Thank you," I say evenly as the door opens behind me. With my attention trained on Violet, I sweep her hair back and place a kiss to her forehead. "I'm glad you're okay."

As I hoist her off the counter, I instruct her to go into her room while I heat up leftover pizza for her. I also need to talk to Bree alone.

Once the door to her room shuts, I face Bree. "Tell your boyfriend good-bye?"

Her lips twist. "I packed up Violet's things." She holds up a pair of tiny shoes with one hand, and the beloved white backpack with a unicorn horn sticking out of the top is in the other.

I remain quiet, stewing with my rattled nerves and frustration.

This was supposed to be a Hallmark evening of cooking spaghetti after a picture-perfect day. I imagined playing a record and enjoying one another's company while the rain outside subsided, and the twinkling lights of the city flickered away.

The night would've ended with Bree and me tucking Violet into bed, as we've done so many nights in the past. Instead, I'm heating up slices of cheese pizza from yesterday while using the rest of my strength to tamp down my flustered anger.

Bree sidesteps me to toss Vi's bag onto the couch, then turns around with both arms crossed. "Ellie explained what she and Violet were up to tonight, and I'm so sorry. It must've been terrifying—"

"Yes, it was," I bite out as I go to extreme lengths to focus on the spinning plate inside the microwave. "I thought something horrible had happened, and I raced home to find you and Tucker cozied up in his apartment, giggling into your fucking wineglasses like you were on a date."

In my periphery, she steps up to the counter, but she doesn't say anything.

"I believe you referred to him as Officer Hot Ass, didn't you?" I finally turn to face her as the microwave dings, punctuating my accusatory tone.

Confusion darkens her amber eyes, until understanding

finally dawns. "Oh my God—that was a stupid joke I made forever ago. Harper was—"

Violet emerges from her room, the princess costume from before switched out for a pair of pink shorts and a white T-shirt with a glittery rainbow on the front. She and her little outfit are painfully cheery, especially compared to the rain clouds hovering over me and my mood. They're much like the ones casting a shadow over the city outside.

I stand up straighter as she tiptoes to the bathroom like she did when she showed me her ballerina moves yesterday, and even the nice memory does nothing to curb my outrage.

As soon as we hear the sink turn on, Bree hisses, "Are you jealous? Is that what this insanity is about?"

"This is about Violet. I thought she was in trouble, and you didn't answer your phone because you were too busy playing house with the neighbor and *my* daughter. You should've asked me before going over there with her in the first place. What if Maggie had popped in unexpectedly like she's done before and found you next door? Our entire cover would've been blown."

She flinches, but as quickly as it happens, it disappears. *Did I imagine it?*

Bree's lips tighten as she says, "I'm sorry, okay? I'm truly sorry I didn't answer your calls. I left my phone in my purse, and I forgot about it. But it wasn't because there's anything going on with Tucker and me. There's *not*," she asserts, clipping the last word like my insinuation offends her.

"It's not that insane, is it?" I laugh humorlessly over the muffled sound of the running bathroom sink. "It's what Bree Finley does, right? A random one-night stand is how you and I met, for Christ's sake."

"I cannot believe you're throwing that in my face, especially since you're no fucking better. You had plenty of your own one-night stands before me too, but that doesn't change what's been happening here the last couple of months." She sears her hurt gaze onto me. "Or is this marriage still fake to you? Is that the *cover* you feared I'd blow? Because it hasn't felt fake to me, not when you were railing me in every room of the apartment and elsewhere. Or, have you just been having your cake and eating it too?"

Violet emerges from the bathroom, seemingly oblivious as she saunters back into her bedroom.

We shouldn't be out here arguing like this, not since she's within earshot, but this conversation with Bree is long overdue. We should've talked about what's happening between us a long time ago, but I didn't want to ruin it. It's always my excuse, isn't it? I never want to face the less-than-stellar parts of myself or my life because I'd rather assume the happy-go-lucky ruse she and I have created.

Pretending is much better than facing the truth.

We've been talking for thirty seconds, and already, it feels like our blissful happy place is burning to the ground.

"What's going on, Wade?" Bree presses. "Because this isn't you. What aren't you telling me?"

"I quit my job a week ago." I lean against the counter, equally relieved and terrified by the confession. I'm glad it's out there, but I'm not looking forward to the backlash.

And if her fierce frown is any indication, I'm not going to like what happens next one bit.

"Why?" she asks, and the simple question holds layers of caution and foreboding.

All I can offer is a shrug because in all honesty, I don't

know how to explain it. What if saying the real reason out loud solidifies what I fear the most—that I'm not capable of being the man, father, and husband I've been striving so damn hard to embody? What if I'm not cut out to live this life I've worked tirelessly for months to build?

"Let me see how you responded to Mick," she says, breaking the tense silence.

"What?"

"You mentioned Mick has been harassing you to go back to soccer. What have you told him? Because I'm not convinced you've refused whole-heartedly enough. Otherwise, why would he continue bothering you? He could be using his energy on other potential players, instead."

"He's just a selfish ass, okay? It's what he does. He bullies his way through the industry, and—"

"Show me your fucking phone."

I don't have to hand it over. It's clear she already knows what I've done.

"That's what I thought." The small, painful smile Bree gives me takes great effort, I imagine. "What do you want, Wade?"

I furrow my brow.

"What do you want from me? From this?" She points between us, and although she keeps her voice down, it speaks volumes. "You came to *me*. You asked for my help, and I've given it to you. I didn't ask for any of this. You're the one getting more out of our agreement than I am, anyway, but I wanted to help. I've changed my whole life for you and Violet. I've done nothing but try—"

"I'm sorry this has all been such a chore for you," I snap and lunge forward, suddenly defensive. She never wanted this, it's true. I'm the one who trapped her here. It *is* my fault, but the bite in her tone strikes a chord. "I'm sorry I ever asked you to marry me. Is that what you want to hear?"

She shoves me backward until my shoulder hits the wall. "You are such an asshole," she snaps as Violet's door opens, and her tiny socked feet step out.

"Is the pizza warm yet?" she asks, the picture of innocence a direct contradiction to our crumbling world.

With a burning lump lodged in my throat, I nod and get back to work on her sad little dinner. When I turn around, Bree is gone. She would've nudged passed me had she left the apartment entirely, so my best guess is that she's hiding in our room.

I don't even blame her. This is a fucking disaster.

"Why don't you eat this in your bed while I read you a story?" I ask Violet, anxious to distract her from any uncomfortable tension out here.

"Mommy never lets me eat in bed."

"Well, I say it's fine, just this once. A special treat for tonight only. What do you think?"

Her eyes sparkle like I just announced we're going to Disney World.

In her room, she picks a book from the shelf on the wall. I read with great difficulty, the words bitter as I mentally replay my fight with Bree over and over again.

As I turn each page, I strain to listen for the door, hoping and praying she doesn't leave before we have a chance to talk more.

To resolve this.

To go back to how we were today while we made funny faces for countless selfies.

We were so in tune and carefree. Bree's rosy cheeks and genuine smile made me whole.

I turned it all to hurt and regret, and we barely even scratched the surface of all our issues.

No matter how big of a dick Mick has been to me, I never answered him. I wanted to cuss him straight to Hell, but I didn't. I didn't even unleash a fraction of the havoc on him that I should have.

I left the door open to soccer, but I didn't mean to. I hadn't even realized what I'd been doing until I quit my job and never started looking for another.

I should've sent out resumes. Made calls. Involved my own wife in the process. Instead, I've been commuting into the city with Bree and spending my days in the park, Times Square, anywhere. I wander around daydreaming of the team. Of sweating my ass off at practices and games with the guys.

I've been fantasizing about LA and the life I used to live there—the old me led a grueling but simple life.

"What do you want, Wade?"

I know what I should've said when Bree asked. That I want all of this with her, because I do. The words should've easily left my mouth.

Instead, I stood there like a damn coward. Why? Why couldn't I fucking say it?

How do I fix this?

TWENTY-SIX

I shared my umbrella with him.

He has no appreciation or respect for everything I've done for him, including the fact that I shared my motherfucking umbrella with him today.

I huff out a watery exhale as I zip my packed suitcase shut, the sound echoing in the otherwise quiet room. It even briefly muffles the rain, which falls harder now.

My phone lights up with a message from Madison, agreeing to do me the biggest favor ever, and my eyes blur with unshed tears.

"I'm sorry I ever asked you to marry me."

The proposal wasn't real. It didn't come from a place of deep-rooted love and affection. It was a desperate plea for his own reasons, none of which involved feelings for me.

I know all that. But his harsh words tonight left craters on my heart, nonetheless.

After everything we've been through, I never expected him to turn on me like this, but I should have. I shouldn't be blindsided like I am now. There have been signs—God, there have been a million signs. From the moment we met, he's held one foot onto an escape route. While I've been reveling in hopes of a happily ever after like a lovesick chump, he's been making plans for himself.

Plans to leave.

I wheel my packed suitcase out of the bedroom and sink onto the couch, my eyelids fluttering as his muffled voice washes over me. He's reading to his daughter, and it's so sweet, my heart aches.

But I can't get sucked in.

Not anymore.

He's played me for the last time.

I busy myself with the outside pockets of my suitcase, tossing away boarding passes and other trash from past trips. I packed in a hurry. I probably shoved countless mismatched outfits inside in my haste, but who cares? I'm not sure how long I'll be living elsewhere, but in that time, it's not like I'll be worrying about my clothes.

I have no doubt my thoughts will be consumed with Wade. Violet. Gaga.

They've become my world, but after this swift kick to the groin of my relationship with Wade, I need space. And he obviously does too.

Violet's door sneaks open, and Wade's tall frame obscures it as he shuts it closed.

With one look at me, he stops in his tracks, his shoulders

hunched. "I'm surprised you're still here."

"One of us has to be the mature grown-up, and it clearly isn't you."

"I deserve that."

"You do, but why exactly do you think you deserve it?"

He walks toward me, but I hold a hand up to stop him from getting so close I can smell his cologne.

Space. We need space.

"I was a dick before." His boundless blue eyes frown, the depths of them full of turmoil. "I'm not sorry I asked you to marry me. Not one fucking bit, and I'm sorry I said it. I was just so… angry."

"Just because you're sorry you said it out loud doesn't make it any less true."

"I didn't mean it. I swear, Bree."

I fold my hands at my waist, stepping in front of my bag. "I know how I used to live before you and I met. One-night stands were my thing. Part of my personal brand, even. I understand how hard it might be to trust me and my intentions, but I thought I'd earned it. After everything we've been through, I thought you valued and respected me enough to return the effort. To tell me when you quit your job. To allow me to be part of that decision since it does affect us both."

"You're right, and I'm sorry for that too. But I don't know how to do this. I don't know how to be someone I'm not." Grimacing, he scratches his head and paces. "I've never been in a serious relationship. You and I must've skipped at least twenty steps. I mean, you met my daughter before we ever went on a proper first date. You met my grandma on our wedding day. We slept together before all that when I didn't even know your last name. It's all been such a complicated mess."

"But we were figuring it out together—that's the difference between our past and this week. We made those decisions *together*," I point out. There are so many things I could say. So many ways to rationalize everything we've done leading up to this moment, but it wouldn't change the solemn truth. I drop my shoulders and all my defenses. "You know what? Maybe you're right too. I inserted myself completely into your life, held your hand through all the changes you've made, and never asked if you even wanted me to do any of that. We never discussed what we wanted after so much changed. You asked for a fake marriage, and somewhere along the way, I gave you a real one before I ever realized it. I believed it had become real, but obviously, you don't agree."

"That's not true."

"Isn't it? You've had one foot out the door for months, Wade. The night we met, you never wanted to see me again. You wanted my number for logistical reasons since you admitted you weren't in a place to initiate an ongoing relationship. When you proposed to me, you just needed a wife, and I was the convenient choice, not only because we'd already slept together but because you didn't even know other women in the city."

The corners of his lips droop into a sad frown as he slumps against a barstool.

"These last couple of months have meant something to me. I might've never wanted another marriage, but you've turned my world upside down. You've made me happy, Wade," I whisper, my voice heavy and unsteady with emotion. "But I can't trust this hasn't all been part of the charade for you.

That you didn't simply get caught up in the roles we've been playing for the world. And I…" I swallow back my confession with painful difficulty, settling instead on, "I feel too much for you to be yet another convenient, practical choice. I've been duped in the past, and I never want to be someone's temporary partner. I want to be someone's everything, always, forever."

His face twists. "What are you saying?"

"I don't miss my old life, Wade, but it sounds like you do," I start and bite my lip as my stomach sinks.

This is much harder to do than I thought.

While I packed my stuff moments ago, I was furious, and it probably would've been easier on my heart to simply walk out rather than face him like this.

But it's too late. This is the right thing, anyway, no matter how brutal it is.

"The only thing I miss is soccer," he admits. "I miss the sport and being part of the team."

I nod. That's not so bad. It's understandable, even. But the thought of him going back and traveling so much—the thought of him disrupting our balanced life here—weighs on my chest.

Is that selfish of me?

"I'm not practical and responsible like Tucker. I'm not stable and boring like Roger. I don't know how to do this, but I know soccer." His cloudy eyes clear as he continues. "What's so wrong with me returning to it? Plenty of professional athletes are parents and spouses too. They make it work, so why shouldn't I at least try? You and I can stay married. We can be Violet's happy parents—together. And I can stop wondering what could've been."

"You totally can, but you know good and well that's not what this is about." I sigh, my temples throbbing. "This is still a decision you have to make, and it can't be a choice I make for you. I can't tell you how to live your life."

I can't tell you to stay.

To pick us.

To love me like I love you.

The unspoken confessions vibrate through my head, each excruciating echo pinching the walls around my thundering heart.

I can't make him do anything, and I don't want to. I thought this thing between us was as genuine and natural as the ocean, wind, or green grass. That our connection was almost earthly—the way of the universe.

But I've had it all wrong.

I reach for my suitcase, which is when his gaze falls on it for the first time. "You're leaving." There's a hint of a question in his voice, but it's also a statement. "Where are you going?" he asks my back as I reach the door.

"We need to get our shit together, and we need space to do it. So, I'll be staying at Madison's for a few days."

"In LA?"

"She and Ian bought an apartment in the city for when they visit. They're heading back west in the morning, but they've agreed to let me stay there for as long as I need."

He sighs as if it pleases him to know he didn't force me to the other side of the country, although he doesn't deserve such relief. He's just lucky I'm too attached to the bagels, my friends, and a ton of good pizza around here.

"What am I supposed to tell Violet? She's going to ask why you're gone in the morning."

"You can figure something out." I drag myself through the door and shut it as a lone tear skids down my cheek.

A slice of guilt cuts through my chest. None of this is Violet's fault, and she shouldn't have to suffer from it. Leaving her guts me, but I meant what I said.

Wade and I need space to decide what this marriage will look like in the future.

One thing's for certain as far as I'm concerned—I don't know how I'll continue being married to him if he decides he's not in love with me.

Is he in love? Has any of our time together meant anything to him? I said so myself that it felt too good to be true, and it fucking was.

I jinxed it. I pushed and pushed until I finally ruined it.

Was my mom right about me? Do I drive men away?

More tears flood my cheeks as I tense in front of the elevator.

"Bree?" Tucker appears next to me. At the sound of concern in his voice, I furiously swipe under my eyes, but it's no use. "What's wrong?"

"Nothing." I shake my head and clutch my suitcase like it's a life raft. "I'm just going to stay with a friend for a few days. She, um…" I clear my throat in an attempt to rid my voice of its tremble. "She just bought a new place and needs help… decorating."

He tilts his head, wearing an expression of doubt.

"I just have to go," I say, fighting a losing battle with my lake-sized tears.

"I was coming over to apologize for tonight. I'm so sorry we caused you two grief, but I didn't realize it was this bad."

"It's not you. Wade and I need to figure some things

out." Since I don't know how much Wade's told him of our arrangement, I leave it at that.

"If a couple can work through anything, it's you two," he bravely—and naively—reassures me. He clearly doesn't know the truth. "I've never seen two people so in love. The way he looks at you is like—"

Another sob breaks loose, muffling out his kind words. I can't hear any more of this. "Thank you, but I should go."

"Please call if you need anything."

Nodding, I step onto the elevator and let my head fall back as I exhale.

It doesn't give me any relief, and neither does the fresh, post-rain air.

I don't imagine a full night's sleep will help, either, not that I could take advantage of such a luxury in my current state. My head spins as I duck into a cab, which puts several miles of distance between Wade and me.

My chest squeezes at the thought of Violet waking up in the morning, and I'm not there to see her off to school.

And I cry some more over how easily such a perfect life was shattered.

TWENTY-SEVEN

Bree

The smell of spicy seasoning tickles my nostrils. The sizzle of hot fajitas buzzes through me. Soft chatter hums from the tables next to ours. It all means one thing—it's margarita night.

And for the first time in years, I don't want to be here. Of course, I love seeing my friends. The bitches mean everything to me, and if anyone could cheer me up right now, it's them.

But I don't want to be in public. I could barely muster enough energy to throw a bra on, let alone enough joy to blend in, and I don't want to talk about what happened with Wade. It all imploded less than a week ago, so it's still too raw and agonizing.

As soon as the sweet and tangy strawberry margarita touches my lips and the flavor bursts on my tongue, I do feel slightly comforted. It's crazy how such a simple, sassy drink can be so uplifting.

"When it comes to all the bartenders of the city, you must be God's favorite," I tell Harvey.

"You and your compliments." He shakes his head, but he doesn't leave without tossing me a wink. It's the same game we've always played—a compliment here, a flirtatious wink there. It's all in good fun.

Was there a point in my life when I'd gladly ride the Harvey train? Sure. He's younger, but evidently, age doesn't stop me from enjoying myself.

But Micah, his ex *and* current girlfriend, showed up out of nowhere and won a date with him at a bachelor auction, during which she whisked him off into the sunset.

It's much like Wade did to me. He swept me off my freaking feet when I wasn't paying attention.

"Fuck," I mutter into my glass after halfway draining it, and the other girls haven't even arrived yet. I got here early in hopes of stewing without witnesses—the strangers surrounding me don't count—but it's not working.

"Strawberry, huh?" Tessa eases onto the seat across from me. "I'm not surprised."

The only answer I offer is a glare over my glass. We save the strawberry flavor for the nights we're feeling feisty, mango is for celebrations, and the classic lime is for every other night. We've really only ever needed those three.

"How are you feeling?" she asks with a wince.

"Like a mix between the worst hangover I've ever had and the time I had mono in high school."

She and I already talked about the whole mess at lunch yesterday. My angel friend met me at our favorite spot for old time's sake. This was after I'd already relayed the sad story in detail to Madison. I stayed with the fiery redhead, after all, so I couldn't escape her. Erin called too, so everyone's caught up.

If only they could advise me on ways to deal with the fallout. Then again, Wade and I are not *over* over, right? I shouldn't start moving on since it can't be the end. We had a stupid fight. Every couple has them, and ours was no different.

But that might just be the optimistic bitch inside me talking. I don't freaking know anymore.

I haven't even heard from Wade. Vi, on the other hand, called me this morning from her iPad while her dad was in the shower.

It's only been a few days, and I miss them.

Madison's apartment is nice enough—far nicer than the one I used to live in alone—but it's lacking a tattooed hunk and a sweet little girl. Without them, nothing feels like a home to me anymore.

"You started without me?" Erin appears with a pout.

"If it makes you feel better, I did pour each of you a glass while I drank mine," I say with a mock innocent shrug.

Out of instinct, I check the door behind her in search of Madison, then remember she's in LA. Will I ever get used to that? She's been living there for several months. My habit of hoping she'll fill the fourth chair every Thursday should've died down by now, but still, I expect her badass black boots to stomp in here and complete our circle.

"Cheers…" Tessa leaves the single word hanging like it's a question—as if she's afraid to have any fun right now.

I roll my eyes and clink my glasses to theirs, exaggerating my enthusiasm. One thing I hate more than cheesy pickup lines and choppy haircuts is pity.

And these two are not hiding theirs very well. I've worked long and hard to ensure no one ever felt sorry for me again. After my divorce, the entire town felt sorry for me. Looking back now, I know they meant well, but as a twenty-year-old, the sad glances and even sadder "chin up" pies were gut-wrenching and humiliating.

I never wanted to feel that way again, but I'm not the same young girl I was then. I'm grown, and I have the spankable ass and perky tits to prove it.

Besides, these are my closest friends. They care about me and want to see me happy. I should at least meet them halfway and talk about it. They obviously want me to.

"When I woke up, six eyelashes fell onto my fingers, and I bumped my head on the shelf right above me. I'm not sure I don't have a concussion." I rub my head for good measure.

"Wait, there's no shelf above the bed at Madi's. How did you hit your head?" Tessa's far too logical brain asks at the same time that Erin asks if I'm okay.

"I fell asleep on the couch after eating an entire pint of Ben & Jerry's, okay? The drool on my chin definitely had some melted ice cream in it, and when I woke up, I hit my head on the shelf. In my defense, they hung that thing too fucking low. But is that what you want to hear right now? Way to kick me while I'm down." I eye the two women, and only silence answers me. Turning to Erin, the earth goddess, I ask, "What does the eyelash thing mean? Am I going to suffer for much longer—what is it like, a day of pain for each lash?"

"How am I supposed to know? I'm not some worshipper of eye gods. I'm not insane," she insists with a flip of her hand.

I can't help but scoff. "You once performed a ritual for a dead spider, who deserved to be in Hell for its mere existence, so…"

"We co-exist with all creatures on this planet. We each play an important role in order to keep it spinning. If one of us goes, the ecosystem suffers, and if too many of us go, then what will be left of this world?" Erin tosses back, her eyes wide and annoyingly serious.

She might have a point, but I'm not in the mood to discuss the greater good. Not when my heart is at stake.

As if reading my mind, Tessa chimes in. "While we agree with you as your friends and fellow humans, I don't think this is the time for a TED talk. But I'm organizing a charity event to benefit New Hampshire estuaries, so feel free to attend and talk about it there."

"What's the date?" Practically in the same breath, Erin adds, "Doesn't matter. I'm totally there."

Tessa claps, then transforms her expression back into one of pity. "Talk to us," she says to me.

I blow out a glum breath, the loose hair over my eye swaying with little zest. "Could the eyelash thing be a sign I push guys away?"

"No. That wouldn't make sense." Erin shakes her head, again entirely too serious, even though I'm partly kidding.

"And spitting on a rose for good luck does?" I blink, recalling a very specific afternoon where she did just that. My quirky friend is superstitious to the max, and just because she spit on one plant, after which it lived longer than expected, she's done it every spring since.

"Touché."

"You don't push guys away, honey." Tessa squeezes my hand. "From what you've said, Wade just doesn't seem to know what he wants, although from what I can tell, he does want you."

"I think he just wants it all," Erin adds.

"Agreed." Tessa nods, and my gaze bounces back and forth as they debate Wade's motivations. "He wants to be a present father, a loving husband, and a busy professional soccer player, all of which would fulfill him."

"But is it all possible? That's the problem."

"I don't personally believe it is. Violet is young, and she's about to start getting busy with more extracurriculars, most of which he'd miss while traveling the country."

"I mean, sure, it would be fun for her too since she'd have the chance to travel with him during the summer. She'd see amazing places."

"But would Maggie even allow it? Three months ago, the woman wouldn't let her stay at Wade's apartment, which is in the same state. I don't see her letting Violet leave the state without her."

"Very true."

"When is it okay for me to join this conversation?" I pipe up, dizzy from their exclusive back-and-forth. Not even professional ping-pong players volley as quickly and naturally as these two have debated my predicament the last few minutes.

I just wish I was actually on the outside of this, but lucky fucking me—I'm right in the middle.

"Of course!" Erin chirps as Tessa waves for me to say my piece.

"I was married once before Wade," I blurt. In truth, I'd forgotten all about this secret I've kept from them, because I was too wrapped up in my newest marriage.

Wade is nothing like Sonny, and I don't regret leaving my ex. There's a lot of blame to be placed solely on his sorry ass, but it changed me. Because of him, I became untrusting. It's why one-night stands became my safety net. I couldn't get hurt if I didn't leave room for it. If I never got attached, I was free to do whatever I wanted with whomever I chose, as were they.

But Wade's different. Being with him has been so different, and I feel more for him than I ever did for anyone else in the past. Did I push myself onto Wade to avoid giving him an opportunity to wander?

"I'm sorry—what did you say?" Tessa squints like she's trying to study me from a distance instead of only two feet away.

"I don't understand," Erin says.

With a sigh, I explain, "I married my high school boyfriend when I turned eighteen, and I left him two years later because he was sexting some hussies around town."

Blank stares land on me.

"No matter how hard I've tried to be a better person since then, I don't think I've accomplished as much as I thought. I just traded in one habit for another. Instead of giving Wade space to do his thing like I did with Sonny, I went the complete opposite and smothered the poor guy like a fucking psycho."

Still, they don't look away, nor do they move at all.

"I hate questioning myself. I've lived the way I have in order to avoid such harsh introspection, but that's why I'm in this mess, isn't it?" I lament as I gulp from my glass. Licking the familiar flavor from my bottom lip, I scoff. "You couldn't stop talking a minute ago, and now you have nothing to say?"

"You were fucking married before, and we're just now finding out about it?" Tessa holds her hands up, palms out. "What the hell? I need a minute to process."

"I don't have a minute," I shoot back. "I need your help. Put on your little thinking caps and light bulbs and give me your best advice. At the very least, please tell me I'm not completely screwed. I'm losing my shit here."

I'm barely done pleading with them when Erin—little miss perfect—dumps the half-full basket of chips in my lap.

"You… bitch," I breathe, disbelief filling my entire body. "What the…"

"You deserve it for keeping secrets." Erin folds her arms across her chest and rests her back against the seat.

Dumbfounded, I stare at my friend until one of us cracks. Tessa is the first to explode into laughter, and Erin soon follows. I can't help my own giggle, either.

I can always count on these two to make me smile—and keep me honest. If Madi were here, she'd have probably taken the good-natured attack a step further and poured the leftover margarita on my head.

And they'd all be right to do it. I've kept things from my friends because I didn't want to face the painful parts of my past. I didn't want them to ruin the life I've built here in the city, but I was wrong.

If I would've opened up and dealt with my issues years ago, maybe I wouldn't be in this predicament. Playing the *what-if* game will get me nowhere, though.

"Start from the *very* beginning," Tessa commands, folding her hands on the table in front of her.

"Okay, but we're going to need a new pitcher and a broom." I point around us, then signal for Harvey.

He takes one look at the mess in my lap and tsks. "You ladies always keep things interesting."

"That's why you love us." I shrug as I scoop up the chips

back into the basket and order another strawberry margarita.

We spend the rest of the night recounting my life pre-New York. I've been called chatty on more than one occasion, but I give the word a whole new meaning tonight. I'm like a broken dam—the truths spill out of me without restraint.

Although I'm exhausted by the end of it, my heart is also lighter.

I needed this. They might not respond with advice I haven't received before, but simply being open and honest is cathartic in ways I never expected.

There's just one other thing I need to do too.

One that requires my suitcase yet again.

TWENTY-EIGHT

"**V**iolet is at a friend's house," Maggie says, half her body obscured by the door. "Roger is picking her up on his way back from work. They'll be here any minute."

"That's fine," I mutter.

"Thank you for coming here to get her. I would've dropped her off at your place, but my car is in the shop. Something about the brake pads. I usually let Roger handle all that." She laughs, but it barely registers, as if I've forgotten the simple act altogether.

When was the last time I fucking laughed?

"If you ever need help with your car, I'm happy to take a look." I flex my jaw, and although my offer is genuine, the gruff edge makes it sound like I'm angry about it.

"Um, thanks." She tucks her hair behind both ears, then nudges me out onto the pretentious porch. They don't have any comfortable furniture out here, so I can't imagine they appreciate this space as they should. Roger probably takes his pompous calls out here while petting the white wooden chairs as a Bond villain might. There's no way he sits in them. They're too damn pristine to be used.

"What's up?" I bite out again, but I swear I don't mean anything by it.

I'm just so tired. I've been out of work for a few days, and I haven't made any progress on finding another job. Part of my argument with Bree was over my career path, and I have yet to address any of it on my own.

Half of me is angry with Bree for making me feel like I have to choose between her and the sport my entire life has revolved around. I have a fucking soccer ball inked on my chest, for crying out loud.

Of course, she didn't explicitly give me such an ultimatum, but it was there, lingering between the lines of what we said.

The truth is, if I pursue soccer, there's a good chance I'll lose Bree in the process. Would she be able to handle the long days of practice? The traveling schedule? The early bedtimes and strict diets? It wasn't a big deal when I was single. It was the perfect lifestyle for me back then, but that was before I got a taste of this new routine.

And what about Violet? I'd have to rearrange the custody schedule to include a lot less time with her, and the thought makes me nauseas.

I've been a jumbled ball of nerves for days.

Maggie leaves the door ajar as she fidgets with her hair some more. "It's probably none of my business, but you look like shit."

She has a point, but instead of making a joke or settling her concern, I pin her under a warning glare.

"You don't have to tell me the details, but for Violet's sake, are you okay?"

A sting jabs at my chest like a needle. "I'm fine." As she inches away, I stop her and blurt, "I lied."

"I know. You're clearly *not* fine, no matter what you say."

"Not about that."

"What do you mean?"

I spin in place as my mind turns in circles too. I didn't come here to spill my guts to Maggie. I've never wanted to confide in her about anything, and I sure as hell never intended to confess what I've done—how fake my marriage really is.

But she's right. For Violet's sake, I need to be okay, and maybe… maybe coming clean to Maggie will lift some of the guilt from my shoulders.

Because I have felt guilty for lying to Maggie. Our lives will forever be intertwined, and I'd hate myself for carrying this secret long into the future. Besides, there's a harrowing chance Bree won't be around for much longer, and how will I explain it then?

"I lied about Bree. About our marriage. About us," I stammer. "We are legally married, yes, but it's not real. We're not actually together. I just needed her in order to show you and the judge that I can provide a stable home for Violet."

The only reaction I get from Maggie is pursed lips.

"I should've told you the truth. If I'm honest, I shouldn't have gone through with it in the first place. I was just so desperate. I'd do anything for our daughter, and I only want what's best for her. Bree has been a saint with her too. I think she's been good for her, and me," I ramble like a frantic maniac.

"And what did you plan for the long run?" she asks, her tone a little too even for my liking. She should be throwing these perfect chairs at my head. I'd be happy to dent them. At the very least, she should be yelling at me for pulling such an idiotic stunt.

"I planned on proving I'm a capable and loving father, so when Bree and I eventually split, you wouldn't consider another custody battle. You'd be comfortable with me caring for Violet on my own." I blow out a breath. "And damn it, I am a good father to her, Maggie. I'm not perfect by any means. Sometimes, I forget the sunscreen while we're at the park, and I cuss on occasion because I forget her little ears hear everything. But as you can see, there's nothing I wouldn't do for her."

"I know," she whispers so quietly, I almost don't pick up on it. Then again, I could just be imagining the compliment. I need one now more than ever, so it's possible I conjured up a fake one.

"I'm sorry?"

"You are a great father," she says more loudly. "You are fun and gracious with her. You and I might've had our fumbles with communication in the beginning, but I think we've even found our own rhythm too."

"We have, haven't we?" I whisper, still slightly terrified to believe this is really happening.

She nods with a hint of a smile on her lips. "As you know, I wasn't your biggest fan at first, but it didn't take long for you to win me over. Bree actually helped your case a lot, even if I wasn't so sure about her at first, either."

A breath of relief shoots out of my mouth, and fucking tears sting the backs of my eyes. I've been waiting to hear this from Maggie for so long, and I didn't even realize how badly I needed it until now. I've been feeling so lousy and confused, but hearing it from Violet's mom—my biggest critic—sends a shot of consolation through my tense veins.

"For the record, I didn't want to take you to court at all. I was prepared to settle it with only our lawyers present instead of the spectacle it became, but Roger insisted."

My eye twitches.

"Don't get me wrong—I totally see his side, and I agree with him to an extent. He has been Violet's father for years before we tracked you down. Even so... after you and I reconnected, I started to feel for you too. I wanted you to have your chance to be her father. I couldn't live with myself if you didn't."

Now, the tears really will burst through the dam of strength I'm holding them back with. I'm about to crumble.

"And I'm sorry for putting you through that. It's just very complicated." Her own voice turns watery.

"It is." I nod. "But since we're being honest, I've never liked Roger."

This earns me a shaky laugh.

"I do respect him for what he's done in my absence, though," I force out as best I can.

It's hard for me to admit, but it is true. Without Roger, Violet wouldn't have had a father figure in her life before I entered the picture, and he really has gone above and beyond for her. The crisp suit-wearing bore truly loves her.

Even though it's not a competition, I, the hoodie-wearing mess, love her too, and I'm glad Violet has both of us to lean on.

After a beat, I hesitate to ask, "So, you're not mad?"

"About your feelings toward Roger, or your lie about Bree?"

"Both?"

Maggie giggles again and shakes her head.

"Really?" Color me fucking shocked.

"I'm not mad about Bree because I think the only lie you're telling is how you actually feel about her." She takes me by the shoulders and gives each a gentle shake. "I don't know what's going on between you. I'm guessing she's the reason you look like shit, and it's safe to assume it's because you were an ass, but it's—"

"This isn't solely *my* fault."

"I didn't say it was, but we have to start somewhere. I'm starting with you because you clearly won't."

I bite back a curse.

Then she asks me for the whole story, and I oblige, supplying the quick version. We have some time to kill while we wait for Violet, anyway.

At the end, I'm sweating as I ask, "What do you think?"

She doesn't immediately answer. Instead, she spends a good few moments chewing on her bottom lip and studying me. Finally, she says, "You don't know what your priorities are anymore."

"My priority is Violet."

"Sure, but what else?" she presses.

"A job I enjoy. If I can figure that out, it's what would be best for Violet because I won't be such a miserable ass all the time. It's what I need to explain to Bree. She'd understand that."

The sympathetic smile she gives is mixed with pity, and it pisses me off.

"What? I'm not wrong."

"Look, I think you try too hard to justify your actions. You take great lengths to prove what you say and do is right, even if it's not."

"I don't do that." What the hell? I've only ever tried to prove I can be a decent man, but what about what I want?

Oh…

I'm totally doing exactly what she's saying, aren't I?

"You literally just did it a few minutes ago," she says. "When you told me you've been lying about your marriage, you didn't even apologize. You spent most of that time explaining why you married Bree when you should've focused on what really mattered—your remorse. The acknowledgment that you did something wrong by lying and that you are sorry for it. That's it."

I hang my head and finally let out the curse I've had locked away since I showed up here.

"Find her, Wade. Do whatever it takes to make this right because when I see you two together, it's anything but fake." She grips my shoulders again. "You love her, and she loves you. You just don't know where you stand or how to move forward. The uncertainty scares the shit out of you both."

"*Ooohh*, Mommy said a bad word!" A high-pitched squeal sounds from behind me, and we both jump. Violet appears next to us on the porch. When did she get here?

Roger holds her little hand as he guides her up the steps, and it's nice. What isn't so nice is the way he eyes me. He's apprehensive, and he has every right to be, especially since I don't love the guy.

But after my conversation with Maggie and the understanding we've indirectly reached, I believe he and I can be civil. Polite, even. For the sake of Violet.

"I'm sorry about that, but your dad and I were having a private conversation. You weren't supposed to hear it." Maggie dots Violet's nose with her pointer finger and smiles. "Let's go inside and grab your things."

A few minutes later, with her bag in hand, I guide Violet to the car. Once she's settled inside, I meet Maggie at the front. "I am sorry," I say, fingering my keys as I retreat.

Never in a million years would I have believed her to be the one to help me out after how unfair I've been. I played her, but she still offered me sound and patient advice. If our positions had been switched, I hate to say I might not have returned the sentiment.

And again, I probably would've justified it to myself, even though I would've been in the wrong.

Jesus. I still have a lot of growing up to do, don't I?

TWENTY-NINE

Bree

"**I**'m in love with my fake husband." I storm past Harper into the narrow hallway of the house, but my steps falter as I'm hit with an onslaught of memories.

Somehow, even after all these years, it still smells like Grandma in here.

As I inhale, the hint of lavender fills my senses. She'd always burn lavender candles, and once I round the corner into the kitchen, I'm happy to find Harper still burns them too.

I slide the tip of my finger along the bottom level of the two-tiered counter, and although I'm heartbroken, I can't help the smile tugging on the corners of my lips.

The irony isn't lost on me that this is exactly where I ran after I couldn't take Sonny's antics. I was drowning in my own tears, and this is where Gran pulled me out from under the crushing weight of my reality.

All I can hope for now is that Harper can do the same for me.

"What do you mean by *fake*?" She wraps her fingers around my arm and drags me out of the kitchen and into the living room.

As we plop onto the couch, I notice one big change to the cottage-style house, which was originally built in the twenties. "When did you add a sliding barn door?" I point to the rustic addition separating this area and the main bedroom. In the past, there was no door at all, and I must say, my sister's idea is both functional and cute.

"Last year." She crosses her ankles and settles her hands in her lap like a prim debutante. "I had a few friends over for drinks one night, and there were just too many jokes and innuendos about my bedroom. So, I needed a buffer—enter the sliding barn door."

"Nice choice." I lift a multi-colored pillow and mock gasp. "Paisley, Harper? We made a pact to let the other ladies in this town keep their paisley, but we would protest the god-awful pattern for the rest of eternity."

She snorts into her palms. "I got those because of the pact. They remind me of you."

"I think I'm equally offended and touched." I set it back down and sigh.

"Tell me what's going on," she presses.

I chew on the inside of my cheek. Wade and Violet are all I've been able to think about for over a week, and I've driven myself to the edge of loonyville.

Talking to Tessa, Erin, and Madi, whom we called during

the last margarita night, was therapeutic, but there's one more person I need in my corner—my sister.

"My marriage to Wade is a sham," I say, each word infused with defeat, which remains as I recount the rest of the sordid tale, ending with, "But I'm in love with him for real, Harper. I don't know what to do, and I fucking hate it. I hate feeling like this lovesick loser, but I can't help it. Wade is the real deal for me."

"This is perfect!" She claps, disrupting her perfect posture.

"How do you figure?"

"Because you're already married, and you're totally in love."

"Have you not been listening? *I'm* in love with him. He only sees me as a gullible little pawn in his game, and I don't even blame him. I was the best candidate to play the role of his wife without getting attached. After all, I haven't been in a relationship since Sonny. All I've done is bounce around the city with my lady boner on the hunt."

I throw my head back against the cushion as the exhaustion from the last few days, plus the flight down South, settles over me. "Except I did get attached—to him and Violet. I fell in love with our family. I can't even believe I'm saying these things. A year ago, I would've laughed in your face if you would've told me I'd be ecstatic over being a freaking wife and stepmom. I would've spit in your face if someone would've told me I'd run to my estranged sister. It's all so—are you crying?" I blink over at Harper, who's been unusually quiet the last few minutes.

Her laugh is unsteady as she reaches behind her for a tissue from the console table.

"Why the hell are you crying? Are you insane?" I shake

my head, completely confused. I know Harper cares about me. She's proven it time and again over the last couple of months, but I don't think the tears are necessary.

Even though I might've shed some of my own on the airplane bathroom on the way here, but that's neither here nor there.

"It's just… you… you came… here." She hiccups in similar fashion as I did while watching *Marley and Me* for the first time. Afterward, I pulled a Joey and stuffed the DVD into the freezer until I finally decided to throw it away for my own well-being.

"I'm aware I'm here," I draw out and cringe as she savagely blows her nose into a tissue like I imagine a lumberjack might, although they'd probably just wipe their snot on their plaid sleeves. Thank God, she doesn't do the latter.

"You came… to me." She wads the tissues into her fist and exhales, her eyes red.

And then it clicks.

I reach across the single cushion between us and squeeze her free hand. "I did," I whisper with a smile as nearly fifteen years' worth of baggage between us is finally laid to rest, once and for all. "Now, can you please stop blubbering and help me?"

"I do have one idea."

"Lay it on—" A sting resonates across my forehead. "Did you just…"

"I did." Her watery eyes slowly clear as we have a staring contest.

The bitch just flicked me.

"Gran did the exact same, didn't she? Back when you ran to her for advice to deal with Sonny?"

"She did, but that was different. Sonny and I were actually married. I thought we loved each other. Our vows were sacred." I search her unreadable expression, and my heart tumbles into my stomach. "Are you suggesting I leave Wade and give up?"

"God, no!" She grabs both my hands and shifts to face me. "This *is* different. Much, much different. You and Wade have the kind of love you never had with Sonny, and it took me all of one hour with you two to realize it."

"We weren't sleeping together then."

"Exactly. It was *that* obvious." She tilts her head. "He loves you, Bree, but the guy's been through a lot of changes in less than a year. Hell, I can't imagine what it was like for you to leave this small town and move to the big city, right? But you only had yourself to consider. He has a daughter he wants to make up for lost time with. A whole new career he was adjusting to, which let's face it—accounting is a snoozefest as it is, but he led an exciting life as a pro soccer player before that. There's no comparison."

My spirits—and hope—lift the more she talks because, she's not wrong.

"Be patient with him, hon. He'll see the error of his ways, and the good news is that, when he does, you two are already married. You can just keep being married forever and have three more kids."

"*Four* kids total? I knew you were insane."

"Just dreaming," she sings.

I glance around the room at the old and new pictures hanging on the walls. Some are of Harper, our parents, and me when we were younger. Others are of her with people I don't recognize.

We've both changed.

I've been beating myself up over this fight with Wade, but sometimes, things aren't so simple. Sometimes, the best thing we can do is have faith in our growth and be patient that it'll take us right where we need to go.

"Where are my manners?" Harper gasps, jumping up. "I didn't even offer you a sweet tea or a lemonade. What would you like?"

Rolling my eyes, I follow her into the kitchen, where she pours us a couple drinks. I opt for sweet tea, which I never get to drink anymore, and she chooses lemonade. Both are perfectly refreshing for this hot day, and it's not even summer yet. The heat has only just begun to show itself around these parts.

"So…" As she takes a sip, she doesn't make eye contact. "How is… everyone in New York?" she asks, setting her drink onto the counter. The glass is covered in lemons, and it is so Harper.

"By everyone, do you mean a certain hot cop who happens to live next door to us?"

"Fine," she draws out with a smile. "How's Tucker?"

"He misses you. You left quite the impression on him during your visit."

"And vice versa," she mumbles.

"What are you going to do about him?"

"Honestly? I don't know." She frowns. "He lives up North with a job, his mom, his daughter… As much as I loved the city, I can't leave Sapphire Creek. I have a life here. I can't start a nursery from scratch up there. I mean, maybe I could, but…"

I can't keep a single plant alive, and my sister cares for

them for a living. That's one interest and skill we don't share. Another is the direction each of our lives has taken.

"Your heart belongs here. This is your home," I say absentmindedly.

"Just like yours belongs in Jersey City with your new family."

And it's true. I might've left this small town because of the fallout with Sonny, but I stayed away because I love the New York area.

I love Wade and Violet. Gaga and the girls too.

I have an entire community of my own up there with so many caring people, just like Harper has here.

"If it's meant to be, you two will find a way." I nearly choke on my own words. I mean them, but I can't deny how incredibly freaking whimsical I sound. This is the new me, I guess, and in truth, I don't hate it.

"Right back at you."

THIRTY

Wade

"**E**llie!" Violet squeals as soon as I open the door.

Tucker and his daughter stand on the other side in the hall, and the two girls don't waste any time disappearing into their own little bubble.

"Remember what we talked about?" Tucker calls out to his daughter.

"No more pranks," the little girl says softly.

"And?"

"I'm sorry, Mr. Wade, for the prank."

"Thank you, Ellie." I give her a smile and tilt my head for Tucker to come inside.

As the girls sink to the floor where Violet was coloring, their giggles fill the apartment.

"I really am sorry for causing you so much trouble,"

Tucker throws over his shoulder as we come to a stop in the kitchen. "I had no idea what they were up to."

"Kids can be sneaky like that, but I think they learned an important lesson—it's not nice to give their dad a near stroke." I reach into the refrigerator for a couple of beers, which I discreetly pour into two black cups so I can hide them from the girls.

"Not a great feeling, no," he adds, the pinch between his brow grim like a man speaking from personal experience.

I tap my full cup to his, and we take a drink in sync.

"Heard Bree went back to Sapphire Creek. When will she be back?" he asks.

Son of a bitch.

"Girls," I call out, my heart slamming against my rib cage. "Why don't you two color in Violet's room?"

"I can show you the tree on my wall. I call him Terry!" Violet tells her little friend while I glare at Tucker.

Red hot rage flares in my stomach. "I didn't know she left New York. How do *you*?"

"Shit. Maybe I shouldn't have said anything." His face pales.

"But you did. Now keep fucking talking," I practically snarl.

I might've been jealous over his little wine date with Bree a couple of weeks ago, but I've had time to cool down. I realized I was being ridiculous and that Bree would never do that to me. Tucker wouldn't, either. We're friends.

But the fact that he knows where my own wife is and I didn't just cuts through me like an ulcer. I can't take the torture of not knowing what's going on anymore.

"I have no idea what happened between you, and I really

don't want to be involved. I definitely don't want to stir up drama for either of you." He backs away, one hand holding the cup of beer high.

I grab his free arm and stop him from tiptoeing his way out of this. "Too late. What the hell is going on? Are you moving in on my wife? Because I swear to God, if I find out—"

"What? You think I'm after Bree?" His arm loosens in my grip, and I let go as the disbelief in his tone washes over me. "Wade, I slept with her sister."

I raise my brows.

"While she was in town, Harper and I started… seeing each other. I really… like her, but when she left, we agreed not to… continue," he stammers.

Is he serious?

"I only invited Bree over that night for wine because I missed her sister, and I wanted to talk to someone close to her. I know it might sound… cheesy or whatever, but fuck… I just wanted to know how she was doing." He swipes at the corners of his mouth, the vein in his neck thick like this is all very difficult for him to confess.

He's definitely never had this much trouble with words in the past.

And I completely get it, although I have a lot of questions.

"How did… Why…" What are words? Because I don't even know how to use them myself. With a frustrated exhale, I sidestep him and slide onto a stool. I need to sit the fuck down. "I thought there was something between you and Harper when she was here, but I had no idea it turned into anything. Why didn't you tell me? Why didn't Bree? How did I miss this?"

"Bree didn't know the extent of it until that night a couple of weeks ago, so she probably just didn't get the chance."

"You and Harper?" I press.

The dopey smile on his face is likely similar to the one I wore when things between Bree and me were good. It's all the answer I need.

He's in love.

"That's what you meant by your Finley girl comment." Understanding dawns. It was never Bree he was after, and I'm the biggest asshole in the universe.

I mean, I never truly believed he'd try to move in on her, or vice versa, but given how confusing things between Bree and me were, I was never sure of anything.

I never knew what was fake or real, but I should have.

I should have trusted Bree, and I should've let myself be vulnerable with her instead of running away when things got difficult. There's no justifying that, except to say fear got the best of me.

"Like I said, I'm sorry if what happened had anything to do with your fight. I never intended to get between you two."

"It wasn't you." I shake my head and frown. "I messed it up all on my own because I'm a dick."

Two gasps sound from the hallway, drawing our attention. I never heard the door to Vi's bedroom open, and considering how loud they've been since Ellie arrived, I figured they would've given themselves away before I said anything bad.

"You can't say that word!" Ellie points at me.

"Mommy says that's a *really* bad one," Violet adds.

"It is very bad, and you two should never say it." Tucker sounds stern, but with a hand covering his mouth, I can tell he's trying really hard not to crack.

"We're more immature than they are, aren't we?" I mutter, suppressing a laugh myself.

Single dad superheroes have faults of their own.

"Want to play a new game I found? It's coloring on the iPad." Ellie beams like she's discovered gold. The excited way Vi follows her into the bedroom again suggests they did find gold.

Once they're out of earshot again, I turn to Tucker. "I'm sorry I was a dick to you too. I was a jealous ass, and I'm a shitty friend for being so wrapped up in my own damn drama that I didn't even know you were seeing someone, let alone that it was my own sister-in-law."

"Wow. I'm just glad the girls weren't here to call you out on all those cuss words. I lost count myself," he teases. "Look, you don't owe me any apologies. We're good."

"Why are you going so easy on me? Maggie did the same thing this morning, but I deserve a lot worse."

"You want us to be mean?"

"It would make me feel like less of a chump."

"I think you feel bad enough," he says, his voice low and somber.

It's true. The one person who has not made this easy on me is the one I need to work on the most. Where do I even begin?

"I had such a clear and focused plan." I hang my throbbing head. "Until I didn't."

Tucker sucks back the rest of his beer and helps himself to another.

"I thought I was doing the right thing… up until I wasn't," I continue. "I don't know what I want or who I even am anymore."

"Sure you do," he states without hesitation, his hand frozen around his fresh cup.

"I don't. That's the problem. I don't have a job anymore because I couldn't stand working for a middle-aged child. I want to play soccer, but that would have so many consequences I don't want to think about."

"What if you got on a team in New York? You'd be around a lot more than if you returned to your old team."

"I would, but we'd still have a ton of practices and away games. I'd be expected to make PR appearances and attend team building shit. I'd drive Bree—and Violet—to the brink of insanity with my dietary restrictions. They'd have to rearrange their lives to cater to me. It would be too much to ask of them."

"I bet they'd do it if it's what you really wanted."

I want to believe him, but mostly, I want to believe this is the best thing for me. I'm just not so sure it is.

The thought of missing a single bagel bar because I'm at practice or sneaking in a weightlifting session makes my chest sink. I can't stand the idea of missing a single day-to-day moment with my family, which is what has kept me from reaching out to Mick. I haven't even spoken with Slater in two weeks. Other than Gaga, my old friend is the only one who knows everything about me, and I haven't even told him I quit my job.

He'd likely swoop in with a list of reasons why it's the perfect time to return to the team, but I don't want to hear any of them.

"I want to be Bree's husband and Violet's father. I want to be present for them. I just don't know how." I lift my sober gaze to meet his.

"I know who can help."

I tap my fingers on the counter, lost in thoughts of what Bree would say right now. How well she'd talk me through this crisis. She'd make me feel better, even though I don't deserve it. Her heart is just that big.

"I don't understand what you're still doing here. The second I told you where Bree is, I figured you'd race out of here with Violet in tow to go after her."

"How do you know Bree is with her sister?" Violet bounces out of her room, sneaking up on us again.

"How do *you* know?" I ask, folding my arms over my chest.

"I talked to her on my iPad yesterday. Mommy said I could."

"She did?" I quirk a brow. I guess Maggie really meant it when she claimed she's accepted Bree. Didn't see that coming one bit.

"She didn't say when she's coming back, though. Do you know?" Violet skips toward me and yanks on my hand. "I want to show her how good I did on my spelling test."

"You haven't even shown me." I clutch my chest.

"You don't shoot confetti at me when I do something good," she argues.

"You shoot confetti in here?" I groan. The thought alone gives me hives. By no means am I a clean and tidy guy, per se, but confetti? That annoying shit can never be cleaned up. It gets everywhere and stays there like mold.

"We go outside."

That helps.

But it also lodges a block of guilt in my throat. Bree is considerate and thoughtful, and she's fun as hell. Vi loves her, and she misses her. Not a day goes by that she doesn't ask about her. Hell, the little girl doesn't let an hour pass without saying her name.

And I'm the reason she's not here now.

"I'll be right back." I grab my phone off the charger and march into my room, calling Maggie's number.

It takes a little begging and an agreement to switch a few days around in our visitation schedule, but I succeed in getting her permission.

Hands out to my sides, I waltz back into the living room and ask Violet, "How about we take a little trip to see Bree ourselves?"

THIRTY-ONE

Bree

"I can't believe I let you dress me." I blow out a frustrated breath and smooth my hand over the high-waisted jeans she picked out for me from Daphne's boutique earlier.

"I still think you would've liked the jean skirt better, but this works too." She winks as I step through the door to the bar for happy hour.

"No way in Hell were you going to get that skirt on me. Not even a date with Chris Hemsworth would've been enough to make me comfortable in such a thing."

"Are you serious?" She rushes up to fall into step with me, gaping. "There's no chance you'd pass up Thor, especially not since you looked hot *in such a thing*."

Although I believe her, I still scoff, playing up my

annoyance because I can't let my sister know the truth.

She can't know I love the outfit she picked out for me. I even loved the jean skirt, but I figured jeans were more practical and trendier for life in New York. Besides, if I would've caved on the skirt, she would've tried talking me into cowboy boots, and that would've gotten ugly. Why ruin this nice visit?

Since I arrived, we've gone shopping, gotten our nails done, and inhaled a few lemon squares from Bready or Knot. I forgot how much I loved them, just as I'd forgotten how charming this small town can be.

Countless people have stopped me to catch up and gush over how great it is to see me. At first, I thought it was a joke. Then Mrs. Marilyn ran out of her antique store on the town square to greet me like I was a celebrity.

It was bizarre but totally… nice.

I was afraid it would be too difficult to come back here. It's not like my last visit was so awesome, not with Gran's funeral, Mom's antics, and the stress. But the last couple of days have been pleasantly nostalgic.

On top of how friendly people have been, the fact that Mom no longer lives here helps too.

"Oh, shit," Harper grumbles, halting in front of me. "Don't look now, but…"

My heart stops when I recognize the man at the bar—the one Harper told me not to look at. How could I miss him, though? He's the tallest, bulkiest of the three guys at the bar. I can only see his profile, but there's no mistaking my ex-husband.

I spoke too soon, didn't I? This was such a lovely visit until now.

"I thought you said he moved to Atlanta or somewhere in Florida," I hiss into my sister's ear, tugging on her arm to hold her back before Sonny notices us.

"He moved to Nashville," she confirms.

"I don't care if he moved to the moon. Why the hell is he *here*?"

"Probably the same reason you are—for family."

"Now is *not* the time to be all smug and reasonable." I peek over at Sonny again. "Last I heard, he got married again too."

Harper steps in front of me. "You are a hot piece of ass with a rock on your finger from a man who actually deserves your love. And it's not just any man, either. Your current husband is a kickass dad who's a former pro athlete. Don't you want Sonny to see all that? To regret his entire existence up to this point and go home with his tail tucked between his legs?"

The twist of my lips softens.

Harper clings to my forearms. "One look at you is all it's going to take for him to know what a huge dick he was and how big of a mistake it was letting you go. And Bree, he totally let you go, no matter what bullshit Mom fed you about it being your fault. It wasn't. Just like this thing with Wade isn't, and he's going to come to his senses." She squeezes my hands, but she might as well have a hold on my heart. Her belief that Wade and I will find a way to make this work runs deep, and I can't help but share in it.

"I guess it wouldn't hurt to toy with his fragile ego…"

"That's right!" She claps. "But also, it doesn't matter what he thinks because he's a garbage human."

"Obviously. This is just good old-fashioned fun."

Harper falls into step with me again, looping her arm through mine as we sashay toward the bar. She was right—Sonny takes a single look at me, and his jaw comes unhinged.

Envy clouds his irises too, which is just the icing on the fucking cake.

"I'll be damned," he says in his deep Southern drawl. His voice used to slay me. It's why I believed so damn hard in his dream of being a successful musician. He has the talent, but he doesn't apply himself. Hard work isn't exactly in his toolbox of skills.

"Sonny," I say evenly as Harper orders us a couple of spiked Arnold Palmers.

"I heard you were living in the big city now."

"I heard you were in Nashville yourself."

He spreads his arms, smug and starry-eyed. "Living the dream."

"Same here."

"Guess our divorce really helped each of us soar."

My laugh is low and sinister. This isn't as satisfying as I anticipated. "Speaking of, where's your new wife? I'd love to congratulate her on how *lucky* she is."

His jaw tics—I'd say I inadvertently struck a nerve. What gives? "You'll get your chance, if you stick around long enough. You're much better at leaving, though."

"Why wouldn't I want to leave? There are much, much better things to experience out in the world." As the jab hangs in the air, I flash my ring and tuck a strand of slick, straight hair behind my ear.

The hint of distaste from before only hardens in his eyes. "What a shame. All that time in the big city must've stolen your Southern manners."

"Yes, it's the city that changed me." I smile, and it's genuine.

In truth, the city did change me—for the better. This excuse for a man has no effect on me, and he doesn't deserve any credit for the person I've become, nor does he deserve any more of my time.

That's never been clearer to me than it is now.

I've halfway turned my back on him to grab my drink from Harper when thick fingers wrap around my arm.

Sonny spins me back to face him, sneering, "Listen here, I don't take kindly to—"

"Hands off."

I blink, bringing Sonny's confused and twisted expression in and out of focus. That sounded like…

"Hands *off*," the familiar voice repeats, but this time, it's far more lethal.

"This is none of your business," Sonny spits as his grip finally loosens.

"It is when it concerns *my wife*."

I turn, coming face-to-face with Wade and his steely eyes. He's out for blood, and I need to cool the impending eruption before it's too late. Besides, Sonny is so not worth the trouble.

"What're you doing here?" I ask him.

"I'm here for my wife," Wade says more softly, covering my hand with his.

My breath catches as his hot skin sears mine, but the welcomed sting is short lived. A pesky shadow looms over us, challenging my patience.

"*This* is the new husband?" Sonny scoffs between us and finally lets go of me. "Is he even old enough to be in this bar? He's a fucking teenage twig."

My eyes never leave Wade's as I smile. "He's a much bigger man than you are, that's for sure."

With a curse, Sonny storms out of here, and Harper skips toward us like we just won some award. "That was so crazy," she whisper-cheers.

I tear my gaze away from Wade as curious eyes burn holes on my back. We've attracted an audience, and while I glimpse a few accusatory ones, the majority are proud. Like they're happy I stuck it to Sonny yet again.

So am I.

"Blake just told me something interesting too." Harper claps each of our shoulders. "It seems Sonny's wife asked him for a divorce and kicked him out. He hasn't performed in almost a year while in Nashville, and she finally got sick of his lazy ass."

"Sounds a little too familiar, which is why I'm not surprised." I put a hand on my hip, recalling his previous statement of "living the dream." It seems his only dream has ever been to sleep well into the afternoon, get up simply to eat, and stay out all night with his buddies while his wife busts her ass to take care of him.

"Good to see you again, Wadey Baby." Harper wraps her arms around his neck and walks backward as she winks at me. "I need to go see an officer about a kiss now."

"What?" I ask, but she doesn't stop to answer. So, I turn to Wade. "What is going on here?"

"I didn't come alone, nor did I work alone to find you." He grins, and my ovaries melt. "Tucker's here with Ellie and Violet."

"Violet?" My heart lurches. I've missed the little girl like crazy. "How is she? How long have you two been in Sapphire Creek? Where are you staying?"

His chuckle interrupts me. "There will be plenty of time to see them, but first, you and I need to talk."

The twinkle in his eyes dims, and I shift under the weight of them—and of him.

I've missed him like crazy too. At night, I toss and turn, endlessly wondering what he's doing. Where he is. What I'm missing with him and Violet.

And now, he's here in my hometown. Am I in the twilight zone or something?

He extends his hand toward the bar, where Sonny's seat is now vacant. "Drink?"

"Please. Although…" I search the bar for the drinks Harper ordered, but I come up empty. Then I remember Blake.

In the corner, the young woman Harper went to school with is cozied up to a tall, dark, and handsome guy in a black dress shirt. The rings on both their fingers shine under the dim light, and I smile.

Coincidentally, Blake is enjoying what appears to be *my* Arnold Palmer.

"Although?" Wade asks.

"Nothing." I shake my head and order another drink from none other than Cole Rivers, Harper's old crush long before a certain cop from New York got under her skin.

Drinks in hand, we move toward an empty booth in the corner for privacy, even though I don't think such a thing exists in Sapphire Creek. There are eyes and ears covering every inch of this town, but this is the best we can do.

I can already imagine the rumors flying after people saw Sonny and me in the same room for the first time in nearly fifteen years.

"I thought you'd be lacing up your boots and running drills right about now," I say.

"I'm not playing soccer."

My eyes flick up to his.

"I won't be joining my old team again, or any other team for that matter. It's not what I want out of a career moving forward."

"What do you want, then, Wade?" I ask, repeating the question I asked him two weeks ago—right before I left his apartment. I hold my breath and hope he has an answer this time.

One that won't absolutely crush me.

But he's in Georgia, for crying out loud. Surely, he didn't come all this way just to break my heart.

"I want you. Us. You, Violet, and me. I don't want to miss a thing. I don't know what the future holds, but I know I want my girls at the center of it."

Tears sting the backs of my eyes. "I don't want to stand in the way of your dreams. If you want to play soccer, I won't stop you, nor will it keep me from wanting to be with you. I just don't want to keep secrets. I want to be a team of our own."

He slides across the booth and reaches a steady hand up to cup my cheek. "That's exactly what I want. It's what I've wanted from the beginning, but I missed the team. I missed Slater and the guys, but I didn't miss being a professional soccer player. Not really. I just… got restless in that office, just like you thought I would."

"I'm not going to say I told you so…"

"Why? You totally should. I deserve it." He laughs, and it soothes my aching heart, until he grows sober again. "I was confused by everything that changed in my life, and I pushed you away the second it got too difficult, because I didn't know what else to do. I didn't know how to properly deal with how hard this all is. I should've leaned on you. I should've trusted you. I *do* trust you, and I'm sorry I ever made you question that."

"Really?"

"I've always trusted you. I think on some level, I didn't believe I deserved you, Violet, or any of the good things happening to me. Even Gaga gave up her life in Florida to be with us, and I was too overwhelmed with the support, as crazy as that sounds."

"It does sound pretty crazy," I tease.

"I should've been grateful to you all, but I've fended for myself for years. My parents are off doing their own thing, and while I had my grandparents growing up, I didn't really have anyone to lean on as an adult other than Slater and the team."

"You have us now. And Slater. You'll never lose your friend. Hell, I have three close friends, and one lives in LA most of the time. We don't let distance change that."

"I realize more and more every day how much of an ass I've been, and I'm sorry. Really, really fucking sorry." He dips his head to kiss the backs of my hands, pleading.

I lower my own forehead and bury it in his silky hair, inhaling his intoxicating cologne. After a beat of silence, I nudge him up to face me again. "You didn't have to come all the way down here to apologize. You could've waited until I returned in a couple of days." I fight my smile because, honestly? I'm beyond damn happy he came all this way to win me back.

"Oh, I didn't come all the way down here to apologize."

"No?"

"I came to tell you I love you."

My lungs collapse. Oh my God. Am I dying? Is this what Heaven looks like—a sexy soccer player confessing his love for me? It sure looks, feels, smells, and sounds like Heaven.

Wade cups the side of my face again and peers deep into my eyes, his piercing baby blues tugging a blush into my cheeks. "You, Bree Finley, stole my heart the first night we met, and I'm completely in love with you."

"It's Bree Jameson," I croak with a watery laugh. "And I love you too, Wade."

He fuses his mouth to mine, and I feel his kiss in my toes.

This is the happy ending I never realized I was missing out on. I once thought I'd be better off with one-night stands and random hookups for the rest of eternity. Figured they'd be the best way to keep my heart safe.

But I was simply waiting for Wade to protect and cherish it.

THIRTY-TWO

Wade

"**C**an we have makeup sex now, or what?" Bree mutters across my lips as we continue kissing in the booth of a very public place.

We've caught the eyes of several patrons, most of whom probably grew up with Bree—or watched her grow up. I'm not from a small town myself, but I can imagine how it works. Everyone knows everyone and everything because they've spent the majority of their lives together.

"We should probably get to Violet first." I pull away with a quiet groan. It's not easy to think straight when I'm under Bree's spell.

"Right," she says, grazing one fingertip across her bottom lip, where I just nipped at it. "Shit."

"What?"

"I'm… frazzled." She chews on the inside of her cheek and peeks up at me like she's blinking at the sun. "This has been the craziest day."

"Good crazy?" I nuzzle her neck and place a kiss at the base of it, my lips tingling from the warmth of her skin.

"*Wonderful* crazy."

I pull back and swipe the hair away from her face. "And you're sure you forgive me?"

"As long as you don't really regret marrying me."

A searing pain slices through my chest and stomach from her words, paired with the devastation in her eyes.

How could I have said something so hurtful and stupid? My temper gets the best of me so often, but I refuse to quit trying to be a better man.

Bree and Violet deserve the best from me.

With both of her hands in mine, I kiss her knuckles, fingers, and palms. "I'm so fucking sorry. I was such an asshole to you, and you didn't deserve it, especially since I never would've survived the last few months without you. You're my rock. My sugar mama. My everything."

This earns me a crack of a smile.

"I've never been in love before," I continue. "I didn't know what it would be or feel like, but when I realized you did end up leaving the state because of me… I lost it. I was lost without you, and not because I needed you to fix the broken pieces of me and my life. It was because you're the reason I'm whole to begin with."

Between more kisses, she mumbles, "We need to go."

I squeeze her hand and slide out of the booth until we're free of the dim lighting and soft country music playing from the speakers.

On our way to the parking lot, I stare at her ass in those jeans. It's a wonder I don't slam into a wall or another car. I'm fucking mesmerized by my wife.

She loves me back.

She has the most loving and forgiving heart. I don't deserve her kindness, but I'll do anything I can to keep earning it day after day—that much I know.

Bree flattens her back against the side of my rental, the lights of which flash as I unlock it. "Kiss me.

"Gladly."

I press my body to hers and slip my tongue between her lips, soaking up her taste as my fingers tangle in her hair. "We're being inappropriate again, aren't we?"

"Totally, but I'm kind of known as the troublemaker around this town." She wraps her hands around my neck and smiles. "I have a reputation to uphold."

Before I capture her lips again, a throat clears to our side. A woman saunters closer, folding both arms across her chest, and I pause. It's not because of the god-awful lime-green purse glued to her body, either. The frown she dons like a bad haircut screams disappointment.

Who is she?

"I heard you were back in town," she says. "Didn't realize you brought back a… treat."

Bree swipes at her twitching lips. "This is my husband, Wade."

Surprise and intrigue color the woman's eyes. "Your mother would be pleased. Have you spoken with her? I don't think she knows about your new catch."

"She doesn't, but I should totally give her a call. I'm sure she'd love to know of at least one thing I've done right, huh?"

She tilts her head, and the menacing grin she gives Bree gives me goose bumps. If Erin were here, no doubt she'd detect some kind of bad, bad energy around this one. "Good to see you, *Breanna*," she says before walking away.

"Feel that?" I ask Bree, who shakes her head. "I got a chill. It definitely came from her."

"My mother turned her into this. So cold and snarky. Some friend they are to each other."

"You weren't kidding about the passive aggressiveness."

"It wouldn't be a proper visit to the South if you didn't experience it firsthand."

"Where is your mom?" I ask with caution. I'm almost afraid to find out, but I'm more afraid of the possibility of running into her unprepared.

"She moved to Tennessee after her husband got a new job. Harper wouldn't give her Gran's house, so she felt like she didn't have a reason to stay."

"Seriously?"

"I only wish I were kidding, but that's our mother. She's always out for number one—herself."

I thread my fingers through hers and hold on tight. "You okay?"

Her smile radiates a glow across her entire disposition. "This has been the craziest day," she says again. "But I've never been better."

On the drive through town, Bree gives directions until we stop in front of a single-story, cottage-style home with a white picket fence wrapped around one side. Two faded rocking chairs sit on the small porch, and the ferns hanging on either side of the door are fresh and healthy. All the plants are. Pink, yellow, and purple flowers decorate the house like Christmas lights.

"My grandma's house," Bree says before she climbs out.

As I follow her up the creaky steps onto the porch, my heart races. This is yet another piece of the Bree *Jameson* puzzle I get to put together, and I fucking love it.

The door swings open, and Harper's smile greets us. "If it isn't the happy couple."

Tucker appears behind her, placing a hand on her hip, and I suppress a snort. "Right back at you."

"Touché." Harper leans back for us to pass. "Come on in."

Ellie and Violet play on a blanket in the living room, their dolls and small clothing items scattered between them. Violet wanted to bring her entire toy chest, but we settled on a couple of coloring books, a stuffy, and her dolls. If Bree were there to help us pack, I'm sure she could've talked her down to fewer dolls, but I compromised the best I could.

Thankfully, I have my partner back, so we can work together from now on.

"Look, Daddy." Vi points to the soccer jersey she put on her doll. "She's a new soccer player, but I think she'll play goalie instead of striker. She's good at stopping the ball like Ladybug in *Miraculous* is at fighting villains. I think she'll— Bree!"

Violet jumps up and races past me until she practically knocks Bree over with a fierce hug. My chest swells at the sight of my girls, and I'm beyond glad we came down here.

I'm beyond relieved Maggie was actually okay with me taking Violet out of the state. After many arguments and trials and error, she and I have finally reached a mutual respect and understanding, which is all I ever wanted between us for the sake of our daughter.

"I missed you, babe." Bree beams, hoisting Violet into her arms.

"Really? Because I missed you a lot."

"Not more than I missed you."

"Uh-huh!" Violet draws out with a giggle as Bree gives her one last squeeze, then sets her back onto her feet.

"Did Aunt Harper show you around?"

"She did. We got ice cream earlier. Mr. Tucker tried the peach, but Ellie and me—we got the cookie dough."

"Good choice." Bree holds her hand up for a high five. "Want to do something else super fun?"

"Sure."

Ellie jumps up and down. "Me too. Me too!"

"This is for everyone, but we're going to need a few things first." Bree eyes Harper, who winks.

"Already way ahead of you, sis."

In the backyard, Harper leads the way toward a skateboard, an old bike with its paint chipped, and a rope with a loop on the end. The women gather each item, while Tucker and I exchange confused glances.

"When Bree and I were younger, we'd play outside all day until we were sunburned to a crisp, and our legs were wobbly from too much running, skipping, and skateboarding," Harper says over her shoulder as we follow her out onto the quiet street. I haven't heard or seen a car the entire time we've been here.

That's new.

And actually, it's pretty damn peaceful. The trees lining either side of the street are green and tall. The houses are all different colors, and every one of them has a porch. I imagine the neighbors sitting on them and chatting with their coffees in the mornings.

It's quaint and humbling here.

"I cannot picture you skateboarding, especially in those shoes." Tucker points to Harper's heeled sandals, which add at least four inches to her height.

Harper sticks her tongue out. "This isn't for me today. It's for Ellie and Violet to try, but we can do it the safer way."

"Yes. I'd prefer the safe route." Tucker runs a hand through his hair.

When it comes to our daughters, I will always agree to the safest way, whatever that means in this case, and I'm not at all surprised that Tucker agrees.

Harper sets the skateboard down, grabs the rope, and tilts her head for Ellie to go first. "Hop on, and hold onto this."

The young girl tightens her grip around the rope, and Tucker helps steady her on the skateboard.

"Remember to bend your knees," Harper says.

Without letting her go, Tucker follows them as Harper pulls on the other end, tugging his daughter along. The wheels scrape along the uneven asphalt, but the sounds quickly drown in Ellie's squeals.

Next to me, Violet cheers for her little friend as they go faster and faster down the street. "Can I try it next, Daddy?"

I scratch the back of my head as I study the trio ahead. Looks safe enough, especially if I mimic Tucker and never let go of Vi. "Sure."

Once they return, Violet doesn't hesitate to jump onto the skateboard and grab the rope. The girl is fearless, but… I am not.

"Let's go slow, yeah?" I say to Harper, and I tremble as we move down the street in the direction the others went. My hands never leave my daughter's waist, and by the time we've covered a few yards, a pool of sweat gathers at my lower back.

I'm a nervous wreck. What the hell is dropping her off at college going to be like? Fucking torture, for sure.

As we approach the house unharmed, Bree holds up her phone and calls out, "I need some shots of this, so say cheese!"

My grin forms easily. She's pulling a Gaga with these pictures, and it's so damn nice to be together again like this, especially in Bree's hometown.

In her own grandma's house.

For the last two weeks, I've felt lost in turmoil of my own making, but now, my world seems right again. Like it's back on its axis and spinning naturally once more.

"Can we go again?" Ellie asks, yanking on her father's shirt.

"You sure can if Harper—"

"My turn," Bree calls out from the porch. Sticking her tongue out in what appears to be concentration, she finishes lacing up her sneakers, then walks the old bicycle onto the sidewalk next to us.

"You're going to do what exactly?" I lift a brow.

"I'm going to skateboard, but there's yet another twist." She shrugs, and she and Harper trade items.

"You think you can still do it?" Harper eyes her big sister, the corners of her lips curling upward.

"Oh, I can still do it." Bree winks toward Violet as she scoops the rope off the ground and hops onto the skateboard. "Once a pro, always a pro."

While the four of us watch with a mix of concern and amusement, Harper ties the free end of the rope to the back of the bike, straddles the seat, and whizzes off, pulling Bree behind her.

And I'm sweating again.

But just like Violet, Bree laughs and hollers as the wind slices through her hair, and the strands whip backward. She practically soars, free and unfiltered. It's magic.

I picture her here as a kid doing this exact thing, and now, she's teaching Violet, although my daughter won't be pulled by a bicycle anytime soon. No need to jump into her true daredevil phase just yet, although I'm sure it's coming.

Reason number two thousand and twenty I'm glad I have Bree—she'll keep me as sane as possible as Violet grows up.

"Ah!" Bree flies off the skateboard, and Harper skids to a stop several feet in front of her.

"Jesus," I hiss as I jump into action and race toward Bree.

Is she hurt? Bleeding? Can she stand?

Fuck. She shouldn't have been on—

"Oh my God." Bree's howling laughter stops me in my tracks a couple inches away. Its echoes bounce off the trees as we huddle around her on a neighbor's neatly trimmed yard.

With a thundering heart, I study her from head to toe. She only scraped her knee, but the gashes look painful enough. "Are you okay?"

"I'm… fine." She snorts and waves us off.

The first car of the early evening appears, so Tucker and I scramble to guide the girls out of the way as a dusty Ford pickup rolls through. But it doesn't carry on. Instead, the guy does the neighborly thing and stops to ask, "Everything okay?"

"I think," I answer, but it comes out as more of a question.

"She's fine, Austin," Harper supplies with more confidence. "Thanks for checking."

As the engine revs up again and he drives off, Bree's laugh

subsides, and I'm so worried my vision blurs. "You could've broken a bone," I chide.

"It wouldn't have been the first time." She eyes Harper, who covers her mouth with both hands.

"Can I do what Bree did?" Violet asks.

"No." My wife shakes her head, her eyes finally sober, thank God. "Not yet, anyway. We can totally get you set up on your thirteenth—"

I clear my throat and wave my hand across it to cut her off.

"I mean, *sixteenth* birthday."

Violet counts on her hands from seven to sixteen. "Nine! Nine more years. I can wait."

"You couldn't even wait nine seconds for your ice cream earlier," I say.

"I don't joke around about ice cream, Daddy."

I hold my hands up in surrender, then help Bree get back inside.

With a bandage wrapped tightly around her knee, I tuck her into my side and guide her toward the couch.

"Rest," I say and kiss her forehead.

"I didn't run a marathon, Wade. I barely scraped my knee."

"The three other bandages in the trash soaked in your blood would say otherwise." I place my hands on both hips like I do when Violet refuses to go to bed.

"Could've done without the gruesome visual."

"It's your fault I had to pull out the big guns."

"And they are big guns…" She wiggles her eyebrows, and I fight the urge to lay her back.

She's hurt, and we're not even close to being alone.

But I'm in desperate need for the makeup sex she mentioned earlier.

"Can we play outside some more? I won't get on the skateboard," Violet promises.

The sun's setting, and if what Bree's told me of this place is true, the swarms of mosquitoes will be on the hunt any second. There's not enough bug spray in the world to fend them off, either.

"I can take the girls outside," Tucker offers.

"The mosquitoes, though…" I twist my lips.

"For a minute, please?" Violet clings to my leg. "We won't be out too long, but I saw a bug through the window. Its butt lit up. Aunt Harper told me it's a firefly, and I want to find more."

"Can't argue with that."

Tucker leads the girls outside. Half of Violet's hair hangs out of her ponytail, and while my hands itch to fix it for her, I learned weeks ago that it wouldn't do any good.

It'll just get messed up again the second she runs off.

Besides, I know what it's like to be seven and curious about every little thing outside. My grandpa used to spend hours with me in the yard while the kid next door and I climbed trees like monkeys and literally rolled through dirt. We also had competitions to find who could pick the most weeds, which was Grandpa Gilbert's favorite game. It meant we did the heavy lifting to clean his yard and actually had fun while doing it.

"I'm going to change. Be right back." I kiss Bree on the lips this time, then hop over a few dolls and her backpack. It's the obnoxiously shiny one Violet picked out—Bree brought it with her down here.

Why is she so damn sweet?

On my way to the bathroom, I sidestep a couple other bags, one of which is Tucker's for Ellie and another is Vi's. I stalk down the hall, stopping only to smile at the pictures of Bree and Harper hanging on the wall. There are only a couple, but they're rather adorable shots of the girls hanging off a tire swing, posing in front of a large mossy oak, and grinning in front of a fireplace on either side of an older woman. It's decorated with garland, so this must've been taken during Christmas. Upon closer inspection, it's the same fireplace in the living room of this house, and I can only assume that's Gran in the middle.

The woman's reindeer antlers light up, and she's grinning down at the girls. Even if I knew nothing about her, I could've easily guessed at how much she loved Harper and Bree from this single picture.

I can also tell she was as fun as Bree has described.

In the bathroom, I shed the sweaty shirt I was wearing. I didn't mention it to Bree, but it got a smudge of blood on it from the cut on her knee.

I stop in the hall again, but this time, it's because I hear hushed tones drifting from the living room.

"We took over your house, didn't we?" Bree says, and I assume she's referring to the mess that accompanied Violet, Ellie, Tucker, and me.

"I kind of love it," Harper chirps. "It was getting too quiet and lonely around here. Oh—and it's *your* house, babe. Gran left it to you. I'm just… a guest."

Bree snorts. "It's yours, sis. You've made Gran's house a home for yourself. All I ask is that we have a room when we visit."

"Anytime. Actually, you can all stay here forever."

I peek around the corner as Bree covers her hand in both of her own in a sandwich of sisterly love and gratitude. "My husband needs to go back, and I'm going with him. I need to go home with my family."

"You didn't call him your fake husband."

"He's real, Harper. As real as he is ridiculous and ridiculously sexy. In fact, I've hung up my lucky one-night stand thong, and I have no regrets."

My lips hike into a smile as Bree wraps her sister into a tight hug as best she can at that angle.

"I'm glad I came to visit, and I know Violet is too. She's taken a real liking to calling you *Aunt* Harper."

"I am her aunt. The freaking coolest too."

"It might even be hard for her to leave."

My stomach twists. I wish we could stay longer. I know Violet is loving it here, and although I could get used to this slower pace of life—and my daughter would surely love the quiet streets to play on—we need to get back. There's so much waiting for us back in New York.

The back door bursts open, and Tucker rushes inside behind the girls.

"We found so many fireflies." Vi beams, racing straight for Bree and Harper as I join them in the living room too.

"Tomorrow, we can bottle some up if you'd like," Bree says.

"We can do that?"

"Of course. Aunt Harper and I will show you both how."

Instead of smiling, clapping, or showing any other sign of joy like I suspected, Violet's shoulders slump. "I wish we didn't have to go back to New York so fast. It's so fun here."

"Your mom misses you, though. We need to get you back to her." Bree lifts Vi's chin. "The good thing is that we can visit anytime we want."

"Can we visit too, Dad?" Ellie turns into Tucker's arms for a side hug.

My friend peeks over at Harper with longing in his eyes—I know that look all too well. "We'll see, sweetheart."

"How about we pitch in to help cook dinner for us all?" I cut in, sensing the pair might need a second. It's clear they haven't yet discussed what any of this means, but it's also very obvious it means something special.

"My sister possesses the burn-everything gene like me, so we will rely on your capable hands." Bree nods, and Violet giggles.

I turn to Tucker and Harper, who are now cozied up together and smitten in the kitchen like newlyweds.

It's what Bree and I should've looked like when the pair first met, but we were pretending then. Every touch and lingering gaze were fake.

But were they really? It's hard to believe there was ever a time when Bree and I were anything but real, no matter how long it took me to realize it.

Which only goes to further show how much of an idiot I can truly be.

That was in the past, though. There's no doubt I'll screw up plenty of times in the future, but I know it won't be as royally as I did two weeks ago. I won't make that mistake again with Bree.

She's mine, and I'll do whatever it takes to keep her by my side.

THIRTY-THREE

Bree

"**W**ill you do me the honor of staying married to me?" I halt, blink, and lean into the closed bathroom door.

"No. Fuck. That's not right." Wade's muffled voice drifts through the cracks of the door, and I cover my mouth to stifle a giggle. "Bree. You are an incredible stepmother to Violet. You are an amazing and attentive and patient wife. You have an enormous heart, and you're sexy as hell. If you agree to keep being my wife, I'll drop down to both knees and reward you so hard you'll—Jesus. That's not right, either. You're not trying to bribe her with sexual favors, you dumbass."

A soft giggle finally escapes, but his long exhale masks it.

"Bree. I'd be nothing without you. You've made me such a better version of myself, and you've shown me a special kind of love. A pure and selfless love, and I cherish it. I cherish you. You're… you're… God. Why is this so hard?"

I should put him out of his misery, shouldn't I? Then again, if I open the door and make my presence known, there's a chance he asks me this very important—and genuine—question next to the toilet. I can't risk it.

Instead, I tiptoe away and into the kitchen, where I busy myself with sweeping. When I'm finished, and he still hasn't given up on his adorable rehearsal, I call out for him.

The door finally swings open, and he rushes out. "What's going on?"

"Just wondering what you're doing," I say with a shrug.

He's so protective and thoughtful. For two weeks after we returned from Sapphire Creek, he cared for my sore knee around the clock like a neurotic doctor. A hot, gentle doctor. He was so chivalrous and kind, I had half a mind to "trip" and hurt myself again.

If it weren't for him and his constant monitoring, I probably would've unintentionally let it get infected. But I wasn't alone. I had Wade, and Violet and I both benefit tremendously from his admirable preparedness.

"You okay? Is it your knee?" he asks, coming around the counter to check it for himself.

"My knee completely healed a month ago."

"Do you feel like throwing up again? Maybe that stomach bug hasn't passed yet."

Instinctively, I clutch my stomach. "That was a horrendous episode yesterday, but I'm more worried about you."

"Why? Why would you… I'm fine. There's nothing… wrong with me." He folds and unfolds his arms over his chest, his hands visibly trembling.

"Clearly," I deadpan.

He blows out a frustrated breath. "Can we go out to dinner later? A romantic date?"

"That would be nice, but Gaga is on her way over with Violet. She picked her up from school and took her shopping. They should be here any minute."

"She takes her shopping just about every week. What more could either of them need?" He spins in the middle of the increasingly crowded apartment. "And where the hell are we going to put anything else?"

"Well, I can at least put away the clothes. That should help." I sidestep him toward the two baskets of laundry on the couch, but he stops me.

Is this it? Is he going to ask me?

Why am I suddenly nervous?

We've literally been married for months, but this feels… intimate. Extremely real. Something we can't take back.

"Will you say goodbye to your lucky thong forever and stay married to me?" His eyes widen as he curses under his breath.

And I burst into laughter. There goes any nervous feeling I had before. What was I even scared of? This is Wade— charming, sexy, sweet Wade.

My husband.

"That's not how you rehearsed it." I snort, and my hands fly up to cover my mouth.

"You heard me?"

"Hard not to. Besides, you were in there for a while. I had to check if you were still alive."

"Shit. This is not how I planned for this to go."

I grab him by the shoulders. "We haven't done a thing by any certain plan since we met. Why start now?"

"We are so backward, aren't we?"

"And yet… we are oh, so right." I smile and fall into his arms for a cozy hug.

"I mean it, though," he whispers. "I want to officially ask you to marry me for real this time. It's not a random idea that popped into my head at the last minute, and it's definitely not a desperate attempt to get my life in order. I just love you. That's it. That's the whole reason I want to be your husband."

I swipe at a tear streaming down my cheek.

"Fuck. I'm screwing this up, aren't I? I didn't practice enough. I would've had Violet help me, but she still doesn't know you and I technically aren't married, even though we are. I didn't want to open that can of worms and confuse her. I'm so—"

I kiss him—hard. "It was perfect," I mutter against his lips, and then I kiss him some more.

The truth is, he could've proposed by the toilet, and I still would've gladly accepted. Nothing could stop me from recommitting to this man.

We cling to each other as we deepen the kiss, our lips smashed together with no space to breathe, and I gladly let him smother me with love.

"All right. All right. Child in the house." Gaga covers Violet's eyes as they waddle into the kitchen, the bags at their sides seemingly making it hard for them to walk.

"Hey, Butterfly Vi." I bend at the waist to hug the little girl.

"Why are you crying? Did Daddy finally tell you he accidentally threw out a box of your magazines?"

Gasping, I pin a guilt-ridden Wade under my glare. "I *knew* some were missing."

"How would you know?" He gapes. "You have a million!"

"You had no right to throw them out."

"They were taking up all the space in storage. Plus, you buy five new ones every week. Where are the new ones going to go?"

"I'm thinking… your part of the closet is where they'll go after I kick you out." My teasing laugh finally breaks loose, and he pinches his brows. "I needed the push. Those things were too close to suffocating me."

"You're welcome, then."

I roll my eyes and grab Violet's hand. "Can you show me what you and Gaga bought today?"

"You got it, babe." She snatches every bag from Gaga, then runs toward the couch, dropping a few items behind her like breadcrumbs.

"Remember, some of those are mine." Gaga points. "I don't imagine you want to try on my pashmina."

"Thank you for picking Violet up from school, Gaga, and for taking her shopping, even though you've spoiled her enough for months." Wade kisses her cheek, and the sweet gesture makes me smile.

Violet puts on a quick fashion show, while Gaga and I rate each outfit. Wade grabs a beer and stands aside like this is his entertainment for the evening. He seems perfectly content with that too.

After all, if he wasn't, he wouldn't have asked me to stay married to him.

In all honesty, he didn't actually have to ask. I would've just stayed here of my own accord. None of them can get rid of me that easily.

As Vi changes into the fourth outfit, Wade holds his phone up and winks. "I need to make a call."

It's probably Oliver. If I had to guess from that wink, Wade's calling him to share the good news about us. The pair is closer than ever, given their shared interests and experiences, but beyond that, Oliver also helped secure a coaching position for Wade. As a principal, Erin's British new fiancé has many important connections, and thanks to him, he got Wade the interview.

Thanks to Wade and his own charms—and his super cool wife—he nailed the interview.

He starts in the fall coaching a high school team. Over the summer, he'll start working toward his teaching certification, which will require a lot of energy and dedication, but he's strong-willed and totally capable.

It also helps that he has the aforementioned super cool wife who will support and encourage him along the way.

Although he hasn't started his new position yet, it's already obvious it's the right choice for him, and not just for Violet and me. Wade is much happier with this new chapter ahead. He's lighter and far less tense. He's open and far more honest than before, like he's finally unburdened himself of the fear that once weighed on him.

And I'm finally free of the nagging cloud of doom and gloom, warning me that the other shoe will drop any second.

"I should get going." Gaga rises as Violet toys with the tag on her new swimsuit. I gave it a ten out of ten, just as I did the others, and she was so excited she wanted to keep this on.

"Stay for dinner?" I ask Gaga, following her into the kitchen, where I grab a pair of scissors to tear Violet's tags off. "I'd say it'll be a warm home-cooked meal, but it's more likely that we'll order out." Before I'm finished with my sentence, I snap my fingers as another idea occurs to me. "Although,

Tessa did drop off a lasagna yesterday, so we could heat that up tonight."

"Is it frozen?" Gaga asks.

"It is, but she did make it from scratch." I furrow my brow. Is that a bad thing? Because Tessa's lasagna is the tits, if tits were made of gooey cheese and a homemade tomato sauce from herbal heaven.

"Keep it for another occasion. What is one of your favorite dishes in the world?" Gaga folds her hands in front of her waist, where the tip of her beaded necklace rests. The turquoise in the cracked design matches her loose linen shirt, and it brings out the blue in her eyes. When Wade returns, standing next to her, it brings out the color of his eyes as well.

I feel his gaze on me, and when I peer over my shoulder for answers, he only shrugs. "Once, I had chicken pesto gnocchi that an old Italian neighbor cooked, and it changed the way I see potatoes."

"How so?" Wade chimes in.

"It's when I realized I will literally eat them in any way, shape, or form. It's the only food I'll happily enjoy no matter how it comes to me—fried, baked, or as a dumpling."

"Chicken pesto gnocchi it is, then, although I can't promise mine will compare to a real Italian's." Gaga raises her hands in surrender, then waltzes toward the door, purse secured over her shoulder.

"What do you mean?" I remain standing in place as Violet emerges from the bathroom.

I recognize the song she hums as one from *The Little Mermaid*, which we've watched a total of five times over the last couple of weeks, much to Wade's chagrin. He doesn't complain, though. He'd literally do anything for his little girl.

The soft notes halt as Violet looks Gaga up and down. "Are you leaving?"

"You're coming too. We're going on a girls' grocery trip." She winks at her, then shifts her attention to me, tilting her head for me to follow. "Wade, will you please take care of the dishes? That way, the sink will be cleared by the time we return to cook."

"*We're* cooking?" I practically squeak.

My attempt to make Wade dinner two nights ago ended with a welt on my finger after I burned it on the pan. The apartment also filled with smoke thicker than any fog I've ever seen, and it set off the smoke alarm. My ears are still ringing from the atrocious sound.

That was embarrassing enough, and I didn't even have witnesses. Giving cooking another go seems like an unpleasant idea, but Violet jumps with joy. Her excitement makes me momentarily forget that I might set the place on fire later.

Even with Gaga's help, there's little hope for me in that department.

"You're going to have to put real clothes on, though." I nod my head to the side for Violet to change.

Five minutes later, I kiss Wade goodbye, give his ass an extra squeeze, and meet the girls in the hall.

Gaga peers over at me as Vi pushes the button for the elevator. "My ring looks good on you." She nods toward my left hand.

"Wait. Are you saying…" I raise my hand and study the ring on my finger with a whole new perspective.

"Gilbert gave it to me the day we got married. It wasn't until a year afterward that he confessed he would've given it to me sooner, but he wanted to wait until we reached the church in the off chance I took it and ran. He wasn't wrong." The wrinkles above her rosy cheeks scrunch tighter as she laughs, a sheen of nostalgia and sentiment glossing over her eyes.

My own laugh releases unsteadily. "This is yours," I say with awe, a hint of disbelief still clouding my heart.

I never stopped to consider where it came from, but I should've known. This kind of ring can't be found in a jewelry shop these days, especially not as quickly as we'd needed it before the ceremony at the courthouse.

It never occurred to me that Wade would give me a family heirloom, for crying out loud. It's too much.

"I don't deserve it," I whisper.

"But you do, honey, and I couldn't be prouder for you to wear it." She squeezes my hand, and I feel the warmth of it spread throughout my chest like water underground, feeding the roots of trees. "You and Wade are something special. I can't thank you enough for what you did for him and Violet back then, and I certainly can't express just how much I appreciate all the things you still do for him. He's a changed man, thanks to you. So joyful and fulfilled. It's… well, it's very special to see my only grandson this well and happy."

"Thank you so much." I wrap my free arm around her and exhale with ease, my chest light and unburdened as we exit the building.

On the sidewalk, Gaga sidles up next to me while Violet continues humming "Part of Your World."

"Did he propose to you yet?" she whispers, presumably so the little one doesn't hear.

"He did. Did you know he would?"

She shrugs. "Of course. He tells me everything, remember?"

"Of course." I laugh, leaning into her as a wave of nausea rolls through my stomach.

Odd. Where is that coming from?

They're probably butterflies from all the pieces of my life finally falling into place, but they've never made me sick before.

I slow my pace as the nausea refuses to subside.

"What is it, dear?" Gaga pulls on Violet to stop us while I clutch my sides.

"I, um, might need to throw up."

EPILOGUE

Wade

Four months later…

The waves slide up the shoreline with ease as the breeze ruffles my hair.

My linen pants sway with the calm wind—the material is so thin and loose that it doesn't take much.

The setting sun casts a glow across the familiar faces in front of me as we all wait for her. This is how it should've been the first time, but better late than never.

We kept the guest list short and intimate, including only our closest friends and family, most of whom make up our bridal party. Instead of having them all stand up at the makeshift altar next to us, leaving no one in the crowd, we agreed to be the only two up here.

But when Bree finally arrives, I wish I had someone nearby to steady me.

I'm not prepared for the vision gliding my way, and I'm dangerously close to using the pastor for balance. I'd probably take the slender man down with me.

Bree is glowing, and instantly, tears prick the backs of my eyes.

Her knee-length white dress is delicately draped around her body, perfectly simple for this beach ceremony but elegant and angelic too—a beautiful bride.

The breeze pulls the material tight around the bump of her belly, and I clutch my chest. She's pregnant with our baby girl.

She's five months along, and some days, it's still hard to wrap my mind around it. It's so damn easy to be thrilled over a new addition to our little family.

When she first told me, she enlisted Violet's help. Both my girls dressed in matching purple shirts, and they had a third tiny onesie, plus a small soccer ball.

I cried.

They cried.

We then shot confetti in celebration.

I wipe at my eyes as Bree closes the distance between us, a bouquet of lavender flowers in her hand. Violet walks alongside her, wearing a soft purple dress and clinging to Bree's free hand—how am I *not* supposed to cry? My two girls are walking together with love radiating from them both. It's what dreams are made of.

When they reach me, I bend down to kiss Vi's cheek before she stands to the side. With Bree, I freeze in a moment of gratitude and joy.

She's beyond my wildest dreams.

"You made it," I breathe. How fucking lame am I?

"Did you think I wouldn't?" She smiles, her eyes sparkling like the sea under the remaining sun. "I know I'm late, but haven't you learned the way I work by now?"

"Oh, I know." I chuckle and lean in to kiss her cheek.

The bouquet in her hands is much like the one Gaga gave her at the courthouse all those months ago. She now hands it to Violet and faces me again, sliding her hands into my own.

All I want to do is kiss her. Hold her. Fucking dance with her as the waves sweep over our feet.

When she first brought up the idea to hold this ceremony at the beach in Hilton Head, South Carolina, I immediately agreed. Even better was the thought of a babymoon, a word I didn't know until a few months ago.

Since we never enjoyed a proper honeymoon after the first wedding, we figured we'd do it now, with our friends and family… and our unborn baby.

Since Hilton Head is very close to Sapphire Creek, Harper's agreed to entertain Violet for a couple of days while Bree and I enjoy massages, relaxing afternoons on the beach, and a few nights to ourselves before this new baby comes.

In the corner of my eye, I see Tucker kiss Harper's cheek, and Ellie lays her little head on her soon-to-be stepmother's shoulder. The trio makes a damn nice family, just like us.

Since Tucker and Ellie left New York, I've had to replace him with Oliver as my meditation buddy, but I'm not complaining. He might be over ten years older than me, but the guy is in better shape than many soccer players I know.

Plus, Oliver needs the healthy outlet as much as I do.

I can't even blame Tucker for moving down here to be with

Harper. Love can't be denied—I know this best of all. And why would we want to? We're lucky enough to experience it, and just like Tucker, I'm holding onto this love for dear life.

Because that's what loving Bree has done to me. It's given me a life that fulfills my soul.

Which is what I include in my vows.

Facing her, I continue with a quote from her favorite movie—I can't help myself. It's smart to kick this lifetime off right, and what better way than to repeat the romantic words of Noah from *The Notebook*?

"We're gonna have to work at this every day, but I want to do that because I want you. I want all of you, forever, you and me, every day."

A light sheen of tears glosses over her amber eyes, and her voice is shaky with emotion as she says, "Wade, I thought being stuck with you all those months ago was my nightmare."

I laugh, remembering how different we used to be. She and I prioritized much different things, but over time, we've come to line them up. In fact, we couldn't be more in sync.

"But it turned out to be the best thing that ever happened to me. It turned out to be a dream come true I never dared to fantasize about before I met you. You made me see the most wonderful side of love and marriage and commitment, and I vow to show you each and every day how much you, Violet, and our little peanut mean to me. I love you so much."

A blissful wave of happiness rolls through my chest as the pastor closes the ceremony with, "You may kiss the bride."

"Finally," I mutter for only Bree to hear.

There are no awkward kisses this time. No hesitation or tension.

Only eagerness on my part. Who can blame me?

I cup both her cheeks and fuse my mouth to hers as our friends clap and cheer for us. Our photographer, Raegan Peters, snaps shots left and right, capturing it all. She normally does weddings around New York, but Bree convinced her to travel down South for this occasion.

It didn't take much pleading and begging, although Bree was prepared to do as much. According to her, Raegan is better than the cake we picked out for the reception, which is saying a lot. Violet's asked about it every day since the tasting.

With my wife's hand in mine and Vi's in the other, the three—four, technically—of us make our way down the aisle while our friends clap us on the back. Gaga's too busy swiping at the tears in her eyes, and my parents cry too. They made the trip out to meet their granddaughter and new daughter-in-law.

It's the first time I'm seeing them in over a year myself, and the reunion couldn't have happened under better circumstances.

At the reception, Bree and I dance in the middle of the room with a chandelier overhead, the reflections drizzling over us in soft drops like rain.

"It's hard to believe I'm the second of our group to get married and the first to be pregnant. How the hell did this happen?"

We both glance around the small space at Tessa, Erin, and Madi. The latter two got engaged within a month of each other, which was also around the time Bree and I found out we're expecting. We've all had so much to celebrate lately, and we're nowhere near close to stopping the good times from rolling.

"I'd say it's because of my magic dick, but I should probably come up with something more romantic since it is our wedding night and all."

"True, but I feel like you used up your romantic juice during the ceremony," she muses, swaying with me. "I can't believe you used *The Notebook* in your vows."

"You shouldn't be so surprised. I'm trying to earn my own confetti party, remember?"

She and Violet might've allowed me to join the one we used to celebrate the baby announcement with, but I've never gotten my own. The two girls claim I'm not yet worthy, and it's become an ongoing joke.

"You sly, sly man." She tsks. "Makes me want to withhold my precious confetti for eternity."

I lean down low to whisper in her ear. "I bet I know how to *coax* it out of you."

"Don't you dare offer sexual favors…"

"Oh, but I am." I kiss the spot below her ear, and she shudders against me. "It's working, isn't it?"

"Only because these baby hormones are out of control."

"I don't think that's the only reason."

"You're right." She licks her lips. "It's because my new husband has no shame, and I'm too weak for him to pretend I don't love his sneaky little games."

I hum as the song comes to an end, and a round of forks clinking against glasses signal for us to kiss. I don't keep them, or my wife, waiting.

We end the evening with plenty more kisses, plus dancing, laughing, and a spontaneous round of karaoke.

It's the most glorious way to send us off into forever.

THE END

THANKS FOR READING!

Want more of Wade and Bree?
Check out where they (and the margarita night crew)
are five years into the future!
Grab your FREE bonus epilogue

https://geni.us/SWTSDBonus

ALSO WRITTEN BY GEORGIA COFFMAN

Stuck with You Series
Stuck with the Billionaire
Stuck with the Movie Star
Stuck with the Boss
Stuck with the Single Dad

Stuck with You Spinoffs
Stuck with a Date
Stuck with the Rock Star

Stuck with You Holiday Spinoffs
Stuck at Christmas
Stuck Under the Mistletoe

The Heat Series
Falling for a Stranger
Falling for a Player
Falling for a Bachelor
Falling for My Roommate

Standalone Novels
Official
Heartbeat
Unbreakable

ACKNOWLEDGMENTS

WOW. I cannot believe this series has come to an end. I started writing the first book in this world over two years ago, during the pandemic. It was during a time when I really needed a laugh. Something light. Something fun. That's how *Stuck with the Billionaire* was born.

But as I wrote the scenes of margarita nights with the girls, I knew each one needed a story. I just *had* to write them, and not simply because I still needed the laughs. I mean, I totally did, but it was more than that. I had the urge to write each of the girls' stories because I'd grown attached to them after the first scene of them all together.

There's just something extra special about a close girlfriend group. They're loyal. Dependable. Refreshing. They're family. And it's so hard to let these characters go.

I really hope you enjoyed these stories. That they made

you smile and filled your days with happiness while reading. Thank you for picking up this book, whether it's your first *Stuck with You* book or your fourth. I so appreciate you trusting me to take you on a fun escape.

Speaking of epic friend groups, I have to thank my own - the KKSB. Chelle, Julia, Claire, and Mae: I can't write a book without y'all. I'm so thankful you continue to be there for me, whether I'm blowing up the chat with rambling nonsense or I'm disappearing for days on end. Just, thank you.

Bobbie Jo, Kelly, Erin, Amy, Angie, Amanda - my beta readers - thank you all so much! I'm always a nervous wreck when sending out raw versions of my writing. My eye twitches for days, but you six made the process so enjoyable. Thank you for your help, from the bottom of my heart.

To my mom - thank you for being my constant cheerleader and my best friend. You've made me believe anything is possible, and I'm so grateful for you.

Last but not least, my husband. Thank you for your unyielding encouragement and faith in me. I wouldn't be writing and publishing if not for you. You opened my eyes to happy endings in more ways than one, and I'm truly thankful. I love you, forever and always.

ABOUT THE AUTHOR

Georgia Coffman is an author of steamy contemporary romances and romantic comedies. She has a Master's in Professional Writing and loves the TV show *Friends*, as well as shopping. She and her husband enjoy working out and playing with their two pups. Georgia loves to connect on social media or through email, so feel free to reach out with any questions, your fave book recommendations, or even a funny joke!

Newsletter
www.georgiacoffman.com/newsletter

Website
www.georgiacoffman.com

Facebook
https://geni.us/GeorgiaFB

Instagram
https://geni.us/GeorgiaIG

Pinterest
https://geni.us/GeorgiaPinterest

TikTok
https://geni.us/GeorgiaTT

BookBub
https://geni.us/GeorgiaBB

Amazon
https://geni.us/GeorgiaAmazon

Goodreads
https://geni.us/GeorgiaGR

Verve Romance
https://geni.us/GeorgiaVerve